C in the ATTIC WINDOW

AN ANTHOLOGY OF GOTHIC HORROR

EDITED BY SILVIA MORENO-GARCIA

AND

PAULA R. STILES

Published by Innsmouth Free Press

Cover illustration: Nacho Molina Parra
Cover and interior design: Silvia Moreno-Garcia

Library and Archives Canada Cataloguing in Publication

    Candle in the attic window : an anthology of gothic
horror / edited by Silvia Moreno-Garcia and Paula R. Stiles.
Short stories.
Issued also in electronic format.
ISBN 978-0-9866864-4-3

    1. Horror tales, Canadian (English). I. Moreno-Garcia,
Silvia Stiles, II. Paula R. (Paula Regina), 1967-

PS8323.H67C36 2011   C813'.087380806   C2011-906106-6

Published by Innsmouth Free Press, September 2011
Visit www.innsmouthfreepress.com

"In the deep shade, at the farther end of the room, a figure ran backwards and forwards. What it was, whether beast or human being, one could not, at first sight tell: it grovelled, seemingly, on all fours; it snatched and growled like some strange wild animal: but it was covered with clothing, and a quantity of dark, grizzled hair, wild as a mane, hid its head and face."

Jane Eyre, Charlotte Bronte

READ ORDER

161	15	115	67
277 (6)	27	129	165
59	93	143	189
181	255 (12)	239 (14)	213
231 (8)			39
105			
267 (10)			

Table of Contents

Introduction: An Open Door

Gothic fiction is one of the building blocks of contemporary horror. Try to picture the current horror landscape without Frankenstein's creature running around, Dracula crawling up the side of a castle, or Poe's House of Usher coming down. *Jane Eyre*, *Rebecca* and *The Haunting of Hill House* have left their fingerprints all over horror literature.

Candle in the Attic Window is an anthology featuring some of the classic Gothic themes, as interpreted by modern writers. This means that, although there are some period pieces, the tales and poems do not take place in a singular, gloomy castle with Victorian characters. The aim of the anthology is not to reproduce exactly the Gothic fiction of yore, but to bring a new spin to it. In short, to take that mysterious house, that wide-eyed heroine, that air of decay, and infuse them with fresh blood.

Picture yourself standing at the curb of the road. Your cell phone has gone dead. A tall, dark house looms upon a hill. The wind whips your coat. You open the iron gate and climb the steps towards the front door. A sickly, yellow light streams from the windows. High above, you think you see the oddest thing, a flickering candle in the attic window.

What awaits inside this house? Cursed objects, love that culminates in destruction, obsessions, ghosts, skeletons, a hidden passageway, revenge from beyond the grave, and, of course, a secret in the attic. Come into our home and meet the horrors we've assembled for you.

– Silvia Moreno-Garcia and Paula R. Stiles

Dwellings & Places

"Hill House, not sane, stood by itself against its hills, holding darkness within; it had stood so for eighty years and might stand for eighty more. Within, walls continued upright, bricks met neatly, floors were firm, and doors were sensibly shut; silence lay steadily against the wood and stone of Hill House, and whatever walked there, walked alone."

The Haunting of Hill House, Shirley Jackson

A Fixer-Upper

By Amanda C. Davis

I had an uncle: very rich.
He died without a child, which
Is how I got the whole estate.
I'll tell the truth.
It's pretty great.

Oh, sure, the wind just howls at night
And branches sway and block the light
And sometimes, just before a storm,
When air is cool and earth is warm,

A mist will rise upon the moor
And drift and slither to my door
And then I think I hear a knock –
Some nights, I lose my breath in shock –

I see a glow upon the terrace –
But then remember: I'm an heiress!
No stupid noise is too much hassle
To occupy this gorgeous castle.

And yes, okay, the nights are long
And, I'll admit, the wind is strong,
And sometimes, from a distant hill
There comes a howl that sends a chill

From skin to bone to nerve to spine.
(Don't worry, though! I'm doing fine.
It's only drafty, just a bit,
And hard to keep a candle lit.)

I'll kill the mice within the wall
And stop that clanking down the hall
And figure out who's screaming when
The windows shiver in the den –

A little plumbing and, with luck,
The seeping pipes will come unstuck.
I'll fix the electricity.
I'll make this manse a home; you'll see.

And then my friends will finally visit!
This place isn't creepy, is it?
Except the mist upon the moor ...
A knock!
Hold on.
I'll get the door.

Amanda C. Davis likes her houses haunted and her moors thick with mist. Her horror stories have appeared in *Shock Totem, Triangulation: End of the Rainbow*, and *Necrotic Tissue*, among others. Find out more about her, or read more of her work, at http://www.amandacdavis.com.

The Seventh Picture

By Orrin Grey

An exterior shot of the mansion through the windshield of a van, pulling up the curving drive. The camera turns until it's looking through the passenger-side window, keeping the façade of the building in view. It looms up, big and dark in front of a lowering grey sky. The kind of fake-Spanish, fake-Gothic mansion that you only find in Hollywood.

The van stops; the camera shakes and jostles as everyone gets out. In a finished film, there would be a cut here, but instead, there's just a tangle of voices and thumps, blurred shots of elbows and knees and the back of a girl's head.

A girl's voice, maybe belonging to that same head, says, "So, we're here?"

The camera stabilizes, the front door of the house in focus now. "This is it," the cameraman's voice says, startlingly close in your ear. "This is where it all happened."

~

Zach Gordon, Director

It was an unexpected coup, getting to use the house. They say no one's been there in years, but if you've ever seen one of Zenda's films, it'll probably look familiar to you. Most of them were shot there. The front stairs are the ones that the Red Death comes down in The Crimson Masque. *There's a hallway that shows up three times in* The Phantom Hand, *standing in for three different hallways. And, of course, the exterior and the entryway show up as the house in* The Enterprise of Death.

They tell me that all those rooms are still intact. Still just the way Zenda left them. The only rooms that the fire got were the ones in the back.

~

The crew goes into the mansion, followed by the camera. The film here is dull from shadows and the interior is black as a tomb, only bits of ambient light coming in through holes in windows and broken skylights. It's next to impossible to see anything, just dim figures jostling in front

15

of the camera, until Caleb York starts setting up portable lights, filling the entryway with a glow that momentarily blinds, then chases back the darkness.

The rest of the crew appear in the light. Danielle Monroe is probably the girl who spoke earlier, the one whose head was briefly in-frame. She stands now, staring up at the domed ceiling of the entryway made semi-famous by countless mid-afternoon cable showings of *The Enterprise of Death*. Off to the side stands Alexia Cole, her once-black hair now shot with grey streaks, though the colour doesn't come through on the camera. Her hair just looks dingy in the semi-darkness. Finally, Thom Dorn, big and jockish, stands and examines the huge round table that dominates the centre of the entryway.

"It's a prop," Danielle says. "It's the table where they have the séance in *The Dancing Skull.*"

"It's not a prop," the cameraman's voice says again. He must be Zach Gordon, the Director. He walks the camera over to get a better shot of the table and his fist appears to rap on it, to demonstrate its solidity. "They moved it out for *Enterprise of Death*, but the table sat here all the time. When Zenda had parties here, this is the table they sat around. It was the one in *The Dancing Skull*, too. Like everything else in this house. Zenda used what he had."

∼

Danielle Monroe, The Dark of the Matinee Blog
Arnold Zenda produced and directed only six movies during his lifetime, five of them with Victor Prince. Prince was born 'Norman Thompson', but he legally changed his name, probably at Zenda's urging, in an attempt to brand himself as a sort of poor-man's Vincent Price.

Prince wasn't Price, though, any more than Zenda was Corman or Castle, the men he seemed intent on imitating. But, together, they made some serviceable B-movies that found decent play, and a few fans on lazy-afternoon cable programs and late-night horror features. Most were low-rent Gothic horrors or supernatural thrillers. The Enterprise of Death *is probably the best-known, a sort of locked-house murder mystery with ghostly tinges à la Castle's* House on Haunted Hill, *but the best of the bunch is almost certainly* The Crimson Masque, *a direct knock-off of the Corman/Price* Masque of the Red Death. *The Red Death costume in it may be straight out of Chaney's* Phantom of the Opera, *but the decadent tone of it works a lot better than you might expect, given some of the other films in Zenda's oeuvre.*

That makes it extra unfortunate that what would have been his seventh film, an immediate follow-up to The Crimson Masque, *never happened. Or, rather, was never finished.*

～

The camera passes through the house. Everything is dim and dusty and festooned with cobwebs. The only illumination comes from flash-lights and hand-held lanterns.

As the crew walks around, different people exclaim about different rooms that have appeared in different movies. Mostly, Danielle points them out, or Zach does, but once Alexia says, "I spent the night in this room once. During shooting." They're standing in one of the upstairs bedrooms. It looks almost indistinguishable from most of the other bedrooms, the pattern of the faded wallpaper maybe a little different, the furniture in different places. "My mom was here with me. I slept in that bed. Or tried to."

"Why wasn't more of this stuff sold?" Caleb asks.

It's Zach who answers: "The house still belongs to Zenda's estate. Some kind of distant relative. Zenda wanted it left alone, so, for the most part, it has been."

They pass through room after room, hallway after hallway, seemingly intent on getting footage, however murky, of them all. Finally, they come to the back of the house, where huge, billowing sheets of plastic bulge and whip in the wind from the growing clouds that threaten a storm at any moment. Everyone stops, staring, and the camera follows their gazes up and out. The light changes, because now, the camera's outside, or near enough, looking through the blackened ruin of the mansion's back rooms. The ceiling here is completely missing and what's left of the walls stand up like charred, black bones.

～

Caleb York, Documentary Crew
Zach knew about Zenda before we got into filmmaking. We both did. We'd seen his movies on Saturday afternoons when we were kids, though neither of us really remembered them all that well. I remembered the monster at the end of Isle of Blood, *but couldn't remember the title of the*

movie, and I remembered being irrationally scared of the crawling hand in
The Phantom Hand, in this one scene where it crawls up onto some guy's
windowsill.

Zenda wasn't exactly an influence on either of us, though. It certainly
wasn't his movies that got Zach interested in doing this documentary. It was
the movie he didn't make. The mystery of it, y'know?

Nobody knew anything about it, except the working title. The King in
Yellow. *It came from a collection of short stories by this guy named 'Cham-*
bers'. It was also the name of a play that showed up in those stories, that
was supposed to drive the people who watched it crazy. Good material for
a movie, right? And right up Zenda's alley. But then there was the fire, and
Zenda and Prince both died in it, along with another person, an actress
named 'Agatha Wray', who was never in anything else that we know of.
Along with them, the fire burned up the only known print of the film. Or, as
much of the film as had been shot by then.

Nobody even knows what the movie was going to be about. Was it an
adaptation of a story from Chambers' book, or was it supposed to be the
play itself? Or did Zenda just pilfer the name?

The surviving actors who'd done any work on the film all claimed that
they were given their scripts a page at a time and that the pages were col-
lected again at the end of each day's shooting. All that any of them ever
remembered was that there were character names that matched fragments
of the fictional play. 'Cassilda' was one, and 'The Stranger'. But that could
mean anything, or it could mean nothing.

Anyway, that's what grabbed Zach, like I said. Not Zenda, but the mys-
tery of The King in Yellow. *Of what it could have been.*

～

The camera is stationary now, steady, obviously resting on its tripod.
It points toward the table in the entryway, and toward the crew who're
gathered around it, but it doesn't focus on them. Do they even know it's
running? They talk amongst themselves, mostly too quietly to be heard
clearly. If they were being filmed on purpose, you'd think they would
speak up.

There are cans of beer sitting on the table. Someone says something
about coasters, and there's laughter. Thom traces his finger across the dust
on the surface of the table and holds it up.

The conversation rises and falls, allowing bits and pieces to be distinguished. They're talking about Zenda, about how each of them heard of him and what brought each of them to this house. Danielle is trying to explain her blog to Alexia, who has never seen it. "Old movies just seem to capture weirdness better than new ones," Danielle says loudly, warming to her subject. "Back when there were smaller crews, when things were made by hand. Weirdness slipped in that way, infiltrated, got in through the cracks and the crappy special effects. When you watch an old, weird movie, you feel like you're watching something real, but also something not real, too. Like something from a dream, or an alternate universe. A universe where the sky's a painted backdrop and fake trees grow up out of the fake ground."

There's laughter and Danielle seems a bit embarrassed by her vehemence. More drinking follows, more talking, but nothing of substance. Eventually, they all agree to get some sleep on the cots they've brought with them. One by one, the lights are dimmed or extinguished and then, in the dark, someone turns off the camera.

~

Alexia Cole, Former Actress

I never wanted to go back to that house. Zach said I was the only actor who'd ever been in one of Zenda's movies that they could track down, but I don't know. I don't know who else was in them, or if they're dead, or in hiding, or working, or retired. I don't know if Zach and his company even tried to track anyone else down. I don't much care.

I was the little girl who gets kidnapped in Gothic!, *Zenda's first movie. I was 13 at the time. After that, I was in a few other movies, always little parts: someone's daughter, someone's niece, a girl someone talked to in a flower shop. I was in some commercials as I got older, and then I got a recurring part in one of those murder mystery TV shows.* Evenings at Sullivan's, *I don't know if you'll remember it. I wasn't a main character or anything. I was a waitress at the titular bar where the amateur detectives got together to solve the crimes. That's it. My hair was always in a braid down my back. Anyone who recognizes me at all these days usually recognizes me from that.*

After my mom died, I quit the business. She was always the one who'd wanted me to be an actress. I bought a partial share in a restaurant up in

Seattle and I never looked back. That sounds good, doesn't it, that I never looked back? But of course I did, or I wouldn't be here.

I'm not honestly sure why I agreed to do this documentary. Nostalgia? I don't think so. The paycheck they offered me for it was a pretty big incentive. Easy money for spending a weekend in Zenda's old house, dredging up the past.

I'd forgotten about the nightmares. They started back up the night after I agreed to the job. I used to have them all the time after filming Gothic! *They'd have been enough to make me quit right then, if it hadn't been for my mom. But I can't ever remember them after I wake up. Just that there's a white hand. That's it. You'd think I'd been in that stupid* Phantom Hand *movie, instead of* Gothic! *But, truth be told, I never even saw it. I never saw any of Zenda's movies, not even my own, and I don't care to.*

⁓

The camera comes back on to darkness. There's nothing to see, but there are sounds. Movement, people talking. "Did you hear that?" a voice says, close by.

"Someone screamed?"

"Is everyone here?"

A light comes on, from somewhere off to the side of the frame, blinding.

"Where's Alexia?" Danielle says. "What happened to Alexia?"

"Maybe she went to the bathroom?"

The camera is lifted up and carried along as the group moves, at first in different directions and then *en masse* toward the staircase. There they find Alexia, standing at the bottom, staring up. She looks strangely white in the dark, as though her clothes got lighter since she went to sleep. She's staring up into the shadows at the top of the stairs and doesn't seem to notice them approach, until Thom puts his hand on her shoulder. She jerks away, turns to stare at him with big, dark eyes.

"Hell with this," she says, after a long, silent moment. "Hell with this!" Danielle tries to approach her, but Alexia pulls away. "No. I'm leaving. I'll call a fucking cab. You guys can take it up with my lawyer how much of that money I don't collect. I'm gone."

She walks away, headed toward the front door. Danielle disappears off camera, following her. The camera stays, swiveling up to peer into the darkness where Alexia was staring. "What happened?" Thom's voice asks quietly. "What did she see?"

~

Thom Dorn, Documentary Crew
Before we got started, I sat down and watched all of Zenda's movies over one weekend. In order. I don't know what I was expecting. Some kind of connection, maybe? Some overarching something that you wouldn't have noticed normally? Some indication of the mystery that was coming?

I got nada. *Zilch. They're just a bunch of crappy old movies. There're some good bits and mostly, they're harmless. Just boring. But man, it's disappointing, y'know? Whenever a movie gets lost, or disappears, or never gets finished, you always want it to be something special. A masterpiece. Something magic. And chances are, this thing, this* King in Yellow, *chances are it was just going to be another boring old horror movie, destined for an eternity of afternoon cable.*

Maybe not getting made was the best thing that could've happened to it.

~

The camera goes off after Thom's question and when it comes back on, Danielle is in the middle of talking, saying that they should stay with Alexia until the cab comes.

"You can," Zach says. From his voice, you can tell he's the one holding the camera again. "We need to see what she saw."

They're at the top of the stairs, standing at the beginning of some upstairs hallway. Maybe the one that recurs in *The Phantom Hand*, it's hard to tell. Thom and Caleb are holding lights.

"What'd she say?" Caleb asks.

"I don't know. She just said she was leaving, that she hated this place, had always hated this place, never should have come back. Something about a dream she had when she was a little kid, something about a white hand."

"Sounds like she had a bad dream now," Zach says. He's walking down the hallway as he talks, away from the stairs, taking the camera with him.

"Bad dreams don't make you call a cab in the middle of the night," Danielle replies.

"Maybe it was really bad," Thom offers, his voice, like Danielle's, coming from somewhere outside the camera's field of vision now.

Their lights splash off the dusty walls, off the wainscoting and the hall tables crowned with statues that throw off misshapen shadows. At the far end, where the hall turns a sharp corner, there's a black space, a door. "Was that there before?" Caleb's voice asks.

"No," Danielle says softly, her voice barely audible.

"It's a secret door," Thom says. "Maybe that's what Alexia found."

The camera draws nearer to it and as it does, the door becomes more obvious, a piece of the wall, well-disguised, that opens outward, now partially ajar where before it was hidden. There's a brief, hushed debate and then Thom's hand appears on the edge of the door, swings it open. As he does, a weight shifts inside and everyone stumbles back, the camera bobbing madly, as a body tumbles out onto the floor.

~

Zach Gordon, Director
Nothing was ever recovered from the fire, from the house. No one ever found any film, so it was assumed that it was destroyed in the fire. No one ever found any bodies, but since Zenda and Prince and that actress, Wray, never showed up again, they were assumed to have been killed. Everything about the fire, about the movie, is assumed, guessed, reconstructed from a lack of contrary evidence. Everything.

How can you hear about that and not *want to solve it, want to look into it, want to try to shed some light, whatever light you can, on what must have happened there that night? What secrets must be buried in that old house?*

~

The corpse is a horror, although the camera doesn't linger on it. What you get are glimpses, impressions. Something disfigured, waxy, melted. Hideous scars long ago ossified, preserved in the space behind the wall. It's dressed in a suit that's decades out of date and holds a fire axe clutched like a baby to its chest.

There are exclamations from the crew, curses. "What are we going to do?" "Who is it?" "Is it Zenda?" "What happened?" "Should we call the police?" The voices are loud, sharp, hard to pin down, but none of them belongs to Zach.

Zach is still holding the camera and it has very little time for the corpse. It swings up, peering into the small, dark, hidden space behind the wall. It's tiny, barely the size of a closet, and there's a bench in there where the corpse was perched. On the bench is a canister of film and the camera approaches it for a closeup on the handwritten label, which reads, in small, tight script: THE KING IN YELLOW.

Cut to: the camera is being held by shaky hands, maybe still Zach's, maybe not, while someone – it's impossible to tell who – feeds a reel of film into a projector. The camera shifts and, for a moment, the screening room in Zenda's mansion comes into focus. Like most of the rest of the house, it's festooned in dust and cobwebs. There shouldn't be any electricity, but it looks like the house lights are on and dim, and when the camera swings back, the projector is whirring to life.

Cut to: the camera lies on its side in the aisle of the screening room, abandoned. The whir of the old projector can be heard from somewhere and a flickering, silvery radiance lights up the shot from the right-hand side of the frame. The only things visible from this angle are the legs of the screening room chairs and, beyond them, the feet of some of the documentary crew.

The film they're screening has no music and the dialogue is so muted as to be mostly inaudible, just a distant murmur, like an incantation in another language.

Gradually, the light shifts from silver to pale gold. Then other sounds join the whir of the projector and the muttering from the screen. First, small noises, breaths and gasps from the audience. A sound like someone crying, quietly. Then bursts of dangerous laughter. Then the first scream.

There's a commotion, a sound like a lot of people moving at once, and something strikes the camera, sends it spinning. When it comes to rest, it's pointed straight into the bloodied face and staring eyes of Alexia Cole.

The camera comes back on. A mass exodus is occurring toward the front door of the house. Everything is a jumble; the camera shakes and jostles in someone's hand, revealing the phantom shapes of running people and dark shadows all around. It's impossible to tell who is where, if the crew is all there, if anyone else is.

"Shut the camera off," someone is saying. "Shut the goddamn camera off!"

There's a scuffle and the camera dips sickeningly for a moment as though the arm that holds it has suddenly gone limp. Then, abruptly, silence. All movement stops. The camera swings slowly back up.

Ahead is the front door, with light behind it, though it's still night outside. In the doorway is a figure. At first, it's impossible to make out; it could be anyone. Some member of the crew separated from the throng. Anyone.

Then, though the light doesn't seem to change and the figure doesn't move, it somehow becomes clearer. As though the camera's eye is adjusting to the light.

The figure revealed is tall and thin, wearing a yellow cloak. Something radiates out from its head, like a halo in an old painting, like a child's drawing of the sun. Where its face should be is a pallid mask.

A voice from behind the camera says a word that sounds like "prince", and then another voice, very clearly, whispers, "No." That second voice is so close and clear that it must be the cameraman, or someone just over the cameraman's shoulder.

No one else speaks as the figure raises its bony hand to its face and begins to peel back the mask.

Static.

~

The camera containing this video footage was found in the front drive of Arnold Zenda's mansion on May 14, 2009. Nothing was left of the house itself but a smoldering ruin. No one from the documentary crew was ever heard from again.

Investigators were unable to determine the source of the blaze, and nothing that could be positively identified as human remains was found in the ashes of the house.

The film has been edited to include excerpts from interviews that were shot separately and that, we believe, give context to certain events contained herein, but none of the original footage has been modified or excised in any way.

❖

Orrin Grey was born on the night before Halloween, and he's been in love with monsters and the macabre ever since. *Never Bet the Devil & Other Warnings*, his first collection of supernatural stories, is coming soon from Evileye Books. You can find him online at www.orringrey.com.

Housebound

By Don D'Ammassa

I believe that ten days have now passed since I became trapped in my own house, but it might be as few as eight or as many as eleven. I am uncertain because there are periods during which none of the rooms I enter have outside windows and all the clocks have disappeared. I sleep when I'm weary, without knowing if it is day or night, perhaps in a bed, perhaps in a chair. The rooms are not always recognizable. I chanced to enter my study the other day, but it wasn't my study, not exactly, although it had some of my things in it.

I found this spiral notebook today, so I have decided to keep a record of my experiences, before I completely lose the gift of language. Where to start is a problem. Perhaps with my name, while I still remember it. I was christened 'Arthur Wade Wellstone'. I attended an assortment of colleges, my curricula designed by my father to prepare me to succeed him at the helm of Wellstone, Inc. It is entirely possible that I loved my parents, but during these past few days, my memories of them have faded. I remember remembering them, but I can no longer actually visualize what they looked like.

The first time I noticed a change in the house was on the second anniversary of their death, which may or may not be coincidental.

I had just returned from a two-week business trip to Europe. I'd been away from the house before, but this was the first prolonged trip since I'd moved back home. I was tired and irritable and somewhat preoccupied when I arrived. Jonas let me in and offered his services, but I dismissed him rather brusquely, intending to go directly to bed. I had chosen not to move to the master bedroom and my feet knew the way to my own quarters so well that there was no need for me to think about where I was going.

Not, that is, until I realized that I didn't know where I was.

My house is very large. There are a total of 20 rooms arranged on two levels, with the servants' quarters in a separate building. There were perhaps twelve rooms that I used regularly, but the rest – guest bedrooms, my father's office and others – were locked up. My first reaction was to assume that I'd made a wrong turn.

It would have been a reasonable explanation, except that none of the rooms had a red door, as did this one. It was locked, or perhaps the door was just stuck in the jamb. In any case, my impulse to look inside came to nothing.

I turned back the way I had come, or, at least, the way I thought I had come. Nothing looked familiar here, either, and it seemed to take much longer than usual to reach the staircase. I was halfway down, intending to interrogate Jonas about the altered door, but decided to wait until morning. This time, I arrived in my room without incident.

The following morning, I went looking for the red door but without success. I concluded that either I'd been so fatigued that my senses had played tricks on me, or that I'd dreamed the entire incident.

For the next several days, I was unusually busy. Situations change rapidly within such a diversified entity as Wellstone, Inc. My father had been an excellent negotiator and had impressed on me the importance of personally involving myself with every aspect of the company's operation. There were dossiers in my office containing the personnel files on all of my key people, as well as expensive-but-occasionally-revealing reports prepared by a private investigator.

During this time, I experienced brief periods of disorientation, both at home and elsewhere, which I attributed to fatigue. Father had always been impatient and irritable when I failed to match his seemingly limitless energy and I could almost feel his disapproval of my weakness. These episodes always passed quickly and I simply told myself that I needed to make time for a brief vacation.

The accident at the Verona plant came at the worst possible time. News of the explosion dominated CNN. The horrible loss of life and associated bad publicity were particularly humiliating because this scenario had been raised by one of my subordinates. The plant was situated in a densely populated residential area, maximizing the potential loss of life in the event of a catastrophic failure.

After spending more than two weeks dealing with the press, local officials and survivors, I returned exhausted and depressed. My nerves were scraped raw and I dismissed Jonas rather curtly, preferring seclusion to servile attendance. My mind was numb, and I drank two brandies for supper and went to bed early.

Some time later, I found myself awake, mouth dry and stomach rumbling. I drank a glass of water then decided to find something to eat. The house was dark and silent, a scattering of night lights providing adequate-but-not-abundant illumination. At the foot of the main staircase, I turned left, or at least, I believed I had, but I was distracted and moved more from habit than conscious effort.

I flicked the light switch in what I supposed was the kitchen, but found myself instead in my mother's sitting room. That meant that I had turned right instead of left, so I reversed direction and crossed through the spacious foyer into what should have been the kitchen. But somehow, I ended up in the greenhouse and the door that would have allowed me to go back inside was secured. Clad in only a bathrobe and slippers, I was compelled to suffer the ignominy of rousing Jonas from his bed in the guest cottage. Jonas retrieved his key without so much as a reproachful look.

Wellstone stock, already anemic, plunged even further. I took a disastrous personal loss. To add insult to injury, the Board had clearly lost confidence in me. My father's admonition never to reveal a wound, however painful, prevented me from resigning.

Three nights later, I woke from a sound sleep in an unfamiliar room. It was arranged roughly in the same fashion as my bed chamber, but it was much larger and the furniture cruder. The closets were bare and the only clothing I could find consisted of a flannel shirt, a pair of well-worn jeans, and some inexpensive loafers. I stepped outside the door with considerable trepidation, convinced that I had been drugged and kidnapped, but to my consternation, I found myself completely alone. My explorations were similarly disquieting. Many of the rooms bore a strong resemblance to those with which I was familiar, as did many of the furnishings, the books on the library shelves, the oriental rugs, the vivid tapestries. But they were arranged in unexpected combinations within the rooms and, even more unsettling, the rooms themselves had apparently been shuffled, so that the greenhouse was now appended to the bathroom and the kitchen opened off the library rather than the foyer.

The foyer itself bore a strong resemblance to my own, with one exception. There was no front door, just an unbroken wall where it had stood.

I soon discovered that all other means of egress were similarly missing. Exhausted, nerves on edge, I returned to the second floor, where the library had been located and where I kept the liquor cabinet. To my utter amazement, the library was no longer there. I was quite certain that it had opened off the hall directly opposite the master bedroom, at least in this version of the house, but when I stepped through the door this time, I found myself in the pantry.

The library, as it happened, was back on the first floor. I tracked it down eventually, found the liquor cabinet and drank myself into oblivion.

There's little else of these past ten days that I can recall clearly. There was food in the kitchen but no electricity, so I was reduced to eating raw vegetables and canned tuna. Lacking power, I could make no use of any of the appliances and the telephones are all missing. Only the lights function normally, although I have noticed that if I leave them on when I leave a room, they have been extinguished when I return.

It finally occurred to me that I might break a window and escape in that fashion. I was thwarted in this, as well, because as soon as the thought entered my head, steps were taken – I have no idea by what agency – to prevent any such deliverance. All of the external windows are now shuttered and I no longer have access to the greenhouse.

I am writing this at the kitchen table. The mess I left behind has been cleared away and the cupboards have been restocked, but I have little appetite. I am clearly imprisoned, but I have no idea what crime it is that I have committed.

~

Another day has passed, or so I believe. Although there seems no point to further exploration, I am restless and have carried this notebook through a succession of rooms. I dare not leave it behind because I might not find it again. It is the only unchanging thing in my environment, or more properly, it is the only item whose changes I control.

A short while ago, I happened upon the room with the red door again. This time, I was able to force it open and enter. At first, I was puzzled, because it was clearly a child's room – a nursery, in fact – and there was no such place in my house. It was only as I was about to leave that I saw a familiar stuffed animal propped against a rocking horse and it was like a key that opened a lock. Memories flooded over me and I slowly turned, re-examining everything with a sense of profound wonder

It was my own nursery, the furnishings long since cleared away at my father's insistence. The shock was so intense that I finally left, consumed by memories, and when I recollected myself, I was in one of the guest rooms. Subsequent efforts to find the red door again have so far proven unsuccessful.

I have a new anxiety today, one which alternately alarms me and gives me hope. I have heard sounds from elsewhere in the house, purposeful sounds, some of which I think might be human voices. At first, I shied away, but once it was clear that I was in no imminent danger, I discovered that my curiosity and need for human company was stronger than my fear. I have since attempted to find my unseen companions, but no matter how promptly I respond, I have yet to see any physical evidence that I am no longer alone.

Later. Still no success, but during my last visit to the kitchen, which was at the time attached to the guest bathroom, I found the remains of a meal, a meal which I had not eaten.

Later still. I have torn several pages from this notebook and written messages, which I have then placed in prominent places, suggesting that we congregate in the foyer. In at least two instances, those messages have been removed, but I have been waiting on the staircase now for what must be at least several hours. Twice, I have heard the sounds of movement, but no one has appeared. I am tired and discouraged, but will try again tomorrow.

~

I grow to understand my situation even less with each passing day. I woke this morning with some enthusiasm, convinced that the enigma in which I am trapped has a solution, if only I have the wits to find it. But just when I think I am beginning to understand the rules, they change.

I found the kitchen clean and orderly and was making myself a sandwich for breakfast, Deviled Ham smeared on a hard roll, when I was startled by an ambiguous sound from near at hand. Before I had time to investigate, something burst in through the open doorway, ran past me, and exited into what should have been the pantry, but probably was not, all before I could react in any useful fashion. I didn't get a good look at it, but it had four legs and fur.

Breakfast forgotten, I spent what must have been hours searching. There were hints of its presence – a clatter of tiny footsteps from over my head, a brief series of bumps and once a crash, as if something glass had been overturned and shattered, but I never caught sight of it again. By

nightfall, or what I judged to be nightfall, I had abandoned the hunt and I
sit at present in the library, dispirited.

~

I must remember to confine my sleeping to a bed. This morning, I
woke in a chair with a stiff neck and a back ache. My mood was somber as
I prepared for the usual morning search for the kitchen. It was nowhere
on the ground floor, so I climbed the staircase and had barely reached the
landing when a commotion broke out below me. I turned and leaned over
the rail, just in time to see my four-footed visitor, which appeared to be a
small doe, bolt across the carpet from left to right. The sight of it was still
registering when a second figure burst upon the scene, a human figure
this time, although an ungainly looking creature. It ran hunched forward;
it wore some rough, colourless fabric wrapped around its loins and it carried a crudely fashioned spear!

I must have called out because it paused suddenly, glanced up in
my direction, and then hurried on in pursuit of its quarry. I should have
followed. I would have, except that something about the creature's face
struck me as oddly familiar. And in any case, I doubt very much that I
could have caught up before the shifting realities of the house shunted it
to some new location.

It was a considerable while later, while passing through my mother's
sewing room, that I happened to glance at the wedding photos she had
arranged in an elaborate triptych on one wall. The face of the savage
hunter was that of my father.

My predicament grows less comprehensible with each passing hour.

~

I have not written here for the past three days, or for my last three
periods of wakefulness, however long that might be. This is not because
nothing of note has happened, but rather because, paradoxically, so
much has.

A low murmuring roused me from sleep, an almost subliminal sound
which drew me out of my room and into the hall, where the disturbance
resembled human speech more clearly. Barefoot and bare-chested, I
walked slowly to the landing and looked down into the foyer. It seemed
larger than usual and was certainly more crowded. Three rough structures
stood in one corner, a kind of hybrid, half-tent and half-hut. Two adults

were crouched a few meters away, building what appeared to be a fire in the middle of the floor. At the far end, a much-smaller individual – a child – was attempting to climb the drapes.

I suppose I should have descended immediately, but my sense of propriety overruled my enthusiasm. Father had always stressed the importance of first impressions, so I went back to my room to dress, a wasted effort as all of the clothes I had been wearing the previous day had mysteriously vanished and the closet and bureaus were empty. By the time this fact had registered, the foyer had been restored to its usual pristine state.

The disappointment was not as great as it might have been. Although I had yet to make contact with my housemates, there had been a clear progression. Sooner or later, our worlds would intersect more determinedly. I was certain of it. But the remainder of that day passed uneventfully and I fell asleep, once more consumed by doubts and apprehensions.

Something touched my cheek and I opened my eyes. A child, a female, stood at my bedside, a rather disheveled-looking waif with round, sad eyes and delicate features. She was quite pretty, but there was a furtive look about her and she recoiled when she saw that I was awake then bolted through the door.

"No! Wait!" I called and followed, but it was probably just as well that I failed to find her, as I was now completely unclothed. I mended that by fashioning a towel into a kind of kilt then conducted another fruitless search of the house, calling out occasionally, trying to speak in a calm, reassuring tone. No one answered; no one appeared.

I made several fruitless circuits of the house and, during my fifth visit to the library, I turned to the liquor cabinet, but instead of the beveled glass containers, I found two bulging, leatherlike pouches, both filled with liquid. The first appeared to be plain water, but the second, though bitter and sour, was clearly alcoholic and I drained more than half of it before setting it aside.

On the small end table beside my chair was a lamp, an ashtray and a small cameo portrait of my mother. I sank down into the seat and stared at it in wonder, for her face, though altered by age, was discernibly the same as that of my young visitor.

～

I have no idea how much time has passed since my last entry. I have been too preoccupied to add to this history. No, that's not entirely true.

On several occasions, I have attempted to record what has been happening, but in every instance, I have been unable to do so. The ability to fashion words into these abstract symbols seems to have become as transient as everything else in my environment. That may be just as well, as there are only a few blank pages left.

But at the moment, the old skill has returned, although it takes me much longer to form each word than it did in the past and when I glance back at what I have already written, it seems an incomprehensible jumble.

It was a tedious process, but I have made contact with the tribe. There are six adults and four children, two of each sex. The three adult males vary in age from late adolescence to elderly; the three women are tiered similarly, although each is noticeably younger than her respective mate. The oldest couple has a son who is nearly grown; the middle pair has a son and daughter, both in their mid-teens, and the youngest has a daughter, the one who visited my bedside. They speak, but no language that I recognize; nor do they respond to mine. Some of their clothing has been fashioned from towels or draperies; the rest consists of animal skins. The women forage for food in the kitchen and pantry, the men hunt the occasional doe. I have seen no evidence of any other animal life, although berry-bearing vines have sprung up in the pantry.

The males all bear my father's face, altered only to reflect their apparent age. The females are variations of my mother. I cannot explain this. They are not close relatives; they are the same.

Although they have a spoken language, it is nothing I can comprehend and they don't understand my words any better than I do theirs. At first, they were wary. The women ran off when I approached; the men warned me off by brandishing their weapons and shouting. Eventually, I managed to win a measure of their trust. They will not share their food with me, but if I bring my own, I am allowed to sit by their fire and eat with them. There is considerably less furniture in the house now, and a permanent burn mark in the centre of the foyer, but they have not touched anything in my bedroom and none of them seems to have entered it since my first encounter with the child.

Until today, I was merely tolerated, but my patience has finally borne fruit. The oldest of the three males approached and I stood before him, eyes respectfully downcast. He muttered another incomprehensible speech then thrust his spear forward, offering it to me. Tentatively, I accepted it, raising my eyes to try to determine what else was wanted.

He nodded toward the cooking fire then rubbed his bare, protruding belly with slow, exaggerated motions. His meaning was self-evident. He wanted me to find food for the tribe. Instinctively, I knew that this was a test, that if I succeeded, I would have proven myself one of them. I smiled and nodded, indicating that I understood, then turned and left them.

There is no apparent pattern to the appearance, or disappearance, of the does. Sometimes, I see several in one day, or perhaps the same one several times; sometimes, I see none at all. I prowled the upper floors at first, reasoning that the presence of the tribe below would scare them off. Room after room proved empty, emptier than ever before. I now wonder what will happen once all the flammable materials in the house have been exhausted. Will we be reduced to eating everything uncooked? Will the house grow cold when winter comes, if it hasn't, already? I have no idea what the date might be.

A familiar fear assails me. What happens if I fail this test? Will I have another opportunity to prove myself or will I be forever disenfranchised? As this possibility grows more prominent in my thoughts, I find my early confidence giving way to nearly paralytic anxiety. What if I cannot measure up to the tribe's standards? What if I am not man enough?

~

It is much later now. I have failed. It would have been bitterly disappointing to have tried and fallen short; it is immeasurably more devastating to have faltered even before making the attempt.

I had nearly despaired of finding my prey before fatigue forced me to sleep. A dozen or more visits to every room had been unproductive. Exhausted, I sank into one of the few remaining armchairs, in what used to be one of the guest bedrooms. I must have dozed off, because I woke with a start, having slipped partway down, banging my elbow painfully against the carved wooden arm.

Eyes stared into mine from only a meter away. It was a doe, head raised from where she had been grazing on one of mother's rugs. She watched me closely but without evident alarm. My spear was resting against the wall, near my right hand, and I reached for it very slowly, not wanting to frighten the animal off. She seemed oblivious to her danger and my heart raced with the prospect of making the kill, winning my admission into the tribe. I closed my fingers around the shaft and slowly raised it over one shoulder. My legs were stiff and sore, but I couldn't strike while sitting, so I pushed up, ever so slowly, until I was fully erect, the spear poised for the strike.

At the last moment, as the muscles in my arm tightened for the final blow, the doe raised its head and looked at me and there was something familiar and almost human about its face. In that moment, I hesitated and lowered my arm. The doe took one last bite of the carpet then wandered off, unconcerned. I never saw her again.

The tribe was no longer camped in the foyer. Even the burn mark was gone, although the missing furniture has not been restored. I don't understand, but I know that I will never be one of them.

~

Later. I am more confused than ever. I found the nursery again, although this time, my childhood toys and furnishings were mixed with more recent items: the desk from my study, the mirror I brought back from Paris.

I have gotten into the habit of avoiding my reflection in the bathroom mirrors, and the haggard and unshaven man who looked at me with panic in his eyes seemed like a stranger. But I paused this time and took stock of myself. True, my hair was long and my beard full, but neither was as disreputable as I had imagined. In fact, the longer I regarded my image, the more content it appeared. There was something familiar about the eyes and the expression, something that I finally recognized.

There was a touch of the doe in my face, or a touch of my face in the doe. I don't pretend to understand that, either, but I think I am beginning to comprehend what has happened to me.

I glanced down into the foyer a few moments ago and something seemed out of place. It took a few seconds to register, but then I realized what it was. The front door was back. Stunned, I turned away, wondering what it meant, excited by its presence but worried, as well, worried about what it might mean, what might lurk beyond the door. Whatever it was would be the unknown; I was certain of that.

Suppressing my anxiety, I descended, but by the time I arrived, the wall was back in place. I expected to feel shattered by the discovery, but that wasn't the case. I know now that when I am ready to face what lies beyond, a world in which the rules aren't known in advance, and in which I have to find my own way and decide for myself what paths are worth following and which are not, the door will be there and I will open it and walk through and never look back.

But first, I have to get my house in order.

Don D'Ammassa is the author of seven novels and three non-fiction books, as well as 150 short stories and several hundred articles related to speculative fiction. He has been writing full time since 2001.

Stone Dogs

By Paul Jessup

Thursday: English Lit

The trees outside of the window are crystallized, frozen into a dance by the ice storm. Mister Harvey is reading a passage from *The Wasteland*. But I can't hear the words.

I only see his lips.

Thick, beautiful lips. The words coming out of them deep and bellowing. I hear some girls whisper and giggle behind me. I know they are thinking the same thing I am – picturing him naked.

Maybe binding him up with his tie to the radiator in the back of the classroom. Gently ripping the clothes from his body. Forcing him to love me, even though it is forbidden. Maybe I shouldn't be writing this down? But that's part of the thrill, I guess. Maybe he will come over, spy my notebook. Spy my trembling hands writing this. Peek over my shoulder and see these hidden words. This language shoved between pages like skin in a sheet.

I get a small thrill, a quick chill, even as I write this. He walks closer. Do I keep the book open? Leave the page naked for him to see? Yes. Of course.

He didn't even notice. Walked past me. Invisible girl. I see his eyes spy the ones behind me. Always the ones behind me, the murder of pretty girls in the back of the room. Those beautiful little waifs, black hair cropped around their shoulders like feathers. The dark, staring, unthinking eyes. Like pools full of drowning children.

All guys look at them. The three of them – all alike. Dressed alike, eyes and hair and mouth alike. Petite, perfect. Like swords lined up in the back of the room.

I will not write their names here. This is a book that will be buried under an ash tree. In a jar filled with broken glass and used coffee grounds. The names and words written here have power. I will not honour them with such a thing. Instead, I shall call them "the crow girls". "The sword girls". "The unkindly ones".

Thursday: Algebra

The numbers on the chalk board do not look like math equations. They look like alchemical recipes. Like magical formulae. Circles, overlapping. Plotted with strange symbols, letters that contain hidden meaning. I wonder if there is a connection, somehow. Between the mental world that imagines such equations and the physical world, where such equations enact out their duties.

Maybe that is what magic is. That bridge between the two. Occult power existing in the actuality – the merging of two worlds.

You may think I'm a strange girl, to think such thoughts. You're right. But that doesn't mean you know me.

The trees outside dance faster. Sped up, animated dance. Whirling wittershins in sleet dresses. The ice smacking against the window. It sounds like a man, sitting outside and rapping against it.

I see snow and ice piling up. The trees are waist-deep now. Frost crystals spread across the pane of glass, like white, spidering fingers, crawling. Fractals. I could plot out their course in equations and predict how they will grow.

There is power in that.

Magic.

Thursday: Study Hall

This is a windowless room. I cannot see the snow, the ice. I cannot see the trees dance. But I feel them, hidden behind the molding, grey walls. Shaking their bodies. They tinkle-tinkle-tinkle when they dance. Like a music box.

This teacher is just an overpaid babysitter. He sits in the back, scolding those who speak. We cannot talk. We cannot do anything. We are supposed to study.

I think I will read, instead.

Did I ever tell you about my favourite book? It's an epic fantasy story, called "*Stone Dogs*". It's very strange, very surreal. I happened upon it by accident at a used bookstore. I saw a wall of the same thing – dragons, elves, dragons. Beneath these rotting and yellowed covers, I saw a single book, on the floor. Face up.

The cover was a thick paper that was textured to the touch to feel like human hair and bone. The illustration on the cover was a line drawing of a little girl feeding on a dragon. The dragon was dead; the girl was petite.

I bought the book with my lunch money.

I've reread it 46 times, already. I can't stop reading it; it is a compulsion. Each time I read it, pages change; words change. Paragraphs are never quite the same with each reading. The characters morph; the landscape changes. Even the map in the back is constantly moving with each read, constantly morphing in shape.

And yet – the plot is always the same.

I'll tell you about that some other time. I only have a half an hour left to read and I MUST read. I feel all drunk and fuzzy even thinking about it. Thinking about that book. In my hands. Like hair on the scalp of a head running between my fingers.

Thursday: Lunch

I usually go outside to eat, Geoff and me walking around the back lot talking and eating. Not today. Today, they said we are trapped inside. That the snow and the sleet and all the ice are far too dangerous for anyone to leave.

I feel caged. Sitting here, in the gymnasium, chewing on a stale salami sandwich. Geoff sits beside me, but he's not talking. He's just looking at crumpled mountains of paper in front of him. Scattered next to him are books on architecture, on engineering. On equations for worlds and universes. And a metal compass. And an ink and quill.

I would bother him, but I know he is working. Designing a world of his own, a galaxy of his own. Geoff is a writer of sorts. A creator. He has over thirty notebooks in his locker, filled with histories of this imaginary world, genealogies, genetic code for various creatures, the planets around it and the number of stars in the sky.

I know interrupting him now would be a big mistake. He gets angry when his work is disrupted; he yells and screams and throws his books at me. He is my only friend. I have no choice but to obey the whims of his imagination. I eat my sandwich in silence.

It smells like feet in here.

I want to go home.

Thursday: Biology

The walls are plastered with the bodies of dissected animals. They are beautiful. Pinned open and revealing their innermost secrets – labeled and categorized with painstaking detail. Like an open pocket watch, the clockwork displayed for all to see.

Geoff's world is like that.

Orderly, open. Naked and catalogued.

I don't listen to my teacher speak. She has a very nice voice, quiet and trembling. Like she is about ready to scream at any moment. A hidden hysteria in the background.

Her actual words are meaningless, pointless. There is nothing to learn when she speaks. Just words. Hollow things. I look instead at the pinned-open body of a pig foetus. The parts are so perfect. Like they are made of glass.

Thursday: Art Class

We have a kiln. But it is out back, covered by snow and ice. We can't get to it to retrieve our sculptures. I fear I will never see mine again. It was a cat with wide eyes. I call it *"Fear of Mice"*.

So, instead, we are treated to a slideshow on Renaissance Art. The boys in the back giggle at the nude women. I hear someone bark out the word "fat!" and another, "chubby chasers!" and I feel ashamed.

Am I like that to them?

At the end of the show, the teacher stands in front of us. Her name is 'Glenda', like the good witch. She has no last name, none that she will let us speak. She is tall and thin; her arms are branches and her feet are roots. Her dress is brown and green, and she looks like a tree. The ice will be coming for her soon. To crystallize her.

She gives the usual speech. About beauty back then being different. That thin people were considered ugly and poor, and fat people beautiful and rich. She looks at me and winks.

I want to kill her. I hope the ice comes for her soon, turns her into a frozen tree, stuck dancing in the sleet and wind. If I see any ice, I will betray her. Give away her location. Let them come, find her. Swallow her whole.

Thursday: American History

We don't learn about real American History. We only learn the same mythology everyone is always taught. About Pilgrims. And Columbus. About JFK's death and MLK's life. We never learn the real stories. The little histories.

My dad has a collection of books in his attic. They are diaries from the Civil War. This is history. I've read most of them but not all. They are by civilians, soldiers. Wives and artists. There are no famous people. No war heroes, no presidents or congressmen.

My favourite one was written by a 14-year-old girl. There was a yellowed picture stuck in the pages. She looked like me. That is why I am writing this. This is real history. This is what happens when you aren't famous. When you are invisible.

My teacher says something. I had to stop writing for a moment there, to listen to it. He got a note from someone outside in the hall. A shadow behind the crooked glass door. The note said that we are trapped. The teacher reads this, tells this to us with an air of authority.

We are snowed in. We cannot even open the doors.

I look at the window and all I see is a wall of white.

I feel like crying, but I don't. I don't want to be known as the girl who cries. That is worse than being invisible.

The note continues. Authorities are trying to find a way to get us out. It could be a day or two, at the least. We are to stay in the gymnasium overnight. The faculty will be laying down beds for each of us.

When the teacher is done reciting, he looks out the window. His face is convulsing, twitching. His eye is moving, like someone is pulling a string and making it go. His lips peel back in a sneer.

He was never attractive. But here, in this state of half-madness, he is downright ugly. I want to stand up, to be excused. But the bell has not rung yet; the period is not over. There are still more lies to be learned.

I am going to pull out my book and read some more. I need to be away from here for a little bit. I need to be someone else, somewhere else.

Thursday: The Gymnasium

I write this in my bed. Well, it is not really a bed. It is a blanket on
the gymnasium floor. With a pillow. The pillow and blanket are grey. The
floor is cold and hard. I can see my breath as I write this. Rising from my
mouth. The ghost of my words.

My pen has a light on the end. It was a birthday gift last year, from my
mom. Before she crawled under the bed and into the tunnels beneath my
house. I am glad she gave it to me. At the time, I thought it was a stupid
gift. Tonight, it is a lifesaver.

I crouch beneath the blanket as I write this. I can hear sounds around
me. Even though they separated us – boys on one side, girls on the other
– I can hear people sneaking and talking. Whispering, moaning. The
shuffling of blankets and the sighs of sex.

I wonder if Mister Harvey is out there. Crawling beneath the blankets
with the sword girls. Just the thought of it makes me sad and embarrassed. And yet, at the same time – very aroused.

I am going to play a game. I hear moaning now, several voices. And
people whispering be quiet – and hush, and please don't get me in trouble. I am going to try and guess who each of them is. Try and figure out
what is going on beneath other grey blankets.

Names escape me. I am awash in the sounds, the rubbing of bodies. I
feel a bump next to me and know that whoever is right over there is doing
something as well. I feel a soft touch of skin, an electric sensation all along
my body.

I am filled with thunder. I hear them, moaning, moving. Thrusting.
Faster. That skin rubbing up against mine. Accidental contact. Motion,
emotion. Flames inside of me.

I have to put the pen down.

I have to put this notebook down.

I know I will feel guilty in the morning, even though I will do nothing
wrong.

Friday: The Gymnasium

In the morning they give us stale donuts and bagels. The donuts
are hard; the bagels are chewy. I eat like it is my last meal. I made sure
to check to see who was lying next to me last night – to see who those

mysterious figures were. Nobody was there. Just an empty grey blanket and pillow.

I read after breakfast. First period will resume at nine am, like it does every morning. It seems there is no reprieve from the schedule. No matter how much the world has changed.

Everybody else chats while I read. I hear them, in the distance. Like muttering echoes from behind a wall. Talking the usual talk. Boys, colleges, work, who is cute and who is not. Who is cool and who is not. The names always change, but the pattern is the same.

I am at my favourite part of the book. The main character is a peasant girl named "Alisandre". She is very pretty, with dirty-blonde hair and intense eyes. In the book, her only desire is to become a knight.

The section I am at now is her trial for knighthood. Fourteen different rituals must be observed. A dragon must be slain. Sacrifice of self and family must be undertaken. Each time I read, it the rituals and trials change. But the result is still the same. She is knighted by the Prince of Butterflies. This is the first time she meets the Prince. When the Prince's hand touches her shoulder, she falls in love.

Now for a little explanation. The magical land where the book takes place is called "Iblio". In Iblio, gender and rank are determined not by birth, but instead by trials that are assigned to each station. With each gender and title come responsibilities and awards, as well as rules for how you are supposed to act and what you are supposed to do and whom you are supposed to marry. What time of the month you are to have sex, what day of the year you are supposed to give birth. What you are supposed to wear and even how you are supposed to wear it.

Geoff would love the appendices in the back of the book. They go into exquisite detail on the different ranks and genders, and the different trials and honours awarded. It is the sort of thing he would read and re-read over and over again.

Even though the prince and the knight are in love, they can never do anything about it. It is forbidden. One of them would have to undergo the trials of the princess, and neither of them wants to do that.

This is where the book's main plot comes into focus. After this point, it is about their forbidden love and the people who want to destroy them. Including the evil princess Earwig, who wants Alisandre for herself.

I hate Princess Earwig. Why would anyone want to be a princess? All day, living under glass. Waiting to be saved or married. Only to be expected have children the minute they are freed. They have no rights, only responsibilities. I completely understand why Alisandre and the Prince of Butterflies acted the way they did. They wanted a relationship of equalities.

I wonder if such a thing is even possible. In any world.

Friday: English Lit

Mister Harvey has a stack of books on his desk. The class moans. He is wearing his glasses and his patched-up smoking jacket. That means what he is about to say is serious. Is deep and intellectual. This is the uniform of his rank.

"Class, I know you are bored in the evenings. A lot of you are. I have certain obligations to your parents – to make sure nothing (cough) happens. So, I have a stack of books here. You are each to take one and to read it tonight until you fall asleep. Understand? I expect a full book report."

He crosses his arms. His eyes look at each of them, meet each eye. The sword girls giggle. I cannot help it, but for some reason, I blush and I think he saw me blush. After a moment of silence to show how deadly serious this all is, he commands us to line up single file and get the books.

I wait and get into the end of the line.

It is so much easier to be invisible from the back.

Each person grabs a book. I see them from where I stand. Big, weighty tomes. Classics. Works that do not involve love and knights and the Prince of Butterflies. Books that are not about the magical land of Iblio.

When I get up – right there, after everyone else is seated and they can all see – Mister Harvey reaches behind his desk and pulls out a book wrapped in leather, with a rope that ties it shut. He puts it in my hand, laying his hand over mine.

"This is for you," he says, "I set it aside just this morning. I think you'll like it."

His breath smells like vanilla and cocoa. His hand is rough over mine, and large and meaty. I want to faint. The moment lasts forever, his eyes staring into mine, his hand over mine. The sword girls giggle, and one of the boys hoots and whistles.

Mister Harvey's hand moves; his eyes move.

I sit back down, but I still feel it. His hand over mine. His eyes staring into mine.

I untie the knot, carefully. Unwrapping the leather around it. It feels soft, smooth, like skin. I am flush, remembering the stray flesh last night, rubbing against mine.

The book.

It is Victorian. On the cover is a naked woman, leaning over a dwarf. The title is "*The Tunnels Beneath the Castle of O*". This might be a promising read, after all.

Friday: Algebra

I cannot pay attention to the equations on the board. Every time I try and focus, my mind swims. Outside is a wall of ice and snow. Inside are the tense bodies, a roomful of trapped teenagers. The teacher sees their stare, tries to avoid their animal gazes.

I open my new book. The pages are thick, heavy. There are no words. Only pictures. They follow a sequential order, telling a story. I blush as I flip through it, closing the book as quickly as possible. I do not want the teacher to see what I am reading. I do not want her to see what Mister Harvey has given me.

They are line drawings, and in each of them someone is performing some sexual act with someone else. Always in the background, hidden in the walls of the castle, in the shadows of the tunnel. Leering at the main characters.

I am not sure how I feel about this.

I open up *Stone Dogs* and read. The teacher's voice drones on in the background. I read about Princess Earwig's glass face. I read about her hair made of gold. I read about her dresses, 230, in all, and no two of them alike. I read about her heart, kept in a box on her stepmother's throne.

And I read about the magic she uses to try and capture the love of Alisandre. Pictures burnt. Words whispered into seashells and buried in a box of mirrors. Blood smeared across the walls and the howls of misery ringing through the castle.

I picture Princess Earwig. And I see her looking like one of the girls in the shadows of the Castle of O. Her face twisted, her mouth wide open.

She is screaming. That is what Princess Earwig looks like. A twig of a girl in a castle of sex.

I hardly even hear the bell ring. One of the sword girls shakes me out of my book, out of my trance. She giggles when I come to, giggles and runs off with her triplets. I want to cut her open. Display her glass organs to the world.

I run outside, into the hall. I see Geoff and wave. He waves back, I see scars along his fingers. Cut into rings around his knuckles.

He talks to a boy. A new kid? I don't know. I don't recognize him. He has purple hair and a trenchcoat. He's cute. His features are very pretty, very feminine. He talks in a thick British accent. He reminds me of a fox, somehow.

Geoff introduces him. The boy's name is 'Nogitsune'.

"He climbed in through the third floor window. He's here to save us."

I smile my best smile. "Really? How come we're still in here, then?"

The boy shrugs. "Because I lied to Geoff; that's why. Although, I did sneak in through the third floor. But I'm not here to save anyone. I'm hiding out. Someone is chasing me."

Geoff sighs. "How could you lie to me?"

The boy puts his hand on Geoff's shoulder. Geoff melts beneath his fingers. "I'm sorry. You just seemed so excited and I just fed you what you wanted to hear."

I know I should ask whom he was running away from. Instead, I do something stupid. I talk about books. "Have you ever read *Stone Dogs?*"

The new boy shrugs. "Nope. Sounds like some weirdo New Agey thing."

I wave my hand excitedly. The more he looks at me, the more I want him. "No. It's fantasy."

New boy Nogitsune puts his fingers to his head. Like a gun. Pulls the trigger, bang. He's dead. Tongue sticks out; head lolls back. "Oh gawd. Not more of that Tolkien shit. I am so sick of elves and dwarves. Don't you guys read anything good? Like Camus? Or Sartre? Or – fuck – I don't know. Flannery O'Conner?"

Geoff blushes. "I read that stuff."

I push him. I don't know why I do it. He doesn't deserve to be pushed. "No, you don't," I say.

Geoff is hurt. "If he can lie to me, I can lie to him."

I see him look at me. His face is red. He's about to cry. He runs off screaming. Nogitsune looks at me and his eyes light up. "Woah, good going, there. I thought he would never leave. So – what did you say your name was again?"

I almost answer when the bells rings.

"Shit. Late for class. Sorry."

I run off; he yells at me.

"Late for class? How can you even care about such things when the world is going to end?"

Friday: Study Hall

I love the prose in *Stone Dogs*. It is unlike any fantasy I have ever read before. The sentences flow over each other. Tripping on the words and melting into a soup of language. I've got some time in Study Hall, so I will copy my favourite two paragraphs here:

The kindly birds, they speak and sing, with knives for beaks and swords for wings; they drip and dance orange light, discarding stray feathers like leaves on the ground. They are the autumnal gods, the speakers of mist; they have come to grant Alisandre 50 wishes, if only she can climb with needle hands and spindle fingers, up the labyrinth halls, past the walking dreams of angels and into the fire of morning light. There, there, burning puppets and the lies of sitars' men. We all know who lives here, the Medusa-spined, the stone singers. The hot and hollow dolls that grab the grass of dreams and weave coats of undying love.

But in corners of anger dwell the archling comedunly, who stretch with milky white eyes and cough and pour starch in the flour. They grab all hair and make them sing and dance. They have fingers; they have eyes. Oh, what burning things they can do to the pretty-pretty. Oh, what holes they can cut into our song boxes.

Absolutely chilling stuff. I have dreams that are written like that, in that same flowing way. Some day, I hope to write like that. Maybe, if I keep reading it and copying the words. Maybe my mind will drink in that style. Will become it.

Friday: Lunch

Geoff is not in the lunchroom. He is not at our normal table, not sitting at his normal seat. I wander around the crowd and look for him. Nothing. Some of the kids in the back wear paper-plate masks, with pictures of the dead stapled over top of them.

I wonder briefly if they are ghosts.

I see new-boy Nogitsune. In front of him, on an intricately detailed plate, is a dead fish. Cooked. With head and eyes still intact. He motions me to sit down.

I set my red plastic tray on the table. Chicken salad. Not bad for cafeteria food.

After I sit, he tells me a story about foxes. About their genealogy. About their species. I am bored and I realize Geoff would love this conversation. It is so full of details.

As he speaks, he eats. Cutting the fish slowly. Leaving the bones on his plate. When he is done, I let the silence sit for a moment. I don't know what to say. I am numb from listening.

"When do you think they will let us go home?"

Nogitsune drums his fingers on the table. "Never. Things have changed. We are in the snow lands, now. They didn't want to tell you, but if you go outside, you will see. There are no more trees, no more roads. We are surrounded by miles and miles and miles of ice and snow. Nothing else."

I stare at the last piece of lettuce on my plate. It is drowned in dressing. It will sting when I stick it into my mouth, coated with all those spices. "Never leave? I don't believe you. You're lying, again."

He picks up his plate and slides it into his trenchcoat. It disappears beneath the folds of clothing. "That's not all. I've seen giants outside. Wandering in that wasteland. You can see them. Their heads scrape the sky. They wait for us. And they are hungry."

Nogitsune gets up and leaves.

It still smells like socks in here.

I wonder where Geoff is.

Friday: Biology

Our teacher doesn't show up for class. They say she tried to leave, tried to go out one of the second floor windows and into the snow. I hope she's okay. I hope she doesn't get eaten by a giant. Nobody else seems to care.

The other students leave. I stay and read. I like the room. I like being surrounded by these pretty dead things. So neat, so tidy. So intricate.

I pull out Mister Harvey's book. Careful, making sure nobody else is anywhere near me. I flip through the pages, looking in the background. The main story isn't interesting. A simple quest of some sort. It ends with the main character, that nude girl, having a threesome with a giant and dwarf.

I look at each face in the backgrounds, at the tiny details of each body. I look in each crack, corner and crevice. There, I find more people, more figures. Doing things I never even thought possible. And I see them stare back at me. All those eyes. Staring right back at me. One of them, I realize, is Alisandre. Just as I pictured her. She wears bits and pieces of chain mail, rubbing coldly against her exposed and naked flesh.

That is not the Prince of Butterflies above her. It is a man. And he sings. And she howls in pain. Staring at me. Pleading for me to come and help her.

I'm covered in goosebumps.

I feel hot, dizzy. Aroused. I slam the book shut. Before things get out of control. It would be a terrible thing if someone were to walk into the biology lab and see me masturbating amongst all of the scientific corpses.

I wrap up the book, carefully. The leather like skin, caressing my hands. I remember the shadow of Mister Harvey's hands and I feel odd. I'm not sure what I want, anymore. If anything is what it really seems to be.

I want to read more in *Stone Dogs*. But I don't have the time. The bell is about to ring. I can feel it, vibrating in the air. Like storm clouds pregnant with snow.

Friday: Art Class

Mrs. Willow Tree stands in front of us. She is covered from head to toe in leaves and mud. This is her winter coat. She tells us in a commanding voice that she will be back momentarily. She is going out to brave the snow. To rescue our sculptures from the kiln.

She has a rusted sword strapped over her back. She is a knight. The Knight of Trees. She will need it when the giants come for her. I only hope that she can stand on her own. It is brave for her to do this.

After she leaves, the boys in the class pull out the slide projector. They turn it on, pulling up the naked pictures from yesterday. They spin and look at me. Look at the two other girls from class. The other girls are a little thinner than me, with curved beak noses. My nose is small, button shaped, and twitches when I get nervous.

The boys crowd around. They have red-lit eyes. Hair like black fur. They remind me of the wolf-kin in Iblio. A race of men whose parents slept with wolves, and begat half-breeds.

One howls.

"Come on, girls. We are all alone. It's time to show us your inner secrets."

They crowd around. Claustrophobic.

I want to run. I turn to look at the exit. Wide open. Ready for escape. I hope the bell rings soon, to give me a distraction.

I see the other girls. The bird girls. They look down at the ground, shyly, sadly. They pull straps down. Bras off. I see them undress and my breath is caught.

They are beautiful and sacred and scared.

The wolfkin are enrapt.

I run, run, run, rabbit-run out the door.

They cannot follow me. They are trapped by the gaze of naked flesh.

Friday: The Rooms Between Floors

I'm still shaken from Art Class. And I have this strange feeling that I survived something. That I got away before something terrible happened. I don't like to think about that. I don't want to wonder what happened to the crow girls. Class seems unimportant now.

Nagitsune was right – why should I worry about going to class when the world is going to end? I skip out on American History and run off to look for Geoff. I know about the secret places. The places he goes to when no one is looking.

He calls it his "cutting room".

It is one of the rooms between floors.

There is a secret into getting between the floors. Most people don't know about it. The janitor showed Geoff the way. One that had a crush on him. I think Geoff wanted to reciprocate, but was afraid. Afraid of himself.

You don't use the stairs to get to the rooms between floors. You look for a green tile on the ceiling. All of the other tiles are dark blue. When you see it, you stand beneath it and close your eyes.

And you concentrate on the sound of the ocean.

Holding your breath.

Still, so still.

If you do it correctly, you will feel water around you. Do not panic. Do not move. Let the water flow around you, caress you. You feel dizzy, your lungs burning. But don't let go – don't breathe just yet. You wait for the water to cover you completely.

And then -

It stops.

You can breathe and it feels like fire.

When you open your eyes, you are in the cutting room. One of the rooms between floors.

I follow the ritual carefully. It is hard to do. I am frightened and want to run. Instead, I think, I flow. I let the water come and wash me away.

I was right. Geoff is here. He lies in the corner of the room. The walls are covered in posters, the only light a single candle in the middle of the floor. It is cramped in here – low ceiling. Stoop down to see everything.

Someone is with Geoff. He is curled up around someone. They turn and look at me, naked beneath a blanket. It smells like the ocean. I see Nogitsune and I sit down, mouth open. I did not expect to see him here.

"Hi," Geoff says shyly. "Did you know the world is going to end?"

I see new cuts. Across his chest. Nogitsune is asleep on Geoff's chest. I see cuts across Nogitsune's back.

"Yes," I say. "It's been ending for a long time now."

Geoff runs his hand over Nogitsune's naked back. I feel a pang of jealousy. It feels odd, bitter in my mouth. I should have seen this coming, but did not. "When did he come up here with you?"

A hand through hair.

"About an hour ago. Are you all right?"

I nod. What else can I do? I can't tell him about the boy-wolves. He wouldn't understand. "Yeah. Why?"

"You look. I dunno. Shook up."

I laugh. "Yeah, a little. I didn't know that he was –"

Nogitsune's eyes spring open. They are red, glowing. His mouth pulls apart and I see tiny needle teeth. "I smell them. They are close. My brothers, my sisters."

Geoff looks down, his eyes squinting. His mouth twitching. I back away, my shoulder against the wall. "Nogitsune? You all right?"

Eyes return, roll back to normal.

"Yeah," he says, "Sorry about that. My family is here."

Geoff seems unfazed by what has happened. I, on the other hand, am spooked. Spooked by his actions and spooked by the wolf kin from earlier. This whole place feels wrong.

"I'm going to head out. Dunno where. Might see Mister Harvey and give his book back to him. I can't keep it; it's too weird."

Geoff doesn't hear me. Nogitsune doesn't hear me. They stare into each other's eyes. Gently, lips meeting. I feel like I am invisible, again. This makes me very sad. I never thought I would be the Invisible Girl to Geoff. I always thought I would be physical and real.

Now, I vanish.

Before his eyes.

I leave the cutting room.

Friday: Mister Harvey's Office

Mister Harvey is behind a large desk. It stretches the length of the room, and is covered in books and maps. Each one is highlighted. Each one has pins in them. Displayed, naked. Like a dissected animal.

He doesn't see me come in. Not at first.

His eyes are down. Head down. He is not talking. Only muttering, fast. Incoherent stream of syllables. I listen, listen closely. Try to find something to stand on. Some symbol to pull meaning from.

His eyes are moving, fast. His lip thickly twitching. His tongue a loose and wild animal in his mouth. I feel an electricity in the air. It is sharp and bites my skin.

I sit down in the chair. I should just leave the book on his desk. Leave and walk away. I don't know why – but I want to say something to him. I want to confront him with the book.

On the cover, I see Nogitsune. In the shadows. Beneath him is a monk, his robes up over his waist. I turn my head. I do not want to see this.

Eyes roll down. Eyelids flutter. Tongue stops moving. He sees me. I am no longer Invisible Girl. He puts his hands on the desk. They have cuts along them. I wonder briefly if he has been to the cutting room.

"Hello! To what do I owe the pleasure of your company?"

The book is in my lap. Under my folded hands. "The book you gave me ...."

He brings his fingers together. Into a pyramid. "Yes, yes. You know that books are magic? All books? They are all spell books of a sort. See, words and images. They carry more than just meaning. They carry the codes to our mental landscape. Books fuck with this. They take the words and change them, take the images and rearrange them. Each time you read a book, you become someone else. Changed inside."

I lean back in the chair. The electricity is still here. I feel it. Under my skin. Like acid. "I don't understand," I say. I feel weak, stupid.

"Did you read the book?"

I nod.

"How carefully? Did you just flip through it? No, no. You didn't. I see the change. It's coming over you, already. You are different now, aren't you? Can't you feel it?"

I do not feel any different. Just the same. Same Invisible Girl. Although, part of me is haunted now. But I am haunted by the things I've seen – the world acting in unnatural ways. That is not the book's fault. But I do not want to seem stupid. "Yes, I do feel different. But that's not the point – you giving me this book. It makes me feel uncomfortable."

That is a part of it. The discomfort. I want him. I need him. But this book made things clear – brought the hidden things forward in my mind. And I didn't feel right after that. Not comfortable. Not right.

He gets up on the desk. Crawls across it towards me. "Yes, yes. It is because you are changing; don't you see?"

I get out of my chair, move towards the back of his office. He has pictures hung on the walls of swingsets and playgrounds without children.

Stone Dogs

"No, that's not it. I don't want this book. I don't – I don't want you. Please. Stop. Just take the book back and let me go."

I move my hand against the door. I feel the doorknob. But it doesn't turn. I shake it, trying to force it to open. It doesn't turn. He is over top of me. Towering.

His hand cuts across the air and I hit the ground, hard. My cheek stings from his fist. I look up to see him pulling his shirt off. Tattoos across his biceps, his shoulders, his chest. Circles. Latin. Symbols I don't understand. He chants under his breath and my knees feel weak.

I try to move, but I cannot. My limbs have gone limp and wooden. I whimper. I try and say something, but I can only whimper. This is how the world ends. This is how the world ends.

A bang on the door from behind me.

He picks me up, moves me across the floor.

The door swings open.

Standing there is Nogitsune.

Mister Harvey does not stop chanting, but I feel different. I feel like I can move. His hands move over top of me, move over top as if they are about to undress me. I can move. I scream and kick him in his balls. He howls in pain.

Nogitsune walks forward. He has a table leg in his hands. He swings it in circles. Geoff is nowhere to be seen. "That's not nice," he says, walking up to Mister Harvey, who lies on the ground, clutching himself. I walk past him.

"Casting that spell on such a little girl. And that book – such a clever trap! But I am stronger than you. I am older than you."

Crack! The table leg breaks glasses.

Mister Harvey's body, curled up like a seashell.

Whimpering. "You don't scare me, Fox Boy. I have followers. Wolves from my world." Mr. Harvey turns and looks at me. "They are here, understand? They are here to feed. We will feed and feed and all of you will be dry husks. Empty things."

Crack! Table leg into the stomach. A howl of pain.

I leave. Quickly.

Without saying a word.

Friday: Roof and Snowlands

I have to see for myself.

I walk up the long steps. Walk up through the shadows. Walk up past the uncounted classrooms. Everyone is gone. Everyone else is in the gymnasium. Probably fucking. They won't miss the Invisible Girl. They didn't even notice I was there, not even when I was being rubbed against and humped against.

The roof is large and wide. I can see no one else up here. Only crows, who dot the landscape like feathered dreams. I want to see the sun. But the sun is gone. I want to see the stars. But the stars are gone.

The sky is a hole.

Nogitsune was right. There is only white, flat snow. A long range of snow plains. As far as I can see. And the only objects in the plain are the giants. They walk, I see them from here. Walk, walk, walk. Their tremendous bodies stomping into the ground, thick hands pounding at their sides.

Their skin is like rubber sewn together. Their eyes are fires burnt into their heads. Their hair is like wire, tangled and broken and strung up on their heads.

They dress in rags.

And they are hungry.

The sight of them makes my blood run cold.

Foxes prance between them, their red bodies like fuzzy fires against the snow. Riding on the back of one is my art teacher, sword in hand. Over her back, I see our sculptures in a brown satchel. I see *Fear of Mice* and feel hope.

From behind, I hear a kicking of a pebble. I turn and see Nogitsune. Walking calmly, swinging the table leg. I see that it is covered in blood and I hate that it has come to that.

It is so cold up here.

"I had to see," I say. I am crying. I need to be the girl who cries. Not invisible. Not to him. "I had to see for myself."

He nods and walks towards me. "I know. They are there. And they wait. My brothers hold them off and my sisters hold off the wolves. But it is only a matter of time before we are outnumbered."

I walk up and put my head on his chest. I feel his arms around me. I cry against his shirt. "Thank you. For earlier."

He runs his fingers through my hair. I feel something against my ear. Like a breast. Like a breast in his shirt. I wonder where it came from. And I look up and he is a she.

"I can be whatever you want," she says. "I can be whoever you want. But I need you now. I need you to want me. I am vague here, flickering. Soon, I will be gone. Geoff was not enough to keep me here. He is barely real, himself. But you – you can keep me whole. You can keep me real."

I say nothing. Only lean my head against the chest. It feels like my mother's breast, and I remember being small and tiny, and sleeping on my mother's breast while she rocked back and forth, rocked back and forth.

He doesn't speak again.

We just stand there and watch a war unfold.

Paul Jessup is a critically acclaimed writer of fantastical fiction. He's been published in a slew of magazines(in print & online) and a mess of anthologies. He has a short story collection out (*Glass Coffin Girls*) published in the UK by PS Publishing. He has a novella published by Apex Books (*Open Your Eyes*) and a graphic novel published by Chronicle Books.

He was also a Recipient of KSU's Virginia Perryman Award for excellence in freshman short story writing in 2000.

You can check out his crazy stuff at: http://pauljessup.com.

The City of Melted Iron

By Bobby Cranestone

Concerning the events in Komplex 5, the industrial part ....

Essen: hundreds of smoking chimneys, factories, melting pots, and steaming iron. Here, where all four elements are centred and put into a new creation. A physically dangerous place, but this is nothing compared to the mental pressure. Decades of hardship, deaths and fears have formed something traceable, as if all those feelings have become manifested into a new form.

There is something out here that lives off your very soul, the guy next to me muttered while munching on his lunch. Not that one actually saw it. But sometimes, if you're turning round a dark corner, there's a light creeping over the walls, and if you're checking the temperatures on one of the kettles, it might happen that you encounter a dark shape leering at you. It changes all the time; it's different, but you know it, anyway, when you meet it. Whatever it is, it's most times faithful. Like the Banshee in the old Celtic tales, it seems to be a foreboding of doom. Those who meet it have little time to speak of this encounter before they die. Yet, the tale spreads, anyway, as tales always do.

~

I was from the lower working class, so no one cared if I was scared or not when I arrived at Essen. I had simply no choice, if I wanted to make a living.

My post was at the Gischt, close to the blast furnace at the very heart of the complex, which seemed, with every passing day, more and more to me like a living being with a mind and will of its own.

The industrial complex included a confusing jungle of tubes and cables that often measured more than one foot in diameter, an iron and steel mill, conveyor belts with melted iron that led over kilometres of industrially-transformed land, high-pressure kettles, several forging presses and other means of forging the gathered iron. On the surface, there were hundreds of buildings of varying sizes, and bridges leading to

watch towers and chimneys. The whole area measured 120 square kilometres aboveground, but there was, as well, a great mining area. A blasted
area, mines and tunnels that led deep down. Five thousand men went to
work each day; some did it reluctantly and with a bad feeling in their guts
that they could not name. Not everyone was given to superstition, but this
place was the likeliest to engender such a belief.

I worked as a machinist at the main gas supply, fixing leakages and
building new mechanical linkages where old tubes were wholly worn
beyond repair. Strangely, they proved unusually short-lived in my area
and the tubes seemed not wholly blasted, but almost torn by claws.

In the glow and the smoke … sometimes, you didn't quite see what
was going on around you and strange shapes showed up that, even when
the smoke was gone, only reluctantly vanished.

The sounds of artificial thunder and whizzing iron were almost
unendurable and the smell was, in some places, dangerous, consisting of
all kinds of unhealthy particles, and you had to wear a mask. The siren
shrilled its warning whenever something wasn't right. Things were often
not right. You could not tame the fire and the treasures of the earth without paying the price.

Maybe the place was haunted, as many old workers stated.

At the very least, it was bizarre. I had worked under similar circumstances, at other mills, but never had I come upon a tube that should be
glowing hot, but was icy cold to the touch.

Young and shy, and the new member of my crew, to boot, I chatted
little with the others, even the friendlier youths like Florian or Karl. I kept
my misgivings and my fears to myself. At least, for a while.

~

On one occasion, the alarm shrilled, as it often did. I felt it like
a certain sign of doom. Panic-stricken men fled to the next point of
safety, anxious and eager to know what had occurred. Hastily, I followed
through the labyrinthine ways of tubes large enough for a man to easily crawl through, iron pillars and supporting beams. It might have been
my imagination, but I thought I felt a warm breath in my neck, which
might have been some other leakage, again, or something entirely different. When I reached the next meeting point, I saw around thirty others
of my shift, with grave faces. Three men had vanished. Just ten minutes
before, when another repair maintenance team had passed them, they

had greeted each other with the ironmakers sign, as it was customary. But ten minutes were enough to change luck into doom and life into death … or worse.

I soon learned other details. There had been an explosion, but only an average one, and the rescue team looking for the missing men expected to find at least some remains of them. However, at the place of the accident, there were no clues. No blood, no shreds of flesh and no bodies. There was no trace to be found of the missing ones.

The source of the explosion was also deemed a mystery, if not such a bizarre one.

A valve had been stuck and the growing forces had finally found the weakest point to get out. Everything in nature was struggling for balance … even if we could not understand it.

The place the explosion had laid waste had to be freed from its ruins and I was among the helpers. What puzzled me was the fact that everything was so clean, so unlike any outburst of gas or flammable substances. I tried not to think too much about it and worked on. What else could I do?

At night, it was hardest. When the flames shone more brightly. Often did I catch the impression of something rushing past me, soundless, yet somehow traceable. Like a shadow with luminous edges, but I was never sure if its source was the fumes that hung heavy in the air or the noises. The dust and the glowing heat could drive any man mad. But even so, I could not wholly shake myself free from the idea that *something* was lurking there amidst the cylinders and tubes.

~

This place was first known as 'Astnide', which was also the name of a Greek priestess who was eventually sentenced to death for having called upon great forces that were neither from Heaven nor from Earth. It was said that she had made a pact of a very mysterious nature, though with whom, I cannot say.

Artefacts from the Stone Age have been found in Essen, proof of some prehistoric past beyond our written and traceable history. Early buildings all centred around one vast temple complex of pits and small lakes. The inhabitants must have paid tribute to some kind of god or other powerful creature, for archaeologists found great amounts of ash, and pieces of plants and shells, as well as pieces of charcoal. The area had been discovered in the early 1920s, when archaeology was still at its beginnings and only the pyramids in Egypt, with their treasures of gold, and the cities of Pompeii and Herculaneum received attention. The temple complex didn't fit into the owners' plans and its buildings were either removed or simply filled in with soil. The past was forgotten, but it was never wholly gone and maybe it didn't care what we thought of it.

~

I was working at one of the great kettles, doing some maintenance, when I had again the strange feeling of being watched. When I turned around, I couldn't detect anything but the spouting kettle and its sounds of working metal that was endlessly heated and cooled down, until it was worn and had to be melted and formed into something new. Somehow, my attention was drawn to the melting furnace, to the small door at its front, and when I moved stealthily forward and looked into it, I thought I saw the flames dance wildly and form some kind of face, fretting at me. When I tried to retreat, I felt a heavy weight upon my shoulder, holding me still. A valve opened and the spell broke and I ran away without any true explanation as to what had just happened.

Only hesitantly did I tell the others on my shift what had happened, and over the weeks, I learned their stories, too.

Florian said that he had seen a big, silvery, shining ball, waiting in one of the hallways. Inside, there was the form of a women leering at him. The face was odd. The head more like an elipsoid and the skin of greenish hue.

When, three days later, his twins were born, something wasn't quite right about them.

And there were other tales, of unexplained noises and lights.

~

The next time the alarm rang, it was in my area. I knew the people of my shift very well now, so instead of running to the next point of safety, I ran in the direction where the alarm was sounding, to see if I could do anything. I stopped stone-still when I saw that my efforts were, and must be, futile. Before me stood, as if built from iron clinker (the iron oxide formed during forging), the human shape of a screaming man. Looking like the human remains from Pompeii that were shown on exhibition at the museum, this thing stood before me, unearthly and yet human. I couldn't help but shrink away. I could discern the features of my coworker, Karl, who had been working in this area, but was nowhere to be seen. Yet, this couldn't be him. How could that be possible? This was a thing beyond physical laws and reality. Yet, it was standing before me.

I heard a faint sound behind me. A shadow flickered over the tubes and bunches of cables. Turning around, I saw a stag beetle buzzing against one of the lamps.

When I turned back, Karl was gone.

~

After the accident, in which we lost Karl – another broken valve, they told us – the air in our lounge area turned serious and our emotions seemed to hang heavy above our heads. Some played cards, but only half-heartedly did they follow the game, they just wanted something simple to do, so they did not have to think about the latest turn of events. You could have cut the air with a knife and the vibrations from the outside world of working machines seemed to us now like the bringers of doom.

"It's not the worst thing that has happened," mumbled Chester..

I raised my head in surprise. "What do you mean by that?"

He rubbed his chin and took a sip of milk. "There were guys before, in my youth. They were not dead when we found them, but the foremen were so hasty in taking them away that there was much room for imagining. Something weird had happened to them. We were not allowed to see them anymore. One of the officers did slip us a word that they were put in some kind of asylum with another man who dared to look ...."

"But what is that thing out there? What does it want?"

"Some say it is some kind of personified evil. It's said it is a man; others believe it's some kind of force, nature-bound, like rain or a heavy storm." This time it was Pit, who always smoked a cigarette, even though it was forbidden to smoke inside Komplex 5.

"However it is ... there is still the *question*."

Chester looked ominously at me, as if this was an especially important detail.

"The question?"

"They say that whatever it is, it asks you a question. If you answer right, you might find some kind of reward. If you're wrong ... well ..."

"And what kind of question is it? I get that you're speaking about some kind of riddle."

Chester shrugged his shoulders. "It's always a different one. A different one, depending on what person you are, what character you have."

~

I could't get the his words out of my head. The whole evening, I worked in a kind of mechanical stupor, I did not listen to the greetings of my ship mates, nor to the call for supper or lunch. Only when my shift ended did I wake up, as if from a very deep dream.

I took up my stuff and turned around the corner. All seemed very silent. Had I lingered too late? Too deep in thought to think about time? The Komplex usually never slept, but the two hours between one and three o'clock were the quietest hours. I should have left four hours ago. Getting my overalls out of my locker I withdrew my hand as if touched by an electrical discharge. The door was icy cold. Hastily, I changed into my fresh clothes, with my mind made up to leave the Komplex as fast as I could. Today was an unlucky day. I felt it with every fibre of my aching body.

Someone opened the door. I turned around, but my eyes took some time before they could discern the person's features in the dark.

There it stood. It was humanoid, but almost double my height. Its skin was red and seemed to steam, while its face was a mocking mask, with very deep and dark eyes that shone like charcoal in its sockets. When it reached out and pointed at me, it seemed to do so in a kind of slow motion. It held out a claw with three fingers. An unearthly voice that seemed to hold at least a thousand other tongues from ancient times spoke.

"What's your desire?" it asked in a low voice.

I was terrified. Only one thought came to my mind: "To live."

It nodded. "You will live."

The light went out.

~

When I awoke, I found myself smeared with a sticky substance. A red fluid spread all around me. Even if this was very puzzling to the men who found me, nothing bad had happened to me. I was whole and healthy, and had survived – they told me later – a rather bad fall down a flight of stairs.

"I guess you won," said Chester, looking strangely at me.

"Do you think it is gone?"

He shook his head gravely.

Things started to change for me. Someone recommended me for a better position and, within a short time, I was climbing the ladder of success. I became, after three years, the partner of Harry Linde, who had been until a few weeks before, the chief of Komplex 5.

Today, I'm running one of the biggest industrial centres of Europe. But a certain feeling of dread has never left me. Day after day, I watch the men going to work. Some won't ever return. I wonder what price I paid and what tribute I deliver.

Bobby Craneston was born in a quiet and ancient part of Germany. She is a musician, poet and author, as well as a student of ancient mysteries. Bobby started writing fiction at the early age of nine and continued working on short stories and books in the years to follow, living the life of a penniless but passionate artist. Accompanied by a small fan following in the UK, through the immeasurable wonders of the Internet, she is eager to spread words of magic and tales of bewilderment to any who will listen.

The Shredded Tapestry

By Ryan Harvey

The thieves who held up Richard Davey on the forest road from Munich to Regensburg must have been in a hurry. They left him with two valuables that men of their lot rarely leave their customers: his boots and his life.

Richard was thankful to have both, but the three men with handkerchiefs covering their faces, and pistols with cocked hammers, had taken away his sturdy horse and its saddle packs, which contained a hundred *thalers* and his sketchbooks filled with the clockwork devices he had studied on his long journey to Prague.

A moment later, Richard realized that the bandits had not ridden off suddenly into the October night out of generosity. Something large was moving through the brush at the road's edge.

Richard, who still had his hands raised foolishly in the air, turned toward the rustling sound. Beech trees and nettles crowded the narrow road and, although the wind was not blowing, the leaves trembled.

Even though fear clutched at him, Richard's mind was busy flipping through memories of the bestiaries he had read. What animals might haunt this stretch of forest road? Wolves hunted in Bavaria, but rarely so close to the cities. Perhaps it was a bear. Neither was a satisfying answer. He settled on a simple piece of knowledge: Animals would only rush a man who tried to flee.

But when the nettles shuddered again, and a low breathing soughed through the air, Richard hoped that a slow, indifferent walk would be almost the same as standing still.

He moved in his original direction on the road. The nettles rustled beside him, matching his steps.

His gut told him to run, but his mind ordered him to move cautiously. He came around a bend in the road and spied an orange light through the prison bars of beech trunks. If the light came from a cottage window, a fast run might get him to safety in time.

He gave thanks for the boots that were still on his feet as he sped up his steps. The movement in the nettles stopped. For a moment, Richard Davey felt that it was nothing more than a phantasm in his ruffled mind.

He looked behind him for assurance.

That was when he saw it.

Against the grey forest, a dreadful black had curled onto the road. It loomed as large as a bear, but its hair spiked wildly, making a diabolic outline. Yellow eyes reflected light without a source. The dark blotch had the feeling of something malignant and *feline*. Electricity, like rubbing the long fur of a cat on a winter morning, rippled over Richard's skin.

When he heard the hiss, a pitiless sound that nothing in nature should make, he started to run. At any moment, he expected to feel the weight of forepaws and unsheathed claws dig into his back.

Suddenly, Richard's fists were hammering against the oak of enormous double doors. He thought he had heard the padding of feet at his back, but perhaps it was only the echo of his own steps. The solid wood under his fists wrenched him back to his senses.

He looked behind him. There was no sign of anything on the road, no animal prints in the dirt. He had run only a short way, out of the eaves of the forest and onto a trail that split from the main road through an open gate.

He stepped back to look at the building he had run to in his panic. It was a large stone structure with a peaked wooden roof that reminded him of a church. But the churches of Bavaria have distinctive onion dome steeples, and this squat thing had no steeple at all – although Richard could sense where one might have stood. Above the double doors was a tympanum with a fresco, but wind and rain had long ago faded it to hazy outlines. In the darkness and the half-moon light, he could see little else except the edge of an outbuilding and patches of earth that could have grown the snowdrop and blue fairy thimble flowers of southern Germany, but instead held only crumbly soil.

Richard clutched at the fabric of his coat and took a moment to regain his composure. He had been years away from home, but never before had he felt so much a *foreigner* on the continent. His inquisitiveness, his skill in losing himself in brass rubbings and sketches of gears, often made him forget that months had passed since he had last heard a word of English.

Richard did not recall that he had knocked, so he twitched as the doors started to creak open. Although he felt foolish after his panic, he was relieved to see someone inhabited the grey place.

Warm light spilled from the crack. "Yes? What do you want?"

"If you please," Richard said in his proficient boarding school German, "I've just been robbed. If you wouldn't mind –"

The voice, which had a peculiar accent, interrupted: "You are out of breath. Are the thieves still near?"

"Uh, no –" Again, he felt a fool, as if he were still walking about with his hands stuck in the air. "I thought there was a large animal after me."

The light spilled out onto the porch. "Inside! Inside now!" A hand grabbed Richard's arm and tugged him between the doors. It happened so fast that he might have left his boots on the porch.

As he entered the vestibule, Richard felt a peculiar sensation around his legs. It was as if a fur shawl were rubbing between his ankles, slipping through the door crack and past him. But there was nothing to see after the man slammed shut the heavy doors and dropped down the bar.

"Pardon me, young man," his abrupt host said, "but the highwaymen here are a vicious class and it's best if they don't spy you looking for help."

Richard was about to mention that the man had reacted, not to news of robbers, but news of the stalking animal. However, the warmth of the inside and the chance for hospitality made him stay quiet. His natural curiosity, which thrived when his life was not in immediate danger of ending, was coming alive again.

The man was grey with age, but had the posture of a saint's statue on a French cathedral. It was an easy comparison to make, for not only had Richard sketched the Chartres and Bourges Cathedrals, but his host wore the habiliments of a monk. His robes were a simple brown, with a heavy topcoat that draped down to his wrists. A black skullcap clung to his silver hair.

"I am Abbot Fletcher," he said, with a bend at the waist. "You will be safe here for the night, and we can offer you modest food and drink. Please come this way."

Richard followed the abbot into a chapel. He was wondering at the abbot's unusual accent, which was familiar but drowned under the heavy gravy of German. "So, this is a monastery?"

"Yes. When the nearby town of Kelheim converted to Luther's heresy, they built this place as their church. Eventually, the righteous returned and burnt down the steeple in anger. That was two hundred and fifty years past. Our brotherhood has resided here since."

Richard decided it was inappropriate to mention that he was a follower of the Anglican faith and had no love for the Pope. But he had nothing against the Pope's followers, as he had learned from the kindness he had met so far in his journey across Bavaria. Highwaymen excepted.

Abbot Fletcher led him along the ambulatory into a room that might have once been a sacristy. Now it was decorated as a small banquet room. A fire struggled in a brick hearth, and an oil lamp added light from a table with Italian-style carvings on the legs. The rug spread across the floor had Moorish swirls, which Richard thought queer for a monastery.

The most striking furnishing in the room was an enormous tapestry covering the wall farthest from the door. While the abbot poured from a flagon of wine into tin goblets, Richard walked up to the hanging. On the thick wool was a distinctive stone bridge arching over a wide river toward a map of a city. Prominent in the middle span of the bridge was a statue of a child with his eyes covered, as if he were afraid to look on the unfinished cathedral at the end of the bridge.

"Regensburg," Richard remarked.

"Indeed. Have you come that way?"

"I'm heading there now." He gave a short explanation of his travels: He was hoping to reach Prague before winter so he could study the collections of Emperor Rudolf II. Richard was an admirer of mechanical devices and contraptions, and the sixteenth-century emperor was famous for his clockwork museum.

Richard placed his fingers on the grey weave of the tapestry that made the bridge. The abbot's face turned stony and Richard pulled his hand back.

"I'm sorry. It's just that I'm eager to cross this bridge. It's one of the finest in Europe, I hear. So firmly built, they say the Devil himself could not break it, although he once tried."

The abbot turned back to the table. "The Devil is said to spend too much time in Regensburg. Too much time."

Suddenly, Abbot Fletcher spoke in clear English with a slight Scottish burr. "You must excuse me, but your accent tells me that what I am now speaking is your first language."

Richard felt a warmth swell that the tiny fire could never have made. To hear his own language, after so many months deep in Bavaria, was almost enough to bring tears. "I had wondered at the name 'Fletcher," he said.

The abbot did not seem as moved to hear his mother tongue. He started to slice a hard rye and serve it onto pewter plates. "Do you see the church with the courtyard in the middle of the tapestry?" he asked. Richard had noted it, since its halo of gold thread dared the eye to look anywhere else. "That is – *was* – the Benedictine Abbey of St. James. Now *this* –" He gestured with disdain at the roof over him. "– is the Abbey."

"The old Scots monastery?" Richard asked. "Are all of you Scotsmen, then?"

"At one time. But we are dwindling and the initiates who join now are more often German." The abbot sat down in the tall-backed chair at the head of the table and motioned for Richard to sit near him.

"Why did you leave Regensburg? I know that the city converted, but I did not hear of them hurling out all the Catholics."

The abbot sipped his wine. "*All* does not mean *none*. It's a pitiful tale, not fit for an autumn night after the fright you've had. The summary of it is that one of our brethren fell prey to the Devil's temptation and committed an ... *indiscretion* ... of which the city had little tolerance."

When the abbot said the word *indiscretion*, Richard felt a prickle around his legs, like touching a brass doorknob in crisp winter. He remembered the strange sensation, as he entered the door, and the imagined feline thing on the road.

"That was before the lifetime of anyone here. We've gone forward in our brotherhood, quietly carrying on God's work." The way Abbot Fletcher swallowed his wine placed a period on the story and Richard asked no further. The abbot moved on to other topics and, at last, seemed to enjoy using his native language with a new listener. He listed the names of his brethren, of whom there were now only 12, and who were asleep in the dormitory attached to the old chapel.

At last, he came back to the events of the evening: "These woods have become treacherous. It must have been a large animal to have scared you so."

"Well, perhaps I was nervous after being robbed. I might have imagined it."

"Ah."

The utterance told Richard that the abbot firmly believed that he had *not* imagined it.

The abbot finished his wine and pointed to the half-full goblet beside Richard's plate. "I do not blame you for not finishing it. It's a watery vintage from Kelheim. We have a wine cellar, but it ages only cobwebs now. There's no need to keep a store for so few and the vineyards shrivelled years ago."

There was something disquieting in the man's tone that flamed Richard's curiosity. But the night already held too many mysteries and exhaustion started to douse his inquisitiveness. Daylight would sweep the mysteries away, and Richard would find nothing more intriguing than a dying abbey and an empty road.

Richard finished his bread and then followed his host to his bed for the night. Abbot Fletcher explained that the upstairs room had once belonged to the Protestant deacon, that properly, the abbot should have it. But he preferred the company of his brothers in the dormitory. The room was a spartan place at the peak of the roof and the triangular shape gave Richard the comfortable feeling of sleeping in an old barn. There was a narrow bed and a writing desk, with an empty bottle of ink and an unlit candle. On the wall hung a garish crucifix, with Christ in more pain than Richard preferred to see.

"I'd be grateful if you could spare a horse tomorrow," Richard said. "I'll leave it at Kelheim and hire someone to return it."

"We have no horses," the abbot said brusquely. "Wild animals have killed them all."

Richard knew not to ask questions. He had been eager for bed, but now he felt even more eager to wake up and be on his way.

The abbot bid him goodnight and shut the door. Richard covered the gruesome crucifix with his coat, feeling a pang of Anglican revulsion at the papist decor. He pulled off his boots and was asleep as soon as his head touched the musty mattress.

~

The wheezing breath woke him. Heavy curtains covered the only window, so he could not tell from the moon shadows how much time had passed. He shut his eyes, but the wheezing came again. It was slow, like a child's hand pressing down a bellows. He remembered the sound in the nettles and the shape on the road, and his chest turned cold and his muscles rigid.

The sound crept just outside the door. Richard listened for it, hoping it was only the noise of his body against the sheets. But he was more still than he could ever remember holding himself in his life.

The sound now turned shrill, like a Yorkshire wind whistling through rocks. Then the shrilling changed into a hiss. *The hiss of a cat.*

Richard recalled the black fiend on the road. Eyes of yellow ichor, fur made from iron spikes gating a cemetery. But ... that had been his imagination ....

He stared into the dark around the doorway. The floorboards outside creaked. A creature was striding back and forth before the door, like a witch laying down a hex. Padded feet stretched the aged wood.

Richard wanted to pull the sheets over his head, but when he reached out, he found the mattress was bare. A childhood fear seized him: the tiny boy who felt that, if he could bury himself far enough under downy blankets, no night evil could touch him. Now, there was nothing between him and the night.

The boards stopped groaning. But then the door started. The wood shrieked from a great weight pushing from the other side. Bared claws scratched down it, mixing the infernal hiss with the peeling of slivers.

Richard backed into the corner of the bed and felt the stucco wall at his back. He tried to pull his eyes away from the door, but he could feel the black monster bristling right outside it.

The thing at the door hissed. But, although the scratching still raked down the wood, the breathing of the thing now seemed to move inside the cramped room. Richard again felt the scrape of fur over his skin. Now it moved across his arms, wending around his torso, tapering off with a sinuous tail. Whiskers like needles stabbed his cheek.

Richard focused his eyes on the vague lump of his coat on the wall, trying to pull his mind away from its hallucinations. The coat hovered in blackness. The wall and the crucifix where it hung were lost in the dark of the room.

Then the coat started to flutter from the wall and drift toward the bed. As it did, the scratching and the hissing stopped.

The coat turned inside out and a black lining flowed out into the shape of a tall woman in robes woven from midnight.

Richard tried to back through the wall. And, suddenly, he succeeded. The wall pushed away, the bed vanished ... he dropped through space.

Above him was a bridge, a huge span of bleak stones. Daggers of icy water jabbed into his back. The air was punched from his lungs and when he drew breath, the freezing water flooded in. Choking, he flailed out his arms.

His hands hit the stucco wall; he fell onto the mattress. The water and the bridge were gone. The woman was still there, a sliver of midnight at the foot of the bed.

"Who – who are you?" He felt as if he were spitting water from his lungs to say it.

A hand slipped from the night that shrouded her. Her skin was the colour of moonlight bleeding through swamp vapours. Yet, it was a relief from the Stygian cloak of the rest of her ... and he had not even dared to try to look her in the face.

Her finger pointed toward the door.

"You – let me – in."

It was a hissing voice and Richard could not tell what language she spoke, except that he could understand it.

"You – will – break – the charm."

Unwillingly, his eyes were drawn to her face ....

He did not remember what it looked like, because the memory drowned as he started falling again ... tumbling from the bridge. He could see the statue of a child on the span above him, a hand covering its eyes as if it could not bear to watch him plunge to a watery death ... to plunge from the bridge that the Devil himself could not break.

The Regensburg Bridge, he knew. And with that, he was back on the bed, cowering against the wall.

One more hissed word came from the woman: *Help.*

The sickly moon glow peeking from the shadows vanished. The midnight shape turned back into a coat hanging from a crucifix.

But the scratching at the door started again. The spectre of the woman was still there, in the shape of the beast clawing to get inside.

Other sounds now exploded through the monastery. Feet pounded up the stairs, and voices called in a hurly-burly of German and English. Then came shouts of Latin, phrases that Richard could recall from murky schoolboy days:

"Et ne inducas nos in temptationem, sed libera nos a malo!"

The beast shrieked and needles of fur prickled across Richard's skin. More voices shouted in unison, *"Libera nos a malo!"* Abbot Fletcher's call followed in a righteous thunderclap: *"Maleficas non patieris vivere!"*

Abruptly, the scratching stopped. The fur uncurled from around Richard Davey and he crumpled forward onto the floor.

A mundane rapping struck the door. The abbot called, "Mr. Davey! Mr. Davey, are you all right?"

Hearing the voice of a living man, one with whom he had drunk wine only hours before, should have comforted him. But Richard suddenly had no wish to see the abbot of this blighted place.

He had no choice. There was no lock on the door and the abbot pushed it open and raised up a candle.

In the first flicker of light, Richard saw the deep furrows of claw marks down the front of the door. He wondered that he did not faint and spend the rest of the night in peaceful oblivion.

The abbot stared at him, offering no aid. Richard staggered to his feet on his own. Other faces peered from behind the abbot, a mixture of elders and novices. They clucked to each other, mostly in German. None of them crossed the threshold.

"Wh – what was that?" Richard breathed.

"It is gone." The abbot squinted. "And you must be gone in the morning."

"I don't understand. What happened?"

The abbot's eyes were lead shots. Looking into them was worse than staring down a highwayman's pistol.

"You let *her* in."

Richard was not supposed to have heard those words. They were spoken in German, as if Abbot Fletcher had forgotten that his visitor knew the language.

Then, in English: "Nothing happened. You will not be bothered again tonight. But be prepared to leave at dawn. I will lay out food for you in the banquet room."

He turned to the others and grumbled at them in German to return to the dormitory. He took one look back into the room, noticed the coat hung rudely over the crucifix, and slammed the door.

Richard groped in the dark to reach the candle. He found matches beside it, struck one, and lit the wick.

The first thing he noticed was his coat. It hung inside out over the crucifix, and he knew he had not done that. He picked it up to turn it back around, and felt a heaviness in one of the pockets. He reached in and pulled out a three-pronged iron key he had never seen before. He dropped it back into the pocket – he needed to take this one mystery at a time.

He turned toward the door. He was frightened to see for certain what he thought he had spotted when the abbot opened the door, but the curiosity of a man who explores curiosities pushed him on. He drew the door open and looked at the marks that ran from the height of the latch down to floorboards.

But he had glimpsed more than that in the abbot's candlelight. He slanted the door and squinted at the marks from a different angle.

No illusion. The beast on the other side of the door was not scratching to get in. It was leaving a message. Four shaky letters: HELP.

～

A taciturn Abbot Fletcher hustled Richard from the room in the morning. The man now spoke only in German, casting aside any brotherhood he might have felt for someone else from the isles. Richard knew better than to ask questions about the nighttime disturbances. He would receive no answers.

The other members of the Abbey of St. James in Exile stood around the staircase as Richard walked down. Some muttered blessings; others gave him stares that he might have classed as "diabolic", if he thought such a thing could be used to describe a monk. He tried to tell which of them were German and which Scottish, so perhaps he might get a last friendly word in his own language before leaving, but their faces were shadowed with fear.

"There is food for you," Abbot Fletcher grumbled, and indicated a burlap sack on the table of the banquet room.

Richard picked it up and slung it over his shoulder. As he did, he thought he felt something different about the banquet room. Something more than the changed air of day. But the abbot hurried him out through the chapel. In all his rush to get Richard out of the abbey, it was surprising he had not conjured a horse to carry him off as fast as possible. Even when Richard tried to offer thanks, the man had no interest in hearing it: "You should never have come here and you should forget that you did."

Abbot Fletcher waved him through the front doors that had welcomed him last night.

Richard walked under the tympanum into the unfriendly morning cold. He expected to hear the creak of hinges and the slam of a wooden beam behind him, but there was only monastic silence. He walked down the path, through the opening in the iron posts around the churchyard. He looked over his shoulder. The maw of the church was open, but the abbot was no longer standing there.

He turned his head back and stepped onto the road that wound toward Kelheim, and then beyond to the bridge and its child protector that crossed the Danube to Regensburg.

Richard Davey was not an extraordinarily brave man. He had the common courage needed to travel across the continent alone, but he would never have survived life as a soldier or in any profession more dangerous than a "seeker of curiosities".

"Seeker of curiosities": That was how he introduced himself whenever he had to explain to lesser nobility why a young man wanted to look through their libraries. Behind him was a curiosity greater than any he had encountered, perhaps greater than the automaton chess player rumoured to be in the treasuries of Prague.

The letters "HELP" scratched in mouldy oak. The hissing of an apparition made of shadow hovering over him. A dream of plunging from a bridge to drown. A key in his pocket that did not belong there. The posture of the abbot, the unease that shrouded monastery.

The daylight could sweep these oddities from most minds, but not from Richard Davey's. They left a blot of ink on his soul, and it was from ink that great tales were written. In him was an urgency, even importance, which was strange to him but stronger than the dark beers of Munich.

He walked only as far along the road as he needed before finding the shelter of a wall of hawthorn. He leaned against an accommodating beech, ate the squishy apple and dry loaf in his pack, and waited until nightfall.

He walked back along the road, staying in the shadow of the trees. The waning moon only peeked out from the clouds in bursts, so Richard had an easy time turning into a shadow himself.

Lights burned in the outbuilding of the monastery. The closer that Richard came, the more he could pick out from the crickets the sound of men's voices chanting evensong. He had heard many evensongs during his sojourn through Bavaria, but this one had an air of fear, not celebration. But if the brothers of St. James were awake, it were better they were enrapt in chanting Latin so that they would pay no attention to an outsider slipping into their church.

The front doors still gaped wide. For a moment, Richard stared in bewilderment; in a countryside filthy with bandits, this was a bizarre sight, making the church a naked man in the middle of a raging battle.

Then he remembered the words of the abbot that he was not supposed to hear: "You let *her* in."

The brothers were now trying to send *her* out, like housewives who flung open their doors to shoo out an uninvited spider or rat. The brothers had no fear of what was outside but what had gotten *inside*.

No one guarded the vestibule. The voices floated from behind the interior doors to the chapel. Richard spied through the gap between them. He saw the backs of some of the monks. They wore red topcoats over their simple brown robes and had gathered in a circle in the apse, where Abbot Fletcher led the song from the center. The simmering Latin reeked of diablerie; there were no simple "*pater noster*"s or "*saeculo saeculorum*"s.

Richard pushed through the doors, making no noise, and crawled on his hands and knees behind the pews, through the nave, past the transept. He managed to move the length of the chapel unseen. The monks were so deep in their ritual that Richard wondered if he could have stomped through the choir shouting "Hosanna!" without distracting them.

It was a relief reaching the banquet hall just to place a wall between him and the unholy chanting. A fire was burning itself out in the hearth, casting enough light for Richard to search for what had seemed different in the room that morning.

He picked it out immediately: The tall chair at the end of the table had been pushed against the middle of the tapestry.

Richard took the oil lamp from the table, lit it with a burning sprig of wood from the fire, and moved toward the hanging. He pulled back the chair, which made a loud *squeak* across the floor. Richard waited, but no one came running to investigate. He pushed back the chair further until he could see what it had covered up.

It was the section of the tapestry showing the haloed Scots Monastery. Richard lifted the lantern; the light seeped over three straight rips down the cloth. A single swipe from the paw of a cat … a paw large enough to slash open a bear's throat.

The lantern shivered in his grip, but he was meant to find this. It was clear as any signpost at a crossroads. He reached toward the rips and pushed his finger through one of them. Then his hand. Then his whole arm. Where a wall should have been was a damp void.

He lifted up the bottom of the tapestry. A fusty cloud met his nose, tinged with the unmistakable smell of fermentation. The question of where the monastery hid its empty wine cellar was answered. Richard ducked under the edge of the tapestry and pulled the lantern in after him.

A tight, circular staircase wound down out of sight. Niter seeped through the stones and the dampness wafting from below explained why the vault at the end of the spiral could no longer keep wine. Either underground water had risen, or something else had contaminated the foundations with liquid stenches. Richard started downward, careful not to slip. He imagined rolling down miles of stairway into an infernal undercavern – or worse, never stopping at all.

The stairway wound around twice and stopped at an iron door. Richard didn't need to think about what to do next; he took the mystery key from his pocket and fit it into the lock. It turned easily, without the expected protest of rust.

The thick air that oozed out was one of willing oblivion. Whatever slept inside did not want anyone to know of its existence, outside of its sworn protectors.

No sooner did the sepulchral miasma hit him, but Richard felt the prickle of fur around his legs and the whisper of sound from inside. It was a woman's laugh, small but victorious.

The lantern flame showed a room smaller than the collection of smells might have indicated. The walls had granite shelves with half-circular depressions to hold wine barrels.

Instead of oak casks, the shelves held vials and beakers filled with murky liquids. Scattered among them were scalpels, knives and tall glass alembics. Richard had seen enough rooms of professed alchemists to recognize the tools of their trade. The walls above the elixirs were scribbled with Enochian letters and less-welcome alphabets.

In the middle of the vault, mortared to the floor, stood an oblong stone vat for the smashing and mixing of grapes. But now it was an open sarcophagus. Inside lay a body draped in cardinal red. The arms were crossed over the chest, skeletal palms pressed against the shoulders. A cross of a wicked design lay across the breast.

But the greatest horror was the feeling that the man was not dead.

Richard approached the robed body. Cat whiskers scraped against his ankles – a feeling almost soothing in the mephitic pit. The lantern lit the man's face, which was like parchment that had been soaked and crumpled, then laid out to dry in an Egyptian sun. But in those sunken cheeks was a flush of life and the lips had a touch of red no undertaker could imitate.

"Brother Skene," said the woman of midnight.

Richard did not jump. He had already seen her necrose glow across the withered face.

"Is he – *alive?*"

"Barely. Infernally."

"The alchemist's art." Richard looked around at the vials and alembics. He remembered what he had once heard from a practitioner in Avignon: "Eternal life in this world is impossible ... but life can be stretched and tautened."

The woman: "He is their charm. While he lives, I cannot touch any of them."

The green hand dropped down into Richard's sight, pressing toward the chest of the thing named Brother Skene. The hand stopped an inch above him and wavered, as if pressed against a glass so polished it could not be seen.

"So weak the charm," she said. "But enough."

Richard pulled against the weight on his eyes and managed to look at her. She was as before: made of night silk. The light from the lantern he had set beside the pit never touched her. Her face, which must have been lovely at one time, flitted between corpse light and Stygian dark.

Richard asked: "What do you want with him?"

The spectral hand turned, seeming to float without a limb attached to it. As the fingers pointed upward, Richard felt the icy river around him again, stinging his eyes and filling his lungs.

"Go back ... to the beginning ...."

As the fingers curved upward, Richard's body followed. The ice water released him and spume hurled him into the air. He spun toward the bridge above, a woman's dress with stains of blood flapping at the edge of his sight. The stone child hiding its eyes came closer.

Then he was on the bridge ... moving through Regensburg, as if he were running backwards ... passing through alleys of a city he had never seen ... through winter markets and past the unfinished Cathedral ... through iron doors into an abbey.

The hand pressed down; he followed the memory. *Her* memory.

Down he ran, into a cell with no windows. Brother Skene stood there. Young now, with mad lust in his eyes and a flail in his hand.

The hand brushed away the vision. "You do not wish to know more."

Richard shook his head to answer the question and to push away the savage crime he almost had to witness.

He rubbed his eyes, and the woman was no longer standing over the body. But Richard felt that she was behind him, taking on her other form that he was afraid to look on. Something scraped on a shelf. Metal scratched against stone and then the object clattered to the floor. It landed at his feet; light glinted off a dagger's blade.

He picked it up. It was then that Richard Davey, a curiosity seeker but also a man of modest bravery, understood what the letters on the door had asked him to do.

He spoke to the shadows. "I can't. I have never harmed anyone in my life."

No answer came except a sibilant hissing.

He held the dagger hilt with both hands. In the blade, he saw his face. It seemed so childish, young and foolish, the way he had felt when he stood alone on the road with his hands up in the air.

"I cannot do it," he repeated.

The corpse-lit hand unfolded from the dark and gripped the back of his hand. The shock of fur touched his neck.

"He is their charm." The voice was in his ears, a purring that formed words. "They make him live ... so I cannot have them. When the Devil has him ... then I may repay them all."

The hand bent Richard's wrist, pointing the tip of the dagger toward Brother Skene's breast. The spectral hand could go no further than a finger's width above the monk's body – but it would be enough, more than enough, to drive the knife into flesh and whatever blood remained in the untimely thing.

"No, no!" His body shook, but he could not move his limbs. A horrible, smothering fur twisted around him, wrapping his body like a tomb shroud.

"Shall I tell you *all* of what he did to me?"

The dagger lowered. Richard's muscles fought, but only his arm seemed able to obey – and it was not strong enough.

"They still call it ... *an indiscretion.*"

The dagger point pressed over the ugly cross ... brushed across a button ... nicked at the red fabric at the collar ... Brother Skene's throat lay bare, a ruffle of breath moving it.

Suddenly, three hands were clasped onto the dagger. Richard's grip on the hilt was pressed between the moon glow of the woman and a withered claw that had struck from inside the pit like an adder.

Richard screamed. He couldn't help himself. The hand of the near-dead thing in the sarcophagus was a touch of maggots. The eyes of Brother Skene, filling the sockets with black, stared at him. They opened onto a soul that had hovered a hands-breath above Hell for over two hundred years.

The force of the two hands pressing against the dagger was so strong that Richard feared his wrist would snap. Smothered from one side, pressed toward a living corpse, he prayed that he might simply go mad and be free.

"*Maleficas non patieris vivere!*"

Another light burst into the room, coming from a single candle. The ghost hand vanished, and Richard was almost thrown into the wall from the force of Brother Skene's arm.

He had a second to see Abbot Fletcher in the doorway of the vault – a candle in one hand and a garish cross in the other, his mouth twisted with cries of exorcism – before all light in the room was choked.

The last image left on Richard's eyes was of claws reaching toward the abbot. The darkness of the cat had filled the room. She bristled her midnight fur and consumed the chamber with her fury.

The abbot was somewhere in the folds of the avenging creature, but it still could not touch him. The abbot's voice shouted protections, snatches of rituals both white and black, and the screeching of the cat as it tried to reach him was a chorus of frustration and fury.

The abbot shouted in German, "You are powerless against us! Go back! Go back to Hell!"

Richard's wrist was burning, but the dagger was still in his fingers. He tried to stand, wondering if he could grope toward the door through the cat's shadow and flee the abbey. His curiosity was finished for the night.

Suddenly, hands like a torturer's iron clamps snapped around Richard's neck and pushed him into the shelf, shattering vials. Brother Skene did not need light to guide him.

The cat hissed throughout the vault, *"Now will you kill him?"*

Richard felt life squeezed from him and was thankful that he did not have to look into the oily pools of Brother Skene's eyes as he was throttled to death. All he could see were glowing spots as he lost consciousness and dropped into endless night.

~

They must have tossed him into a pauper's grave. No coffin, not even a pine box. He felt the weight of bare earth on his chest. But then his eyelids fluttered and opened. It was still dark, but his body felt room to move. He tried to roll and the weight slid off him. As it dropped away, light reached his eyes.

The lantern glowed from the edge of the vat where he had left it. Beside him was a body in red robes. A dagger stuck up from where the heart should be. The falling weight of Brother Skene had driven in the knifepoint as he had strangled Richard. All that remained of the monk was a dust outline and a few bones rising through the gaps in the robes. He had finally dropped the last hand's-breadth to Hell.

But Brother Skene looked more pleasant than the remains of Abbot Fletcher. The cat's claws left nothing behind that even the most hardened undertaker would wish to bury. Once the charm of the undying man on the floor was gone, the rage of his victim was worse than anything that Richard, an imaginative man, would have imagined.

He snatched up the lantern and climbed the stairs. He followed the clawed prints stamped in blood. He did not need to lift the tapestry; it was ripped from the wall and crumpled on the ground.

He walked through the chapel. It was the fastest way out, although he feared what he might find there. He walked quickly through the nave with his head turned away from the apse. He got only a few blinks of the red ruins of the rest of the Benedictine Abbey of St. James. They had paid for keeping a sinner so long from the Devil's grip.

It was still the deep of night when he stumbled outside, but the sky had cleared. He stepped past the gate. The moment his foot touched the road, he sat down in the dirt to wait for her.

She flowed from the eaves of the beeches, still a thing of midnight. But the green of her skin had flushed red. She was more beautiful that way, fulfilled in her wrath.

"You could not drive the knife in yourself." The words came easily now. Hate no longer held onto her.

Richard nodded. "You are the Devil."

"Only a servant." The redness began to fade. "'Vengeance is mine, sayeth the Lord.' But that is a lie. The Devil may also repay, when he has been falsely accused and long denied. Some men do not need the Devil to make them do what they do. What they *have* done."

Her eyes – was this the first time he had seen them? – were filled with sorrow but not for what had just happened.

Richard looked toward the open doors of the church. The scent of blood wafted from it. "Revenge should be – cleaner."

Her eyes were on her own body. "The crime was unclean. Yet, I was no maiden at the time. And I took my own life. God would not have me, but the Devil welcomed me. He welcomed revenge. It is repaid. And you are still clean."

Richard Davey did not feel that way. But he was the weapon that did not want to be drawn. The sword did not have the guilt of its wielder, no matter what the blood said.

She spoke: "At dawn, it is finished for me. But I have a reward for you."

From behind, passing through her body to reach him, trotted a familiar horse with bulging saddlebags. Richard stood up and placed his hand onto the animal's forelock.

"The thieves – they did not get far."

It was the last sound he heard from her. When he turned to ask what she meant, he saw only the orange glow of the dawn.

As he mounted the saddle, he tried not to look at the claw marks that crossed the leather, or the bloodstains on the animal's hoofs. He turned in the direction Regensburg. He did not enjoy the thought of crossing its bridge and the icy waters below.

❖

Ryan Harvey has crossed the Regensburg Bridge and seen much of Bavaria (thanks to his sister living there), but has spent most of his life in Los Angeles, where he resides with an ever-growing and space-gobbling collection of books and Blu-rays. He is a recent winner of The Writers of the Future Contest, and his winning entry, "An Acolyte of Black Spires", is collected in *L. Ron Hubbard Presents: Writers of the Future Vol. XXVII*. He has worked as a columnist for *Black Gate* magazine's website for three years and has two upcoming stories in the print edition. His fiction will also appear later this year in the anthology, *Roar of the Crowd* (Rogue Blades Press). Aside from writing, Ryan is a pulp literature nut, avid swing dancer, and wearer of 1930s fashions in LA's vintage scene. His Latin is far better than his German.

Lovers & Desire

"O what a black, dark hill is yon,
"That looks so dark to me?"
"O it is the hill of hell," he said,
"Where you and I shall be."

The Daemon Lover, Popular English Ballad

Obsessions
(or Biting Off More Than One Can Chew)

By Colleen Anderson

Dream, dream divine, my dear
of dark's loving, sheltered clasp
immortal hopes in mortal sleep
gaslit vapours drape, shape
the land restless
with its secrets
lurid phantoms shift within
a discordant haze of consumption and gambled lives
hollow hooves ring cobblestones
turn and there is nothing
the dust of Morpheus mists your vision
while Poe and Wilde linger at the tomb
discuss portraits and Annabelle Lee

You will descend, my dear
steps from reality to mad cacophony
hidden laughter chimes its manic bell
your perfected self is heedless
until spectral hands chill your face
a sibilance of whispers writhe and burrow
hook their glinting cause within, though you are the apple
from which that worm has crawled
your bosom white as casket lilies shudders, yet
you cannot, will not pull free of darkling touch
the canvas more garish as you work, daub in
Venus's flytrap, the nightshade bloom, narcissus
at its center, the inferno melts your brain and heart

Try to turn away, my dear
Elysian fields hold no mystery once you've tramped eternal blooms
you pollinate your dreamworlds with blood dust

cradled in blossoms soft as funeral silk
bony fingers that snare your imagination, then your arm
are mutilated, corrupt and it is paper that you feel
not parchment flesh that scratches
you seek a demon lover through lifetimes
black-lace parties, angst-filled wine and candlelight
rotting breath and broken, blackened teeth chew
greedily your neck, your heart wants more
selfish hunger – you taste false remorse
one-time friends and lovers have turned to morsels

Do not believe it all, my dear
Gypsies caged by flame and shadow
pass bottles more than ancient secrets,
down warmth not found in guarded eyes
smoke sour tobacco, torture tamed wood until it screams
before the flickering fire, cracked bone dice rattle
they lead between the worlds
to crystal balls gorged on lies
half-truths are none at all in clearing the air
your future still awaits, meek and willing
in morning's scowling light, the Gypsy camp quiets
turn away – you won't see the poor and persecuted
you have cloaked in mystery, caravans and well-traveled tales

Wait forever, my dear
for a bloated, blood moon full
from forlorn howls, the shaggy man whose beast is
not contained, who pursues you, yet tames
his bite, sees, scents through lupus rage
your nobility does not hear his soulful whimper
prey to mange and blood-sated fleas
his flight, blinded, betrayed by Moon
wolf-pack tracks, slavering to kill
nature's aberration – he cries out, *lunatic*
I am not welcome anywhere, two halves that cannot join
you fancy to have leashed the noble beast
the wolves, or he alone, would hunt you if they could

Search ever on, my dear
the shambling, bolted simulacrum is not the sum
but the beginning, a mind hinged to flesh
monster made by machines diabolical
project of a madman who, in creating life, honours it not
the divine escapes as you try to simulate by writing
reconstruct the myths; believe them toys to sunder
yet born a byblow of contrived machinations
these frankensteins serve to scar the pages
journal entries assembled for pity and distress
what sorrowful imaginings, Victorian preoccupation
hoping to be discovered and saved from certain fate
conundrums erected to your mad genius

Be yourself, my dear
not like limpid Gaimanettes, pallid leeches
wrapped in ebon leather, sweating perfume
unsure if they exist outside a frame of reference
or were fabricated within the nimbus of a thought
without the molten core to heat their lives, they try to fit
discarded casings, fallout from courtesy and composition
one sudden solar flare would etch distinction
with the half-life of attention as long as youth
they willingly open any orifice to suck
fame from their dark prince, grow on his glory
you shine as bright in any galaxy, yet set
your sights on this year's fleeting asteroid, forgotten in a moment

Dream divine, my dear, in dreams
leave life's nightmare, escape death's coma
wander the ornate halls of opium infatuation
the shallow dance of guttering candles
pipe smoke curls, a seductive foreign screen
unveils a massaging marriage, hallucinations
delirium's slow, sensual lovemaking
caresses as you court romantic death
you will not leave, cannot exit quickly

until life has bled youth and vigour
assisted by your ghoulish thoughts, vampiric verses
then, shattered beauty discarded, attired in neither dream nor mystery
Life, a jealous lover, will toss you to death's portal.

Colleen Anderson writes in various genres and has over one hundred 100 published stories and poems appearing in magazines and anthologies, including, *Evolve*, *Chizine*, and *On Spec*. She has a BFA in creative writing, received an honourable mention in the *Year's Best Horror* for her story "Exegesis of the Insecta Apocrypha" in *Horror Library Vol. IV*, and is an 2010 Aurora nominee in poetry. She also edits for Chizine Publications. New work will appear in *Polluto*, *Witches & Pagans* and *New Vampire Tales*.

Desideratum

By Gina Flores

Another sleepless night, with only the dim glow of her cigarette for company.

Lorena turned on her side, using her elbow for support, and stared out the window. Sweat pooled in the hollow of her breasts and the backs of her knees, at the nape of her neck beneath her thick veil of hair. It was September, time for rain and cloudy skies, cool breezes, but they were elusive this year. She inhaled deeply, using nicotine to get rid of the night-taste inside of her mouth, and pitched the butt out the window. Watched the pale-orange ember until it hit the walk with a small show of sparks.

A few lights were visible in other buildings. Parked cars lined either side of the street, but nothing moved. Only Lorena, awake in the dark. Alone. Wishing for a cat, a television – anything to break the monotony of waking up every night at the same time, to stare out at the same emptiness with the same yearning that kept her from sleep. But cats were not allowed in the building and the television was nothing more than a stand for dying plants and lost books. Books also covered the single sagging shelf in the corner. Two boxes without tops sat on the floor in front of it, leaking paperbacks; stacks piled against the wall wherever there was room.

She ran her hands over the books nearest her bed, her favourites. Traitors, all of them; not one could numb the yearning she felt for real human company.

She thought, as she always did when loneliness got the best of her, of her mother. Her mother loved to talk, even if the conversations didn't last long, and usually wound up in bitter arguments. Lorena sat up and put her hand on the old tan phone before remembering it had been disconnected over a week ago. That was probably for the best. The call most likely would have ended with Lorena feeling guilty, while her mother tried to talk her into coming back home. Most of the time, being alone, independent, was what she wanted. Except on nights like this, when the heat was unbearable and the shabbiness of the apartment grated on her.

On nights like this, she wanted more, something she couldn't describe, even to herself.

Sighing, she absently braided her hair and continued looking outside for something, some kind of variation. The last few weeks, she had felt a horrid yearning, but she didn't know what for. It was just a pull at her stomach, her brain, her heart. A pull that made her stare out the window for long hours. As she worked the plait, she wondered why she kept her hair so long, when all she ever did was to pull it back and away. But Lorena's hair had always been long, a comforting shield to hide behind when she wore it down, something to swing around and play with when it was bound back, and to pull on when she got nervous. Comfortable. She looked out the window again to see if anything had changed. A few pieces of trash blew around near a sewer grate, but that was all. She secured the braid with an elastic band and flopped back on the bed, sighing loudly.

She knew she wouldn't sleep much, if at all, the rest of this night, so she got up and pulled on a pair of cut-off sweat pants. The walk was becoming a nightly ritual. She grabbed her cigarettes from the bed and stuck them in her waistband, after slipping on a ratty pair of tennis shoes she had bought on sale at work.

The outer hall was dark with imitation-wood paneling on the bottom, faded yellow paint on the top. The smell of rot lingered in the hallways, emanating from other apartments and fast food bags left in the corners. *I can't wait 'til I'm outta here. Just a few more months.* Lorena had been saying that to herself since first moving in over a year ago. She hated the hall, the narrow stairway, the apartments and the people in them. Her life. But not enough to go home.

She walked around the block five and then six times, willing somebody to come out and rape, rob, mug, stab her.

No one obliged, so it was back up four flights to her one-room life. Maybe she'd get an hour or two of sleep before work. The walk had exhausted her physically, if not mentally. *I want,* she thought. *I want.*

The want stayed in her thoughts until she got up and paced the small box of her apartment. Even then, it ran like a train in the back of her mind. *IwantIwantIwantIwant.* She pulled on her hair, nervously twisting the ends with one hand while she alternately smoked and paced. Finally, she went to the kitchen and dug around in the messier of the two available drawers. Found a pair of scissors. The shears were old and rust-spotted, not as sharp as they used to be. *Kind of like me, ha-ha.* But they'd do.

She went into the bathroom and looked in the mirror. Same plain face, brown eyes, brown hair. Nothing special leapt out at her. A few freckles dotted her nose, but even they were light, difficult to see if you didn't know they were there. *Like me.* She reached around and grasped the thick braid with her left hand, brought her right behind her and closed her eyes. *What am I doing?* she thought.

She cut.

It was tougher than she'd expected to get through the twist and the scissors didn't cut quite straight. Holding the thick braid of hair in her hands made her realize what she had done, what she had really, actually done. Cut off something that had been there most of her life. A phantom weight remained on the back of her neck, telling her she really hadn't gone through with it. She reached back and felt her neck, the feather-light strands on her skin. Short intake of breath and even smaller exhale of laughter, and she hacked away, then, at the stray wisps that hung haggle-straggle around her head, evening them out the best she could. She did the back without a mirror, feeling, instead, with her fingertips. She hoped it was straight, but did not bother to check.

At last, Lorena looked in the mirror and saw her new head. Her face looked smaller, her eyes larger. It was certainly different. She didn't bother to clean up the bathroom, just stripped off her shorts and crawled into bed.

She lay on her side and smoked a cigarette while looking out the window. Someone was walking down the street. He was tall, with dark hair pulled back in a tail. Familiar. Thigh-length black jacket and dark pants. Boots on his feet. Their heavy tread echoed below. He was thin, almost sickly, and beautiful. So familiar. She'd seen him somewhere before. *Where?* Lorena ashed her cigarette out the window and inhaled again, watching. Not many people were out at this hour and she always studied those who were, trying to guess where they were off to, where they might be coming from.

He looked up, then, and *Ohmygodhesbeautifulthemostbeautifulthingi' veeverseen*, his eyes, large dark eyes she could see even from her window, held hers for a moment before he put his hands in pockets and walked on.

She shivered with excitement under the covers. *What just happened?* It wasn't much, but it was what she'd wanted – something different. Enough, perhaps, for her to finally be able to sleep. She wondered what he looked like up close and why she thought he was beautiful, when all she'd really seen was a coat and dark hair. But his eyes, they seemed to look right at her. And she could have sworn she knew him from somewhere. But where? She wondered if he would be back tomorrow, wondered if she dared walk downstairs if he was, wondered and eventually fell asleep.

~

She awoke to rain misting her face. It finally felt like September. She glanced at the clock and saw it was 7:00. She had gotten nearly three hours of sleep, the most she'd had at one time in weeks. But instead of rested, she felt edgy. Eyes haunted her mind as she got up. Dark eyes that searched hers.

The bathroom was a mess. A fine drizzle of hair covered the toilet seat and long strands clumped together on the floor. Her braid, now coming undone at the top, was on the small ledge between medicine chest and sink. She picked it up, surprised at how much it weighed, and brought it with her to the kitchen as she smoked her morning cigarette.

"Well, what am I going to do with this – glue it back on? Send it to Mom?" She giggled, as she thought of her mother opening up a package to find a chunk of hair, and tossed the braid in the paper sack she used for garbage. She'd take it to the dumpster before going to work. Which, she realized, she had less than an hour to get to.

She grabbed a clean Family Mart shirt before hitting the shower. She kept the water lukewarm and enjoyed the goose bumps it produced. Such a relief from the heat of yesterday. Hopefully, summer was over for good. She wet her hair, running her hands through it until they reached empty air, still expecting to find a long mane. She smiled a little to herself at her forgetfulness and closed her eyes as she lathered in shampoo. It felt good to have so little to go through. She found herself thinking of the man she had seen the night before, how he had looked up before walking on. But had he really seen her? What if he had? And where had she seen *him* before? Her mind wandered as she went through the motions of shaving and washing, and focused on work. Family Mart, the grocery store where she was manager and sole employee of the tiny floral department. She hated the store itself and the job didn't pay well, but she enjoyed the plants and flowers. Something about their crispness, their perfection, appealed to her.

And then Lorena remembered where she had seen him before. It was a Friday evening, not the busiest of times for her department. He had shown up wanting a white rose. All she had were the usual red, yellow and pink, and some that were white with pink-tinged edges. He selected one of those and, when she wrapped and handed it to him, his hand had touched hers. Only for a second, but she shivered, remembering. She hadn't noticed much about him until that point, but whatever it was that came through with his touch really made her look at him. His green eyes caught orangish flecks from the overhead lights. Those eyes were the most remarkable thing about him, dark and enticing. His body was skinny, too thin, dark clothes hanging off of him like an exotic scarecrow, but exquisite just the same.

The water became cold, startling her out of reverie and into the present. She had accomplished something. She knew where she had seen him before. Small victory, but it made her morning brighter.

Her mind continued flashing pictures as she dried off. Of the dark coat. The hair. His eyes. Why was she so concerned with someone she had seen for a grand total of six or seven minutes? Because he was her ideal. Sure, she didn't know a thing about him, but all of her fantasies to this point had involved a tall man with dark hair. His face changed with her fantasies, but his features remained constant. Long, thin arms and legs that were lightly muscled. Long fingers on strong hands. What if she were to walk downstairs tonight and just go up, as in one of her late-night fantasies, and put her arms around him? What would he do? *Probably tell me to get the hell out of his face.*

~

Work passed in a blur. It was order day, so she spent her time clipping stems, pricing, rotating product and making arrangements. She did the work by rote, nodding and smiling at the infrequent customers, clipping and pricing, but the whole time, her mind was on the man with the hypnotic eyes. *Who is he and why do I keep thinking about him?*

That night, Lorena tried to sleep but kept waking up to peer out the window, expecting *him* to be outside. But, of course, he wasn't, and the only thing she gained was more circles under her eyes. The rest of the week was much the same. She saw him from the window twice more and both times, he appeared to be watching her apartment. Of course this was imagination, wishful thinking ... but it satisfied her. And each night, she looked for him, hoping for more than a glimpse, for the courage to go outside and speak to him. Her nightly walks had stopped; she was afraid she would miss him if she left her watch at the window.

The sickness began a few days later. Even the thought of food repulsed her. Some of the other employees said something about a flu going around, but everyone else seemed to get sick for a day and bounce right back. Lorena languished. She was not sure whether the fatigue was the result of her late-night wakings or from being ill. She woke at night to smoke and keep vigil, before falling into uneasy dreams.

～

The following week, she was sent home from work, with instructions not to come back until she had a doctor's note clearing her from illness. She dragged herself home and immediately fell asleep. She woke four hours later. Her head pounded with every beat of her heart and her mouth was fuzzy. Lorena closed her eyes and tried not to think. Her eyes throbbed with every breath, white flashes colouring the movement. She opened her eyes and the flashes persisted at the edge of her vision. Her stomach roiled, clenching and releasing, until she couldn't take it anymore. She made it to the bathroom and dry-heaved for what felt like hours before a thin stream of bile made its way out. Her eyes watered, nostrils burned. She turned on the faucet and stuck her mouth on it, tasting the grimy, unwashed metal.

She looked up into the mirror. Her eyes were larger than ever, but lined with shadow, faded, watered down. Her skin was paler than normal, highlighting her freckles.

She needed a cup of tea, some chicken soup. She hadn't bought food, her mind focused only on the man outside the window. She would go to the corner store, get what she needed, then come back and rest.

Leftover rain formed puddles on the sidewalk and a scent of decay drifted up from the sewers. She walked slowly, one foot in front of the other, careful not to fall, avoiding puddles the best she could so the water didn't get into her ripped tennis shoes. Her head spun, still pounding. Her fingers rolled over and over the money in her pocket, feeling the crumpled bills – a ten, a five, a one – rolling over and over three quarters, pressing them in the clefts between fingers. One, two, three.

Someone was behind her. She heard the footsteps, almost in time with hers, and hoped that whoever it was wouldn't give her trouble. She didn't think she had the strength to deal with it tonight. She concentrated on the money. Three bills, three coins, three and three. Three more buildings to pass before she got to the store. Light shone out of its front window, brightening the sidewalk and making her headache worse. She stared at the ground as she walked. *Tea bags, soup, aspirin.* Three things to get.

The footsteps grew louder and a shadow drew up beside her. Water splashed onto her feet, making her shiver. "Sorry," a deep voice said.

She looked up and forgot to walk. It was *him*. Dressed in the same jacket, dark pants, beautiful face. He was tall , as she looked up, she noticed that stubbled shadow lined his upper lip and chin. His eyes were pools of darkness fringed by long lashes. Under his coat, white letters stood out on a black t-shirt, but light from the store made her squint so she could not tell what it said. He didn't seem as thin or sickly as he had from the window. He looked at her, waiting.

"N-no problem," Lorena stammered. She smoothed her hair back, feeling how greasy it was, wishing its mass was back so she could hide behind it. *Why did I cut it?* She wondered what she looked like through his eyes.

"Watch out for those for those puddles," he said, and continued walking. "You'll catch a cold."

She stayed where she was, reveling in the sound of his voice as shivers racked her body, afraid she would fall down. If only she had been feeling better; if only she hadn't cut her hair. If only he wasn't so perfect. If only. She breathed deeply, trying not to think, hoping the dizziness would pass, watching him walk up the street, wondering where he was going. The outside lights to the corner store blinked off and Lorena remembered why she was here. She quickly went in and completed her shopping.

Climbing the stairs back to her apartment was agony. She had to stop several times, panting deeply. The bag weighed a ton. She dragged it on the floor behind her, half-tempted to leave it on the steps, but the emptiness in her stomach pushed her on. At one point, she forgot where she was going, wondered what she was doing on the stairway and whose stairs they were. She noticed the stains on the wall, as if for the first time, and gazed at them, trying to make sense of things. Eyes stared out of the wall. *His* eyes. Searching.

"I'm here," she whispered. A face formed around the eyes, blurry. She smiled, happy he had sought her out. His body came into focus and then his clothes. Baggy jeans that looked newer than new, a bright-yellow t-shirt. Curly brown hair.

"Whachoo lookin' at, psycho? Think the wall's gonna help you up these steps?" The laughter continued as the man pushed her out of the way, bounding down the steps.

Home. If she could just get home and something to drink. Her throat was parched, head throbbing more than ever. She had become used to the rhythm, though, a second heartbeat *Soup. Water. Tea,* she chanted mentally, as she shuffled up the stairs. Somehow, she made it the rest of the way. The bag ripped, but nothing fell out except the corner of the cracker box. She shut the front door and latched it, made her way to the bed. She was hot and cold, hungry and tired. The cracker, dry as a page from one of her books, held no appeal. She struggled with the cap to the soda bottle for a few seconds before giving up and sipping water from the glass that had been sitting on the table all day. There wasn't much, but it wet the back of her throat, eased the ache. The walls pulsed with the beat of her head and heart. She wrapped herself in a blanket and shuffled into the kitchen to put a pot of fresh water on the stove.

By the time the water boiled, Lorena was curled into a corner against the cabinets, shaking. It took an eternity for her to pull herself up and rescue the pot, pour some of the water into a cup with a tea bag, spilling most of it on the counter. Some splashed to the floor and burned her feet. She was so weak at this point she decided to forgo the soup and, instead, took her tea to the bed. She propped her pillow up on the wall and rested her back against it. Sipped tea while watching the night and closed her eyes before finishing the cup.

Sleep came in fitful sweats of tossing and turning. And dreams. When she woke up, she felt worse than before, her head a metronome of pain, face on fire. She made it to the kitchen for water and aspirin and soup. Her throat was too swollen to swallow the pills, but she sipped at the water and carried the soup back to the bed in a chipped blue bowl edged with stars. She settled into bed, spilling on herself, and leaned back against the wall while she ate. She glanced at the clock. 3:38 a.m.

Half-closed eyes gazed outside. A car drove down the street, leaving drunken laughter in its wake. A woman walked quickly past Lorena's building, shoulders hunched, hands in pockets. The wind blew and Lorena caught the odour of oncoming rain. She loved that smell. It reminded her of childhood, brown leaves and brown eyes. Brown, brown eyes that never left her thoughts. She didn't want – or need – to think about the man who had been haunting her the past few – had it only been days? It felt as if she had first seen him ages ago.

The soup gone, she set the bowl on the floor next to the bed. She'd move it in the morning. Her throat was still parched and she glanced toward the kitchen. It wasn't *that* far away, but it would take too much effort to get there and find a glass, turn on the faucet and then come all the way back. Her throat clicked and she sighed. Got out of bed and made her way to the kitchen.

~

Sunlight and cold linoleum woke her up. Her face was pressed against the cabinet under the sink, feet curled up behind her. What had happened? Why was she in the kitchen? She sat up weakly, muscles protesting. The groove etched in her face from the cabinet began to tingle and she rubbed it absently.

The daily sounds of passing cars and people drifted in through the open window. She stood up and drank half a glass of water, filled it again and took it with her back to bed. She thought about calling work and decided against it. She wasn't to come back without a doctor's note, so she supposed she would not be going back at all.

She sipped at the water, which was gone too soon, and lay back on the bed. Looked out the window. A group of people walked by, laughing and pushing each other jokingly. The group passed, but one person stayed behind. He stared up at Lorena's window, dark eyes locked with hers. It was *him*. Still in his leather jacket and jeans. Didn't he own any other clothes? Maybe he was like the guy she went to high school with, who owned five black t-shirts and three pairs of Levis 550 jeans. He thought it was a big joke that everybody thought he wore the same thing every day. Maybe that's what *he* did. She had the urge to run down and ask him. To run her fingers through his hair, pull his face toward her and not let him go. She ran fingers through her own hair, feeling the spikes of early-morning hair, the grease from days of not washing it. Like he'd let her anywhere near him. She looked down, again, and he was gone, again. *Dammit.*

Her stomach twinged. She stumbled to the bathroom and saw how wasted she looked. Pale skin and wizened eyes. At least ten years older than she had looked last week. One thing she had to admit, though, was that she'd been sleeping better since she'd been sick. Not, she noted, that it seemed to be doing her much good. Always thin, she now looked anorexic, like she'd been starving herself. *Goddamned flu. Maybe I will go to a doctor. I can hike to the bus stop and go to ReadyMed.*

Shower first. All she needed was a few minutes under the spray, but Lorena didn't think she could handle even that. She grabbed a shriveled washrag from the rack in the shower and ran it under cold water in the sink. Wiped at her armpits and under her breasts, breasts that felt like tight little bags too close to her skin. She grimaced in disgust and stuck her head under the running water, soaking her hair and washing it with liquid soap. She splashed her face and patted it dry. Ran a toothbrush through her mouth. Rolled on deodorant. She sat naked on the toilet seat for a few minutes, trying to catch her breath, to let her muscles stop screaming at her. Breath came too quickly and her head began its slow beat. If she could only get dressed and then to the doctor, she might be all right.

She grabbed the faded black shirt she had left on the towel rack two days ago and pulled it over her head. Shuffled the few feet back to the bed and lay down. Just for a moment. A short rest on top of the sheets and everything would be fine. She'd go the bus stop, to the doctor.

~

Lorena woke to feel the t-shirt soaked with sick-sweat, the cotton clinging claustrophobically. Not today. No way would she make the doctor today. She glanced over at the kitchen counter and saw there was only one more can of soup left, but she still had the box of crackers, three of the plastic packages still unopened. She'd be all right until the flu passed. She just needed to rest.

She wrapped herself in covers that stank of illness and once again looked out the window. Slept.

The next time she woke up, she knew it was now or never. She had to get help. The sun had set, so she knew the clinic would not be open, but the hospital didn't close – did it? She'd find out. She pulled on sweat pants and tennis shoes and made it over to the front door. Opened it.

"Hi," he said. He leaned on the doorframe as if it were the most natural thing in the world. As if they knew each other. As if he belonged.

"Hi," she said, surprised. "I, uh, I'm on my way out." Her voice was a croak, not hers. She tried to stop her hand from running over her still-wet hair, attempting to fix it in some sort of attractive style.

He walked in, as if invited. "I needed to see you," he said.

"Excuse me?" Lorena was sure she was dreaming. Who was this guy? He looked different somehow. His cheeks, the bones still prominent, were more filled in. His eyes brighter, the orange flecks more solid than the green. Even the way he stood was somehow different. *How can I know this from seeing him a few times?* "Why would you need to see me? You don't even – I don't even know who you are." *Liar,* her body said. Even if she didn't know, her body did. It stood at attention; every muscle seeming to call out to him.

She wasn't sure how it happened, but the two of them became tangled. It didn't matter that her mouth was full of fuzz, that she smelled like a sickbed. It didn't matter that she didn't know him, his name or who he was. She was not altogether convinced she wasn't dreaming. Things like this didn't happen in real life. His lips were firmer than in her fantasies. Warm and smooth like his hands, his hips. It didn't matter that the wooden floor was hard and dirty, because he was hard and clean, smelling faintly of red licorice, tasting of lemon. She took him inside of her, blocking out thoughts of AIDS and herpes and unwanted pregnancy. Nothing could happen to her here. This was bliss, a dream.

When she grew tired and sore, she opened her mouth to tell him, to ask him to take a break, but he covered her in kisses, her traitorous body responding. She was unable to speak, her throat too dry. Her stomach sent sharp, shooting pains through her body in rhythm with his thrusts. He would not stop.

She gave up and lay under him, limp as a rag doll. Arms and legs too weak to move, stomach clenching and unclenching. Her mouth moved, but no sound came out, just the exhalation of old, stale breath. She prayed in her mind for help, for an end. For it to stop for good. She fought to keep her eyes closed, from looking into his eyes. They were pits of darkness, ready to swallow her up.

She fell asleep or passed out, and woke as he dressed and left the room. She crawled into bed, shivering, and pulled the blankets up over her. She felt skeletal, as if her flesh was just a thin cover for brittle bone. A glimpse in the mirror showed her a husk of her former self. Lorena rolled over on her side and looked out the window, trying to remember how she had gotten here. Her breath was shallow, coming in gasps as if she had run a long race. She looked out the window at the people walking by, some well-dressed, others casual, everyone with some apparent place to go. But not her. Lorena lay and stared out the window knowing he was gone, had left her to rot, but too tired, and oddly satisfied, to care.

She noticed, as she looked for one last glimpse of him, hoping that he would do her the honour of looking into her window one last time, that he had left a white rose on the windowsill.

Gina Flores lives on a beach in Texas with her husband, a 90-pound lap-dog, and a cat. She writes stories to stay sane and teaches at a university to pay the bills.

Victorians

By James S. Dorr

The first thing I remembered of my early childhood was the fog. I must have been only five years old when I left the house that I had been born in – beyond that, my mind was still pretty much blank – and I would not have returned even now, more than thirty years later, except that I had finally married. Her name was "Amelia" and I had met her in Chicago, but now I traveled home alone. I had determined to open the house first and, only after it had been restored to a liveable condition, to send for my bride.

I crested a hill. Just as the road hooked down toward the river, and to the town I would find across it, I caught my first glimpse of the house my father had been born into – the house he had died in and that my mother had fled from just after, never to come back. That, at least, was what they had told me after I had been taken away, to another state, to be raised by a cousin on my mother's side.

The fog, a persistent feature of autumn during those first years of my life, had always been thickest nearest the river. Above it, however, under a pale late-afternoon sun, I could just make out the eight-sided top of the great central tower – the Queen Anne tower that dominated so many Victorian homes of its age – as well as the tips of three of the highest pinnacled chimneys.

Memory came back in driblets and pieces. I knew that, when I approached the next day to take possession, I would recognize below them the sharply peaked hip roof, broken at angles by the main gables that clutched the tower within the ell they formed at their crossing. The tower itself, with its latticed, oval, stained glass windows, would soar a full story over even the tallest of these, a clear rise of nearly seventy feet from its base to the scale-shingled dome that crowned it.

Memories continued to come back unbidden. I followed the road down a series of switchbacks, until the top of the double lane iron bridge I knew I would find loomed out from an ever increasing fog. By now, I had lost sight of my parents' home altogether, but in my mind, I could hear the voice of a young attorney reading a will.

The will specified that the house would be mine, but only after I had gotten married. The young attorney, a Stephen Larabie – really no more than a clerk at the time – explained to me what my older cousin protested seemed an unusual provision. "Your father," the lawyer said, "fully expects you not to marry until you've tasted somewhat of the world, just as he did. But, at the same time, you must eventually take on the obligations of manhood, as well as its pleasures, and settle down. The house, that you will not obtain until you do so, is intended to be a reminder."

My cousin who, in that I was a minor, had been court-appointed to speak for my interests, had laughed at that. "You mean young Joseph" – he gestured toward me – "is being told that he has permission to sow his wild oats when he gets a bit older, but, until he's grown out of such urges, to stay out of town. In other words, not to keep out of trouble, but just out of scandal."

The lawyer cleared his throat. "Something like that, yes. I doubt you knew Joseph's father well – as you do know, he was always reclusive and rarely visited even immediate family members after his own marriage – but he, like his house, was quite Victorian in his nature."

"You mean that he was a hypocrite, don't you?" my cousin asked.

I remember now that the lawyer had glanced in my direction to see if I had understood anything of what he and my cousin were saying, but I had already begun to play with his pens and inkwell.

"Some people claimed that of him, yes. At least, that he might, at times, have followed a double standard." He cleared his throat a second time. "In any event," he said as he stood up, having come to the end of his papers and seemingly anxious to usher us out, "the will specifies that this firm will keep the house in trust until Joseph is ready."

And now I was ready, by my father's will. The firm, now owned by Stephen Larabie, had apparently kept an eye on my own various comings and goings, as well as the house. And so, three days after Amelia and I had returned from our honeymoon, I received the telegram that had brought me back to this place, at best still scarcely half-recollected, that yet had so overshadowed my first years.

So ran my thoughts now as I reached the bridge and, turning my lights on low, carefully picked my way across it. Fortunately, the fog seemed less thick on the river's town side and, even though it was starting to get dark, I found the hotel I had made reservations at with surprisingly little trouble. Since I was tired from a full day's drive, I checked into my room, and showered and changed first, then decided to have a couple of drinks and something to eat in the small restaurant I had earlier spotted just off the lobby.

When I sat down, the hostess smiled at me. Somehow, I found that I couldn't help thinking how much the opposite, and yet, in terms of the abstract of beauty, how much the same she was as Amelia. Where, for example, my own wife was blonde and her figure slender, the restaurant hostess was every bit as buxom and dark. Where Amelia was quiet, the hostess appeared, as other customers came to be seated, almost too vivacious. And afterward, when she winked at me while I took out my card to pay the bill, I learned that even her name was much like my wife's, and yet unlike it, as well.

Her name was "Anise".

When I returned to my room later on, I placed my wife's picture on the dresser and went to sleep quickly. The first thing next morning, I looked up Attorney Larabie's office. As soon as I strode in through the door, I was struck by how quickly my mind recalled the tiniest details of my visit, some thirty years past, down to and including the stain on the wood floor where I had dropped one of the young lawyer's pens. The man who confronted me now, however, must have been fifty-five or sixty.

"Mr. Parrish?" he said, extending his hand. "Mr. Joseph Parrish?"

I nodded and accepted his handshake.

"Are you Stephen Larabie? I got your telegram ...."

"Yes," he said, before I could add more. Still gripping my hand, he pulled me over to a table and sat me down, then produced a thick sheaf of papers. "Couple of things I'll need you to sign first," he continued. "That'll most likely take up the whole morning, so, unless you have some objection, I thought we might have a quick lunch after that and then take a look at the house together."

I nodded, wondering somewhat distractedly if lunch would be at the hotel restaurant and, if so, if the hostess, Anise, would be on duty for that meal, as well. I shook the thought away and, soon enough, became lost in contracts and deeds, instead. Lunch, in fact, turned out to be a quick affair at a hamburger place just outside of town, on the way to the bridge. And then, as river fog started to thin, giving some hope of a clear if not wholly sun-filled afternoon, we found ourselves on the steep and winding road up the cliff on the other side.

Larabie turned to me while I was driving. "How much do you remember of your father?" he asked. "Or, for that matter, of your mother?"

"Very little," I had to confess. I searched my memory and nothing came, yet I had the feeling that if I just waited – waited until I was inside the house that they had lived in ....

"You do know, at least, that your father was murdered?" Larabie paused, reacting, perhaps, to what I imagined was my blank expression. I had no such memory.

"That's what the police said, in any event," he finally continued, after some seconds. I *did* remember that when, with my cousin, I had been in his office before, the younger Larabie had struck me as being every bit as taciturn about giving out excessive information.

"Did they catch the man who did it?" I asked. Again, attempt to recall as I might, I had no memory – at least not yet – and hence no real feeling one way or the other. But I was beginning to have a foreboding.

"Figured it was probably a drifter," Larabie answered, his voice sounding thoughtful. "A lot of people were moving from town to town in those days – mostly farmers who'd been foreclosed on. Big farms forcing out smaller holdings. And you've got to realize that this was a small town. People generally disliked sharing local troubles with outsiders. So, the police just poked around a little outside the house – set up a few roadblocks – but they never did catch him."

"M-my mother wasn't murdered, too, was she?" It had suddenly occurred to me what he might have been trying to hint at and, while I didn't really remember her any more than I did my father, the thought of my mother's death by violence somehow *was* shocking.

"Oh no," he said quickly. "In fact it was her who phoned the police. Figured she must have been out when it happened and had you with her, but came home just after. Sort of a lucky reversal for her, though, that that's the way it worked out." He hesitated for a moment.

"What do you mean?"

"It was your father who usually went out while she and you were the ones left behind." He hesitated, again, then frowned. "I may as well tell you; your father was somewhat of a ladies' man. Good-looking man even in his late thirties, just like you, and everyone knew it – except maybe her. Used to be a whorehouse where the hotel is now and some said he spent more time in that than he did in his own house."

"Really?" I asked. I was about to ask him more when we reached the crest of the hill we were climbing. The road widened and, just at that moment, a ray of sun burst through the clouds overhead. The house could now be seen suddenly rising, dominating the next ridge over, in all its flamboyant, old-fashioned splendor.

As we approached, it loomed higher and higher, the light glinting off the gingerbread scrollwork that framed the huge front third-story gable. I pulled up into its curving driveway, got out of the car and let my eyes wander – below the trim of the gable, in shadow, the arch of a balcony pointed yet higher to the great tower, half-impaled by the slant to its right, and the cast-iron finialed crest of the main hip roof behind it. And yet above that, thrust to the sky, the three major chimneys – the tallest one crowned with a wired, glass-balled spire that was meant to catch lightning, my new memory prompted – added their own bursting streaks of colour. An almost blood-coloured patterned-brick red, when the sun struck full on it, that, in the jumbled gray and white of friezes and rails of the building below them, was matched alone by the stained-glass red of the tower's downward-spiraling ovals.

I walked, as if in a dream, to the house – apparently long-repressed memories came back of the tower windows lighting a second and third-story staircase before it curved backward up into the attic. Others of diamond-panes in the front parlour. I scarcely noticed Larabie's presence until we stood on the broad front veranda.

"You'll notice we kept the property up for you, Mr. Parrish," the lawyer said. "Painted it most recently only last summer, in fact." He pulled a notebook out of his pocket, along with a large, old-fashioned iron key. "You'll notice we nailed up the lower-floor windows with furring strips – this far from town, why take any chances? – but, once we're inside, the smaller fireplaces you'll see sealed off were boarded up in your grandfather's time. After they put in the central gas heating."

I nodded dumbly. Yes. I remembered. One of the lesser, back-left chimneys went down to the basement. I watched as he twisted the key in the door, only half-noticing that it opened with hardly a squeak. I smelled the fresh oil – they had, apparently, kept up the inside as well as the outside – not just of hinges, but of the darkly polished woodwork that surrounded us as we stepped into the shallow, box-like reception hall.

"Just a moment, now, Mr. Parrish." Larabie spoke in almost a whisper. He handed me the first of the keys then produced a second. He twisted it in a smaller lock, across from the entrance we had just come through, then pushed back the double sliding doors that opened the wall to the huge, oak-paneled, main staircase hall.

"Your mother went with this house, Mr. Parrish," Larabie said, as he stood aside to let me look. To try to remember. Second only in size to the large formal dining room, the hall, with its stairs angling up to the right and around the back wall, was the dominant feature of the first floor. "Your mother was frail, white-skinned and slender, with pale-blonde hair," the attorney continued. "There were times when she would descend, the white of her clothes standing out, as well, from the dark wood around her, and look the perfect Victorian lady. Times when I'd come here on legal business ...."

I nodded. I saw. I remembered my mother on that staircase, saw in her now, in retrospect, the thin, almost-sickly Romantic ideal that would have held sway, not so much in her time here, but generations before when the house had been first constructed. I longed now to climb the stairs – now I remembered how she would pause at the corner landing, letting me dash to her so we could go to the main hall together. But first, I had to know something more.

I turned to Larabie.

"You told me, just before we came to the top of the cliff, that my father was murdered. But not my mother ...."

"No, Mr. Parrish. She was the one who called the police – I think I may have said that, already – but, when they arrived here, they came through the sliding doors, just as we did, and the only person they found in the hall was you. You told them your mother had gone away. That was all you would tell them. But when they asked you about your father, you pointed, silently, to the rear archway that leads to the kitchen."

More memory came back – the memory of blood. Of *wanting* to forget what I ....

"Under the circumstances," I heard the attorney continue, as if at a distance, "no one blamed your mother. For leaving you that way. She must have been so horribly frightened – and she did keep her wits about her long enough to make sure help came. She had always been such a frail woman ...."

Incongruously, I thought of my wife, then – fragile and pale. The bride I would send for who, people might say, would fit comfortably in with this house, as well. Then – stark contrast – of yet another detail I suddenly found I remembered. My father had been murdered in the kitchen, had almost staggered out past the pantry, past the back stairs and into the service hall, when he had fallen.

An axe in his back.

I must have begun to look Victorian-pale, myself. I felt the attorney's hand on my shoulder. Now I remembered the men in uniform, blood being cleaned up in the kitchen later by neighbours, my own panic at missing my mother. My wondering when I would see her come down the main staircase again.

"Mr. Parrish?" Larabie's voice was very low. "Mr. Parrish – perhaps you'd like to come out for some fresh air?"

I shook my head slowly. "No," I answered. "Everything does look in order, however, so why don't *you* wait outside if you'd like to. I just want do a little exploring on my own, to get an idea of how much work it'll take before Amelia – before Mrs. Parrish and I can move in."

Larabie nodded. "Upstairs, you'll find we pretty much left everything alone. May be dusty, though. Didn't even put dropcloths down much above the second floor."

"I think you've done an excellent job with what I've seen so far," I assured him. I took a deep breath then looked at my wristwatch and glanced toward the front door. "I shouldn't be any more than an hour ...."

I waited, gazing up at the main staircase, until I heard the outside door close, then turned to the back hallway and the kitchen. On my left, I passed the downstairs parlour first and then the dining room, noting the bay window in the latter – the first-story bulge that jutted out onto the side veranda, forming the base of the four-story tower. Once in the kitchen, I took a deep breath. I saw, at least in my mind's eye, the stains. I thought for some reason of the ink I had spilled, myself, on Larabie's floor as I imagined my mother calling me, saw her standing over the sink, the door that led to the yard and the woodshed behind the house still yawning open, her hands red with blood.

My mother's hands. *Why?*

I watched as she washed them then followed a trail of water stains, this time – pale, clear drops diluting a deeper red – back toward my father. It circled, minced, avoided expanding pools of crimson, as it reached the telephone in the hallway, then returned to the door by the pantry that led to the back stairs. The stairs my mother would never use because, as she used to say, "It isn't proper."

The stairs that rose toward the outside wall then curved and spiraled up through the tower, until they angled back into the attic.

A child's "secret passage".

I followed the trail.

I heard my mother's voice.

"Joseph," she said, as we climbed the spiral, "you must forget everything that you've seen. It's only a game, like the games your father played down in the village. Games I might have been told about, but had never believed until he came home, more drunk than usual, early this morning."

We reached the top, where the stairs straightened out again for their final climb up to the attic, and the sun suddenly shone through the windows, filling the tower with spotlights of blood-red.

"While he was sleeping," my mother continued, "I thought of a game, too."

My mother had always used the front staircase. The back stairs were dusty. And one had to stoop to get from the attic into the tunnel beneath the front gable. But this was different – this was a game.

I straightened up, bumped my head, realized I stood in the attic, myself, now.

I had trouble breathing the stuffy air. I leaned against a rough brick column – the front parlour chimney, my memory told me – and felt the flange where it thrust through the roof brush against my shoulder. I blinked my eyes, hard, to clear my vision and, when I opened them up again, I saw what still looked like a pool of blood.

Again, a memory – a recognition. I was already within the front gable. The red that I saw was the light of the sun, spilling out from a second low arch where the gable roof met the tower's final top level. I heard my mother's voice warning me to be sure to brush my pants carefully before, once the game we would play was ended, I went back downstairs. I saw my mother kneeling next to me as we crawled through the final tunnel.

We came to a child's hidden pirate castle. A room of oval stained-glass windows that served as portholes, of worn-out sheets and ropes, carefully hung from the open beams of the dome roof above as a ship's sails and banners.

I helped my mother build a tower within the great tower's uppermost room, helped her make a stair-like heap of the boxes and trunks I'd dragged in for years from the main attic proper as pirate treasure.

"Now you must help me with one thing more," she said, when we were finished. She climbed to the top and began to pull on the ropes that hung toward her. "Hold my legs. That's right. And now I want you to promise me that everything that has happened today will be our secret. Do you promise, Joseph?"

"Yes, Mother," I said. The memory was clear now.

"I want you to think of this as a game. Like playing pirates. Do you understand?"

"Yes, Mother," I said again.

"Good. Now your mother must walk the plank – just as in a game. As soon as you feel me move my feet, I want you to push me off these boxes and knock them over, just as if you were a real pirate captain pushing me off the plank. I want you to go downstairs after you've done that, without looking back. Some men will come later and all you must tell them is that your mother went away. Do you promise, Joseph?"

I had promised.

I blinked again. I stood alone in the tower now. Raising my eyes to the dome above me, I gazed at my mother, her flesh long since shrunken into a parchment against her body, still hanging in the red light of the windows, just as I had left her.

And somehow, for no reason whatsoever, I thought of Amelia, who so resembled her, walking down the front, formal staircase. Amelia, my bride, also somewhat reclusive, who, I was sure, as soon as the house was cleaned and ready, would come to love it and make it her own.

And then, without willing it, I thought as well of the restaurant hostess. I could not help it.

Of dark, round-curved Anise, who lived in town and would be waiting.

James Dorr has published two collections with Dark Regions Press, *Strange Mistresses: Tales of Wonder and Romance* and *Darker Loves: Tales of Mystery and Regret*, and has a book of poetry about vampirism, V*amps (A Retrospective)*, out this year from Sam's Dot Publishing. Other work has appeared in *Alfred Hitchcock's Mystery Magazine*, *New Mystery*, *Science Fiction Review*, *Fantastic*, *Dark Wisdom*, *Gothic.Net*, *ChiZine*,

Enigmatic Tales (UK), *Faeries* (France), and numerous anthologies. Dorr is an active member of SFWA and HWA, an Anthony and Darrell finalist, a Pushcart Prize nominee, and a multi-time listee in *The Year's Best Fantasy and Horror*. Up-to-date information on Dorr is at: http:// jamesdorrwriter.wordpress.com.

New Archangel

By Desmond Warzel

From: Ivan Vasiliyevich Furugelm, Governor, Russian American
Company
To: Otto Furugelm, Helsingfors, Finland
June 30, 1859

Dear Father,

Nearly a week has passed since my arrival in Novoarkhangelsk and
my assumption of the mantle of Governor of Alaska. I wonder if perhaps
someone simply wishes me out of the way, for there could be no worldly
place in less need of governing. In fact, I fully expect Imperial interest in
Alaska to fade completely within ten years. My predecessors have already
wrung nearly every pelt from this land, and we are forced to squabble
over the rest with the British and the Americans. As a result, there is precious little to do here.

One curiosity: I spoke at length with Voyevodsky, the outgoing Governor, and a more relieved man I have never met! During our conversation, he chanced to bring up a legend that has sprung up here over the last
decade or so. It seems that Voyevodsky, one or two of his predecessors,
and several of their guests over the years, have all claimed to see a curious spirit roaming the halls of Baranof Castle, a lady in blue. I humoured
the man, of course, for I have seen what this place is like and I could not
begrudge its residents any harmless tales they might conjure to amuse
themselves.

Or so I thought, Father, for I have now seen this ghost myself! She is
a lady of indescribable beauty, dressed in sumptuous blue wedding attire,
with hair blacker than night. I promise you that I was neither dreaming
nor imbibing! I looked her directly in the eyes, but she seemed to stare
straight through me; though I was also looking through her, after a fashion, for she was in no way solid. She never stays in one place; indeed, she
never stands still at all. She is seeking something.

My inquiries have turned up a tale of a princess or noblewoman who killed herself and her lover in 1844, but there is no one in the castle with firsthand knowledge of this alleged tragedy. Would that it were so easily ascribed to that event, but then where is the lover's ghost? He is nowhere to be found and he has more reason to haunt than she, for his demise was both violent and unplanned. Perhaps there is some logical explanation, if logic holds in the affairs of the restless dead, but I fear it will forever remain hidden.

I will write again soon, Father, but in the meantime, I charge you with delivering my greetings and good wishes to the rest of the family.

Your loving son,

Ivan

~

From: Brig. Gen. Jeff C. Davis, Commander, Department of Alaska
To: Maj. Gen. Horatio Wright, Brooklyn, New York
March 19, 1868

Dear Horatio,

I can only imagine the expression of shock that graces your countenance as you unfurl this missive! You never expected to hear from old Jeff, and I never expected to write, having resolved only to trouble my friends with letters if something noteworthy were to occur here in Sitka (the Indian name with which we rechristened the town, since no one could pronounce that ludicrous name the Russians had foisted on it; there are no angels in this place, for certain). Well, something has happened: an unfortunate and curious circumstance.

Last evening, I had the ill luck to discover an officer of mine, Lieutenant Paul McKenzie, dead in his quarters. Damn good man, too; such a shame. We committed his body, today, and now it will fall to me to write Paul's family and inform them of his death. This is a duty I do not relish at the best of times, but I find myself arrested by an even greater hesitancy in this case. It is the manner of his death, you see, that gives me pause.

Paul was murdered, stabbed in the back with his own sword. He cannot have done it himself, obviously, yet the guards swear that no one entered or left the castle all evening. I believe them, for I am scrupulous at monitoring my men when they are at their duties. Likewise, I can account for the whereabouts of everyone else in the castle (There were only a few). We are therefore looking at an impossibility, it would seem.

Whispered speculations have been circulating in the castle today regarding the involvement of the Blue Lady. I have put a decisive end to these. Of course I know the story. The outgoing Russian Governor, one Prince Dimitri, related the legend to me during the hullabaloo surrounding the transfer of Alaska to the United States. I will admit that Dimitri could spin quite a yarn; so much so, in fact, that there were occasions, early on, when I actually thought I glimpsed a flash of blue in the corner of my own eye, disappearing around a corner or down a staircase. Such illusions are easily dismissed by men of our intellect.

Poor Paul. Bad enough his death must remain a mystery, but he had nearly completed his duties and was set to leave Sitka for home within the month. Though his body must remain in this godforsaken place, thank Heaven that at least his soul has escaped.

How are things in Brooklyn, Horatio? Have you begun building that silly bridge, yet? What a common task for such a valiant warrior!

Your friend,
Jeff

~

From: James Sheakley, Governor, District of Alaska
To: D. P. Packard, Greenville, Pennsylvania
March 19, 1894.

Dear D. P.,

Baranof Castle burned yesterday and we are well rid of it.

Perhaps the Blue Lady has found that which she sought; or perhaps she has finally claimed her ultimate revenge for whatever slight has tied her restless shade to this place. It may even be that the fire was righteous rather than diabolical, that the Good Lord has at long last seen fit to scour her from the Earth.

I am not given to flights of supernatural speculation; your father, God rest his soul, once called me the most stolid and skeptical man he had ever met. But I cannot deny what I have seen since my arrival last summer. And yesterday's destruction marks 50 years of such horrors– 50 years to the day, D. P.! Real horrors, not apparitions; lives have been lost.

The things I have witnessed! I will tell you when I next see you, rather than commit an account of these atrocities to paper; if the Blue Lady has gone from this world, let her remain gone.

If we may indeed hope that the Blue Lady's reign ends with the immolation of her demesne, then a new beginning is called for. I think the fire is a sign; I have long been for moving the capital away from Sitka, perhaps to Juneau. Sitka is a trapping town and there are few animals left to be had. America's future in Alaska, if it has one, lies with gold, or some yet-undiscovered treasure. The Lady has had done with us; let us have done with Sitka.

I have done my best, in my short tenure, to give Alaska those things I think it deserves: better schools, greater stature in the Republic, a peaceful existence for the Indians. My reward has been to be hounded throughout my home by a spectre whose grievances I can only speculate upon. I could hardly stand to set foot inside that place and lodged elsewhere when I could. Perhaps I shall now have peace.

How I yearn for the hills of Pennsylvania, D. P.! I have some years left here in Sitka and I would not think of shirking my duties. I will remain here and better what I can. But you may rest assured that I am headed straight to Greenville the moment my successor arrives. I cannot imagine I shall ever live elsewhere again. The things I have seen have made me appreciative of the comforts of home.

Your friend,
James

~

From: Olga Feodorovna, Novoarkhangelsk, Alaska.
To: Iryna Dvorkin, Saint Petersburg, Russia
July 20, 1840

Dear Iryna,

My most heartfelt apologies for the tardiness of this letter; surely, one who has been such a devoted lifelong friend and companion deserves greater consideration than this. But such is the degree of my distress that it has taken me over two months to become sufficiently accustomed to living in this wretched place that I might take pen in hand and produce anything more sensible than the ravings of a madwoman!

This is not to say, mind you, that there is anything of consequence to relate. Even a simple pleasantry such as a discussion of the weather is precluded by the simple fact that, much of the time, there is none. And on those occasions when we are blessed with weather, the skies rage so as to exceed the reach of the Russian language to describe them. As for life on Baranof Island, it is simply a mockery of aristocratic life as you and I had known it. Baranof Castle is drafty and dreary, and it is only with the utmost charity that one might call it a "castle" at all; are not castles built of stout stones rather than stacks of logs? And Novoarkhangelsk is no proper town but a seamy den of hunters and trappers; and where we are not surrounded by the ocean, we are fenced in by savages.

Despite this, Uncle Adolf insists that his appointment as Governor of Russian Alaska is a reward rather than a punishment! Though, of course, he is Finnish by birth and so, is easier acclimated to such an inhospitable locale.

Now, Iryna, stop your scoffing! You know I love Uncle Adolf with all my heart and shall ever be grateful to him for taking me in. I have only the most sincere best wishes for him, which is why I would have him finish his tenure as Governor as quickly as possible so he might move on to greater things– and that we might return home and leave Alaska behind forever!

I miss you greatly, dear Iryna, and will endeavor to write you regularly.

Your friend,
Olga

~

From: Olga Feodorovna, Novoarkhangelsk, Alaska
To: Iryna Dvorkin, Saint Petersburg, Russia
May 11, 1843

Dear Iryna,

It is nearly three years into my Alaskan exile, and three years you have had to tolerate my monthly letters in which I relate my misery and little else. I had intended that this letter mark the end of my correspondence with you, to be resumed only upon the occurrence of some event momentous enough to justify its chronicling. I wanted to spare you the endless cycles of anticipation and disappointment that my missives must surely produce. But no sooner had I made this resolution, when something happened that saw me racing to my desk and fumbling madly for ink and paper.

You see, I have met a man, Iryna!

Oh, I have met many men, as you well know. Uncle Adolf, the dear, as though sensing my discontent, has assumed the role of father as best he can, doting on me and being a lovable nuisance; in doing so, he has realized that I am of marriageable age and has taken upon himself the burden of alleviating my spinsterhood. The arrival in Novoarkhangelsk of even the lowliest of noblemen is grounds for an elaborate ball, that I may be presented to my latest suitor. All are horrid boors, of course, as you might expect in this dirty corner of the Empire.

But this month, a ship graces our port, the grandest naval vessel I have ever seen. Baranof Island is simply riddled with sailors; to be besieged by so many vulgar gazes is enough to put one off ever leaving the castle. With one exception, none of them has the slightest conception of how to act in the presence of a lady.

But, Iryna, what an exception! He is a lieutenant, and his name is 'Pavel'.

How can I describe him to you? In truth, I cannot. Though he is handsome, his qualities extend much further, into the deepest reaches of his soul. How long it has been since I met a man who could converse at all wittily? And yet, when Pavel and I talk, hours go by in the space of a minute. We walk together every night along the bank of a little river that flows nearby.

In your wisdom, Iryna, you are now wondering how Uncle Adolf can possibly approve of such an arrangement and you have guessed the answer: He does not know. Except for Pavel and me, only old Yevgenia, my maid, is privy to our assignations. She is my confidant and willing accomplice, and finds great sport in plotting a new escape each night; now you are my confidant, too! It goes without saying that you must tell no one of this. A lady's reputation is her most fragile possession.

Perhaps, next month, I shall have even more news for you!

Love,

Olga

~

From: Olga Feodorovna, Novoarkhangelsk, Alaska
To: Iryna Dvorkin, Saint Petersburg, Russia
June 22, 1843

Dear Iryna,

Discovery!

I admit I was careless. I wished Pavel to have a favour, to remember me during the times we could not be together, and so, I presented him with one of my ribbons: blue, of course. You remember how Uncle Adolf was always having new clothes made for me, and always the same colour. He said it went well with my black hair, which he claimed looked blue in strong light, and he called me his "blue lady". Here, in Novoarkhangelsk, he has maintained this harmless eccentricity. So, my closets are seas of blue.

Pavel wore my ribbon at his wrist but underneath his sleeve. One day, Uncle Adolf was down in the town and chanced to pass him in the street. The ribbon had slipped, unnoticed, below the cuff of Pavel's shirt and Uncle's eye was naturally drawn to it. He recognized it and confronted Pavel, demanding an explanation.

Pavel responded admirably. Although he feared for my honour, he refused to speak falsely before a Governor of the Empire, much less before the father of the girl he hoped to marry. He confessed everything and professed his love for me.

Uncle will have none of it, of course. He refuses to allow me to marry a "common sailor". This from the Governor of Alaska! As though sailing the seas for the glory of Emperor Nicholas is any less noble than sitting hunched over a ledger tabulating otter pelt yields!

Pavel has Uncle's grudging respect; I have his boundless love. I can only hope that, together, these assets might be enough to change his mind.

Pray for me, Iryna!
Sadly yours,
Olga

~

From: Olga Feodorovna, Novoarkhangelsk, Alaska
To: Iryna Dvorkin, Saint Petersburg, Russia
July 8, 1843

Dear Iryna,

Uncle Adolf has dispatched Pavel's ship on an extended voyage. He
will be gone a year or longer.

Uncle wishes to arrange my marriage to a wealthy friend of his,
Vladimir Titov.

I have given my assent. What else can I do? Uncle Adolf wants what is
best for me. I could never bring myself to show ingratitude.

We are to be married next spring. Perhaps you can arrange to come. I
feel I may need you.

Love,
Olga

~

From: Olga Feodorovna, Novoarkhangelsk, Alaska
To: Iryna Dvorkin, Saint Petersburg, Russia
August 17, 1843

Dear Iryna,

I have much to tell you and I hope you will read to the end of this letter before dismissing me. You may find it unbelievable, but I am a desperate lady and I have discovered that there are few lengths to which I would
not go to escape my situation.

What you will not find unbelievable is that, though my love for Uncle
Adolf persists, I simply cannot marry Vladimir. To begin with, he eats
like a swine and looks like one. His manners are atrocious; his hygiene is
questionable; and ever since our betrothal, he has inflicted any number of
unwanted physical visitations upon my person when Uncle isn't watching, asserting his immediate ownership of that which has merely been
promised. Since Vladimir came, I have been subjected to abuses that no
ordinary serving-girl would allow, much less a lady.

Iryna, I would gladly submit to this if I thought that my future were
foremost in Uncle Adolf's thoughts, but I know this is not so. Various

fragments of conversation that I have chanced to overhear have revealed that Uncle hopes to benefit from certain friendships and associations of Vladimir, after his term as Governor is ended. I should have seen it. I am not his daughter, after all. And what is the life of one girl where the promises of wealth and comfort are concerned?

Having learned Uncle's true motives, I knew I must make a decision soon. I spent the better part of a day locked away in my rooms, praying for guidance; alas, nothing came of it. I fear I have spent my life amused and distracted; now that decisive action had become necessary, I found myself paralyzed.

It was Yevgenia, my maid, who forced me out of my helpless state. She came to me with a brilliant new escape, only, we were to make this egress together. She laid out trousers, shirt and sturdy boots for me and, just before midnight, she spirited me out of the castle.

Yevgenia has been at Baranof Castle forever, it seems, having served governors for almost as long as Alaska has been part of the Empire. She has seen much, and knows a great many things about this island, most of which had held for me no fascination at all. As I discovered, she was privy to secrets I couldn't have imagined.

I had seen the local savages before, of course, though I had naturally always kept my distance; they often came into Novoarkhangelsk to sell their pelts. It is my understanding that there are similar tribes practically everywhere on the continent! I cannot imagine the nuisance they must pose the Americans, French and Spanish. I should have gladly kept away from them my entire life, but it was not to be.

Yevgenia and I left the town behind and soon found ourselves thrashing through the most vulgar, brush-infested woods. I was glad of my trousers, though when I had first put them on, I thought them quite scandalous; how snug they were at the hips, Iryna! We went on forever, old Yevgenia practically dragging me at times. I was perspiring in a most uncomely way. Just when I had had my fill and was about to insist on our retreat, Yevgenia stopped and pointed.

Ahead of us was a dilapidated house– a shanty, really, with a small fire blazing nearby. Sitting in the doorway, in a battered wooden chair, was one of the savages! The 'Koloshi', we call them, though I understand they call themselves the 'Lingit' or 'Tlingit', or some similar gibberish. This particular Koloshi had taken note of us, staring in our direction without blinking, like a lunatic.

Yevgenia bade me remain and went to the man, engaging him in whispered conversation, occasionally gesturing in my direction. He nodded slowly, once, and held out his hand. Yevgenia withdrew a small sack from her pocket and emptied into the savage's palm several gold coins, no doubt liberated from my personal funds.

My maid motioned me forward. As I approached the fire, I got a proper look at the savage. Iryna, he must have been older than Moses! Beneath his ragged clothing, his skin clung to his bones like wet silk and the lines etched into his brown face looked like the veins in an autumn leaf. His eyes, still unblinking, were black pits.

Yevgenia explained that he was what might be called a 'shaman'. He had been here since before the Russians came, and he would tell me my destiny, so that I might determine the proper course of action.

When he spoke, his voice was faint from age, but unwavering: "You are the blue lady." My surprise was twofold: that he spoke passable Russian and that he knew Uncle Adolf's pet name for me, especially because, for the first time in years, I was wearing no blue. My borrowed men's clothing lacked that shade completely. Yevgenia swore before God that she had not told him and I believed her.

"You are bound to two men. One rope you grasp willingly. It stretches into the sea. One rope has been tied to you by another. Its end bears a great weight." He can only have meant Pavel and Vladimir, Iryna. Are shivers running down your spine as you read?

"All that you see around you was once our country. The Russians have it and, though there has been conflict, we are content to live under your law. For now, it is profitable for us. But hear me. This land is still Tlingit. The land obeys Tlingit law and no Emperor can change that.

"For the Tlingit, there is the light and the dark. The water and the earth. The ocean that gives food and the forest that gives danger. The soft, wet cold of the outside, which causes sickness, and the sturdy, dry warmth of the inside, which protects from sickness. All things are two.

"You and your sailor are one. This I see. And, being one, you are two.

"You can never truly leave this island. And the sailor can never truly remain. He can come, but always, he will be drawn away again. You may go, but never far and never for long."

He rose from his chair, doused the fire with water from a rusted bucket, and retired to his shanty, shutting the door behind him.

Yevgenia and I walked back to the castle in silence. She held my hand the entire way.

What do you make of this, Iryna? If the savage was able to guess at my identity and my situation, was he also right about my future? Must Pavel and I be apart forever?

I wish I might talk about this with Pavel. He is intelligent and logical, and would know what to do. Alas, I will not see him until after I am to be married to Vladimir.

I must think. Perhaps, I might find the answer myself, as I have some months to consider the problem. I shall make certain you are informed, my dear.

Love,
Olga

~

From: Olga Feodorovna, Novoarkhangelsk, Alaska
To: Iryna Dvorkin, Saint Petersburg, Russia
March 18, 1844

Dear Iryna,

I am a married woman. What choice did I have? I do so wish you could have come, but I would not wish that terrible voyage on anyone.

Uncle Adolf is happy. He gave an immense banquet afterward. Everywhere I looked, his friends and associates indulged their appetites, both for free victuals and for lewd conversation. Vladimir ignored me save for the occasional leer, though I sat at his right hand.

As the desserts were brought out, Yevgenia crept in and whispered to me that Pavel's ship had been observed entering our harbour. Curiously, it was not flying the colours of the Empire, but rather, displayed a standard of brilliant blue. Pavel has returned for me.

I have dispatched Yevgenia to locate Pavel and tell him all that has transpired, including the sore truth that that he is mere hours too late. If he will still see me, she will bring him to my rooms. We have much to discuss, certainly.

I am in my rooms now, Iryna, finishing this letter to you, so that I can entrust it to Yevgenia when she comes. It is hard to say when I might be able to write again and so, I had to inform you of all that has happened today. You have always been so kind and understanding.

Now I hear two sets of footsteps in the corridor outside. My Pavel is coming. I believe I know what I must do.

Love,

Olga

~

From: Adolf Karlovich Etolin, Governor, Russian American Company
To: Count Sergey Petrovich Volkov, Saint Petersburg, Russia
March 21, 1844

My dearest Count Volkov,

How is life in the State Council? I surely envy you the excitement and intrigue of life at Emperor Nicholas' court!

I had happily anticipated reporting to you the joyous occasion of my niece Olga's marriage to the gentleman Vladimir Titov, whom I believe you know. I am afraid that, instead, I must relay a great tragedy.

Though Olga and Vladimir did indeed wed three days ago, misfortune reared its head on their very wedding night. While Vladimir and the rest of our guests celebrated in my great hall, Olga was in her chambers, consorting with a sailor of her acquaintance; the maid admitted to arranging this shameful tryst and it was she who interrupted the serving of the wine with a hysterical account of her discovery.

Both were dead, you see. My little Olga had wrested the sailor's sabre from him, thrust it through his heart, and then done likewise to herself. It was a horrid scene that chills me yet; Olga was slumped across the mariner's body with the sabre protruding from her chest. I have no idea of the nature of the dispute between them, though he cannot have reacted well to the news of her marriage. Her motive, regrettably, must remain a mystery, though she had previously harboured an infatuation with the man. It could be said that they finished their lives together after a fashion, as she once wished, but obviously, humour, even black humour, has no place in these circumstances.

As for my own duties, you may report to the Emperor, with all confidence, that his interests in Alaska are being well attended to. We have been living in peace alongside the Koloshi for some time, and that cooperation has led to an unprecedented harvest of seal and otter pelts, whose shipment to Russia is being expedited even as I write this. Though I know I risk my good name by speaking with such optimism, I daresay it will not be long before the Russian American Company shows an actual profit!

Yours,
Adolf Etolin

Desmond Warzel's curiosity about the Blue Lady of Baranof Castle was stymied by the near-absence of concrete details concerning her legend; he has now graciously rectified this historical oversight. In the past year, his stories have appeared in *Daily Science Fiction*, *Redstone Science Fiction* and *Shelter of Daylight*, and more tales are forthcoming in several anthologies. He lives in northwestern Pennsylvania.

The Snow Man

By E. Catherine Tobler

I loved – but those I love are gone;
Had friends – my early friends are fled:
How cheerless feels the heart alone,
When all its former hopes are dead!
Though gay companions o'er the bowl
Dispel awhile the sense of ill'
Though pleasure stirs the maddening soul,
The heart – the heart – is lonely still.

– "I Would I Were a Careless Child", Lord Byron

The dream was always the same, except when it wasn't. The season was cold, fog stretching low across every hill and meadow, tucked into the valleys and over the rooftops, and no wind did rise to stir it. Even the sails of the old windmill stood still. Should something move in the gloaming, it would seem odd indeed, for no one ventured out into such weather and the air was, all about us, still.

He would take me by the hand – his own not gloved, fingers twining warm and firm about mine – and lead me through the fog, up the hillock with its dew-wet grasses (faded to amber with the coming of autumn), and into the meadow beyond. The gate would unlatch, the sheep unseen, and we would make our slow and steady way toward the windmill, which rose in dark relief within the clouded air. The bare oak and apple trees made a fringe behind the old mill, only half there in the gloom; he pulled me through thorn bushes which caught at my skirts and tried to hold me back.

Inside the mill, he would lead me up and up and up to the top room, beyond all the gears and strange mechanisms that made this building-machine work. He would draw me to his side with a whisper and then dance me across the old wood floor. That flooring made a music beneath our feet every so often, depending how we stepped. I was conscious of it

129

only for a moment and then there was only the warmth of his arm around me and the soft clouds of fog that began to intrude into the room.

The walls were rough slats and smelled of old corn, and they splintered under my fingers as he pressed me backward into them. I dug my fingers into the old wood, thinking to shatter the entire windmill under my force. Much as I tried, it never came to pass. But his mouth did pass across my own, his breath mingled with mine. He had lips as would any human man, lips that tasted of wintergreen oil, but his eyes were far gone – and so, too, his nose – and yet, in the dream, this did not bother me. It simply was. His hands were no longer those of a man, either, but skeletal. Long, pale bones stroked over my cheek, my hair, and curled around my throat. I thought I should scream, yet the touch was warm, rousing, and I leaned into it. Even when he bade me not to, even when he told me only I could stop him.

I didn't wish to.

~

I first saw the man on the rocks near sunset. He stood on one of the highest outcroppings of jagged cliff stone, his face toward the churning lake. The tails of his greatcoat whipped in the wind, snapped at the gathering mists like bird wings, while the wet rope of his hair lashed against his cheek. He reached up with a gloved hand to tuck the sodden mess into his coat collar.

The wind threw more rain against the windowpane, beginning to freeze into flakes of snowlit ginger by the remote sunset. I wondered why anyone would venture out on such a dismal night. I pressed a hand against the glass and could hardly tolerate the cold that slid into me. The man seemed small under my palm, as though I might wrap him in my fingers and thaw him. At the least, I could take him a mug of cider, but when I lowered my hand and looked again to the rocks, he was gone. A thin layer of snow dusted the ground, snow that was not disturbed by a single footprint.

"... gone and lost your mind. Turned 17 and it's just gone."

I turned away from the chilled window, to free the golden velvet curtains from their loops. Wrangling their considerable weight across the windows helped close out the frigid night from Aunt's house. Once done, I turned to look at my sister. Across the room and bundled before the crackling fire, Louisa clucked her tongue at me. Like an old woman might, though she was all of 15, black hair smoothed into a shining cap that my own hair could not manage. Louisa looked like a butterfly tangled in its own cocoon, with – With *my* sketchbook across her knees!

"There *was* someone out there," I murmured.

"I meant *this*." Louisa jabbed a finger into the sketch she had exposed.

I lunged for the book, grasping it by the corner to pull it out of Louisa's lap. She didn't try to keep the book and I closed it against my chest, upset that the man outside had distracted me. No one was allowed to see these drawings. No one.

"It looks like the cliff without the house," Louisa said, turning the small tie that bound her hair. "Tangled thorn bushes, shadowed skeleton men caught inside ... Why do you draw such awful things?"

Because I dream them, I would have said, if I wanted to gift Louisa with the truth. Being that I didn't – for she would simply brush my answer to the side, again – I shrugged. Still, I couldn't stop my heart from lurching into a frantic rhythm. A shadowed skeleton man, not in the black thornbushes of my mind, but on the snowy rocks, pressed beneath my palm for the merest of moments. I could feel all the ice that covered him melting in my palm, running down my lifeline, over the pad of flesh near my thumb, down into the shallow loveline where it would greedily overflow.

The book made a gentle protest as I closed it, its binding groaning under the slight motion. It was an old book, a gift from Grandmother. She claimed it had been her own as a girl my age, though she had never used it. And now? Now, it was seeing use, with a fresh set of pencils from my mother, who came into the room just then, offering Louisa and me cider. Louisa took hers, but I was content to let mine sit, hugging my sketchbook against my chest, looking to those ugly velvet curtains.

"Making lists, then?" our mother asked, and settled onto the couch, which Aunt had always claimed was host to the cream of the celebrity crop. Why any of them had ever come here was beyond me: this small town, with its ancient windmill, and roads in need of decent service. Perhaps people came here to escape the modern world, but – I laughed at that idea. No one came here to escape, but maybe to get lost.

"Aunt kept a green-striped scarf, didn't she?" I asked, before Louisa could reply to Mother's question.

Mother's nose wrinkled, but soon enough, her frown turned to a laugh. "Why would you want that old thing?"

I shrugged, for how could I explain that such an item would be perfect for the man upon the rocks? "Just a keepsake," I said, and that was when Louisa launched into how strange I'd become since we had arrived. Aunt's house was clearly haunted and the spirits were sinking down into my bones, taking me over, turning me into someone I was not. I said nothing, but slapped Louisa lightly on the head before I left the room, climbing the old staircase up and up and up to the small corner room that had always been mine.

Aunt had never married, though she could tell you one tragic tale after another about the men she had loved. Oh, certainly, she wished to wed (a dozen times, if you believed her), but the men she loved always seemed to flee onward to something else, leaving her behind, a memory, a ghost, although she was a living girl – until two weeks ago.

Without a family of her own, Aunt made us her family, treating Louisa and me as her own daughters, which, at first, made our mother prickle and scowl, for we were *her* daughters, not those of her sister. Aunt snapped during one argument they had – faces heated to scarlet as they screamed, making me and Louisa wonder, as we crouched under the kitchen table, if such a sound might indeed break the kitchen windows. When the glass *did* shatter, oh, the four of us simply gaped. We looked all afternoon for the stone that someone had surely hurled, but there was no stone, no brick, nothing physical that might have caused the pane to break. Only those terrible screams.

Aunt snapped, yes. Said, of course she knew we were not her daughters, but where was the harm in giving us a place of our own, a place to run to should we need, a place to dream? And when she cried, tears running down her hot cheeks, our own mother also snapped, gathering her older sister close to hug, and rock, and wipe her cheeks clean. So, this house and its countless rooms were dear to us. Though even Aunt had fled, going to that great unknown, I still felt her here. Felt her in every shadow as a warm hand, guiding me along.

My room was cold, however, the very windows beginning to ice up in the corners. I shivered and bent to the vent in the floor, finding it tightly shut. The little lever did not move until I cursed at it. Even then it moved with a squeal, as though I'd stuck a knife into a living creature. It even seemed to wriggle under my fingers. I pulled my hand back quickly, wiping my fingers on my jeans. Disgusting.

I straightened and set my sketchbook upon the desk that ran under the windows, windows which looked out onto the lake. The storm was deepening now, the moisture in the air and that in the lake combining to throw snow every whichway. At the dark flicker at the edge of the window, I leaned forward, pressing a hand against the chilled pane. The shadow skimmed the lakeshore, seeming like a bird in flight, but there were no wings ... only arms wrapped in a dark great coat. The tails snapped in the rising wind. It was him – out on the lake!

The window creaked beneath my hand, so loudly that I looked down. My hand had made a foggy impression upon the glass and condensation ran downward, warm enough to melt the hint of ice that had begun in the corners. But there was a strange shadow pressed against my hand, only the creaking glass between. I stared at it for the longest time, trying to fathom what it was, and then I realized, it was another hand.

Another hand, and it had no warmth, for where my hand left an imprint of fog, this hand left a deeper imprint of ice and snow. My head came up sharply, so sharply that it hit the edge of the lamp on the desk. But the light was unlit and, through the window, I saw him, the man at the lakeshore, the man upon the rocks. The man crouched upon the roof just outside my window – how many times I snuck out via that little ledge, I could not tell you, but in the summer, there were sweet vines to help me find my way safely down – and pressed his shadowed hand to the glass. He had no eyes – nor even a face, I suppose – for with the swirling snow, he seemed only the impression of a man.

"Mädchen."

He only whispered my name, but it came clear to me, through the very window. His breath, if it were his breath and not simply a random puff from the storm, swirled against the window and reached me, smelling of wintergreen oil. Sharp and strong and dark, like the planks of the old windmill.

"Come to me."

I screamed and jerked my hand back from the glass. In that moment, he dissolved, like a snowflake upon a tongue. There and then gone. I was left to wonder if he had been there at all, or if perhaps Aunt's house was laughing at me, turning shadows into whatever it would.

"What on earth is wrong with you?"

Louisa's voice came from the doorway and I turned to look at her with eyes that must have been wide, because she came forward with a look of concern. She even reached for me, taking up my hands. Her mouth fell open in a soft O.

"You're like ice! Did you check your vent?" She squeezed my hands and crossed the room to check it. "Mine keeps closing on its own – something to tell the handyman about, I'd guess ... yeah, yours is open and there is warm air. Mädchen –"

I shoved my hands into my pockets, forcing a smile for my sister. "Just a long day and I – I miss Aunt, don't you? This place is different without her. She's here and yet, she's not." It was a good cover – because it was entirely true. My strange behaviour could easily be blamed on missing our aunt, and Louisa – trusting, sweet Louisa – nodded.

"I do feel her here, but she's still gone. I think they call that a paradox?" She shrugged and then reverted to her 15-year-old self. "Dunno – I'm not thinking about words until I'm back in school. Storm's getting worse; Internet is down. I may not survive the night!" With that, she stomped out of my room and toward her own, as though she hadn't just shown me concern a moment before.

I closed the door behind her and looked to the window, thinking to see nothing, but there on the other side of the glass was the clear outline of a hand in ice.

~

Aunt's house was something of a legend in the city. It was not uncommon for tourists to drive past, snapping photographs, or to even stop and take more detailed shots. Aunt had once found a man prostrate in her vegetable garden (on top of her very kale, she would tell you!), for that, he claimed, gave him the best angle on capturing the uppermost tower room of the build. "The build." Oh, those words were poison to Aunt. It was not a mere structure; it was her home, she informed people, and quite often called the local police to come retrieve those who took to poking around.

It was not only that it was a spectacular build, mind you; it was that the house had established a history all its own. People claimed it was haunted (We had counted no ghosts) and that chains could be heard all hours of the night (Not one clink), and that sometimes, if you were very still, it would snow in the middle of the living room (That only happened once; I believe I was nine). Candlecliff was well-known for miles and miles; some famous photographer had even won an award for a photograph of the house, a photograph at which I now stared, for Aunt had received the first print.

The photograph hung in the uppermost hallway, which the photographer had taken as an insult, believing Aunt wanted to hide the image away. But no, Aunt had assured the woman, it wasn't to hide it, but to allow the photograph to receive the best light it could. The lower floors were too dark, but upstairs, in this hall, there was a clever little window of leaded glass, which allowed just enough light in to illuminate the photograph as though it were in a gallery. Still, the photographer's mood could not be assuaged and she had never spoken to Aunt again or come to her house. (So she claimed, for seven years later, I would have sworn that very photographer was crouched in the cornfield next door, camera in hand.)

This photograph was much like my own drawings, I came to realize as I looked at it the morning following the strange incident with the hand upon the window. Candlecliff had been captured in black-and-white, the house standing in stark contrast to the pale sky. Brambles and bushes tangled around the house, looking rather bonelike in certain instances. Though I was certain it was my imagination, I would have sworn there was a skeletal man amid them, holding a hand up as if to ward off the camera's magic.

It made sense to me, then, I decided as I walked back to my bedroom. I had seen the photograph too many times to count and those images had imprinted themselves on my young mind. I had simply sketched the photograph, hadn't I, pulling these strange images from it, rather than my own mind? It was comforting to believe that, if only for a little while. When I reached my room, I found the green-striped scarf resting on the foot of my bed. Louisa's footsteps thundered down the wood stairs.

"Left that hideous thing for you!" she called.

Her voice and Mother's floated upward as they worked on sorting other things. Aunt had many things – much of which would likely be sold at the estate sale – but we wanted a complete inventory before we jumped into that phase. I didn't want to have the sale at all. I wished this house might stay forever ours, for what would we do without a place to dream?

I closed the door behind me and curled into bed, with the scarf held against me. Just a little nap, I told myself, and then I could join Mother and Louisa and pick through the remains of Aunt's life. I didn't want to. Didn't want to.

Her scarf smelled like spearmint and tansy, and I thought of the small sachets she liked to make, to keep the moths away from all her most precious things. None of us knew where this scarf had come from, for she always seemed to have it. Not even Mother could place it. "But then, your father is that way, too, isn't he? Just always been there ...." She would say it with a soft laugh, but you could tell she was partly serious. Her life before him had been a thing entirely different and now, she could not fathom him gone, so he had simply always been there.

The dream was different this time.

The windmill stood as it always had, a deep shadow beneath a moon that looked about to burst and send milky light everywhere. But this night, there was a soft wind which turned the sails; they creaked much like the glass beneath my hand had. If you listened long enough, it sounded like a low moan. This agony carried across the fields and seemed to saturate everything. Even the trees seemed to bend their bare branches low under this unhappy sound.

I waited for one sail to pass before I could step into the slight doorway and press against the door. But the door did not give and the next sail was rapidly approaching – surely, the sails did not reach to the ground, I told myself, but I could feel the wind that pushed it and so, too, the wind that the sail itself made as it hastened toward me. I gripped the doorknob, shaking it and crying out to be let in (for it never occurs to the sleeper to simply step backward and out of harm's way, does it?), but still, the door did not open.

The sail caught my left shoulder, knocking into me hard enough to set me off balance. My other shoulder slammed into the door, just as it came open, and icy hands gathered me up before I might fall. My name was a whisper on his mouth then, dark and somehow full of secrets, as he bore me deeper into the windmill and the sails outside continued their anguished dance.

Over and over, he whispered my name, but did not draw me upward to the top room as he usually did. He pressed me back into one of the work tables, iced fingers sliding against my throat, where they started to melt. I could feel the trails of water running down into my blouse.

"This is the thing you must do," he said.

His voice was its own agony, rising and falling with the sound of the sails. His face was clear before my own – I could have touched his cheek, but my fingers curled into the old table beneath me.

"Tell me what – what must –"

But before I could finish and before he could tell me, the windmill broke apart. The hideous sound shattered around us, as the sails broke free from the old mill and took the upper deck with them. Centuries of dust and wood and memories fell down upon us. The moonlight showed us how the sails toppled into the old fields, running, running, until at last, they gave a final breath, and fell still, shattering amid the corn.

"Come to me," he said and I woke up, tangled in the green-striped scarf.

I flailed in an attempt to free myself, for it seemed a snake, a tentacle, something cold and slimy, meant to hold me down. I flung the fabric onto the floor and stared at it, slowly coming to believe otherwise. It was just a stupid piece of fabric. Nothing more.

If this house was our place to dream, I thought that I only need go home. Perhaps I had conjured him to life, from the photograph or the sketches, or some combination thereof. Driven mad by my sister's need for social media, even in the midst of a winter storm, I sought the opposite refuge, that of imagination.

But when I saw the footprint, I reconsidered. The footprint gleamed in the low afternoon light, just inside my door. As if someone had been walking in snow and paused here, long enough to leave a wet impression. Was the snowman melting?

~

According to the police reports – and sadly, there had been such a thing, because the neighbours didn't know who else to call – Aunt was found just outside the door to the windmill. She was in her nightclothes and barefoot, her hair unbound, as though she had just come from bed. Being a woman of some seventy years, no one had been too surprised by her death, but its means remained a mystery. Had she simply wandered outside, fallen, and perished there in the night? The medical examiner thought that the most likely scenario and Mother seemed to accept it well enough – for it was easiest. Asking more questions was tricky.

Why had Aunt been wearing such a smile? Did the dead smile? Why had Aunt been carrying a spring of rosemary? (It had been broken from the large rosemary bush she kept in her kitchen, dirt scattered around the pot as though she had been in a hurry.) The old do curious things, so I was told, time and again. Who could truly understand the mind? I wanted to, but how did one understand a mind that had already moved on?

If there were clues in the house, I could not see them. Everything looked ordinary. The kitchen felt as though Aunt had stepped out, but would be right back; even the teakettle that Mother had heated left me thinking it had actually been my aunt, for there sat her favourite cup with the white violets on it. Her room was still scented with the fragrance of her powder and there, by the bed, sat her slippers. Slippers she had not put on the night she had wandered outside to her death.

"Curious old lady," I whispered, as I turned circles in her room, looking for something, for anything.

When I noticed the thin line that ran up the far wall, I stopped spinning. The wallpaper was slightly curled up, yellow on its underside. The paper crackled when I touched it and I thought it was unlike Aunt to leave something so worn. She was proud of her house, though she wanted the public to stay away; she made certain it was well-kept in all ways. Yet, here was an oddity.

I ran my fingers along the paper, beneath it, where the glue had turned hard and had, in some places, flaked off entirely. There was still a little scattering of glue bits on the floor there, which I was prodding with my shoe when a hidden latch disengaged and the wall swung outward.

Alice in Wonderland was familiar enough to me that I was wary of such doors. I peered inside and saw a bare lightbulb with a dangling chain. One tug on the chain sent light spreading over a small space that looked like a closet, but that featured stairs leading upward. At the top of the stairs (Of course I climbed those stairs, which groaned and seemed likely to give way before I did reach the top) there was another door, shorter. Through that door (for how could I not go on?), yet another door, and this one had me crawling through a small space that seemed more like a heating duct than it did storage. Surely, nothing was kept up here – but I was wrong.

A small box sat at the far end of the space. I pulled it toward me, through the dust of ages, and pried up the small latch that kept the lid closed. Inside the box sat another box, and inside this box, a delicate ring. It was nothing complex, a loop of white gold or silver, holding one small diamond aloft in a simple filigree swirl. It seemed a thing a bride would wear.

There came a shout from the lower part of the house and I jumped into motion, wriggling out of that small space, even as I jammed the ring box into my jeans pocket. I came down to find the bedroom quiet and dark. A glance out the windows showed me that, somehow, the day had flown. I closed the secret door and left Aunt's room, but as I stepped into the hall, a terrible cold seized me.

"Louisa! Mother!"

There was no reply from them. I was shivering by the time I reached the stairs and pulled myself back before I slipped down them, for they were coated in ice. Long daggers of ice draped the banister and small bits of snow swirled in the air. I stood there for the longest time, thinking I was dreaming, but a sharp twist of the skin near my wrist seemed to prove I was awake.

I picked my way down the staircase, only slipping once when I neared the bottom. I thumped down those last steps and entered a world that seemed unreal. Snow had drifted to the foot of the stairs and against every wall. The wind blew a gale from one end of the house to another, ice and snow tracing over every wall, window and door.

It was the front door that was open, a mouth for the storm to howl through. I could not close it, for the snow had drifted in such a way to make it impossible. I cried out for my sister and mother, again –

"Mädchen."

It was *his* voice, though, not theirs, that rose above the shriek of the storm. I turned, fully expecting him to be there, but I was still alone in the snowy house. All around me, the house moaned, like Aunt once had as the cold burrowed into her, down to her bones. Oddly, I wanted to soothe the house, make it better, but instead, I fled.

Out into the storm, where that dismal voice hailed from. All through the blowing snow, the sculpted drifts, I stumbled half-blind, reaching frozen hands out to push brambles and branches back. I slipped on ice and staggered when the cold seeped into me; I could not feel my feet, but kept moving, not away from the house, but toward that voice.

"Who are you?" I screamed the question, expecting no reply, but one came.

The skeletal arms closed around me, nearly warm the way they had been in the windmill. Dream or awake? Awake, I told myself, over and over, as I turned in those arms and looked up at his face. And yes ....

He had lips as would any human man, lips that tasted of winter-green oil when they crossed mine, but his eyes were far gone and so, too, his nose. Yet, this did not bother me. It simply was. His hands were no longer those of a man but skeletal. Long, time-worn bones stroked over my cheek, my hair and curled around my throat. I thought I should scream, yet the touch was warm, rousing, and I leaned into it. Even when he bade me not to, even when he told me only I could stop him.

"What do you want?" I whispered. Though my breath turned to frost between us, I still watched as it melted the snowflakes upon his rotting cheeks.

He could not speak – I saw that now. As other parts of him had rotted, so, too, was his throat gone. There were no muscles that might make such sounds. He had never spoken my name, had never told me anything. Then who?

Though his eyes were clouded over – perhaps they had once been blue – I saw some frantic horror still within them. He needed me to understand, but he could not speak. He needed me to know. He was wretched and terribly lonely. And Aunt had never married ….

I shoved a hand into my pocket, barely feeling the scrape of cold denim over frozen skin, and pulled out the ring box. With shaking hands, I lifted the ring from its box and held it up, showing him how, even in the storm, it managed to gleam. That diamond was small but lovely, almost like my aunt.

There was a recognition in his eyes and maybe, just maybe, he had offered this ring dozens of years ago, so long ago that none could remember – but Aunt had remembered. Had shut the box away in a secret place that only another dreamer might find.

I saw them then. He would take Aunt by the hand – his own not gloved, fingers twining warm and firm about hers – and lead her through the fog, up the hillock with its dew-wet grasses (faded to amber with the coming of autumn), and into the meadow beyond. The gate would unlatch, the sheep unseen, and they would make their slow and steady way toward the windmill, which rose in dark relief within the clouded air. The bare oak and apple trees made a fringe behind the old mill, only half there in the gloom; he pulled her through thorn bushes, which caught at her skirts and tried to hold her back.

Aunt said no and forever regretted it. Forever.

I held the ring between us, like a shared secret, and his milky eyes blinked. Did he gasp? Did he – Ah, Reader. The dead *do* smile.

E. Catherine Tobler lives and writes in Colorado – strange how that works out. Among others, her fiction has appeared in *Sci Fiction*, *Fantasy Magazine*, *Realms of Fantasy*, *Talebones*, and *Lady Churchill's Rosebud Wristlet*. She is an active member of SFWA and the senior editor at *Shimmer Magazine*. For more, visit www.ecatherine.com.

In His Arms in the Attic

By Alexis Brooks de Vita

The first surprise was that the two hundred-year-old townhouse was still intact in the heart of the French Quarter, even after Hurricanes Katrina and Ike, and the rebuilding of New Orleans into an adult fantasy of itself.

Ave Marie de la Croix pulled her antique 914 black Porsche over to the curb that dipped between the narrow-bricked sidewalk and the cobblestoned street. She shoved open the driver's rusted door and unfolded long, lean, jean-clad legs to slide out and confront her childhood holiday playground.

Then Ave had her second surprise.

She thought she heard a voice, hushed and urgent, call her name: "Ah-vay!" She jerked her head up toward the townhouse's second floor. And something slipped like a razor-edged knife between the wrought-iron balcony and the glass panes of the French doors.

A bird as it flew overhead? A squatter scuttling back into hiding?

Ave waited. Watched, barely breathing.

But no bulky darkness shifted behind the dusty glass. No hesitant hand pushed aside tattered lace to peer down at her upturned face. Nothing moved again.

Ave muttered, "Jumping at shadows."

She threw a cautious look back over her shoulder. No frustrated residents were out running errands, and no lost revelers wandered in search of bars or breast-baring college girls. Even with Mardi Gras night fast descending, this little side street remained empty and still.

Her neighbours had probably all fled the seasonal festivities for suburban relatives' homes. Ave would be alone in the townhouse tonight.

She squared her shoulders. Tossed back her head and yanked out the hair-tie that held together a lopsided bun at the nape of her neck. Braids and dreadlocks cascaded down to her narrow waist.

She had not driven all this way from San Francisco just to play the scared, little, big-eyed girl again. She was all grown up now.

And ready to believe in ghosts. On the theory that, once you believed, there was nothing left to fear.

Ave kicked shut the sports car's door and strode across the cobbles and bricks. She jangled through the ring of rusted keys she'd retrieved from a Bay Area safe deposit box until she found one with curled masking tape, faintly labeled: "Front Door."

She worked it into the lock. Grabbed the scratchy latch. Twisted and shoved.

Hesitation seized her with the panic of a virgin who has changed her mind just seconds too late. *No!*

And then came the rush of rotted air and the sweeping view through darkness to abandoned things huddled under stained sheets that always meant coming home.

Only, this had never been her home. Ave had never been more than a holiday visitor here, puzzled by the grandmother and aunts she loved so much.

Ave lifted a booted foot across the threshold. Eased her body behind it like a dancer poised at the edge of the stage.

Surely, someone was here. She could feel someone. "Sheridan?" Ave called. She couldn't resist the hope.

But nothing stirred.

Ave pulled herself together with a little mental slap. Of course that was not the way to invoke a spirit.

Ave flung out a hand and patted the wall to her right in search of a light switch. Felt an old-fashioned knob at the end of a long, wire-covering tube. Turned it.

No lights flickered on. The electric company hadn't come through.

I should have brought a flashlight from the car, Ave scolded herself. But she suspected that if she went back to the Porsche now, she would leap into it and drive straight to Canal Street to search for a hotel room. *Mardi Gras Night, there won't be one.* So, she'd end up fleeing the Crescent City all the way back to the Golden Gate Bridge.

"And what will you do there?" Ave challenged herself out loud, just to hear a voice. "Jump off of it into the Bay?"

If she hadn't jumped or overdosed during her zombie-state in the blighted seasons following Sheridan's death, there was no point doing it now. *Just see this through,* Ave urged herself.

Maybe he will come. Perhaps he is already here.

Watching her. Counting on her to bring them together again.

Ave crossed the dust-coated hardwood floor to the closest lump of furniture hidden under dust covers. Grabbed a handful of cloth and yanked.

And screamed as a spiky clump hurtled across the toe of her boot, squeaking and trailing a bald tail an inch above the floor.

Ave was back on the street and had already grabbed open the Porsche's resistant door before she got hold of herself. "Just a rat," she panted and, "What did you expect?" she chided herself. "No one's been in that house since the honeymoon."

And with the accidental resurrection of that blessed, fairytale memory, she bent her face into her grimy hands and let belated tears of loss and despair gush free.

It felt good to cry. She sank against the Porsche's side, her curved back pressed against Sheridan's gaudily stenciled "914", and sobbed.

Flashes of memory: Sheridan openmouthed like a child as they cruised the French Quarter's narrow streets. Sheridan emerging from his gleaming Porsche, laughing and shaking his head with disbelief at the sight of her inheritance, this dilapidated mansion.

Sheridan coaxing her up the curved stairs, a candelabra in one hand and her wrist in the other. "Come on, babygirl. Aren't you even curious to see if the old stories are true?"

They had been married in San Francisco on a long-ago Valentine's Day before they rushed their honeymoon Gulf-ward. Sheridan so wanted to celebrate his first Mardi Gras in New Orleans: to revel in the streets and stack his neck with gaudy beads flung from masqueraders floating by in the night air.

Wanted to get into the townhouse attic by midnight and see if the ghostly Mardi Gras ball was only a spinsters' story told to a gullible Creole child. As if, in this sunken city where history and myth trembled at the edge of the encroaching sea – holding back the final devastation – magic still lived.

The two newlyweds never made it into the attic. Ave thundered down the steps and out onto the street, cursing Sheridan's insensitivity every step of the way.

He'd come after her. When he caught up with her among the revelers groping her rear end and waving strings of bright beads to tempt her to share her body, she slapped him. "That's my childhood you're making fun of, Sheridan! It's not funny. And I don't want to see whatever comes into the attic at midnight!"

Sheridan had laughed off his shock, kissed her, and swept her up into his arms to carry her back to the townhouse. Watching all this, the revelers cheered.

They'd spent the night out on the balcony. It was his idea. They'd told each other favourite childhood memories, and made love in a sleeping bag against a backdrop of fanning fireworks and the drunken laughter of merrymakers.

"Oh, Sheridan." Now, as the sobs eased, Ave dabbed at the muddy paste her tears made as they mingled with the dirt she'd gotten on her hands when she pulled off the first dust cover. "Tonight I'll make it into that attic for you, my love. Be there for me, too, Sheridan." She pulled herself to her feet.

Ave looked toward the wide-open townhouse door. The ring of keys glinted in the dark parlour where she'd dropped them when she'd fled.

No way could she go back in there now. But she'd go get some candles, see if she couldn't put in a call to the electric company, and maybe the gas and water people, while she was at it. Go do some groceries, as the locals called shopping, maybe find a few of Sheridan's favourites. Then she'd be back.

When Ave returned, she drove the Porsche through the narrow alleyway behind the townhouse to its carport. The walk through the alleyway around to the front door, lugging four bags of food and cleaning supplies with a flashlight, normalized her re-entry. The flashlight's beam swept ahead of Ave and sent vermin skittering out of sight to the edges of the dark parlour.

"Uh," she groaned. She'd be anxious to get into the attic by midnight and, if no one was there, get out of here.

Could she bear to think that no one would be there?

That Sheridan was gone? *Grief does things to your mind.* How many times had Ave heard this from her university's counselor, her aunts and girlfriends, in the blisteringly lonely months since Sheridan's death?

"I just have to try," she said aloud, a habit these days. "Sheridan believed in ghosts." Which led to that unspeakable hope: *Maybe his belief can bring him back.*

It was worth a try. What did Ave have to lose? *Sheridan will try to come back to me. If anywhere, here. He will know I need him. He will know I stayed alive just to come here for him.*

She would go into his arms once more. This thin thread had tied her to life. Because the worst thing about death was that it came without giving fair warning, one last chance to fill up your soul with enough love to last as long as you had to keep going.

A winter ago, Ave had prepared a lecture on war-and-water literature for her university students as she tossed together a soup and salad for Sheridan, on his way home from a Deans' meeting. But Sheridan flung aside his trenchcoat and briefcase to gather in his arms a rape/murder victim in an alleyway and was shot along with the fleeing culprit by the arriving police officers.

Struggling to hold onto life at the hospital, he'd weakened so alarmingly before she even got there that just kissing his cracked lips seemed a cruel imposition. As she waited and watched the emergency team work on him, Ave never doubted for a moment that he would revive.

But the doctor pulled up the sheet to cover Sheridan's face. He looked up as Ave started to scream and shouted for help, tugging her out past the curtains of the emergency room.

She fought all the way, shrieking Sheridan's name. But he was gone. And her first coherent thought, struggling up out of layers of shock and sedatives, had been that they would never make love again.

Not easy to say to her aunts when they came to her loft apartment with plates of steaming greens, spicy cornbread, and savory dirty rice. "Eat, Ave Marie. You're not in the grave yet, no matter how badly you wish to be." Not easy to explain to friends who asked her to a party, a club, a blind dinner date. "Maybe it's time for you to meet someone new, girl."

I'm not through with Sheridan. I have to hear his voice. Tell him I love him. Feel his arms around me again. If another man touches me, I'll kill him. I'll die. I need to make love with Sheridan. Maybe then she could finally say goodbye.

Sheridan would have understood exactly how she felt. And if he came to the Mardi Gras ghostly ball ....

By now, Ave had snatched off dust covers all the way from the front door through the dining hallway and up to the kitchen. They littered the floor behind her, waiting to be gathered up and dumped into a washing machine.

And there was just such a machine where she remembered it in the corner of the kitchen: frontload, European-style.

Ave deposited her load of candles and cleaning utensils and a handy camping lantern on the kitchen worktable, and went back for the dust covers. She jammed them into the washing machine and took a deep breath before she snatched open the broom closet.

Shushed sounds of brittle things scuttling out of her way.

Ave stood her ground. She shone her light bravely around inside the cramped storage space, driving hideous creatures before her, back into the darkness. Only brooms and a dustpan, a bucket, and a collection of string and sponge mops remained.

The water and gas companies had done better than the electric people. Soon, Ave had mopped a disinfectant trail throughout the downstairs rooms that was guaranteed to send vermin staggering back into the city's sewage system.

Nothing scampered at the edges of the darkness now, she thought with satisfaction as she dumped the muck into the gutter outside. She really should finally close the front door when she went back into the pine-scented townhouse. Close herself in with her ghost.

The latch clicked loudly in the silence.

Seemed to echo far away, upstairs.

Ave's heart stutter-skipped. Could an echo carry that far in here? All the way up to the attic? "Hello?" she called, after the sound ricocheted off the dark cathedral ceiling.

No answer. No more sound.

She should go back outside to the Porsche 914. One of its two trunks held Sheridan's battery-operated sound system and his favourite CDs. She should play Sheridan's music so she wouldn't have to listen to sounds she couldn't explain while she prepared to see him again.

Ave left her cleaning bucket to wedge open the heavy front door, even after she returned and set up Sheridan's music system.

Blues would be good for the invocation. Soon, Bobby Blue Bland crooned, "I'll take care of you. Please let me take care of you."

Now for a romantic dinner.

Ave retrieved a candelabrum from the mantelpiece in the parlour and carried it to the dining hall. Had she and Sheridan eaten at this very dining table before they went in search of the ghostly ball? Was this the same candelabrum Sheridan had carried upstairs? Ave couldn't be sure.

That one honeymoon night they had spent at the townhouse was hazy, entangled as it was in her mind with so much fear and desire.

Ave fitted new white candles into the holders and debated lighting them this early. Decided against it.

She went, instead, to the kitchen, and washed and dried a collection of fragile plates from the china cabinet. She set out a circle of brie, a baguette of fresh bread, some buttery mascarpone cheese, and clusters of willow-green and violet-black grapes. She covered all these under upturned serving bowls on the dining table, in case the vermin crept back in while she was away, up in the attic.

Last, she set out the very same Hungarian cut crystal goblets that they had toasted their love with out on the balcony. "To us," Sheridan had said.

But she placed a bottle of clear water on the table tonight. Ave had not dared drink anything stronger than coffee since Sheridan's death. Depression always threatened.

"There." Ave stood back from the table, hands on hips, to survey her spread. Perfect.

And a black line as thin as a hair caught in the viewer's eye moved just out of Ave's line of vision.

At first she thought it was a hair. She wasted precious seconds fluttering an eyelid and tugging at her eyelashes.

Wait. No pain.

There was nothing in her eye.

Ave jerked toward the doorway between the dining hall and kitchen. Something slipped away just ahead, as she turned.

"Sheridan?"

The slamming in Ave's heart took forever to calm. She had to reason with herself that Sheridan wouldn't come to her like this, slithering around at the edges of things. This was her imagination. She had always been frightened by the attic as Mardi Gras midnight drew near.

And a memory surfaced like a swimmer breaking through ice to gasp for air.

Ave's grandmother, bathed and scented with lavender, wisteria, and mimosa oils from the local *Voudun* shops, draped in delicate white lace, her fine golden fingers sparkling with her wedding ring's diamonds and sapphires as they ran along the keys of the baby grand piano, while she waited for that blackest hour.

The candelabrum's flames flickered roseate spatters against the darkness all around and drew a courageous little Ave down the curved stairway to sit at her grandmother's side. "Why are you still up, Grandmamá Marie? Why are you so dressed up?"

Ave had looked up into her grandmother's face. The fullness of her grandmother's youth had been carved by passing decades into contours of tenderness and grace lovelier than any of her young wedding photos.

"I want to be with him again, little one."

"Be with who, Grandmamá Marie?"

Grandmamá Marie had raised her beautiful face to gaze up the pitch-black stairway toward the attic.

Ave turned there now as Bobby Blue Bland's song died away. In the sudden hush, a footstep sounded high away at the top of the stairs.

And brought a memory of Ave's aunts struggling to restrain the one of them who fought in their arms to go up the stairs at Mardi Gras midnight, dressed in red satin, her hair straightened into undulating waves of perfumed blackness.

"No!" Ave screamed before she collected herself.

The footsteps stopped. Or had never sounded. Ave couldn't be sure. She breathed deeply. Swallowed the sudden panic.

Grandmamá Marie's bath. Of course. A scented hot bath would ease Ave's mind and put her in the mood for a possible encounter with Sheridan. And wasn't she in luck? Water and gas were both turned back on.

It was harder to mop the upstairs bathroom floor and scrub the tub in what was now the pitch darkness of nighttime. Ave was very aware that the front door downstairs was still open to the street, to wanderers, revelers and burglars. But she wasn't yet able to bring herself to close it again. She kept remembering the sound of that distant latch closing way upstairs in the attic.

Ave kept her cell phone off to save its power, but placed it carefully on the bathroom floor between the bathtub and the lit candelabrum, in case she needed to call for help. Then she stepped into the old claw-footed tub.

The warmth eased her legs and back. She moaned with pleasure and relief.

And came awake, thinking it was silly to be afraid to close the front door. Rats and roaches were nowhere near as dangerous as rapists, thieves and drunks. She would go close that door right now and then come back and finish her bath.

Ave clutched the edges of the tub and rose. Water sluiced down her sinewy *café-au-lait* thighs. Sheridan used to kiss her thighs like sipping coffee, the cream of the sunless season whipped deep into her skin's end-of-summer mocha.

Dizzied by sleep and reverie, Ave stepped onto the newly cleaned floor and gathered up the sheet she had taken for a towel during her foray into a linen closet. She rubbed briskly, wrapped the sheet over damp skin and tucked the end between her breasts.

Paused. Listened. Called sharply, "Who was that?"

Someone had just whispered her name. Ave was sure of it this time. She leaned forward and shoved the bathroom door closed. Latched the flimsy hook.

She fumbled for her cell phone. Snatched it up and powered it on with shaking hands. Waited an eternity for it to beep into life so she could call 911.

And then thought, *A burglar wouldn't know my name. That has to be Sheridan.*

"Sheridan? Sheridan, is that you, honey?"

Ave shut the phone just as she glimpsed the time. Nearly midnight. Already? *Finally.*

She slid the cell phone back to the floor and reached for the candelabrum, instead. *How long did I sleep in the tub?*

Went to the bathroom door and leaned her cheek against it, listening. Nothing moved. No one spoke again.

"Sheridan?"

Ave gathered up her nerve. She had survived nine months when she would rather have been dead. She had driven halfway across the continent to meet with Sheridan one last time. She must not falter now, hiding from him in the bathroom, cowering in fear of the unknown.

Ave forced her free hand up to the latch. Flipped the hook free. Lowered her hand to the knob.

Twisted it open. Pulled the door wide.

She raised her candelabrum and peered into the darkness. "Sheridan?"

How she hated the pleading in her voice! She tried again, more forcefully this time. "Sheridan, I'm here. It's Ave."

Ave stepped out into the hallway and looked up toward the closed square of the attic door, still half a flight of stairs higher.

He would be in the attic.

Ave had not meant it to be like this. She had meant to be bathed, perfumed, dressed in his favorite colours, with her hair cascading from a pretty clip atop her head.

But what if he was up there already, waiting for her? How alone he must feel, suspended between the world of the dead and the world where they had shared their lives together!

Ave closed her eyes and thought of the warmth within Sheridan's arms. The hard strength when he pressed her against his chest and abdomen. Their passion.

She opened her eyes and forced herself to move up the last curve of the stairway. Of course it was Sheridan up there in the attic, waiting for her. What on earth else could it be?

Another flash of memory. One aunt's sharp hand across the cheek of the aunt who struggled and wept.

"You don't even know what's up there."

"But Mamá always went up there every Mardi Gras."

"And you don't know what she went up there to meet."

"Papá. Daddy was up there for her."

"You don't know that. She never said it was Papá."

"But who else could it be?" the aunt in red satin had asked desperately, just as they all heard the tinny thin music of the ghostly ball begin.

Ave paused beneath the attic door cut into the third floor ceiling. What had the aunt in red satin done, in the end?

But what did all that matter? What else besides the spirit of the man a woman loved could possibly be in that attic?

Had her grandmother ever explained? To any of them? *No.* She was sure Grandmamá Marie had never said anything beyond, "I want to be with him again."

But Ave hadn't been there to hear the last words when her grandmother died. Couldn't even remember her grandmother's waning years. Couldn't begin to guess at the "he" that Grandmamá Marie meant.

In fact, it seemed to Ave that she could remember nothing worthwhile, figure out nothing, just now when she needed so badly to remember and figure out everything.

And finally, for the first time ever, she wondered if the culprit whose crime cost Sheridan his life had survived that double shooting. How ironic, if he had. How cruel of fate.

In a flash, un-tethered memory – a hissed warning to the aunt who struggled : "Carnival is the night when spirit becomes flesh, you fool. *Anything* could be up there."

This had stopped the aunt in red. And now it stopped Ave.

She faltered. Struggled with indecision.

Became impatient with herself. Really, what did all these memories matter? *Surely, nothing at all!* She knew with all the power of her love and devotion that Sheridan would come back for her, no matter what, just as she had held on, survived the pain, and come all this way just to be with him.

And anyway, if something else was in the attic when Sheridan came for her, he would protect her from it.

Of course Sheridan would protect her.

By now, Ave had arrived beneath the attic door. Bolstered by the thought of Sheridan's protection, she reached for the rope that would open the door and drop down its collapsible ladder.

They would be together again.

Only as she gripped the rope did Ave wonder if Sheridan might not yet have arrived in the attic. Who or what else might know her name?

Her hand on the rope lay still.

Ave thought of the limbo of nothingness Sheridan had to have come across to return to her. She shivered, damp from her bath in the humid chill.

And maybe just a little frightened?

Ave realized she was waiting for Sheridan to call her name again. This close, she would recognize his voice. Or know if it was something else that called her.

But nothing called.

The cell phone was back in the bathroom. Maybe she should go get it and call her aunts in San Francisco, to ask if one of them had ever made it into the attic at Mardi Gras midnight. Maybe they would tell her what waited there, once they discovered it was too late to stop her from coming to the townhouse.

Ave let go of the rope.

And the music of the ghostly ball started.

So faintly at first that she wasn't sure she heard anything, only that pleasure and sweetness had stolen into her mind and eased away her worry, the music seeped through gaps between the attic door and the ceiling just above her head, and swelled into fullness as she listened.

"How lovely." Ave could not recognize a tune. Only the tinkling harmony of archaic instruments. A mandolin? A harpsichord? Bells?

The ghostly ball had begun! Was Sheridan just a few feet above her, even as she hesitated? Would she soon be in his arms in the attic?

Excited now, Ave reached for the rope, pulled it, and opened the attic door.

Blackness and melody surged down the descending doorway and engulfed her. The flames of the candelabrum guttered out as the music drew Ave up the ladder.

Topping the last rung, Ave climbed forward onto the attic floor, into the blindness.

Far below, she heard the front door slam.

Ave swung the useless candelabrum around. "Sheridan?" The attic door creaked shut behind her bare feet. "Sheridan, it's Ave." Her voice shook. "We can be together again."

Silence.

Why would Sheridan frighten her so? She would ask him as soon as she could unclamp her throat and speak again.

And then, so faintly she wasn't sure at first that she felt it, a touch on her ankle.

Lighter than a wisp of dust. Weightless as a gossamer insect's wing floating upward on a draft, a trickle of feeling drifted against gravity along her leg.

She wasn't sure she felt anything until it spread behind both knees and clambered up to seize the insides of her thighs.

She screamed and hurtled the candelabrum. Heard it crash as she tried to backpedal toward the ladder, out of the attic.

Found she couldn't move.

What had happened to the music? When had it stopped?

And what was this that roiled just in front of her? Darkness boiled thicker than the darkness it drew from.

She whimpered, mute with terror and hope. And sudden, deep, humiliated pleasure. Her trapped legs spasmed.

"Ssshhh." Oddly, the sibilant shush quieted her as the pitch mass surged against her trembling, welcoming limbs.

It eased her to the floor, pierced her body with white-hot chill and splintered her mind with light. Pleasure fled before awe. She succumbed in amazement, unsure that this thing that embraced her could ever have been Sheridan, gathering ethereal fragments of himself to swarm back to her from his oblivion.

Alexis Brooks de Vita has published literary theory in *Mythatypes*, an historical murder mystery titled *The 1855 Murder Case of Missouri versus Celia*, a translation of Dante's *Comedy*, beginning with *Dante's Inferno: A Wanderer in Hell*, and has contracted with Double Dragon/Blood Moon to publish a series of Atlantic Slave Trade dark fantasy titles, beginning with *The Books of Joy: Burning Streams* and *Blood of Angels*. She can be found at: alexisbrooksdevita.com.

Objects & Mementos

"As we hastened from that abhorrent spot, the stolen amulet in St. John's pocket, we thought we saw the bats descend in a body to the earth we had so lately rifled, as if seeking for some cursed and unholy nourishment. But the autumn moon shone weak and pale, and we could not be sure. So, too, as we sailed the next day away from Holland to our home, we thought we heard the faint distant baying of some gigantic hound in the background."

"The Hound", H.P.Lovecraft

The Ba-Curse

By Ann K. Schwader

They asked him if he feared the mummy's curse,
That blameless maid he'd stolen from her tomb.
The excavator laughed; he'd heard far worse
In every local *souk*. As twilight's gloom
Suffused the valley like the Nile at flood,
He lit a lamp & tied his tent-flaps tight,
Then, with a flourish fit to freeze the blood,
He poured a dram & bade his prize goodnight.

They never knew what savaged him, although
He shrieked it very clearly as he died:
"*Ba! Ba!*" A madman's babble ... Even so,
His men won't speak of things they saw inside,
For neither time nor whiskey can erase
That black-winged nightmare with a maiden's face.

Ann K. Schwader is the author of five speculative poetry collections: *Werewoman*, *The Worms Remember*, *Architectures of Night*, *In the Yaddith Time*, and *Wild Hunt of the Stars* (Sam's Dot Publishing, 2010). *Twisted in Dream*, a comprehensive collection of her weird verse, to be edited by S.T. Joshi, is forthcoming from Hippocampus Press. Ann lives and writes in Colorado, USA. For more about her work, visit her Web site, http://home.earthlink.net/~schwader/ or read her LiveJournal, Yaddith Times: http://ankh_hpl.livejournal.com/.

Hitomi

By Nelly Geraldine García-Rosas

"The pupils dilate and shine with the thousand facets of a kaleidoscope with an abyss in the centre."

— Clemente Palma

~

The fire that floats in the hallways purrs, whispers my name.

~

I was in the last stages of writing a thesis about Japanese literature. The classes were over and the summer, which one could foresee would be severe, reminded me of the imminence of the deadline.

I read, as part of my investigation, an odd little novelette titled 'Hitomi', written by a woman called "Tsukino" during the first years of the Edo period in Japan. It was a complex text with a plot revolving around insomnia; the characters seemed to be one alone, repeated infinitely, who, with a different costume, moved from house to house to escape the impossibility of sleep. I, insomniac by election, did not wish to escape, but had no option.

Like the infinite faces created by Tsukino, the rigour of summer forced me to find a new place to live: a return to my parents' home was not an option. Besides, Mexico City had something that demanded I stay, search for a roof atop the ancient lake, traverse its subterranean veins inside suffocating, sweaty trains; the same "something" which took me that day to Donceles Street.

~

The squires, the *donceles*, are no longer that sweet nor young. From the parking lot that bears the same name of the street, it seems a labyrinthic cave opens up; at its entrance, an impassive, worn, three-story building stares back: three heads which question my entrance, but allow my passage. I penetrate a web of centuries-old neoclassical constructions, which close above me. Although it is noon, the sun barely lightens the sidewalk; there is a cold that slices the bone, but I keep walking. I walk by the theatre, Fru Fru, amidst a thick rain of black feathers. I see, on each side of the street, photographic businesses in niches full of humidity, some which are, ironically, illuminated by candles of trembling light. The bookstores of used books, like angels of a cemetery, open voluptuously. Amongst the angelic businesses shines "Miracle Alley". I enter this store as though an external force conducts me to the shelf at the back. On the third bookshelf – dusty, damp and covered with a black jacket – is the book. I pay 13 pesos. I walk. The street also smells of mildew; it is cloudy, full of dust. The used bookstores invade the sidewalks. I walk as if possessed. I walk.

I stand before a newsstand. On the right side, a thin, very-white sheet is pasted. With beautiful calligraphy, it offers a room for rent. There is no phone number, only an address on this same Donceles Street. I take the rice paper and ask the newspaper seller for the address.

"Right ahead, miss," he says, pointing to a moth-eaten wooden gate.

At this moment, I realize I am pressing hard on the book. I open it to the first page and place the white sheet of paper as a bookmark. The dust from the street lodges in my throat when I realize the book, *Bakeneko Monogatari,* was written by the author of *Hitomi.* Not only that, but on the margin of the paper, the same name is written in Japanese: 'Tsukino'.

Heart beating, I touch the knocker. She opens at once and, with a gesture of her enormous eyes, invites me in.

~

To live in Tsukino"s house was like going blind: The small building from the dawn of the 20th century had been trapped between another two of greater size. For this reason, it received very little sunlight. The electrical wiring was old and failed constantly, so our daily life depended on the faint candlelights, which shone yellow because of the humidity.

Despite this impenetrable darkness, I grew used to living in this place with airs of used bookstore: There were rooms full of dusty books and a central patio which, I can swear, is the source of all the humidity in the world. At night, Tsukino walked the hallways in the company of her three cats: Hitomi, Kasumi and Ayumu. From my desk, as I made annotations on the thesis, or from the bed, I would see the brightness of the flame travel the house and hear the meows and purring of the felines. Later, I would feel how one of the cats jumped on my bed and snuggled against my feet.

I had not seen the cats. I knew them by their cries and because Tsukino mentioned their names during her nocturnal walks. Once, I tried to caress the fur of the one sleeping in my bed, but it fled when I reached my hand towards its back. Surely, the darkness and loneliness of the house had made them unsociable.

One night, I bumped into a bookcase while searching for a candle to replace the one that was extinguishing. The book that I had bought on that occasion at "Miracle Alley" fell and opened on a page: "The pupils dilate and shine, with the thousand facets of a kaleidoscope with an abyss in the centre ...."

The light went off.

Kneeling at the threshold, I was able to glimpse a reddish light coming closer down the hallway. I heard Tsukino calling the cats and they responding with loving meows. I heard, too, my name. When the light came closer, I realized it floated like a will-o'-the-wisp over the robust body of a beautiful white cat with two long tails, which, with elegant steps, entered Tsukino's room. My hands shook, I sweated cold sweat, but I managed to drag myself to the main room. What I saw can barely be told with words: On the bed, wearing the clothes of my landlady, the white cat devoured the bloody flesh of a creature which I am unable to describe.

The tails quivered, ethereal, happy: Kasumi, the mist, and Ayumu, the apparition. The white cat turned, looked at me, and with a gesture of her enormous eyes, invited me in. Hitomi, the pupils ....

I felt myself watched into the infinite by those abysmal eyes, which eat away the flesh and soul. I ran outside towards the dirty air of Donceles, where the moldy bookstores grow and spread like mushrooms over the asphalt, and, like the infinite faces of Tsukino, I began to escape eternally to rid myself of those eyes ....

~

I still feel her lying at my side at night. I hear her whisper lascivious words in a language I do not understand. Each night, I imagine her eyes and I feel her snuggle next to me, and I am paralyzed and I am lulled and I slowly fall asleep, while she, wickedly, purrs her bestial prayer.

Nelly Geraldine García-Rosas is a Mexican writer and a freelance copy editor. Her stories have been published in local independent magazines and anthologies like *Historical Lovecraft* (Innsmouth Free Press, 2011). She loves cats and has been working on a thesis on Gothic Literature for so long that it's not sane, anymore. She can be found online at: www.nellygeraldine.com.

I Tarocchi dei d'Este

By Martha Hubbard

The Magus

Lurking in the sharp morning shadows, I, Zoesi Bianfacchio studied my niece in the courtyard below. I schooled my long, saturnine
face to display little emotion, only my narrow mouth puckering as if I'd
just ingested a rotten lemon. *Look at her*, I thought. *Jumping about like a
demented chicken.* There are times I think my niece should be sequestered
somewhere quiet for her own safety – other times, – I'm certain of it. Holy
Mother of God, it's a hanging not a circus.

"Alicia! What are you doing?" I commanded, leaving the shelter of
the portico.

"Oh, Uncle, can't you see? There's to be an execution – actually, three.
I do adore hangings. All those dangly bits flipping and flopping about,"
the girl burbled. "I love watching the workmen – look at those muscular
arms – setting up the scaffold for the hangings. I hope the hangman is
incompetent. I like it so much better when the knot isn't tied true; the
victim dies slowly: gasping, gurgling, tongue protruding as his life ebbs
away."

As Alicia rattled out this obscene monologue, I wondered, not for the
first time, if installing her in the household of my Lord's wife Parisina had
been a mistake.

True, there weren't so many hangings these days. The long reign of
the d'Este family had enabled a period of peace and stability that meant
most citizens of Ferrara were too busy scheming up ways of pulling in
more florins and soldi to foment troublemaking, while the Duke usually
preferred the swift finality of beheading. Sad, really – a proper hanging
could be an occasion of unbridled festivity. Tomorrow, there would be,
not one but three droppings: pickpockets, thieves – lowlife – in plain sight
of the entire court and populace of Ferrara. It would be the high point of
a boring, lonely summer for Alicia.

Nonetheless, that was no excuse to behave with such an appalling
lack of dignity. She should consider herself a very lucky young woman.

Had not I, her uncle, Chamberlain to His Lordship the Marquis of Fer-rara, Niccolò d'Este, secured a brilliant position for her with the Marquis' beautiful young wife, the Madonna Parisina Malatesta? If she would only apply a bit of discretion, a judicious combination of hard work and well-judged flattery would see her named Chief Lady in Waiting. From that place, she would be of genuine use to me. I would repay her usefulness to the fullest.

Instead, the stupid girl had fallen in love with the Marquis' bastard son and heir, Ugo.

It disgusted me to watch. Whenever she was not otherwise occupied, her eyes tracked his every move. When she and Parisina walked to chapel, the young prince glanced in their direction with the sweetest, most ten-der expression in his coal-black eyes. My stupid Alicia believed that his tender glances were for her. It had not taken me long to discern the truth – that the boy was enamoured of his stepmother. This was something I could use – but how?

You ask why I would want to harm my beautiful young mistress? I tell you my hatred of this spoiled, self-indulgent beauty burns like a smoul-dering fire, ready to burst into blazing fury. She possesses the singular item I want most in all the world and now, she has claimed this exquisite boy, as well.

I know it is so. Damn her! Surely, no man can look at a woman the way he does without feeling the same stirring in his loins that I feel in my most private places at the sight of him. If only that stirring were for me. I cannot bear it. For months, I have sought a means of bringing down my cruel mistress. Now, perhaps Alicia has shewn me a way.

The High Priestess

My life was not easy. Do you imagine it a wonderful fate to be mar-ried at fourteen to the greatest lecher in our city-state? The magnificent Niccolò, hero of ditties sung in every tavern: *On this and the other side of the Po, everywhere are the sons of Niccolò.* How could any woman, after experiencing his masterful lovemaking and potency, desire another? Let me tell you true. In bed, he was a dud: fat, pimply, foul-smelling, and fast. The buck in its cage takes more care of his partners' needs than my Lord Niccolò.

Nonetheless, I was a Maletestina; well-trained by my father, Andrea, I knew my duty. Surrendering my dignity, I acquiesced to his ruttings, even on occasion pretending he had pleased me. My reward was two beautiful daughters, Ginevra and Luiza. Of the boy wrenched from my arms too soon, I will not speak.

On balance, my life was not unpleasant. After a few years, Niccolò, determined to continue the goal of planting his seed in every nubile female residing in Ferrara, demanded his husbandly dues less and less. Monetarily, he was not stingy to me and mine. Thus, unlike many of his other spawn living in the palace, we had proper clothing and the rushes in our bedding were changed before too many ticks and lice could take up residence in them.

I did what I could to help my stepchildren, but my primary concern was my daughters, their well-being and their education ... and my cards. Oh, my cards, my pretty playfellows!

Desiring to find a way to understand and endure my place in this life, I had become interested in the Sacred Inner Teachings. Any wise man will tell you of the two key pathways to Supreme Knowledge. One of these is the Sacred Tarot. In its powerful, mystical images, I hoped to find the conduit to an eternal and happy life. To this end, I had begun collecting decks of *tarocchi*. How beautiful were these packages of sublime ideas! Each artist brought something new and different to his own creation. Using an allowance from my father, I sent my servant, Zoesi on journeys throughout the breadth of the peninsula, to most of the city-states: Venezia, Mantua, Bologna, Ravenna, even into the lair of the Popes themselves, not so many years returned from exile in Avignon. Who would have believed that the most treasured and dangerous deck of all would be found so close to home – in the greedy, mercantile city of Firenze?

In the spring of 1423, whispers reached me of the birth of a very special deck. Discreet inquiries returned the news that, indeed, such a deck, containing entirely new images and with covers wrought with fine gold, had been brought into existence by the painter Giovanni della Gabella. The story making the rounds the drinkers in the *Firenze enoteche* was that these extraordinary images had appeared to della Gabella in visions, that for the seven nights he worked on their creation, he neither slept nor partook of food nor strong drink, so powerful was the urge to render out this creation. He was said to be demanding the unheard-of sum of 40 gold ducats for this valuable pack of cards. Was he insane, I wondered. What stack of paper images could possibly be worth so much?

Excited beyond the point of reason, I nightly dreamt of them. The idea of them, how they would look, their scent, their cool, portentous feel in my hands. What hidden knowledge they might reveal possessed me. At last, I sent Zoesi to secure them for me. I had realized the outrageous price by selling my dead mother's wedding ring, one of my dearest treasures. At the time, it seemed a small price to pay, to acquire an object so extraordinary.

The Magus

By the time Milady ordered me off to Firenze to collect the latest of her trinkets, I had become disgusted to my core by being made to act as her errand boy. Arriving in that glittering, giddy metropolis, my first thought was to secure lodgings. I had no intention of returning to Ferrara the same day. A bird released from its cage will fly free as long as it may. Inquiries about the house of the painter Della Gabella produced the news that the painter had left his home and family, and was living in a house of ill-repute with Angelina, the exquisite beauty who was said to have been the model for some of his cards.

Certain that, with these changes in his fortunes, he must now be in great need of monies, I reasoned that procuring the mistress's cards would present no problem. The house, so-named '*Garden of Earthly Delights*', was on one of the narrow alleys leading away from the Ponte Vecchio. It was not difficult to find. Reaching a massive wooden door that guarded the entrance to this 'garden', I knocked several times, only to have it opened by the largest, shiniest Moor I have ever seen. The head was shaved, the massive body entirely encased in a voluminous robe, making it impossible to determine whether this creature be man or woman.

"My good lady or gentleman," I began.

"Ha." Don't know what to make of me – do you?" the creature mocked. "'Merisondé' will do. How may I help you? From the look of you, you aren't the type to require the kinds of services we offer here."

"You are correct in that assumption, Merisondé. I seek the painter Giovanni della Gabella. I am told he is to be found here."

"Oh, you want the lunatic. If you can take him off my hands, I'll make it worth your effort."

"He is mad, you say?"

"Not so as you'd notice outright, but something about him upsets the other customers. My regular business has fallen off since he took up residence."

"I'm sorry to learn that. Perhaps I can help."

"Somebody has to. He's been keeping one of my best girls from working. And now, neither has set foot outside his room for two days."

"Direct me to him and I'll do my utmost."

"Right this way. If you can shift that miscreant out of my house, I'll give you personal service, myself – free of charge."

Tempted as I was to find out what was under that kaftan, I declined.

A stirring in my chest, a vague new hunger, was pulling me upwards to the painter's room. I knocked, knocked harder, called the painter's name – all to no avail. So it was, uninvited, that I entered the maestro's lair.

The scene that greeted me should be indescribable. Even now, I wish those images were not forever burned onto my memory. The once-beautiful model lay, sprawled naked on a bed, her shaved sex open to all eyes, her blue-white body a mass of cuts and stripes oozing blood and pus. I feared that she was dead, but a soft moaning, like the purring of a dying kitten, told me that life still flowed in her.

On the floor nearby, in a pool of urine and excrement that had attracted the attention of a host of flies and other insects, the painter sat staring with cloudy eyes at the beautiful deck laid out in the traditional *Spread of Destiny*. As I entered, he looked at me and moved to shield the cards from my glance. From what I did see of the pictures, his future was not going to be pleasant.

"Go away! " he cried. "You cannot take my beauties."

"You have promised them to the Madonna Parisina. Here, I have money for you."

"I don't want the filthy bitch's coins. She cannot buy my love."

"I thought your love was the model Angelina, there."

"That," he gestured with his head toward the bed, "that is dross. It knows nothing, sees nothing, is worth nothing. Only my beauties here can speak the truth." He stroked them with a lover's touch. I winced to see him fondle the lovely images with his filthy hands.

At that moment, Merisondé arrived, a shadow falling across the carnage in the room. "You beast! Monster! What have you done to my beautiful Angelina?"

"Not so pretty, anymore – is she?" cackled the painter.

Turning to one of the blond giants who had followed her, she ordered, "Get that foul creature out of my house! Throw him into the Po so he doesn't stink up our streets."

Then, kneeling on the bed, cradling the dying whore, she commanded, "And fetch the doctor. Now!"

"Well, Signor from Ferrara," Merisondé said to me, as the wretched painter was dragged, crying and screaming, out the door, "It seems you have forced an ending to this sorry tragedy. There, take those accursed cards. Get them and yourself out of my house, as well."

I was only too happy to oblige her. Scooping them into a pouch I had prepared for this purpose, I thanked her and departed. I was already crossing the ancient bridge, with its mercantile temptations, when I realised that I was unexpectedly 40 ducats richer.

Returning to my lodgings as fast as my shaking legs would carry me, I ordered a magnificent supper, along with a basin of warm water and some scented soap to be sent up to my room. Once my feast had been laid out, the curious eyes of the servant had departed and my cleaning materials set out, I removed the miraculous deck from my pouch. My first thought – to remove all trace of that painter's contamination from the lovely images. As I worked- oh, so carefully – wiping the grime and mire of his fingers from the beautiful faces and gowns, I felt a warmth growing in my breast. A stirring of love such as I had felt for no living creature in my existence.

When my toilette of the cards was complete, I poured myself a goblet of golden wine. Before bringing it to my lips, I dipped my finger in the warm liquid and turned up a card, touching a drop of wine to that first card, *The Empress*. The card and I shivered as one. She was pleased.

Throughout the long night, I brought forth one and then another card, each succeeding image more beautiful than the previous one. Truly, Della Gabella had been a master. The miraculous pictures shewed story after story: dreaming cities where nothing living stirred, peopled with strange, angular towers of jade and obsidian that twisted and turned, seeming to disappear into themselves. That night, the cards took me to places that mere mortals had never been – even in dreams.

By morning, I was exhausted and exhilarated beyond words. The perfume from the images, exotic hints of violets, earth and despair, had lodged itself in my brain. When the peal of the carillon announced it was time to return to Ferrara, I experienced an anguish that wracked my bones, causing me to tremble in the fibre of my being. I now was certain of only one thing. I must possess them ... this ... miracle – but how?

The High Priestess

Zoesi's appearance when he returned from that excursion – spinning, fizzing with unharnessed energy – frightened me. It told me that something untoward had occurred.

"Were you successful?" I questioned.

"Oh, yes, My Lady, beyond all expectations." His voice was so low, so slurred, I could barely hear him.

"May I see them?" I said, holding out my palm. As he slipped his fingers inside his tunic to retrieve the deck, his hand shook like an ancient's crippled with palsy. Claw-like fingers gripped the gilded packet as I wrenched my treasure from them. His pallor spoke of torment at relinquishing the prize. But it was his eyes, the rage in his eyes, which set my heart racing and my limbs shaking with fear.

"Thank you, Zoesi. That will be all."

"My Lady." Without another word, he turned and stalked out of my chamber. Observing his retreating back, I knew I had made an enemy.

In the days after his return, I observed Zoesi's behaviour. His eyes, when he watched me, were twisted with lust and anger. If I did not know that he preferred the hard, smooth limbs of young men, I might have mistaken this as frustrated desire for my own favours. I knew better. Zoesi's passion was for my golden *Imperatori Tarocchi di Firenze*.

He could not, would not have them. They were mine! The minute those golden gems settled like a lover or a child into my tiny palms, I knew that we had been intended for each other. The blackness of his eyes told me that Zoesi wanted my treasure. How far would he go to possess them? This would be a battle to the death, if need be. I trembled with fear at thoughts of the outcome.

I was girding myself for the conflict, rehearsing reasons I could give my husband for dismissing Zoesi, when I received an unexpected boon. Plague had spread its ugly countenance over the rat-infested streets of

Ferrara. My husband, fearing for my safety, ordered that I withdraw for the summer to the countryside and take my stepson with me. I determined to take the golden deck with us, believing that removing the cards from Zoesi's proximity would diminish his lust for them.

Ah, if that had been the only snare of which to be cautious. A far greater danger awaited.

Codigoro, away from the miasma of Ferrara, was lovely that summer. In the long, clement evenings, Ugo and I would sit close together in a bower by the River Po. Sheltered and screened from servants' prying, in our canopy of vines and willows, we laid out the cards again and again, letting the magical images transport us to gardens filled with rosy fruit and fantastical, half-seen animals.

The scent of lilac, hyacinth and violet flowers pervaded the air around us. Their miasma gave the impression we had been transported to a new heaven. Experiencing ourselves high up in a crystal tower overlooking the entire Delta, we could see all the way to a strange ocean, alike and unlike the familiar Adriatic. Ferrara and my husband seemed an eternity away. In those nights, transported by bliss, we became lovers. It seemed so natural, inevitable ….

I say to you, that summer was the one period of my life when I knew true happiness. Alas, too soon, autumn rains washed away our idyll. It was time to return to reality.

The Knave of Hearts

That summer, Alicia, left behind, had become one with the gryphons guarding the roofline of the castle. Daily, she occupied the high, west-facing rampart scanning the horizon, as if by her presence she could will an apparition into being.

"Oh, I am so unhappy!" she cried to the clouds. "Has ever any mortal suffered such pangs as I? Where are you, my beloved?"

She might have enjoyed the respite from work occasioned by her mistresses' absence, had not the thoughtless Marquis also sent away his son, heir and her beloved, Ugo, to accompany his stepmother.

The endless, steaming days and soggy nights plodded along, interminable. The flat plains to the north of the river steamed and festered, while Alicia endured nights twitching and writhing in a frenzy of frustrated desire. In the morning, sodden bedclothes stank from the sweat of fantasy lovers.

On this day in late September, her vigil bore fruit. A thunderclap of approaching hoof-beats heralded the end of her blighted existence. The onset of autumn, with its cooling rains, had dispersed the pox, calmed the Duke's fears for the safety of his loved ones, and brought about the return of her mistress and the adored Ugo.

"At last, I shall be released from this itching which wracks my days and torments my nights," she cried to the approaching cloud. "Surely, after this intolerable separation, he will be emboldened to speak of transforming our dark needs into reality."

Time, wretched thing that it is, passes. Oh, evil fate. With each unresolved day, Alicia became more distraught.

That fateful morning, she stood in the arcaded loggia just outside her mistress' chamber, shredding a silken chemise, her fingers enacting on the thin fabric the resentment she felt at his betrayal.

"They have been back a week today – an entire week. He hasn't spoken a word to me," she hissed at the ravaged chemise. "I have ceased to exist. My heart is wrenched into jagged pieces."

Her eyes narrowed, remembering. "His fingers linger over-long on my mistress's hand. I am filled with the most stinging bile at this betrayal." Her nails raked the innocent silk.

Never one to endure frustration for long, Alicia decided to search her mistress' chamber while she was at table with the Marquis.

When the contemptible lady appeared, flouting her betrayal in ruffles and lace, Alicia accompanied her mistress to the small dining chamber and saw her seated opposite her husband. Ignoring a speculative look from the Marquis, and wishing them *"Buon giorno"*, she retreated.

Secure in the knowledge that the Lady would not return in less than an hour, Alicia ransacked the chamber, looking for evidence of Parisina's treachery until her fingers seized upon a new clove pomade. Opening its secret chamber, she found a ring hidden inside.

At first glance, she recognised it as Ugo's – *her* Ugo's. When she tried to place it on her finger, it would not fit. The flimsy trinket had been cut down, made smaller to fit the hand of a faithless wife. Looking more closely, she espied the inscription traced on the inside: *To my enchanting Parisi, long may this remind you of our love.*

Her eyes were thrown open, her heart stabbed with betrayal. Tossing the wretched thing into the fire, Alicia ran out of the chamber, only to collide with her dear Uncle Zoesi, upon whom she collapsed in a flood of tears. As she sobbed against his chest, he was so supportive that soon, she had confided to him all her sadness and resentment.

The High Priestess

My maidservant Alicia was Zoesi's niece. She had served me faithfully for two years and could rightly expect a prosperous marriage, with a proper dowry, after her time with me. Such was my habitual way to reward those who had pleased me. Concerned about Zoesi's intentions, I determined to question her about her uncle's habits and activities – perhaps to confide some of my fears to her.

When I returned to my chamber, Alicia was nowhere to be seen. What was to be seen was a maelstrom of overturned tables, bottles tipped onto the floor, powders and tablets trod underfoot. All of my bedclothes had been torn from the mattress and thrown about the chamber. Ignoring these, I searched frantically for my clove pomade. Finding it open under a pile of pillows, I knew without looking that Ugo's ring was missing.

Only Alicia had access to my room. Only she could have done this. Why? Ordering her brought to me, I cleared debris from a stool and sat down to wait. On first entering the chamber, she feigned astonishment at the sight.

"My Lady, what is this? What has happened here?"

"Alicia, please do not insult me with falsehoods. Only you have keys to my chamber."

"I ... no ... There are others ... the Marquis ... My Uncle Zoesi ...."

"The Marquis was with me, as you know. Are you accusing your uncle of this ... this abomination?"

"I ... no ... I don't know."

"Come, come, Alicia. Stop this play-acting. Where is the ring that was in my pomade?"

"What ring? I know of no ring."

"Alicia – stop. I shall have you searched – by two or three of my men. They would make a very thorough experience of it. Would you like that?"

"No, please ... no."

"Then tell me what you did with the ring and we shall put this behind us."

"It is ... I threw it into the fire."

I rushed to the fireplace and, grabbing a poker, began to search through the ashes. Finding it in the far corner, I said a silent prayer to the angels for Alicia's lack of dexterity and turned back to my cowering servant. If ever I had thought her a friend, she was now anathema to me.

"Why would you do such a thing?"

"My Lady, I was trying to protect you. I saw the ring was a man's and too small to be the Master's. In a fit of panic, I threw it onto the flames, lest other eyes should happen upon it."

"Alicia, I don't believe you. Do you think I have not noticed the way your eyes seek out Ugo, undressing him with your hungry thoughts? I cannot stand the sight of you. You are dismissed. You will be beaten before quitting this palace forever."

The Magus

What a fortuitous fashion in which to begin one's morning! To comfort my niece, I had feigned great distress at Parisina's behaviour. Alicia did not know that I was only-too-aware of her stupid passion for young Ugo. As if the heir to the throne of Ferrara would ever use a servant girl for more than a moment's distraction. I feigned shock and dismay at learning of my mistress's infidelity – and with her stepson, no less. I cautioned Alicia to say nothing to anyone, lest the guilty couple learn of our intentions to expose their secret. At last, her rage assuaged, my silly niece walked away, head bowed, but no longer weeping.

My heart leapt into flight, like a butterfly exiting its chrysalis. Could this be the tool I needed to extract the miraculous *tarocchi* from the clutches of its undeserving owner and punish her for her selfishness? Yes! I would make it so.

From that moment on, I began to observe their actions. To my great delight, I was soon able to prove the veracity of my niece's accusations beyond all doubt.

Despite knowing the need for caution, the lovers were unable to control their illicit passion. I overheard them fix times and places of assignations – assignations that I watched from the shadows. How beautiful they were, these young lovers in passionate embrace, their hands and limbs entwined in desire, bodies like white marble in the candlelight. The aesthete in me was saddened to think that this beauty would be defiled – but it must be so. I would defile the Virgin herself to recover my beautiful *tarocchi*.

Perhaps I have misled you – allowed you to believe, that my actions were solely motivated by my desire to possess the unique deck I had procured for Parisina? I cannot deny that, from the first moment these cards snuggled into the palm of my hand – as if they had been created to sit – just there, I became determined to make them my own. But what is a courtier to do? My task was to protect and defend the interests and well-being of my Lord and Master. My duty was clear. I must inform Niccolò of his wife's treachery. First, I would need a way to demonstrate their perfidy beyond all possibility of denial. Their passion, boiling out of control, soon made this possible.

I learned that on those nights when she was not called upon to be with the Marquis, My Lady had become accustomed to spend the hours of darkness with her beloved in her chamber. What bliss they experienced in those hours together.

What terrible frustration the boy suffered on those other nights when his mistress was required to lie in the arms of his rival – her lawful husband – his father. During those times, I watched him pacing the ramparts in turmoil. How I longed to take him into my trustworthy arms and calm his frenzy, to save him from the dreadful fate approaching. Alas, now that I was certain of the terrible truth, there was no alternative but to tell the Marquis.

~

"What is this evil spewing from your mouth? Are you mad?"

"My Lord." I was on my knees before a raging Marquis.

"I would that I was. I would gladly take upon myself the agony of madness if it would preserve thee from this terrible betrayal."

"You are telling me that Parisina – my wife Parisina, mother of my children, is enjoined in incestuous union with that ... with my bastard Ugo!"

"My Lord, I am deeply saddened, but it is so."

"But she is my wife. How could any woman I have honoured with my favours, especially my wife, entertain thoughts of taking another into her bed?"

"I have no idea, My Lord." In my mind, I compared his blotched, heavy-jowled face with Ugo's fine skin and lustrous black eyes. "But she is young, as is he. I believe the affair began when they were thrown together in exile last summer in Codigoro."

"Don't tell me these things. I will not entertain such foulness in my home."

I shrugged my shoulders. Lecherous, greedy pig he may have been, but he was my master and he was mortally wounded by these accusations.

"I don't want to believe this atrocity. Have you proof?"

Nodding my head sadly, I said, "The proof of my own observations. I have seen them in unholy congress."

"I would also have this proof. Arrange it."

"As you will, My Lord." I backed out of the audience chamber.

∼

To this end, I secreted my master and myself in a carved, wooden garderobe in Parisina's bedchamber. The Marquis had earlier sent word to his wife that he would be away for the evening. I had every confidence that the lovers, believing themselves free for the night, would soon unite before us.

My unhappy confidence was not misplaced. The Marquis, seeing his wife in the arms of his son, burst out of his hiding place. "You whore! Defiler of marriage beds and the good names of good woman. I am sickened by you both."

Surprised at the moment of coitus, Parisina and Ugo struggled to find blankets and sheets to cover their nakedness.

Turning his attention to Ugo, the Marquis grew more incensed, "You viper in my bosom. You are my son. You would be heir to my kingdom. I loved you!"

"My Lord, Father …," Ugo tried to say.

"Shut your lying mouth. I will hear no more words from those deceitful lips." Niccolò turned away from his son. "Guard. Take this bastard to the dungeon. When I have finished with this whore, I shall observe his beheading."

"Father!" Ugo screamed as he was dragged away.

Niccolò was not listening, his attention focused on Parisina cowering in the middle of her bed. He screamed, "You faithless bitch! What did you

want that I did not give you? Was it too much to ask that you be faithful to your lawfully wedded husband?"

"Niccolò ...."

"No, don't speak. No more lies from you, either. You will watch
your paramour separated from his head before also paying the same
price for your betrayal."

Turning his back on her imploring eyes, the Marquis buried his
face in his hands. "Guards, watch over this chamber. Let her prepare to
meet a vengeful God. Make certain she has no opportunity to speak to
the bastard before he goes to his Maker."

The Chariot

Alas, we are undone; Zoesi has ruined us. He will have his cards.
I caressed them and held them in my hands for the last time; I cursed
him with them.

"My treasure, may you bring him no joy – only pain. May his days
be empty and alone, his nights filled with demon-terrors, and may he
end his life forgotten, a rotting corpse plucked apart by scavengers."

I had been a fool, blinded by first love. How could I have been so
stupid to believe that our passion would remain undiscovered? If I
could so easily read the truth of Alicia, why then should I expect others
not to see the joy that lit up my face whenever Ugo approached?

It would be possible to say ... to excuse our behaviour as the fruit
of a lonely exile in Codigoro, but I am no hypocrite. From the moment
Niccolò announced his intention to send the boy with us, I *knew* what
would happen. My pretty cards foretold it.

"I am entrusting my beloved son and heir to your safekeeping," he
said. "You are his stepmother; I know you will look after him as one of
your own."

Dear God, Niccolò, were you blind or too puffed up with vanity to
see that he and I are the same age? And now, it is too late. *The Wheel*
has turned and we must accept our fate. My sorry part will be to watch
my lover lose his head for loving me.

The Lightning-Struck Tower

Dressed in white, Parisina stood in the loggia overlooking the courtyard, waiting her turn at the block. I, Zoesi, author of this sorry tragedy,
waited in the shadows. Tearless, she watched Ugo's execution and moved
down the steps to take her place. As she reached the bottom step, Niccolò
appeared in the same archway.

"Parisina, attend me."

"My Lord." The proud girl bowed her head, waiting.

"Madonna, although you have betrayed me and our marriage vows,
you are still my wife." the Marquis paused.

Parisina's eyes never left the ground. She spoke not a word.

Unsure now, the Marquis struggled to continue. "I realize that I have
... not always been exactly fair to you."

"And so ...?"

"I offer you a chance to save your own life. If you will repudiate
your vile affair, confess your sin before Almighty God, and retire for the
remainder of your life behind the walls of the Poor Clare's, I will allow
you to live."

"My Lord, I cannot live a lie, nor do I wish to live without my
beloved. I go to my death with joy, for in that sweet place beyond life's
sorrows, I know I shall be reunited with him."

"Then die. Go with your lover to Hell!" The Marquis turned and
stalked away, shaking and trembling.

So it was done. Afterward, the Marquis arranged for the bodies,
wrapped in white shrouds, to be conveyed to the cemetery of San Fran-
cesco and there buried beside the Campanile.

Standing there in the gloom, I watched Parisina's head separate from
her body and land with a soft plop in the waiting basket. Certain that
she was well and truly dispatched, I dashed to her chamber – my only
thought to reclaim the miraculous *tarocchi* that had so claimed my heart.

To my unbelieving eyes and hands, the deck was dead – dead as its
mistress! It would not wake for me. I screamed and cried, pleaded and
begged. My sorrow was so intense it brought the guards at a run. Finding
me beside myself, raving in my dead mistress' chamber, they dragged me
before the Marquis, who demanded an explanation. I could only gibber
and plead.

"Bring her back, please ... Bring back my beloved, my only love ....."

The Marquis, hearing my cries, became convinced that I, too, had been his wife's lover. He ordered me locked in this stinking cellar, my only companion these now-mute, useless pieces of paper. How ugly they seem to me now.

He further ordered the banishment – the permanent banishment – of my now-insane niece Alicia, who had played such a sorry role in all of this. After being escorted from the palace, she would be strangled, her corpse taken by boat downriver and released into the Po Delta. The fish and creatures of those sodden waters would make a proper feast of her body and her madness.

She was allowed to visit me just before she left. Her eyes glittered as she babbled and giggled, while relating how Parisina had used the miraculous cards to curse me.

I was not surprised to hear this. I know I shall soon be dragged to my death. I can neither eat nor drink nor sleep, but pass the wretched hours screaming and moaning for the loss of my beloved *tarocchi*. I daily beg to be dispatched from this earthly torment. Soon, if God will have mercy on me, the Marquis will no longer be able to tolerate my existence in this world and I, too, shall find a home in the stinking waters of the Po. Perhaps, in death, I shall be allowed to return to the dreaming cities. I pray, to whatever god resides there, that it shall be so.

Martha Hubbard lives on an island in the North Baltic Sea. For 1000's of years a place of strange gods, mysteries, tragedies and wonder, Saaremaa Island provides the perfect bed-rock for a writer of dark fantasy. Previously she has been a teacher, cook, stage manager & drama-turg in New York City's Off-off Broadway community, a parking lot company book-keeper and a community development worker. Recently she put aside some of these activities to concentrate on her writing, but is still the Consulting Chef for the local Organic Farmers Union. Her story "The Good Bishop Pays the Price", appears in Innsmouth's anthology, *Historical Lovecraft*.

Elizabeth on the Island

By Joshua Reynolds

In the sea was an island. And on the island was a house. And in the house was a woman. And in the woman was a secret. But, like all the best secrets, the one upon whom it centred was completely unaware of its existence.

Her name was Elizabeth and she had never seen her face.

Elizabeth had been born out of the sea, like Aphrodite. A classical allusion that she clung to in order not to think about the circumstances of her birth – the cold fangs of rock that she had clung to all unknowing, and the hard scrabble for the grim, grey shore through the freezing waters. Bloody and dripping, she had emerged from the womb of the sea to stagger onto land and into the house that seemed so familiar, despite her inability to recall how or why.

Shuddering and weak, she had reached out to touch the door and it had swung inward, as if in welcome. Inside, there were a table, chairs and shelves of books. All of it waiting for her. All of that and her name, as well, inside a locket that lay forgotten in a pile of clothing covered in stains.

On the back of the locket were the letters 'V' and 'F', and when she had opened it, a woman's face had returned her stare. There was a name opposite. 'Elizabeth'. Her name and perhaps her face, though the angles she traced with her fingers did not seem to fit those of the woman in the picture.

She lived hard, eking out an existence on the barren rock, at night hunting the innumerable rats that scampered out of the island's guts when the lightning ripped wide across the black sky. With the rats, she ate the moss that clung to the rocks and, once, a seabird that drew too close to her.

Elizabeth had strong hands. She wielded rocks and driftwood with all the dexterity of a Norman knight swinging his sword, but, often as not, she relied only on her fingers and stalked through the scrub of the island's high places on ten toes. She did not cook the meat she caught, but felt no ill effects from chewing it raw. Indeed, she could not imagine dousing the taste of the flesh through fire.

She had clothes which she did not wear for fear of ruining them. There were trousers and a shirt, neither of which truly fit her, perhaps having been meant for a child, and an apron which stank of chemicals and other, less pleasant things. The latter she rolled into a ball and buried behind the house.

In truth, the constant rain that drenched the island felt good upon her skin and her nakedness became more about comfort than consideration. Her flesh was invariably flushed with an unrelenting heat when it was hidden from the air. Sometimes, when the lightning curled and coiled, it burned as well.

There were two other houses on the island, besides hers, but they were both ruins now, broken and empty. In the evening, as she gorged on rat, she wandered among them, exploring their secrets.

By day, she read. She read the anatomy texts and alchemical treatises that filled the shelves of the house to bursting, and when those grew dull, she gorged on Byron and Shelley and Voltaire. Of those, she preferred the latter. There were twenty-seven books in the house and she had read them all, in random order, seven times apiece. That some were in Latin and others in Greek, French and Arabic did not matter, for she could not tell one language from the next. It was all the same to her.

When she had finished the last book and waited to begin the next rotation, she would sit on the rocks outside her door and stroke her arms and legs, which ached sometimes in the oddest places. It was as if she were filled with old hurts and ancient wounds that her eye could not see and fingers could not reach. A bone-deep itch that scuttled through her at lonely intervals, dragging with it images to her mind's eye.

Some of those images were comforting. Others made her pull out her own hair and drum her heels against the rock. Once, possessed of a rage that echoed out of a glimpse of a memory of mismatched eyes, she had bounded across the island, screaming and howling and flailing at the lightning with a club of driftwood.

Only when the club had broken, and her fists had been rendered bloody and bruised from battering the unheeding stones, did she at last return to sensibility.

Her wounds healed, and quickly, if the medical texts were to be believed. She watched the bruises lighten and fade over the course of hours, the golden skin returning to its normal sheen.

The scars never healed in the same way as the bruises. They remained, but then, they had always been with her. They were thin strands of pale yellow that stood out against the gold of her flesh, rising and falling across her arms and legs and belly and elsewhere: a latticework of marks that she could not recall the origins of, nor, indeed, did she wish to.

Sometimes, when she touched them, she got the strangest sensation that she was waiting for someone. The true owner of the house, perhaps. She touched the locket and traced the initials carved on it. Who was 'VF'? Was that whom she was waiting for?

Elizabeth was stroking the locket when she caught sight of the boat for the first time. It was a blotch of pale colour on the vast darkness of the water. She half-stood as the wind whipped her hair about her face in a frenzy. Unconsciously, her hands clenched and she warred with the sudden impulse to flee.

She had never seen a boat before, but the word and the shape lurked in her memory. And with the word came fear. Hard, cold fear that clambered up into her belly and sat lodged like a lump of badly-chewed rat. Elizabeth did not know why she was afraid, and that only made the fear worse.

Breathing hard, she crouched and watched the boat for minutes, then hours, watching it draw closer and closer. As it grew dark, she lost sight of it at last and the trance was broken. Abruptly, she turned and dove into her home, slamming the door and latching it. Head down, she let a wracking sob escape her and trembled uncontrollably. Her stomach heaved as she pushed away from the door and she looked around wildly.

Suddenly, the house, her home, seemed horrible. Everything sent a razor-caress of disgust across her nerves – the anatomy books on her shelves, the odd table that sat in the centre of the room with its runnels and score-marks and the stains on the floor. Her hand flew to the locket hanging from her neck and she squeezed the soft metal.

Eyes closed, she slid down to the floor and sat weeping. And then, after a time, she sat sleeping. She dreamed that night of the sea and her birth and the way the water had smelled of iron and oxygen, and how that smell had clung to her for weeks following. She dreamed of how she had hurt all over, as if her limbs were held on by red-hot pins, and walking brought new agonies each and every day until finally, the pain had faded.

She dreamed of those first days, when the books had been full of blurry hornets rather than words and how she had destroyed three in a rage, scattering pages across the island. Three books full of cramped writing, with neither pictures nor poetry. She had torn them page from page the way she tore rats and had watched the white shreds become caught in the cold wind rolling off the sea. The sight of it had calmed her immediately, though she could not say why.

Elizabeth awoke with a start. Her nostrils flared as she took in the smell of the day and the sea. She pushed herself to her feet and away from the door. Her hand hesitated inches from the knob. Then, with a growl, she yanked the door open and stepped out.

Birds cried out as they swooped over the beach. She gazed at them, then down towards the path that led to the beach.

The boat sat among the rocks where its occupant had pulled it ashore. She bit back a whimper and contemplated running back inside. But the house wasn't safe. Nowhere was safe. Not now.

Elizabeth didn't know why; she simply knew it was so. Safety had been an illusion, now stripped away. Slowly, unwillingly, she started down the path, pausing only to scoop up a length of driftwood.

The boat sat silent as she approached. She circled it, stepping unheeding through the surf, her bare feet dancing awkwardly over the rocks. She tapped it with the stick and when no response was forthcoming, her lips peeled back from her teeth. She had strong teeth, capable of breaking bone and grinding muscle to paste. She bared them now as she climbed into the boat and searched it for any sign of its occupant.

Wet tarps and empty boxes filled it. She swung a tarp around her shoulders, suddenly cold, and used the stick to smash a hole in the bottom of the boat. Then, grunting with the strain, she shoved it back out into the water. The rocks shifted loudly beneath her feet as she pressed her shoulder to the prow and heaved. The boat glided along against the current then began to dip as the water blossomed through the hole she'd made.

Elizabeth could not say why she had done what she'd done, but it was satisfying all the same. A blow struck against ... whom? She shook her head and turned, the driftwood creaking in her grip.

Above her, at the top of the path, a man-shape watched her. Her heart stuttered in her chest and her eyes sprang painfully wide. She stumbled back and the sea clutched at her ankles, shocking her back into herself. Above, the man-shape ducked out of sight.

Elizabeth screamed. A moment later, the tarp fell from her shoulders as she sprang into motion, running up the path, the driftwood swinging wildly. She fell several times as she scrambled upwards, such was her hurry. At the summit, she hurled the driftwood blindly and it clattered against the house.

There was no sign of him. Breathing, she whirled, head cocked like a hound's as she sniffed the air. Familiar scents dug into her mind, but she could not bring the memories they had hooked into the light. Frustrated, she hissed and swung her arms.

Where was he? Where?

Her eyes fastened on the door. It was open, ever so slightly. She grunted, as if struck, and shivered. Was he in there, in her house? Was he watching her even now?

Her breath came faster, painful rasping knife-stabs of oxygen that bruised her lips in their escape. Her hands writhed into fists and sprang open again over and over. She took a clumsy step forward, but then hopped back.

Why was he here? Why had he come back? She shook her head and whined. Had he come back? Who was he? Why was he tormenting her? Her fingers dug into her scalp and she yanked at her hair, shuffling back and forth as her eyes stayed locked on the house.

Finally, explosively, she lunged for the door, striking it with her shoulder. The hinges popped and squealed. She was very strong, and not just in her hands or feet, and the door fell in and she fell with it. She was up a moment later, crouching on all fours. Books sat on the table, neatly piled as in preparation to be moved. Clothes were folded and placed in a trunk. She scrambled around, peering beneath the table and behind the bookcases. Where had he gone? He had been here; she could smell him.

Where was he? Where was he?

Rocks crunched together. She froze. Her eyes cut to the door. A shadow, rippling in the wind. In her mind flashed again that long-ago nightmare of mismatched eyes. A voice like the thunder rattled in her head.

Her hand flew to her locket and she screamed. She flung herself at the closest window and broke through, heedless of the scratches and splinters in her skin. What she could not ignore was the splash of pain that rippled up her leg as her ankle twisted and refused to bear her weight. She tumbled forward.

"No, no, no, NONONONONONO," she whined, her voice long unused now slipping forth like metal scraping metal. The shadow stalked her, gliding across the ground like a hunting dog ahead of its caster.

She met his eyes across the distance. Grey like the rocks and harder still. They widened as they took her in and she felt the memory of scalpels and cold ointments. He opened his mouth to speak, but then she was moving despite the pain, moving up and towards him, shrieking like a hawk. She lashed out and he fell back, no longer a monster but a man, the same as any in the anatomy texts. Berserk, she threw herself on him.

As she bore him down, images pinwheeled through her brain like scraps of paper caught in a wind. Images of the man before her examining her with grey eyes and a surgeon's smile, and of another whose mismatched eyes blazed hungrily, hatefully in her head and whose voice cut across her soul like razors stropping stone.

Her fist rose and the man squirmed away from her, babbling inanities. She reached for him, feeling the strength coil through her. She could rip him in two like a rat and crush those hateful eyes. As she dragged him back, fear filled the grey eyes. Fear and something else.

Her face looked back at her, contorted in rage.

"Elizabeth," he said. But he wasn't looking at her. His flailing hands snagged the locket and, as she jerked back in surprise, he tore it loose. She stood and stepped back, her hand flying to her throat.

Then, hands dangling, she looked down at him as he grovelled in the dirt, sobbing and clutching her locket. No, not hers – his. His locket. His Elizabeth.

She wasn't his. She had not been waiting for him. A darkness crept upon her and she saw those mismatched eyes again, alight this time with a devil's flame. Her hands clenched then, abruptly, relaxed.

"No," she said. "No."

On his knees, he reached for her, babbling. She stepped back. "No," she said again, more strongly. She brushed fingers across her throat. The weight was gone. The weight of Elizabeth. Of memories not hers. Of designs and desires that she had no part in.

She was not Elizabeth. She had never been Elizabeth. And she had not been born in the sea. But to the sea she would return.

Leaving the man with the grey eyes behind, she walked away from the house with its secrets and down towards the water, her golden limbs moving much more smoothly than they ever had before. Before she knew it, she was running.

As she entered the water, she wondered, just for a moment, whether her intended bridegroom would be upset by her absence. She imagined his mismatched eyes wide with rage and his hands, so like hers, shaking in fury. Then, pushing that thought aside, she wondered what her new name would be.

In the end, there was only one way to find out. With strong, smooth strokes, she began to swim.

Josh Reynolds is a freelance writer of moderate skill and exceptional confidence. He has written a bit and some of it was even published. For money. By real people. His work has appeared in anthologies such as *Cthulhu Unbound 2* from Permuted Press and *Specters in Coal Dust* from Woodland Press, as well as in magazines such as *Innsmouth Free Press* and *Bards and Sages Quarterly*.
Feel free to stop by his blog, http://joshuamreynolds.blogspot.com/, and cast aspersions on his character or to give him money.

Dark Epistle

By Jim Blackstone

I pressed the skull to my stomach. I only looked down once to investigate it again, while I fled for my life, and only because my fingers had slipped into what I can only imagine to be ocular orifices that should not have been there. The skull was demonic to the core, triangular, and as black as the darkness beyond the stars.

Forgive me. In my haste to start this letter again, I have begun in the wrong place. Each day, I run, hide. Like a rabbit in winter, desperate for sustenance, I sense the proximity of those who hunt me. I know that my time is scarce.

Yet, I will try for the port of Tyre, or for the crossroads at Constantinople, or for escape to undetermined lands far safer than home.

First, however, I will do my duty. I have to report.

~

It was never my intention to wander so deeply into darkness. I could say the same about so many things: I never intended to live in a blighted wilderness on the edge of the Holy Land; I never intended to join a suspicious religious order of knights; and I never intended to fall in love with a woman – "Abide even as I," said the Apostle Paul to the unwed, and such was my sacred aim. Then the Pope involved himself.

I write these words that, through blasphemy, truths might be revealed. The Western World needs to know those secrets rising covertly from the Orient and invading, through stealth, the lands of my nativity. All must know of the conspiracies, political manipulations, usurpations, demoniacal plots, and the hidden fight for survival, the silent war that we are on the verge of losing. Indeed, the first draft of this letter, I had addressed to the Holy See in Rome, the Church Father himself. Yet, I fear that if I do not change my account – offer truth in the *lingua franca* of my people – that these things unspoken and unspeakable, which may have been known by the Ante-Nicene Fathers and to some who came later, might continue to slumber in dark Vatican vaults, whilst a greater shadow seethes westward across Europe.

189

Born Jacques de Ronnay, I was a spy from the womb. I watched by mother sin and my father do worse. I am witness to the wickedness of siblings, neighbours, even regal authorities. I heard the words, "Thou shalt not kill," and then learned of murders and strifes uncountable. "Thou shalt bear no false witness," said the sheriff in my district, who then chose his words carefully and hid truth whenever he thought appropriate. I felt myself an outsider. I dedicated myself quickly to the labours of Heaven.

My father was a man of distinguished honour who fought in holy wars across the Mediterranean. From my youth, I heard endless tales of conquest, the bloody dispatch of the heathen. I, too, would one day follow my forbears and travel far, to kill the evil Saracen hordes and carry back the booty of honest endeavour (or what I called in my heart of hearts, 'honest hypocrisy'). I would serve the Holy Host.

My agreement to this duty, covertly amended by my desire to *really serve the Creator of Heaven and Earth* according to His dictates and teachings, sustained my quest to enter into holy orders and the reception of sacraments consecrated to those who would be the greatest servants in the Church, even the administrators and leaders.

Yet, my hope to become a priest was thwarted by complications owing to erroneous physical competitiveness with certain brothers in the seminary – *errare humanum est*. The words did not serve as excuse enough. Father Soissons banished me on a mission to Rome, I went in the company of the Lady de Siverey, who would visit the Pope. When attacked by brigands beneath the Alps, I beat them off, splashing the red fluid of the wicked over the Lady's cart. She told me not to apologize. She said that I had performed my calling. What really happened was this: I fell in love with the young widow in that very moment, though three tiny dots of enemy blood speckled her cheek like a constellation of heavenly winks.

In the Holy City, I made my honourable desires known. I was informed that our Papal Father was in need of a confessor on a trip to Avignon in Arles. My deeds and sacred longing were again brought to his attention, along with descriptions of my birthright and heritage. He summoned me. Prostrate, I swore my undying and unquestionable allegiance to him, making sure to clarify my aspiration to stand as far from the sword, and from the women of the world, as possible. I sought more sacred endowments. Perhaps I sinned in my request.

In the middle of the night, I was awakened and directed to visit Pope Nicholas IV himself, for a special assignment.

But this is all history.

For the greater part of a year, Our Church Father would not release me from my penance for lifting the sword against fellow Christians. I begged forgiveness for my selfishness: "Thy will be done, and not mine." At length, I was pardoned. Immediately, I would receive ordination to higher office.

There was an order in which St. Bernard himself had endorsed the sustaining of an array of knights whose particular obligation was the protection of all pilgrims and crusaders from all parts of Europe and throughout the Holy Land. Having captured the Temple in Jerusalem, they called themselves the "Knights Templar".

Yet, like my fathers before me, their activities were in question. After Saint Bernard's edict, the Knights of the Temple quickly became the wealthiest branch of the Church: They did not pay taxes. They did not even pay tithes to Rome. No royal hand could touch them.

And now Rome was feeling a tearing pain that, again, is unimportant for me to belabour here. Nor do I need to explain the rift and scandals, the disputations between Church Doctors – I fear these terrible issues do not matter, not with the secrets I have uncovered: There are far more foul things in the earth than any of the quarrels of men. You must know. All must know. Or, I am certain, all will perish.

~

Quickly, papers were drawn up: recommendations, the highest praise, lists of experience and sacrifices – lies to which I was forced by the holiest and most perfect of all living men to admit as truths, that I might fulfill my mission.

I was admitted as a novice into the Knights Templar. It was a humiliating and dehumanizing initiation, full of boisterous humour. Did I flinch? Never. I was doing all – I would sacrifice anything! – to serve Him on High and wash myself clean of the blood and sins of this generation. Whatever horrors and atrocities that I beheld and in which I participated, I knew my real purpose. It was a sacred secret. And I would report to my Father, the Pope, personally.

My first crossing of the Mediterranean, I fear, shall be my last. The visions that I have uncovered are too dark, far deeper than the mysteries that the Cardinals expected me to uncover, so vast in their empty depth, in fact, that I suspect that the Pope already knows. I do not think that any who were aware of my mission imagined that I would really *see*. It is a true miracle that I am not completely blind. After the horrors which I must confess to you? It is a wonder that I still live.

There we were, upon the boats that would bring our black-and-white banner to Moorish shores. I remember viewing the stone faces of older brothers, their bone-white or brown or black habits, with red crosses flapping hard and loudly in a mean sea breeze, intent on pressing us away from the beach. I remember the coast all aglitter, prepared for our arrival: pikes to spear European knights, scimitars, oriflammes, halberds, and a wall of shielded men, madness in their blackened eyes.

There was a great stink – that familiar smell of the corpses that the Crusaders had hung from captured city walls to be picked by crows and riddled by ants and maggots, warning all infidels that Christians were present and would not be denied their death-dealing victories. Such a rot carried on the Mediterranean wind. The foetor choked my nostrils as I saw the off-coloured bodies.

~

In Acre, I saw her.

From a staircase, the Lady de Siverey peered on me with eyes so majestically black and painted, she looked like the most beautiful of Egyptian infidels. A shadow roiled inside of me. I wanted to flee, like Joseph in the House of Potiphar. But she remembered me.

"Jacques de Ronnay, you have come to the Temple as a Knight of that holy order. You have reached the Holy Land at last."

I felt that she had the power to see into my mind and soul. I *felt* it, but I did not believe it. Not until now.

With these words, de Siverey offered her hand to be kissed. Yet Knights Templar, by their monkish rule, are not allowed to touch or kiss even their mother or sister.,

To avoid slighting this lady, who clearly had important ties with Rome, I bowed, lowering my forehead near to her signet in righteous esteem. Even so, the brother with me frowned at this impertinence.

She laughed. Perhaps she was mocking me, but all I heard was music to my heart. I heard the whisper of the Adversary in my mind, telling me that I might run away from divine ordinations and live happily ever after with this gorgeous female. I rose and retreated.

De Siverey smiled at me, her head to one side, her hair spilling and casting a lovely spell over me. In her eyes, the colour of deep Frankish woodlands, I thought I saw understanding and admiration. Mine must have shown a bit of shame, much adoration, and a determination to live every moment of my life as I was meant.

I did not see her again for more than sixteen months. Also, I left Acre but not the fiendishly hot countryside. I was transferred to a small garrison overseeing vineyards outside Acre.

⁓

There was a great peace between the Templars and the Sultan. There were so many different tales told. Forsooth, the Knights of the Temple were experiencing a sort of heaven on earth. The uneasy peace allowed them the time to cultivate their vast vineyards and olive groves, and rebuild their battered fortresses, even as their share of the Holy Land slowly and inevitably shrank under the encroachment of the Infidel.

There was also incredible evil. The sins rumoured to the Pope were true, for I was witness to much fraternizing with the Infidel and infernal compromises. I was expected to participate and mandated by the Church itself to do whatever pleased the Commanders.

And this I did. And to this day I regret it all, for it led me toward the horrible hidden mysteries and sciences discovered and kept by Judean and Saracen mystics.

⁓

I learned that certain Knights of the Temple resided close to the Sultan's dignitaries. Their friendships disturbed me. More than once, I was reminded that the primary task of the Knights Templar was to provide safe passage to Christian holy sites; the Saracen and Jew sought the same: Jerusalem was sacred to them, too.

The topics made me ill. How could my "brothers" in the Order speak as if Saracens knew of the Bible? How had their hearts lost sight of real sacred callings, to promote the Church Visible until that great and dread-

ful Day of the Lord when the King of Kings would come again to rule all
– even the infidel – on the Earth? I could not understand. Nor would I,
until I discovered the depths of their evil gaze.

~

In Acre, I was brought, as a servant most trusted in the Order, to the
house of Grand Master Guillaume de Beaujeu. His rooms in the com-
mandery were small and houses himself and his staff.

The Grand Master expressed interest in my history. First, he praised
me for my acts in the Order; then he referred to fictionalized aspects pro-
vided by Papal letters. He asked me questions. I gave prepared answers.
Then his eyes seemed amused.

It was as if he knew the truth behind my mission, but that the game
was only getting started.

I wish I had trusted my instincts. I might have fled and been happy
with my delusions of simple hypocrisy in the world.

"Brother Jacques de Ronnay," he said, "What do you know of true
religion?"

"Grand Master, I am a humble slave and would rather be the lowliest
doorman at Heaven's Gate than spend a moment out of His service."

"But what do you *know*?"

I did not understand his inquiries. Did he wish me to begin at Creation and tell from memory all that I could from the Bible, as little as I
knew?

I began, with humble voice, in Latin, "*In principio creavit deus caelum
et terram*," before the old warrior held up his hand.

"Do you believe, Brother de Ronnay, that God knew all things from
the beginning?"

"Yes."

"That he taught many of his greatest secrets to our father Adam in the
Garden of Eden?"

"Of course."

"And that he has taught the same, through angels and other ministers,
throughout the centuries to other important individuals, seers and revela-
tors, such as John the Beloved?"

"Certainly. Praised be His name." I felt like slapping a hand over
my mouth – in my devotion, I had spoken almost like an Arab, who so
quickly attributed all to Allah: I had heard plenty of their mumblings in

the street. Their devotion is unquestionable, mirroring my own. I could see how time among these people had disturbed the Grand Master's mind, for I felt it disturbing mine own.

"Yet, the Bible does not record a single holy sacrament," said the Grand Master.

Chills rolled over my back. I was sure I had heard blasphemy. I could only say, "My lord?" for he seemed more regal and less holy to my instincts.

He smiled at me. "You know the Holy Writ?"

Ah, I thought. This is a test. "I study as a meager disciple. I learn all that I can. Will you teach me, Grand Master?"

"Where does it tell us the words to be used in the Baptismal prayer?"

I opened my mouth. The answer failed to come forth. He wanted me to quote scripture, yet I could not – not for this quest. I had forgotten the words for the baptismal rite, for the Templars, being monks, were not allowed to raise children over the font.

"Do not fret, Brother de Ronnay. None of the sacramental acts are given specifically within that sacred collection. My purpose in turning your attention to these facts is to assure you that, while all truth has been revealed since the beginning, not all has been handed down ... to the lowliest of servants. Yet, we of the Order are obligated to protect these same ancient secrets! What do you know of Jericho?"

"I know," I thought about it, with astonishment regarding the implications he inferred, "I know only what the Book tells us."

"The City of Jericho existed before the Children of Israel came into this land from Egypt. Do you agree? Search your training."

"I do agree, Grand Master."

"The City of Jericho was old, with Sodom and Gomorrah, before Lot and Abraham arrived from Haran and Ur. Search your memories of these accounts. Will you not confirm what I have said?"

I could find no disagreement with his words and stated as much.

"Jericho was built on a town formed in the desert over a village built of wood and brick, over a desert hamlet constructed by ancients so old and forgotten that ..."

His wide eyes had fallen with the weight of his knowledge and listed away from me along with his words.

"Yes, Grand Master?" I prodded, after a minute of silence in which I heard his staff slipping and moving around us like snakes under grass, privy to these blasphemies. I could not abide that sound. "Grand Master?"

He did not look at me. His tone dropped. "I have sent four on missions to discover the secrets beneath Jericho. You see the box on the table against the wall?"

I looked and saw an ornate construction, wicker woven, lined in exquisite brass and touched with gold.

"It is filled with trinkets from the street: cheap jewelry typically sold to pilgrims on their way home from Mecca, easily scooped out. Beneath, you will find a bottom that can be removed if you press hard upon the far left corner. In the cavity beneath, you will find on papyrus the copy of a map. This map reveals an entrance found by a certain servant of the Lord."

I bowed.

As I followed his instructions, he said, "None who have gone before you have returned. You must know, Brother de Ronnay, that I am confident of your discovery. I have ... read fragments of texts testifying of those present in Palestine before the Flood of Noah washed the Earth clean of all evil."

I was shaken. "What shall I do?" I said when I held the scroll in my hand. I felt that I was, at last, reaching the heart of the mystery that the Pope wanted me to reveal to him. With this final mission, I would learn the reason for all concern, all Templar blasphemies, and the true goal of Knights. I suspected that I knew enough already, but going to Jericho would provide me ... with – Oh, if only I had not gone! If only I did not know!

Forgive me. I will compose myself.

The Grand Master leaned forward and answered my question: "Bring me a skull."

I left with a detachment of turcopoles, native mercenaries working for the Order, who would be required for only one part of his orchestration: They would distract all eyes and ears while I traveled with a small contingent of black-robed Templar sergeants already present in the city.

Along the way, I thought of Grand Master de Beaujeu's final warnings. None of the previous brethren had returned. I had detected the faintest hint that some might have lived and that the possibility of their continued mortality was of greater concern to the Grand Master than the possibility of their terrible demise. I recall thinking that he seemed to mumble some words to the effect that the Knights of the Order would find any of those traitorous survivors and deal with them swiftly and justly. But I may be mistaken, for I was overcome by thoughts of a one-way assignment that I needed to endure, if ever I would fulfill my instructions and purpose on this Earth.

Now I know that my death is absolutely necessary. This is my purpose in writing this dark epistle to all, that all mankind – all human kind – might be edified, might fear what needs to be feared, might thereby live with full knowledge of the beast and his infiltration among us.

~

I began this version of my account in reporting that I was charged to serve the Pope in Rome. I told you that I have changed this recording after great and terrible thoughts: The Church Father seemed to know something that he would not reveal, as if he wanted me to learn it for myself – I can only guess at his purpose.

And I recall that as I left the Grand Master in Acre, he looked upon me with that same expression. He even grinned, as if everything he had told me had been constructed of half-truths and that he knew far more than he was revealing there. Did he know that I would die? Did he know the horrors I would experience in those black caverns? Knowing I had, unlike most of the brethren, learned how to read and write during my priestly duties, he told me to record any writings, even if the letters and drawings were expressly foreign to what I had heretofore experienced. Perhaps that skill was why he had chosen me. But foremost, I was to bring to him a certain relic – a skull, the kind of which, he said, would be plentiful in that place, for so had lost legends reported.

We must, perforce, because the Saracens had ruled the town since the dread day of Hattin a century before, travel in secret and in disguise. Ere I reached Jericho, I felt as a lamb being led to the slaughter, a man sent from dungeon to execution, a chess piece about to be sacrificed in my conflicting masters' game.

Jericho was a beautiful town from the outside, though fallen in decline since crusader times. Watching it from a nearby hill, I could easily imagine how years had piled up dust and sand, fallen towers, natural growth, death, and more years, burying city after city until the mosques and churches were built.

To the Saracens, I spoke the peaceful words of snake and Templar, as taught to me by the Order, and was accepted within the rebuilt walls of Jericho as a Jewish pilgrim.

For three days, I fasted alone in a cell, following my instructions while the detachment sent with me waited in a secret camp beyond the city.

On the fourth day, I ate. As expected by de Beaujeu, I discovered the city's inhabitants in a nervous uproar regarding reports of bandits in the hills outside of the city. All attention turned outward, and mistrust of pilgrim visitors sought out those foreigners like myself inside Jericho's mighty walls.

Did a loud noise really topple this city once upon a time? I do not doubt it. But now I suspect with terrible seriousness that after the feet of Israel tramped and tramped and tramped around the city ... I wonder if something beneath their feet *awoke*. Something mighty and far more evil than anything recorded with clarity in the Bible. I wonder about the noise.

The Jewish house, wherein I had been preparing myself, was over-run with Saracens. The Jews who had, unknowingly, taken me in, were dragged into the street, questioned, tortured, and slaughtered. I would have been one of them.

But one who propelled me forth, while I was yet in my weakened condition after three days away from food as the Grand Master com-manded, threw me into a wall at the side of the house, cursing me with a guttural tongue that makes the husky German barbarians sound like fine singers.

I attempted to speak the words of peace between Muslim and Jew, but I was hit in the face, silenced, thrown deeper into alleyways, laughed upon by the crowd who could not follow.

Then I saw the steel raised above my foe's head. And I praised Mother Mary and all the saints, so grateful that my time had come to join them as a member of the Church Invisible. Yet, a part of me also recalled the mission I had received from the Bishop of Rome himself, and I leapt into action.

Before I could tear out the throat of my enemy, I heard *him* say the secret words of peace and treaty between Sultanate and Templar, followed quickly by words describing the need for illusion: "It is the only way to let you live! Do what I say, or you will be killed as a spy!"

I was a spy. A spy for the Pope. A spy for the Order. A spy sent from Heaven to live among men.

I told him none of this. He feigned domination over me, casting me into another alleyway and then through a door, which he quickly shut and barred once the game was over. "I will check the front," he told the darkness, and left me.

Then I smelled a woman. "Jacque de Ronnay? We meet again."

I bowed without understanding. "Lady de Siverey? You are trapped in the city of Jericho on this terrible day?"

She laughed at me. "I am trapped nowhere. Dress in these."

My eyes grew accustomed to the darkness as I pulled myself into the clothing of an Arab soldier. I did not have my sword with me, but the hilt of a desert weapon felt equally good in my hands. I could see de Siverey, her eyes alone peeking through exotic clothing appreciated most by sheiks and those who believe it sinful to see any part of a woman but the eyes. She smelled of rose oil, more powerful than a garden itself in all its splendour at springtime. And how powerful were those eyes! They bewitched me. I had no idea what a Frankish woman was doing in this city. Perhaps she had been captured by bandits.

She spoke as one with authority. "We must go now, while the distraction is at its height. You will walk ahead of me, my escort, yet I will whisper to you the way. Do not look upon me when we are in the street. Are you ready?"

"Will they not recognize the face of a Frank?"

She laughed again. In my heart, I knew then how men could become drunken on the sweet music pouring from a woman's throat. "You think too highly of Franks. No, they will be too busy to notice your heritage at all."

We left forthwith.

~

Not knowing beforehand where I would go, and not allowed to remove the map from its hiding place, I walked blindly through the city, sinking lower and lower along streets and staircases and alleyways as she whispered behind me.

We came to a sunken building. Inside, we passed though three more doors, the buildings interlocked, and each stepping lower until no window light was able to warm a room with the sun. Then we followed a staircase down and met a man, to whom de Siverey spoke passwords that I could not have repeated if I tried. From this place, we delved into another, and another, following a ladder into a room no longer lit with lamps.

"Carry this," she said, handing me a Jewish lantern, and all I could think of was sin and fright. Her voice and this close intimacy with her – foreign and forbidden to all monks and priests – made me want to run away from this darkness and intrigue, to flee with her and love her forever. Instead, I watched her as she took the lead. I watched her as we scurried like rats through narrow passages. I watched her until, at last, I realized my mortal wretchedness and infantile anxiety and weakness of flesh were vanquishing my spirit when I would demand it otherwise.

I fought a war within myself. I stopped looking at her. And that is when I saw the warning on the walls.

I did not recognize the Hebrew script. I could not translate the words. But I did well at deciphering the pictures.

I saw the light of heaven and the Holy Ark firing rays over armies of black demons. I saw winged beasts in the sky fighting angels – I cannot describe the beasts to you, for they had, as it were, the heads of stars and the bodies of squid and the wings of torn dragons. They were like nothing I had seen or read about anywhere.

I was slowing. The Lady de Siverey berated me. So, I tried not to look upon these painted mysteries. I clung to both lamp and edged weapon, my hands filled so that when, running behind de Siverey, I slipped upon a sandy slope. I dropped straight through the hole in the ground that I did not see.

The lamp shattered before I could cry out in pain. The oil spread and caught fire. So that, for a brief time, there was plenty of light to behold this sunken place.

I was in a vaulted room with a doorways in each of three corners, each aperture easily fit for Goliath or – as I now know – something much larger.

Above me, I could hear de Siverey's enchanting laughter, a musical chuckle, pleasure. I never saw the Lady again.

I called for her. In whispers at first, then louder, and then in whispers again as my eyes watered before frescoes depicting the most horrible scenes.

On the wall, I saw men who were not men worshiping at the Mediterranean's edge. I saw a nightmare larger than the moon, black and indistinct now that the paints and tiles had faded so. It was a form of art unlike any made by man, but it was so old now. There was something Egyptian about the wings that filled all the sky from the South to the North, as if saying that Heaven was this: only darkness, a night with every star blackened out.

And then I remembered, in my quivering state, how the Earth was without form and void in the beginning. How, after the waters were separated from the waters and the land appeared, there was a time theologians and doctors, to my memory, never bothered to portray. I felt that I understood: This time was too terrible for man to recall, even after it was revealed to him in the Garden eastward in Eden. For after, there was a sea and there was dry land; *the sun and the moon and the stars had not yet been created.* Oh, there was light! Yes, there was light – I could see on the walls that there was light. And there was grass, the herb yielding seed, and the fruit of the tree yielding fruit after its kind. But, as my training confirmed to my memory, the sun and the moon and the stars were created as signs and for seasons and for days and for years and set into the firmament "to rule over the day and over the night" ... but not until the *Fourth* Day.

I had risen, one ankle throbbing with pain that I dismissed before all my fear. I fell again. I was looking upon the Third Day, upon details unspecified in the Bible, and felt that this Day, this period of creation, must have lasted for aeons.

And who were these nightmares infesting the Earth before Man was placed in the Garden?

I had heard of dragons. These were not dragons. There were fiends cast from Heaven along with the Devil – I imagined the angels depicted in the Hebrew halls now far above me, and the words of John the Revelator, who described Michael and his angels fighting with the Dragon and his angels. Was this what I saw? Were these entities those beings who had been cast down from on high?

It was too simplistic. This place and its horrible secrets ran deeper. I did not want to know more. But the fire, which had spread and grown bright in the oil, was eating through it quickly and would soon be gone.

At the thought of being left alone here, deep underground in the ancient darkness, my heart pounded as if expending all of my life now before giving up the breath that had started it.

I found, in the rubbish of bodies heretofore unrecognized, the cloth and bones necessary to construct a crude torch. The bones were human. Why did I find solace in that? As I righted my traveling flame, my eyes took note of Templar red-on-white scattered among heaps of skulls with hair and flaking skin. I turned away from what must have once been a mountain of desiccated soldiers, swept aside as if by a great foot away from one portal. In each brick about the frame, I saw the faces of scream- ing men and women carefully etched and carved, like trophies of memory from bygone wars.

The fire on the floor died at last, though I managed one small torch from it. I pondered fearfully which way to go.

The hole above me was dark. I could not imagine the Lady de Siv- erey alone up there in those endlessly black passageways, forced after her laughter of insanity to travel alone. But I also could not comprehend how easily she met these horrors and keenly knew the way to this pit. I could not reach the top of that domed ceiling if I wanted to. And the artwork staring down at me brought a whimper of childish panic from my tongue; I would not look up there anymore.

One thing was certain. The Lady de Siverey knew what I would find. Others knew. How many? Who else? The Grand Master? The Pope?

I thought at that time about the Bible, about the wisdom of the Church Fathers, about a library in the Vatican of which I had heard respectably rumoured whispers. Surely, the Pope at least had an idea of this ancient knowledge upon which I had stumbled. I reminisced about my enthusiasm and how my former teachers looked down upon it. I suspected that I was a fishhook, used by a fleeing Roman bishop to snag a fish of mystery or simply die in cold waters. I wondered, in that moment, if anyone on Earth cared about me at all. For I had also heard that often, crusaders were little more than troublesome sword owners, that the Church nudged them toward death in the Holy Land to free Europe for more peaceful living.

There were tears on my face. I thought I might die down here. And the thought of exiting this mortal life gave me reason to go on: If I was cursed and doomed to die, I would at least see behind this temporal veil and look upon the unspeakable secrets of the Earth.

But which way?

A spark inside me whispered that I still had a purpose. I recalled de Beaujeu's map and drew it forth.

The rough sketches *began* with the drawing of a triangular room with a doorway in each corner. I studied the lines, saw passages twist beneath one another, enter what seemed to be halls so vast that entire castles might fit inside without touching the walls.

Only two of the passages were sketched forth. The third had not been taken.

The third, I saw, was the one once blocked by a mass of bones and dead men that stood higher than my head.

I walked that way.

A new resolve took hold of me. In their apathy and humour, my masters had sent me into the grave. If I could, I would return. The Grand Master wanted a skull? I would find one for him, if possible, one that would reflect the horrors to which I had been witness; I would fling the skull at his feet and leave the Order forever. Let them hunt me down for breaking my vows. The Church wanted the secrets studied and carried forth by the Knights Templar? I would bring this map, my report, and any drawing or writings I could copy onto the paper. I would deliver my promises and then disappear with my knowledge, if they did not kill me first as a heretic. Either way, I could not see how I would exist anymore among men. Especially if any of these ancient beings still lived.

Oh, the madness! Again, I am ahead of myself.

~

I did not think about *them* living until I came to the place of the skulls.

It was as if the Grand Master knew the room existed. The chamber was octagonal, with dread corpses nailed to the walls in unholy admiration. At first, I saw skulls, but could not identify them as such. They were somewhat triangular, like the heads of a mantis – which insect always looked particularly demonic to me. Each skull was as black as the things hanging on the wall, shiny like metal where lines of light reflected my struggling torch. Each was stacked with the utmost care. These demon heads were treated with reverence.

My eyes rose to what seemed to me hanging decorations, at first. As my eyes studied and grew accustomed to the details above me, I thought I was seeing the hung carcasses of something like those winged monstrosities that fought the heavenly angels painted on the ancient Hebrew walls so far behind me. Could this be their slack remains?

What had the war been like? My belief that these creatures were cast down from Heaven fled, as I renewed the horrible image in my mind of the giant evil in the sea and the crowding worshipers on the beach.

The wings were staked, as I said, to the walls. Stretched as far as they could be, the wing of one beast touched the tip of another. And so it was, all around the eight-sided room, until they came together again.

I stared up at their heads hanging loosely over bodies of amassed tentacle that seemed to begin in the region of a mouth and ran to a nethermost point. It was then that I collaborated the images above me with the stacked heads along each wall around the room and knew that I had found my skull at last.

I reached. I grabbed.

In that instant, I spotted movement from the corner of one eye. My military training saved my life. I spun, dropped, yet not quickly enough, for a whipping tentacle lightly grazed the side of my face and sent my torch flying. I was on the ground, face down, the skull in one hand and the map in the other.

Also in that moment, a terrible screaming filled the room.

Almost as quickly as I hit the ground, I turned onto my back, drew my little Saracen sword, and looked up.

I tell you, I did not feel the pain.

It was only the screaming, and the distorted sight of those creatures on the wall, alive, writhing, flailing about, trying to reach my flesh, tacked to the wall and yet fighting to tear themselves free.

A great wetness like tears covered my mouth and nose.

Yet, I was more cognizant of their living alarm, horrified by any being that would permanently bond its own kind to walls and leave them positioned at the ready against thieves or invaders like myself. I could only imagine what their screams would draw into my presence.

The wetness ran to my mouth, and I tasted metal that wasn't there.

I needed to leave.

My neck became covered in tears as I rose, slicing at tentacles thrashing to catch me.

From one doorway, one pit of Hell, I heard a hurried rustling that made me think of wet spiders the size of horses from the frozen north of Europe.

At last, I touched my face with the back of the hand I was using to carry the skull.

With a glance, I saw, in the light of the torch left on the ground, the blood there. I realized, when looking at the door from whence the unhallowed ruckus issued and looking at the creatures on the walls, and looking for an escape, that I could not discern distance accurately.

And the pain of my open eye socket was rising to the fore.

So.

What can I tell you next?

Did I go insane? Would it be a wonder if I somehow did not? I was half-blind, and even more blinded by a growing agony. I was surrounded and fighting off tentacles worse than any stinger that I feared as a child. I was lost in an ancient underground, with no way out, committed to missions that I was absolutely determined to complete. And ... they were coming.

I fled. I know that much.

I ran with the black skull pressed tightly to my bosom. I no longer used my one eye, for the torch was left in the room far behind me. My hands and fingers, like tentacles, saw horrible things. I heard terrible sounds from the mouths of beasts, sounds that could not be copied by the most skilled singers or creative actors of our race. They sought me. I ran.

And I am sure that, for a time – a continual epoch, perhaps, if only days or weeks, while I ate the hemp I wore and drank whatever moisture I splashed through– I will agree that I was insane.

~

When I came to ... which is to say, when I remember thinking clearly again ... I was in the bed of a well-lit room. The soft lips of a woman were pressed, cupping and lovingly over my mouth. The scent of roses and potent oriental blossom cradled me.

The Lady de Siverey sat over me, a smile of softness upon her face.

I shut my eye, afraid of the horrors attacking once more, afraid of the consequence of my sin of kissing a woman's mouth.

When I looked again, she was standing near the open door of the room. "Well done, Jacques de Ronnay. Now, go, and do thou likewise."

I told you before that I never saw her again. I am not sure that I did even then. For I wept and studied the door through which she might have passed. It was tightly shut, as if it had never opened to admit her. Perhaps this was my troubled mind and nothing more. Perhaps I have still never touched a woman so and am therefore clean before all the Saints and Mother Mary.

I assure you that I am now quite rational. Likewise, I know that I shall run and hide for the rest of my life.

I never laid eyes on that skull again, though I know I carried it for as long as my memory will replay. I also lost the map.

Yet, my story must go forth.

There are people, humans on the errands of nasty fools prancing as educated,, who would have us nurture and protect ancient secrets, as if to harness them in some future day or be harnessed by them as servants in reverence to unholy and alien gods.

Please. In holy houses and elsewhere, copy this letter. It must be shared with all. It is my testimony that this witness is correct in every account and that Man must know. These secrets cannot be trusted with the uncouth soul any longer. And you need look over your shoulder and into the night, forevermore.

Jim Blackstone is a scholar, educator, and writer with a passion for foreign languages and history. His most recent science fiction novel, *Interference*, was recently released by Golden Acorn Press.

Broken Notes

By Maria Mitchell

Broken notes, anemic strokes,
and withered snakes of wire
Incited the fear. The frenzy. The fire.
What was the reason?
What was the threat?
What horror was so dire?
Dust. Distortion. Solitude.
The truth of this room without
artistic interlude.
Rust. Contortion. Ineptitude.
The truth of this mind
without artistic interlude.
One hand can do many things
while the mind and horror sing.

Maria Mitchell read the poem "We Organized" from Patricia McKissack's compendium *The Dark Thirty* in elementary school. Compiled from actual slave narratives by the Library of Congress in the 1930s, it had a vivid imagery of tyranny, slavery, Gothic horror, and retribution that motivates much of her poetry today.

Ghosts & Death

"There are two bodies – the rudimental and the complete; corresponding with the two conditions of the worm and the butterfly. What we call "death", is but the painful metamorphosis. Our present incarnation is progressive, preparatory, temporary. Our future is perfected, ultimate, immortal. The ultimate life is the full design."

"The Mesmeric Revelation", Edgar Allan Poe

The Malcontents

By Mary E. Choo

Curious,
I planted the seedlings
just as the catalogue said:
on the stroke of midnight,
in late spring,
when it was more than warm.

They did well enough
in that part of the garden
behind the secret gate.
Some rose as high as my shoulder,
their lush leaves unfolding.
I was delighted at first
when they all sprouted heads
with succulent eyes and mouths.

Still, if it rained during summer,
they were quick to complain
about pests and blight.
Most grew feet
at the base of their stems
and wanted to walk;
shocked, I refused,
though I cried when I cut their feet off.

As the weather grew colder,
they challenged the frost,
demanding blankets;
if smaller, their feet did grow back.

Damp and shrivelling,
they began to whisper behind my back,
so I heaped them with cuttings
and latched them in,
hoping they'd die.

One winter night,
I could hear them plotting
in their hidden place,
the uneven tread
of small, softened feet,

and on the chill air,
sudden as the snapping of twigs,
their louder voices, angry,
calling me Mother …

the rusted gate hinge
creaking.

Mary E. Choo's speculative poetry and fiction has been published in a wide variety of magazines and anthologies, as well as online and electronic publications. She is a two-time Aurora finalist, and has received a number of honourable mentions in *The Year's Best Fantasy and Horror* and *The Best Horror of the Year* (online lists). Her short story, "The Man Who Loved Lightning", appears in the anthology of fusion fiction, *Like Water for Quarks*.

Liminal Medicine

By Jesse Bullington

After the journalists discovered the killing fields and Tuol Sleng, the whole world knew about our ghosts. The metaphor is a strong one, I'll allow: Just as the spectre of Nanking haunts the Japanese and Mao's revolt made the tale of the hungry ghost more palpable, so, too, did the Rouge grant us our own haunted legacy. Movies and books and articles and television and a rather morbid tourism industry all parade the ghosts of Cambodia before the pitying eyes of the world, and even down all these years local witticisms, such as *It is better to lose one leg than both,* remind me that countless landmines wait like vipers in the fields, that the phantom of the Khmer Rouge will haunt my country for many lifetimes. The summer I returned home, the news fixated on the arrest of a deranged American murderer and I thus discovered another appropriate allegory for what the Khmer Rouge did to my country – cannibalism.

My grandfather, like many Cambodians, had a ghost arm; unlike many, he lost his during the civil war and not afterward. He claimed that, had he found and cremated the limb, it would not have haunted him, but even as a child, I suspected this tale was told for my amusement, the waxy stump wiggling for my edification alone. After my uncle whisked me out of the village and bounced me from town to Phnom Penh to border to Bangkok to University, I ran across an article on the phantom limb phenomenon. I translated and copied it to show my grandfather, but by the time I graduated and returned home, he had found his way back to the arm the Khmer Rouge had taken so many years before.

After the train and boat and taxi and bus and rickshaw, I found myself on the familiar road home, debating how to approach my grandmother, as a cat mewled somewhere in the cab and insects hummed and the mud squelched under the tires and the jungle pulsed with all the sultry wetness of summer. Much to the curiosity of the two well-dressed men sharing the vehicle with me, I made the driver stop a kilometer outside the village to walk the rest of the way in; the lengthy journey from my new life back to my old had not been nearly long enough to prepare myself, and I thought returning as I had thousands of times before might help. Naturally, as soon as the mud coated my sneakers and the taxi resumed bouncing down the road to deliver my bags, I regretted my decision, the heat turning my dress to sticky rice paper.

I paused in the shade of the mango tree overlooking my village and smiled. Unlike many of my scholastic compatriots, I felt no shame regarding my rural upbringing and, after the intensity of Bangkok, I relished the notion of a neighbourhood not constantly throbbing with noise, traffic and electricity. Had I any intention of staying longer than the summer, I might have thought differently. That in itself was strange, I ruminated, that the one place I always considered home I now saw for what it was – a quaint and antiquated little hamlet that would likely become intolerable within a few months.

The mango tree above me wilted pregnant over the road, its fruit crowning down, almost within reach. City living had not made me too proud to hop in the mud like a gibbon and soon, I netted my fingers over a plump, ruddy orb and rent the fruit loose of its moorings. My heel slipped in the muck as I landed and I fell backwards, knocking the wind out of myself as I slapped down in the road. My initial panic at how my grandmother would react to my soiled dress brought on a giggling fit – that particular mango tree had brought on more than one lashing from similar circumstances.

"Are you a bitch, cooling yourself in the mud?" the thick country accent made it impossible for me to tell if the speaker was male or female, and I scrambled to my feet in embarrassment.

"I fell picking –" but I stopped as I turned and saw the witch scowling at me, her own dress blackened with mud halfway up her spindly legs. A basket hung against the sharp jag of her knees and she looked even more horrible than she had when I was a child, if such a thing were possible. Yet, I was no longer a child and studying medicine, I had of course thought often of this poor, maligned woman whom the village shunned, yet turned to in place of real medical attention. "Hello, ma'am. It's good to see you, again."

"Eh." She squinted at me then cracked a yellow-toothed leer. "Jorani's granddaughter."

"Yes, ma'am. My name's Malis," I said, resolute to make up for –

"You used to throw rotten mangoes at my house," she said, warily eyeing the fruit still clenched in my hand. "And worse. You and that Phirun child."

"I'm sorry ma'am," I said. "We were just –"

"Nasty little things," she muttered. "You know how he ended up after you left, that boy you ran with? You hear the bad end he came to?"

My grandmother had answered every letter I wrote and while, over the last few years, I had not found the time to write as often, she had never mentioned anything happening to Phirun in her replies. We had terrorized this lonely old woman, Phirun and I, and gauging by the sadistic glitter in her eye, something dire had happened indeed. Perhaps noticing the worry on my face, she grinned even wider and fumbled in her basket.

"What's happened to Phirun?" I said, when I realized she had no intention of volunteering the information. Withdrawing a hand-rolled cigarette and a matchbox, she lit up and blew an ivory cloud in my face.

"Gone," she said, her ghastly face obscured behind the smoke. "Met a bad end."

"What happened?" I snapped, remembering I was no longer an ill-behaved child to be talked down to.

"Run off with a Viet," she took a drag on her cigarette. "Went to Ho Chi and ain't come back."

"That's it?" I asked, relieved.

"Bad end, eh?" The witch was clearly disappointed Phirun's desertion of the village had not disturbed me. "Living with the Viets?"

"Let me help with your basket," I said, the mud drying all over my back and legs encouraging me to get on with my penance or abandon it all together.

"You sound like a Thai," she grumbled, but handed off her basket, and together, we walked slowly down the road, the emptied taxi soon passing us on its way back out of the jungle. "Why're you talking like a Thai now?"

"I've been in Thailand," I looked off into the eye-scalding brightness of the verdant foliage to hide my smile. "I've been training to be a doctor and –"

"Doctor?" the witch took a long drag. "Why'd you leave, then? Think a Thai knows more than me?"

"No, ma'am," I said, leaving the road and following her onto the trail leading to her hut beside the landmine-riddled Dead Field. "I just wanted to learn a different kind of medicine."

"Different?" she snorted. "Shitty Thai medicine's different than the real thing, sure enough. That's where you've been? Learning Thai tricks?"

"Ma'am, setting bones and stitching up cuts aren't tricks" I said, reminding myself that her racism and hostility were but results of her upbringing, and she probably had dementia besides.

"Could've taught you that and more, had you shown a bit more sense."

"As I said, I'm sorry –"

"Had another skilled set of hands about, could've saved your grandfather."

"What?" I stopped, allowing the mosquitoes to swarm me and the fronds she had held back to whip my legs. "What about Grandfather?"

"Was my master what saved him when he lost that arm, but I helped, yes, I did. And had I a helper when we tried to get the demon out, it might've worked." She clucked her tongue. "Get along, then. I've got guests waiting."

"Yes, ma'am." I followed her, blinking the sweat and tears out of my eyes. Grandmother wrote when he fell ill and said she was taking him to a doctor, and by the time my response received a response of its own, he had passed away. I assumed she had taken him out of the village, to a real clinic instead of –

"Coated him in chili oil, bound him tight, and kept the coals good, but it was tough, didn't want to go. Took him with it."

"Coals? Chili oil?" I stopped again, but seeing her advance over the twisted roots, I had to continue as well. "A demon? He had a fever, didn't he?"

"Burning up," she nodded, ducking under a plump vine. "So, I got him on the coals, but it still wouldn't come up. Toughest little demon."

I could hardly believe what I was hearing; I knew rural healers like the witch used genuine natural remedies in conjunction with liberal quackery, but this seemed beyond all reason. That my grandmother would allow it surprised me even more, for she was a smart, semi-educated woman. Fevers can be fatal if medicine is not received, of course, but to roast him over coals would be a virtual death sentence to even a healthy man of my grandfather's age.

"You witch!" I blurted out. "How dare you!"

She stopped and turned, her hut jutting out of the jungle over her shoulder. Her narrow eyes and sharp nose appeared stuck halfway between scorn and pity. I noticed the two well-dressed, middle-aged men from the cab standing by the door to her hut, watching us, but did not think anything of it until much later, after my anger and disgust were shed with the quarts of sweat flowing from me.

"I only work when I'm paid," she said, snatching the basket from me. "And I'm only paid when folk come here. Me and the Thais got that in common, at least. You come back at dusk and I'll teach you something they won't have showed you. He won't live out the night, to be sure, and looks like they've brought what I need."

Much as I wanted to slap her or scream at her or even somehow calmly explain to her how what she did was wrong, wrong, wrong, I did what I had always done as a child when the witch told me something horrible – I turned and ran down the trail without looking back, her cackling laugh sending the cuckoos into flight. By the time I entered the village proper, I had calmed somewhat, and then my neighbors took turns swooping me up, and praising my maturity and beauty, and laughing at my bedraggled appearance, and welcomed me home with an embarrassing amount of fanfare. Grandmother saw at a glance that something other than emotion at my homecoming had darkened my countenance. After we had all eaten together in the village centre, she spirited me inside her – our – sweltering stilt-house to have a proper talk.

"You took him to see the witch," I said, when she finally ceased her interrogation of my (long and dangerous) trip, my (obviously poor, without her cooking) health, and my (not *too* trampy) appearance.

"Now?" she asked, setting her glass of nectar down. "You've just got –"

"Now," I nodded. "Why didn't you take him to the clinic? Pho's still got his jeep; I saw it."

"He wouldn't listen," she said and I realized with irritation her sorrow had more to do with my reaction than Grandfather's death. I guiltily tried to rein in my frustration and, unlike the witch, she had the decency to continue without being pestered. "I'd taken him to that clinic a dozen times. When the last fever got him, he said, 'No, take me to her.' What could I do? He was dying, Malis."

The heat and the sun streaming into the room sapped some of my melancholy and I simply felt exhausted. Grandfather had rolled cigarettes as fat as his thumb, worked shirtless in the jungle, drank mostly rainwater, and essentially lived a life as far removed as possible from what I would come to consider healthy. The only real surprise was that he had lived as long as he had, the weathered old veteran, and after what the Rouge had done to him, being slathered in chili oil probably seemed more an indignity than a torture.

"Who told you?" she asked, in her slightly nosey, high tone. "I didn't hear anyone mention it at lunch."

"You know how I walked in and had the driver drop off my stuff?" I nodded towards the small bags crowding a corner. "I saw the witch on the road and she told me. Probably couldn't believe her luck to deliver some bad news."

"That poor woman." My grandmother suddenly looked her age, thin, silver hair clinging to her sweaty forehead like spider silk.

"She –" I began to say, when something the witch had said finally sank through my heat and emotion-clouded consciousness. "The witch said something to me about tonight, about a patient she had that wouldn't last until dawn. And two men, city-men, shared the car in with me and didn't say a word, and then I saw them waiting at her hut."

Grandmother clicked her teeth and reached for my glass, but I snatched it up and drained the last of the bright-orange, fibrous juice. "You shouldn't meddle in her business."

"Who's meddling? She invited me herself, to watch whatever mummery she's got planned, and there's no chance I'm going to sit here while she cooks another patient. I've got some aspirin in my bag and I'll bet my magic little pills will do more than her exorcism, regardless of the malady."

I offered her my empty glass and she snatched it; her eyes narrowed in the angry expression I had missed so much.

"You're not going, and that is that. I saw those men who got out of the cab, and I saw them yesterday when they brought in their sick friend. They're Rouge, girl, and you are minding your business under this roof tonight."

"How do you know they're Rouge?" I asked, knowing full well she would not have said as much if it were not true. You do not lose a daughter and son-in-law to monsters and then invoke their title flippantly. Grandmother turned away, rather than answering my question, and looked out the screened window into the dense greenery swelling up behind our house.

"Pho thinks it may storm later," she said, eventually, and although the obedient part of me willed my churlish mouth to be silent, I would not let it rest.

"A sick man is a sick man," I said evenly. "No matter who he is or what he's done, it's my duty to help. That witch said whoever it was wouldn't live the night and, unless I examine him, I don't doubt it. I didn't spend all those years away from you to shirk the very responsibilities I have accepted."

"Please," she whispered, sitting back down across from me and taking my hands in her own gnarled fingers. I winced at the sight of the arthritis-swollen digits, realizing how much agony writing me all those letters had been. "You're old enough I won't try ordering you about, but listen to me – she will do everything in her power to save him and if she can't, then I know what will come next. They brought a black cat, didn't they?"

At this, my scorching skin went Pacific and my mouth became dry and clammy. One of the men had an occasionally purring pet carrier between his legs on the long drive, a detail I had found curious and then forgotten. I felt her sweaty palms shaking against the backs of my hands, and her tongue flicked nervously over her teeth. I had never seen her look so uncomfortable in all my life, and this unnerved me even more than her comment about the cat.

"I don't know if it was black," I said, suddenly curious as to the speed of my pulse. "But they brought one, yes ... is she going to sacrifice it or something?"

"Bah," Grandmother released my hands with a smile. "The cat will be fine and they'll get exactly what they deserve, Rouge bastards."

"I'm going," I said again, although my voice did not sound so steady, anymore. "I told you; it's my responsibility. I can't start my residency knowing I ignored an ailing person, even if he's Pol Pot."

She spit at the hated name and cursed quietly, immediately cleaning up the smear of spittle with the hem of her skirt. "I won't tell you again, Malis; stay away from that hut. She's half-ghost, herself, and those men are all-demon. What can a doctor do for devils and ghosts?"

"I'm going," I whispered resolutely, growing ever more nervous at the superstitious turn the conversation had taken. This was the woman who had chastised me a thousand times for calling the witch a witch, after all. "I don't have a choice, Grandmother. This is who I am."

"Why won't you listen to me? That sick man, he came from here. He's the one who took your mother and father! And you want to help him?" Grandmother trembled all over and wagged her finger at me. "A good doctor, yes, but what kind of daughter, then?"

"I –" had nothing to say to that, nothing at all. Never in my life had I dreamed a face could be attached to the end my unremembered parents had come to. That I would be put in such a melodramatic moral quandary struck me then, as it does now, as a contrivance more fit for a Thai soap opera than a life. Maybe that is why I recovered so quickly and told her, "I'm still going."

"It'll be all right," I heard my grandfather say. "I'll keep an eye on her."

Grandmother wearily closed her eyes. I snapped my head around and there he was in the doorway, smiling softly like he always did when we were having a spat and he interrupted. Light-headed and wondering why everyone had tricked me into thinking he had died, it took me an instant to notice that his left arm terminated in a wide-palmed hand instead of a knotted stump. Then I did what any grounded, logical young doctor would do in my situation – I screamed and fainted.

When I came back around, they were arguing quietly and rain rattled the house. Most of the details of that afternoon are lost to me, but, somehow, I made peace with the impossibility of the situation. When I recovered, I inspected my grandfather with the sort of stoic practicality that only absolute shock could grant to one in my position. He appeared identical to how he had in life, khaki pants and a wide-brimmed hat his only attire. With a slight grimace of effort, he could pass through solid objects, clothes and all, but my trembling fingers were able to settle on his frigid skin. At this realization, I threw my arms around him and cried.

The rain slowed and finally withdrew, fog and twilight conspiring to provide a more appropriate atmosphere for the evening. Grandfather ate bowl after bowl of rice, and both Grandmother and I politely pretended not to notice that he kept a larger bowl underneath him as he ate to catch the food that fell through him onto the floor, so that only the same two bowls of rice were consumed over and over. Grandfather eventually set down his bowl and Grandmother joked that the reason for his insatiable appetite was his extraction – Grandfather had fled Southern China when Mao's followers descended on his family farm like locusts, and emigrated to Cambodia to avoid the brewing war and famine in his homeland. He often lamented his ill luck in that regard, and now was no exception. Finally, the happy, surreal reunion came to a close, as the fog blotted out the setting sun, and Grandfather and I rose to leave.

My grandfather pecked my grandmother on the cheek as we descended to the bog of a road. When I later realized they both suspected they were seeing one another for the last time, I marveled at the brevity of their goodbye. Then again, few couples are afforded the reprieve that they were and they surely knew this. The jungle inhaled us into its misty belly, and I would have lost both my way and my grandfather had he not taken my hand in his. My fingers crept reflexively to his wrist, even though I knew nothing pulsed there.

"Malis," he said, as we walked, "while you were asleep, Jorani told me you were planning on interfering tonight."

"Not interfering," I said defensively. "Helping. There's a difference."

"You think you can do more than Theary?"

"Theary?" I had forgotten the witch's real name. "Oh, yes. I hear she rubbed you down with a nice chili oil liniment."

"That didn't burn as bad as the coals," he laughed. "But look at me now! I owe my current condition to her skill. I approve of your work, but can the medicine you learned perform as well as hers?"

He had me there and he knew it. The damp, cold mud filled the sneakers I had foolishly forgotten to leave behind, but otherwise, the evening walk was as pleasant as any we had taken before ... before he died, I made myself think. The ethereal road vanished before us. I nearly panicked at the thought that I had somehow died and he was escorting me to whatever lay beyond.

"The sick man," Grandfather said, his voice low and sad, "Jorani's told you who he is?"

"She said he was the one who sent my parents to Tuol Sleng."

"I went there, after the Viets took over." His voice sounded harsh in the way it always did after he had been looking at my mother's pictures. "They called it a prison. We knew then, but to see it – oh, Malis, can you imagine? To do such things to other people? And for what?"

I knew of no answer, nor did he expect one. I squeezed his hand and we came to a stop, the miasma thinning around the mouth of the trail to the witch's hut. He rubbed his eyes and then squeezed my shoulder; I felt his phantasmal tears dampen my neck.

"He grew up here," Grandfather went on. "That man and your mother played together, like you and Phirun. I never cared for him – he was cruel and cowardly. After the war, when your father came here and met your mother, I knew that little coward would cause a stink. But how could I know? How? We all deserved peace. The coward joined up right away, gone from the village overnight. Your father returned to Phnom with your mother and then you were born. By then, things were getting bad ...."

He stared past me into the mist, haunted by his own ghosts. When he finally continued, his voice had steadied. "They were going to come and stay with us, rather than risk being sent to a farm, risk being separated. Then he showed up at their apartment, and I know it was him because your uncle was visiting, recognized him through the window and knew enough to go out the backdoor with you. Then they took your mother and father to that hell, and your uncle took you to us. That is why I could not leave, yet, Malis."

"What?" My own eyes were blurry, as much from confusion as from the details of the story I had never before heard in its entirety. "Why can't you leave?"

"I can," he corrected himself, his voice harder, sharper, "but I won't. Not until I see what happens to that monster who took my daughter."

"But how could you know he'd come back? And so soon?"

"Soon? I died over a year ago, Malis." He smiled at my guilty frown. "And I knew he'd be back because he's a coward and, no matter what faith they might profess, all cowards fear death. I knew he'd do everything to stave off his end and that would mean coming home. He knows how powerful Theary is; everyone who lives here does."

This last seemed to have the air of reproach in it, but I felt far too unnerved to defend my beliefs. Perhaps sensing this reluctance on my part to acknowledge the witch's prowess, he adopted a different strategy. As he spoke, he again took my hand and we began threading our way between the hazy trees towards our destination.

"You know I'm not some traditionalist stooge," Grandfather said. "I've always respected your decision to practice the new medicine. But don't you have a responsibility to respect the wishes of your patient?"

"Of course," I allowed. "But if they don't know what's best for them, sometimes a doctor must make a decision for them."

"The coward's dying," Grandfather said, almost happily. "Like most of his compatriots – like those two lackeys who came here with him – he's been taken into the fold of the new government. No arrest, no tribunal. Don't you think a man in such a position, if he desired it, could receive better western treatment than a young doctor without her tools in the middle of the jungle?"

"I suppose ...."

"Those folk at the clinic helped me enough that I know the good your stuff can do. But the Rouge spit on your learning. Many less might have died had they not outlawed any but Theary's way, for hers is a special sort of medicine and requires more skill than you might think. So this patient, if you must call him such, this dying, murdering coward, he has come all the way out here to receive treatment far different from any you might provide. And yet, you insist you must interfere?"

I stayed quiet, the only sound my sneakers pulling in the mud and slipping on roots. I wanted to tell him how badly I had wished for such an excuse not to even look at this man, to stay inside my warm childhood home and bore my grandmother, and have her bore me, until we both passed out from exhaustion. But I was prouder then and, even believing as I must have that I either dreamt or hallucinated the ghost leading me deeper into the jungle, I did not give him the satisfaction of an answer. We both knew, though, and as the lights of her hut appeared like the eyes of a smoke-wreathed demon, we approached the side window instead of the front door.

A stool waited for us in the mud beneath the window. From within came the chanting of the witch. I slipped out of my filthy sneakers and socks, rather than risk slipping from my perch, and stepped onto the stool. Grandfather floated higher off the ground to watch beside me. I felt a strange giddiness, as though I were a child peeking in on a secret adult activity.

The heat, the stink, and the light pouring out of the room blinded me, but when my eyes adjusted, I almost laughed at the ridiculous sight before me. Prostrate and still on a bed, in the centre of the one-room hut, lay a man swaddled in damp bandages from head to toe. Three other figures danced around him in pursuit of a trotting black cat. They followed it around the room, but my attention shifted to the patient, who was not breathing. The witch and the two men from my car-ride goaded the cat towards the patient, but the cat seemed intent on avoiding the man and made for our window. Before I could duck out of sight, Grandfather leaned forward and the cat jumped backwards, preferring the chase to confronting a ghost in the window. The witch saw us, even though the men did not, and she smiled.

Then one of the men startled the cat from the other direction, and it deftly leapt onto a chair, only to have the other man direct it back towards the bed. At this, the cat dived over what I now took to be a corpse and the two men cheered, their faces bright and sweaty. Glancing with confusion at Grandfather, I saw him grinning. After another few minutes, the cat again found itself on a chair and again pounced over the corpse, and at this, Grandfather floated behind me and gripped my shoulders tightly.

The two men exchanged wary looks and cautiously approached the corpse, and the witch put herself between them and the door. I leaned closer, as did Grandfather, as did the two men. Then the corpse sat upright on the bed and I jumped, falling backwards off the stool. Grandfather smiled even wider and beckoned me back up, whispering, "You'll miss it; look quick!"

Inside the house, the men were shouting and I quickly righted the stool, my legs trembling and my brow drenched at the knowledge that all my childhood fears of the witch were justified. I clambered back up, soaked in mud and puddle-water, and saw one of the men on the floor, the risen corpse squatting over him. The other man had a machete and wrestled with the witch in the doorway. I realized he must have cut her when blood began soaking the neck of her dress. I was so transfixed by the sight that it took the corpse bellowing a wordless, terrible cry to startle me into action.

Even if my grandfather's presence beside me had left any doubts that the dead can return, the scream of that bandaged corpse now straddling his fellow would have dispelled them. I had put in several eighteen-hour shifts in the emergency room, and heard every manner of sound the human body can produce, and that shriek dwarfed them all in its fury and pain. The sound made me sick to my stomach. Then the man underneath the crouched corpse gave a very human scream of his own. Before I could move to help, the corpse brought its mouth down on the pinned man's throat and ended the wail by biting through every major artery in his neck. Blood jetted over them both, Grandfather cackling with glee beside me.

The cast-iron stomach I thought I possessed revolted at the sight and I stumbled down from the stool just as the bile rushed up. I hunched over in the shadow of the witch's hut and vomited as I heard the second man scream from within, Grandfather now taunting them through the open window. Then Grandfather went quiet and I felt his chill touch on my neck, even as my stomach projected more mango and acid into the widening puddle.

"Malis," Grandfather said, his mirth suddenly replaced with an edgy desperation. "Run home, now!"

Shuddering from my convulsing stomach and the scene repeating itself in my head, I somehow managed to stand up. Instead of fleeing, however, I shakily got back onto the stool. That idiot pride in my recent graduation would not allow me to leave without first ensuring none could benefit from my ministrations, the fractured state of my psyche such that the horrors of the night paled beside the thought of failing to uphold my convictions. Or so I told myself; perhaps I was just too scared or fascinated to run.

The man the corpse had bitten bled out on the floor next to a toppled chair, his head nearly severed from his vicious neck wound. The witch – Theary, I corrected myself – lay twitching in her doorway. Beside her, the man with the machete she had fought lay sprawled, his head snapped all the way around. The risen corpse had vanished and then I heard footsteps in the mud rounding the hut to my left.

I slowly turned, fear bringing my nausea back with renewed vigour, and then Grandfather's frigid fingers slapped my cheek and passed partially through, saliva freezing to my teeth. The blow invigourated me to flight, just as the murderous corpse rounded the hut and saw me. Then it and I screamed together as I tumbled from the stool and ran. Grandfather was shouting, and before focusing on the mist-masked trees blocking my way, I saw him drift between me and the pursuing corpse. My bare feet sank to the ankles with each step, but I propelled myself faster and faster through the mist, wet leaves slicing and slapping as I ran into the night jungle.

That wretched wail came again from just over my shoulder, and then a fallen tree reared out of the fog to trip me. I hurled myself into the air, clearing the rotten wood but entangling myself in sharp, thin vines. Grandfather shouted again, somewhere nearby in the mist. I clawed at the vines, but, in my panic, I could not get a grip on them and so, instead, yanked and thrashed and rolled until I came loose, shallow gashes opening all over my slick, muddy body. I stumbled away from the wreckage of the dead tree and the vines. As I frantically spun myself in a circle, nothing moved in the ever-thickening fog. The vegetation had thinned somewhat and I hurried forward, but after only half a dozen paces, came up short, a sudden epiphany freezing my legs and darkening my vision in the manner that heralded another blackout.

Forcing myself to regulate my breathing, the black rings closing in around the fog widening and fading, I staved off unconsciousness. Not vines but wire had caught me, I had suddenly realized, meaning I could only be one place: the Dead Field. Another echoing howl rolled out of the fog, the corpse of the man who had killed my parents loping closer, my feet paralyzed by the justified fear of what lurked under the mud.

Biting my lip until the pain returned my body to me, I spun around and carefully stepped back the way I had come, hoping the fact that I was still bipedal signaled a clear path.

Click.

Not even two steps, I thought, clamping my eyes shut and setting my jaw, willing away the sharp metal digging into the sole of my left foot.

A shadow darted through the mist before me and I screamed. I had to; otherwise, I would have moved my legs, my body demanding some response to the approaching shape. I resolved to lift my foot just as the evil corpse reached me, in the hope that it would share the deadly blast. I was too scared when the time came, however, and instead found myself babbling at the corpse not to kill me.

"Shut up!" Grandfather hissed, his profile solidifying through the fog. "Shut up, Malis, please."

I squatted down in the mud, too scared to cry.

"We're in the Field," he said. "We have to find you a ... Malis?"

I shook my head frantically, the silence of the Dead Field even worse than the baying of the corpse had been.

"Are you ..."

"Yes," I managed, my voice cracking. "My left. Will it hurt? Tell me, I –"

"Shut up." He knelt down in front of me . "Stay still and jump back when I tell you. This may hurt; I don't really know."

Grandfather laid his cool palms on the top of my muddy left foot and pressed down. It felt the same as the first time I swam in the ocean instead of a sun-fermented pond, my entire body charged with a cold so intense it burned. I saw the backs of his hands disappear through my foot, his wrists now brushing its top.

"Now," Grandfather said, "jump backwards."

I did, staring intently at the ghost of my grandfather. His hands were buried in the muck, his face taut, and then I saw his failure. His eyes widened and we both heard the trigger rise without my weight on it, his spectral palms lacking sufficient corporeality to keep the weapon from discharging. All this transpired in an instant, as my foot lifted and I stumbled backwards.

Nothing. I did a nervous little dance in the mud until I finally suppressed my body again. Grandfather blinked and raised his palms towards me, a smile tickling his cheeks.

"A dud. You are so lucky, Malis," he said, with the same tone as if I had brought a pit viper into the house thinking it a water snake. "Now, do not move. Please."

Before I could answer, Grandfather jumped about with his back to me and planted his arms to the elbows in the mud. Then he began pushing forward in a crouch, amid the scrub growing in the Field, resembling a monk cleaning a temple floor. I carefully followed where his footsteps would have been. Through the fog, I saw the wire fence tangled in the fallen tree and quickened my pace, only to realize my grandfather could no longer protect me.

The corpse hopped over the fence with surprising agility and I remember praying – actually praying, for the first time since I was a child – that it would trigger a mine. Grandfather shouted and tried to shoo it away, but I do not know if it could even see him. It saw me, though, and I backed away as it advanced, no longer caring if I stepped on another mine. Then it pounced and I screamed and screamed and screamed, the stench of excrement and pus and fever-sweat and mud enveloping me in a nightmare haze as it pinned me under its knees.

Maybe it saw something of my mother in my pale, wet face, or maybe it simply enjoyed hurting more than killing. Regardless, it twisted its fingers through my hair and stretched its other hand towards my eyes instead of opening my throat like its first victim. I felt another panic attack swelling inside me, the jabbing pain in my chest almost equal to that in my plucked scalp. I must have screamed, because then its fingers were between my teeth, chili oil burning my mouth as the slimy digits tried to seize my tongue.

Grandfather floated in and through and around the muddy, swaddled corpse that pressed me deeper into the mire with its weight, but still it did not acknowledge the ghost's presence. The soiled bandages dangling from its face brushed my own and I bit the fingers, only to have it snatch its hand free and begin pummeling my cheeks. I saw its teeth shining through the dark and the fog, its whole face glowing phosphor green.

I saw its eyes brighten with the same unnatural luminescence, and then another punch struck my temple, but it lacked the strength of the previous blow. I squinted, to bring my eyes back into focus, and saw that it looked past me, the jade light bathing its bared teeth and bulging eyes and dripping nose. I heard raspy breathing from behind me, saw Grandfather retreating behind the corpse, and then the thing howled and fled, departing as violently as it had arrived.

The fog had nearly swallowed the running corpse when the green light warmed my own cheeks, but before I could turn, an explosion shook the earth and I tucked my knees to my chest and whimpered. Parting my rapidly swelling eyelids, I half-expected to see my mother and father returned to rescue me, their ghosts tinted lime and their motives pure.

Instead, I saw the witch for what she truly was and closed my eyes right back up, holding my knees even tighter in an attempt to ward off the crippling pain in my lungs.

"Come on, Malis." Grandfather shook me gently. "He's gone and that means I'm to be off."

This, combined with the endorphin cocktail stirring through my body, brought me around enough to sit up in the mud and put my arms around him. He hugged me and already, I noticed his sweet smell of tobacco and wet leaves was fading into nothing. Pulling back, I saw he grew more translucent by the moment, the shining witch-thing visible through his bare chest. I shook my head in a childish effort to dispel it all, but he took my hand and helped me up. I slipped as I did, his fingers no longer able to grip mine. Together, we approached the witch and the once-more-inanimate corpse.

"Thank you, ma'am," I managed, disgust and pity and fear jostling around my taxed brain. "I'm sorry for everything I said. For everything I did, when I was little. I didn't ..."

I could not finish, for she looked up from her meal and smiled at me. The man with the machete had not cut her throat, as I had assumed, but she had simply loosed herself through some means of her own. Her bark-like face and stringy hair tilted upwards, the light cast from below now brightening my face, just as it darkened her own. Her teeth dripped a mixture of feces and meat, the carcass of the raised and killed-again

Khmer Rouge captain splayed before her facedown in the Dead Field, one leg missing and the other shredded beyond recognition.

She dipped her head again, burying her jaws in the corpse's cratered posterior, teeth cracking bone to better access the ripe bowels. Only the complexity and the completeness of her organ structure allowed me to ignore my climaxing nausea. Watching her swallow, I saw no visible change in the skin of her neck, but where the exposed organs dangled beneath, I could clearly see the bulge of the food traveling down until it plopped into her surprisingly large stomach. I marveled at the emerald radiance her heaving lungs shone onto the scene, on the surreal impossibility of a living human head floating in the air, with all of its entrails and organs intact and functioning without the benefit of a body.

"Told you," the witch said, meat and ordure pushing out between her teeth. "Learn something tonight, eh?"

"We were right," I said, remembering our childhood theories regarding the witch's true nature. "What did we call it? You? *Arp*? *Krasue*?"

"Call me by my name, girl," she said, with a leer, and by the brilliant light emanating from her lungs, I saw that she had eaten all the way down to the man's stomach. "Call me 'Theary'. Or, if you like, 'Teacher'?"

"You ate babies out of women." I sat down heavily in the mud. "You'd float through their windows ...."

"Nonsense," Theary snorted, her face and mannerisms so normal compared to the rest of her. "Might've helped a girl now and again get shy of a problem some boy gave her, but I'm no thief. Do I take what others throw away? Well, I'm not too proud. Children can think such things, but you're a doctor now, aren't you? Like me?"

"Yes," I said and from that moment on, I truly was. How could a mere mangled body bring on nausea? How could a simple wail of agony chill my nerves? How could mundane suffering and death quicken my pulse?

I heard Theary laughing beside me, smelled the sour smoke and shaved metal and burned meat and raw waste, and choked on my own revulsion. When I could again breathe without gagging, I turned toward my grandfather, but he had already dissipated into the fog. If not for the wet slurping noises of one monster eating the other, I would have convinced myself then and there that I had hallucinated the entire ordeal. A good doctor believes what she sees, however, and I had no choice in the matter.

I left the Dead Field without triggering another mine and returned to my childhood village of mangoes and rain puddles, and what I did from that night on is my own business. I try to help people and I try to keep my past where it belongs, and if I only succeed some of the time on both accounts, then that, too, is my own business.

I miss my grandparents. My grandmother joined my grandfather the year we finally had tribunals for the surviving officers of the Khmer Rouge. She passed quietly in the clinic. I will not say, "Too little too late," but even with the last of those monsters banished through the medicine of the courts, I know their ghosts still thrive and lurk and maim and kill. I do all that is possible to set things right, but in my heart I suspect that my Cambodia is a country forever haunted.

Jesse Bullington is the author of the novels *The Sad Tale of the Brothers Grossbart* and *The Enterprise of Death*. His short fiction has appeared, or is forthcoming, in various magazines, including *Beneath Ceaseless Skies*, *Chiaroscuro*, *Jabberwocky*, and *Brain Harvest*, as well as in anthologies such as *Running with the Pack*, *The Best of All Flesh*, *The New Hero II*, *Historical Lovecraft*, and *Future Lovecraft*. He currently resides in Colorado and can be found online at www.jessebullington.com.

At the Doorstep

By Leanna Renee Hieber

From the desk of Mrs. Evelyn Northe

November 1, 1881

Day of All Saints. May every single one of those hallowed souls be with me now.

It is true that I live in a haunted house.

You wouldn't know it to look at this fine, glorious Fifth Avenue town home filled with all the stained glass, marble, carved wood, and other opulence you might imagine of its prime Manhattan location. But the moment I trim my gas-lamps low, I am too aware of the chill, of the comings and goings of spirits. And never have they been as active as tonight. I can't usually see them. But I always hear their steps.

Never one for letter writing, diaries, journals, or any of that nonsense, I haven't had time for such sentiment. But considering I might be seized in death's grip, I ought to have a record. If nothing else but for my friends, so that they might know what became of me when the footsteps got too close to ignore.

I hear the tread far off now, like a dull drum, one after another. Soon, they'll creep up the stairs and stand upon my threshold. While I find the temperature of spirits uncomfortable, it's nothing compared to the dread sound of those steps.

I wonder what my poor friends might do without me, they whom I've drawn into my madness. No. Not my madness. It began long before me. And it called me. It called my friends. It will soon cry out for the world.

Who can say when the spirit world split in two? Who can say when that in-between place of sleep and awake became a true battleground for the soul?

I will always blame the War. Once a country pits brothers against brothers, and has more mangled corpses than it knows what to do with, it's hard not to think of humanity in terms of war.

At some point in history, men began to fracture their hearts, minds and souls. It wasn't enough to simply send a dead spirit on to Heaven or to Hell. There was born a proving ground between, and a new breed of restless dead and restless living began to walk the land. It got worse, *so* much worse for the heart of New York when it lost so many twenty years ago, when our country lay in bloody tatters and hundreds of thousands of bodies lie in pieces in the dirt.

New York City, you gorgeous gorgon. You manifold monster. You have made the evil industrious. You have made the striving hungry. You are still broken and grieving for those bodies, and you have *ignored* your pain. I saw you when you were on your knees with manifold losses. Too many to fathom. You ignored your sorrow and you sewed patches onto yourself and stuffed all your empty parts with just so much meaningless straw, making rag dolls. With one strike of a match, this whole city would ignite like young girls incinerated in garment factories.

But how can I blame you, my fair city, when I have done the very same? I, too, have patched my grief over loved ones gone, over my husband taken from me – not in battle but in health that failed too soon. I wonder if I shall see Peter Northe yet this day, if he waits for me. No, his mind went; he wouldn't remember whom to look for. Perhaps that's best. To enter the passage without attachment. But I would like to hear him say, "Hello, old friend," just once more, his greeting to me since our youth, when we looked into one another's eyes and glimpsed inner life far elder than our years.

Society would have nothing to do with me had my husband not made an absurd amount of money on what could have been a failure. But his venture succeeded. Life is full of those two walks: the winners or losers, the broken or the triumphant, the beautiful or the ugly. And each of those paths wears deeper the tread of those who restlessly watch the results. Destiny is not preordained. Your walk is not writ for you. You make choices along the way.

I made one today.

There is a letter near my hand. It sits upon my writing desk, glaring up at me with my own shaking script, addressed to a man I despise. But I know that he is going to die. My gifts have told me. And I should let him die. He's made the city worse; he's hurt innocent people; he knows not what he toys with when he perverts a séance and goes grave-robbing in foreign lands. I am aware, with a knowledge as mysterious to me as ever, that his train will derail and that he, along with many other passengers, will die.

So, he should, by all intents and purposes, be left to it so the devils may take him.

And yet.

I was not left to die that day when everything changed. My life was once spared, on a winter's morning in '63.

On the West Side, near the mid-town piers, I watched a boat come in, brimming with wounded soldiers up from the Carolina coast. It was not long after the Proclamation had been signed and announced, and New York was buzzing with the news, nervous murmurs of what it could mean for the Union, though it didn't bring a swift end to the war.

"Mr. Olmstead's on that ship," I heard a woman say, nodding towards the waterfront. "Sanitation officer for the Union. I hear he's seen more than his poet's heart can bear."

F. L. Olmstead. The visionary behind Central Park. An architect of natural beauty presided over unnatural, ugly and twisted remains of men that were once whole.

Two walks.

It was cold, there by the pier, and the crowd was anxious, women swaying from foot to foot, their hoop skirts moving to and fro like silent, tolling bells. Tolling for the dead. Hopeful for the living. Those assembled likely had a relative they were praying to see disembark. I wanted my cousin returned, James, a vibrant young man who was like a brother to me. As if it were a spell, I kept murmuring his name, an enchantment to bid him into my arms. I was not prepared for what would come.

Since childhood, I'd seen phantom shapes in corners, things I passed off as shadows, and I had a way of knowing unknowable things. Mother, sensing tell-tale signs, owned a similar ability and guided me with calm practicality, insisting I never make a show of what I had inherited. But my talents were unpredictable and inconsistent. The fate of James, for instance, to my chagrin, remained entirely shrouded to my senses.

But as I stood watching a vessel approach, its stars and stripes flying (the Confederates may have flown their own stars, but our flag remained that of the United States), I knew it was involved with the War. Goodness knows there weren't pleasure crafts docking on these weather-worn planks; they had their own piers to separate themselves from the hard truths of the city. But not just the grey trappings of the ship anointed it as war property. It was the chill and the odd haze that surrounded it. Cool as the winter air may have been, it was suddenly arctic as the ship neared. And a halo came off her bow, her stern, a haze overpowering the haggard faces in Union blue peering from the rails ... hungry for their city yet haunted for it ....

While I couldn't make out distinct forms, I sensed that I was watching as many dead come home as living, aboard that ship.

My nose started to bleed. A garish drop of crimson upon the bell of my pale wool skirts. Damn. A shift to my psychology was one thing, but messy physical reactions were quite another. I glanced about. Was anyone else affected by this dread chill and the aura around the ship, making it, too, seem like a phantom? It didn't appear so – mostly, people simply scanned the paper listing recent New York dead and kept looking anxiously back to the boat, to see if anyone able to stand on the prow was one of their own. But a few knew. A few could feel what wakened in me.

Six average men and women held hands, facing the river as if they were bracing for a storm. Their noses weren't bleeding like mine, but they stared *around* that ship. Did they see that same halo? They held tight and bent their knees as if anchoring themselves against a tidal wave of secondary impact – as if barricading against whatever that boat carried in its wake. One of them turned to glance at me, a striking middle-aged woman.

"It is up to us, those who see the world in ways the rest cannot, to *affect* the world for the better," she said, and then smiled as if I'd nothing to worry about and turned again to the west.

It wasn't until James floated face to face with me that I truly *saw* a ghost. And when that beloved face – transparent, grey and hollow – met my eyes, I fainted. Too close to the edge where I'd wedged myself in for a better view, I took a nasty tumble right into the Hudson.

A blow to my head took care of my consciousness.

Yet, I shall never forget what I saw in that in-between state.

The two walks.

There, on the edge of life and death, in this soul-defining moment, distinct presences were on the move. Threads of light and columns of dark, thin coils moving in different directions, were buffeted like leaves in a breeze down an endless corridor. Along this passage were windows, windows onto small scenes. Intimate, or epic. A family dinner. A coronation. A first kiss. A last wish. A battle scene. Somewhere in that scene lay James' final breath. My hand seized at my chest, as if to massage my faltering heart. I, and these shafts of illumination and shadow, together we were captivated by the window-boxes of human existence. Both the lit and darkened threads vied for the scenes, pushing and pulling for dominance over these slivers of time. My life hung suspended between the world's moments.

Then, all at once, it was as if the threads noticed I did not belong. I was mobbed. The light surrounded me and gave a huge push, while the dark matter simply hung to the corners, watching. Waiting. A vibrating string, positively singing with light, grazed my ear:

"You see the currents of life. Take your gifts and go. But do not overstep your bounds. Do not weave the threads of life and death with your own hands."

I did as I was told, responded to the demand to go on living, and gasped painful, cold air.

Dock workers had pulled me from the river; the mass of piers and ships blessedly buffered the undertow. I never did get the chance to properly thank those workers and I still regret it. A doctor who happened upon the scene took charge and so, I was bid to lie still. Coats were thrown over me, women glad to have something to fuss over that was not their dead relation.

I put my hand to my face and touched a bloody gash on my forehead. My nose still bled. The six I'd glimpsed were nowhere to be seen. But that was all right; they'd given me something. That woman had inspired in me confidence to be an anchor against forces pressing in all around us and the light had only confirmed it. I knew then it was my duty to aid the living while I lived. I patched my grief. I steeled my heart, stuffing it with purpose and pride. These things may yet be flammable.

As for whether I'll help the dead once I've crossed onto that shore is knowledge for another day. Yet tonight, perhaps, but not *this* moment.

My duty is to life while I have it. What knowledge I have I must use. I mustn't stand back and let a man's train derail and kill him, even though I abhor him. The lantern at my elbow is lit; the smell of oil is distinct. The letter is in my hand, addressed to Mr. Bentrop. It simply says:

If you take that 8pm train into the city next Tuesday, it will derail and you will die. Sincerely, your second chance.

My hands shake. I return to these pages after having dropped the note in a mail box, despite the dark, dangerous lateness of the hour. Countless spirits attended my wake; I could feel their icy tendrils bouncing behind me. A drunkard or thief wouldn't have dared accost me; the air at my back would freeze the standing hairs on the bravest of necks. I was the Reaper. Off to delay tidings of death.

But did I, in doing so, inappropriately weave the forbidden threads?

And for a man such as *Bentrop*, of all people? What of the other poor souls on that 8pm departure? Do they not matter? Yet, I sense Bentrop has a further part to play in matters in which I am engaged, and I must act on instinct, even if it violates instruction. What *good* is a gift untapped?

Bentrop is in part responsible for the needle which is about to come to the city. A vast stone obelisk from the sands of Alexandria. "Cleopatra's Needle", it is called and it shall sit beyond the steps of our lovely Metropolitan Museum of Art. Men like Bentrop see in the artifact a vast power. Men like Bentrop need to be curbed. Yet, there I went, warning him against the closing jaws of prophecy. Still, he has to take the advice. There is choice involved. Two walks. Two paths. Bentrop has helped to bring a tower into our city that boldly points to the sky, as if in a demand ... must he not be prepared for how the skies will answer him? Must not I, too, be prepared for just such a reply?

Ah. Pardon the dark mark upon the pale page.

My nose has begun to bleed. Damn.

The steps are on the stair. Landing. Stairs. Landing. My hallway. Far worse than the cold, I maintain.

I confess I'm not ready to again face that passage where angels tread and devils pace. What force will win me this day? Who is closer to seizing any of us, the angels or the devils?

As God is my witness, I rattle my saber. I shake my bones. No matter what takes me, the angels or the devils, I am not finished here, upon this Earth. I am *not* finished.

I will walk, my friends, my loves, all those I've yet to meet.

I will walk the passages. You will hear my footsteps. There, the creak upon your floorboards. That will be me, what I may yet become. It's always one of us, for good or for ill. I pray the angels win. But it's always war, just beyond the limits of our flesh and the corners of our eyes.

Every sound you hear.

Every whisper, every creak of a settling house.

You're hearing war.

You cannot end it; you cannot avoid it; mankind made it and seems unable to do without it. Even without bodies, it wages on for you.

Listen, friends, and take up whatever arms you will.

Listen: It is at the doorstep.

Leanna Renee Hieber graduated with a theatre degree and focus in the Victorian Era. While performing as a professional actress, she adapted 19th-century fiction for the stage and her first publications were hot-headed little plays which have been produced around the U.S. Her novella, *Dark Nest*, won the 2009 Prism Award for excellence in Futuristic, Fantasy or Paranormal Romance. Her *Strangely Beautiful* series debut (Gaslight Fantasy), *The Strangely Beautiful Tale of Miss Percy Parker*, hit Barnes & Noble's Bestseller lists, won two 2010 Prism Awards (Best Fantasy, Best First Book) and has been optioned for adaptation into a Broadway musical, currently in early stages of development. A proud member of Science Fiction/Fantasy Writers of America and Romance Writers of America and also a member of actors unions AEA, AFTRA and SAG, Leanna works often in film and television. She lives in New York City with her real-life hero and their beloved rescued lab rabbit. "At the Doorstep" is set within the Gaslight Gothic world of *Magic Most Foul*, releasing November 2011 from Sourcebooks Fire, beginning with*Darker Still: A Novel of Magic Most Foul* Please visit her at http://leannareneehieber.com/, on Twitter @leannarenee and Facebook.com/lrhieber.

Frozen Souls

By Sarah Hans

"Are you nervous about tomorrow, Li?" Shen asks, between mouthfuls of rice.

Lien shrugs. "I've done it before." She sips her tea, watching him over the rim of the tiny porcelain cup.

"I would be scared," Shen says, trying to goad her into an embarrassing confession.

Lien knows this trick and deflects the conversation.

"I know. That's why they send me instead of you."

"They send you because you're the smallest," Shen replies. This is a dance they have done before; he knows the steps.

"They send Li because he's the bravest," the ordinarily reticent Bao adds. "He volunteered and you did not."

Lien lowers her head, a show of respect whose real intent is to hide her blushing cheeks. Her affection for Bao has become bothersome. Sometimes, she even thinks, when he defends her like this, that he knows her secret. Earlier today, his hand brushed hers while they worked and, though he seemed not to notice, the unexpected contact drew a shuddering breath from Lien. Her skin touching his was like an electric shock, sending a tingle to parts of her that she has long ignored.

The flap of the canvas tent opens and the Foreman enters. Though the crew is almost entirely Chinese, the Foreman is a huge Irishman. He counts on his enormous size and grizzled appearance to intimidate his workers; he does not know that they call him "*Maxì Tuán Xióng*" – "The Circus Bear" – mocking his size, hirsutism, and the way he takes orders from the Superintendent, always ingratiatingly willing to please. 'Storbridge' is his name, but when he enters, Bao boldly says: "*Xiong*! How can we help you today?" in heavily-accented English.

The others stifle their laughter at the mocking name behind sips of tea and mouthfuls of rice. Many become engrossed in their reading or chores.

"Will Li-Li be ready tomorrow?" Storbridge demands, his voice deep and rasping, with an edge of menace. 'Li-Li' is the white man's nickname for Lien, who is one of the tiniest of the Chinese workers.

"Yes, Li will be ready," Bao replies, nodding to Lien. She averts her eyes, not wanting to attract the Foreman's attention.

"Good. Be up at dawn so we can get to work."

Storbridge lumbers back to the tent flap, a blast of freezing air rushing in as he exits.

Lien shivers, pulling the rough wool blanket closer about her shoulders.

Shen starts laughing, first, and the others join him in low, appreciative chuckles.

"Bao, you are too bold!"

Bao ignores the laughter, looking at Lien.

"Sounds like the blasting did not go well today."

Lien nods.

"It's too cold; the rock will be too hard. But the Superintendent demands satisfaction, so the white men ignore our engineers and the blasting will proceed."

"With our lives the ones at risk," Shen says bitterly.

"We knew the risks when we signed our contracts," Lien reminds him, but her voice is bleak, and she stares with regret at her cracked and callused hands.

The tent flap opens again, and the assembled men groan and mumble about the cold as a few more workers enter. They rush to the cooking fire to warm their frostbitten hands, ill-covered in mittens full of holes. Lien counts them and finds only six.

"Where is Fa?" she asks. There is a hard knot in her belly while she awaits the answer.

One of the men by the fire turns slowly to her, a warm bowl of soup held in his palms to warm them. His expression is sorrowful. "He fell," he says, and the others nod somberly.

Lien tries to fight back tears. Like her, Fa was small and nimble, perfect for the dangerous work of blasting the cliffs. He had taught her the ancient Chinese art, and had been the quickest and most agile of all the dynamite-setters. She can't believe that he fell. Her mind reels with conspiracy theories, but just as quickly, she dismisses them. The work is dangerous and men die blasting the tunnels for the railroad every day. It was only a matter of time before Fa, too, met his end.

She can't allow the other workers to see her tears, so she rises and hurries out of the tent, with the blanket still clutched about her. She has to be stronger and braver than the others to prevent suspicion. They have seen many men perish in the grueling work on the railroad and she has cried for those who were her friends, but always in secret.

So much of her life is a secret.

Lien finds her way through the tent city to the latrine pits, which are thankfully less noisome in the extreme cold than they are in the summer months. No one wants to venture far from the warm tents, so the men have been urinating in the snow nearby, rather than make the trek to the designated area. The latrines are virtually abandoned, a silent sanctuary for her tears.

Lien takes a few moments to empty her bladder, squatting on the far side of the latrine behind some snow-covered bushes. Once relieved, she feels a little less like weeping. She stands near the pits, forlorn, unwilling to return to the tent but unable to cry. She thinks of Fa and tries to mourn him as he deserves, but she has been exhausted by the sorrow of the last terrible weeks and can't muster much beyond a few sad sniffles.

While she stands there, knee-deep in snow, waiting for the cold to leech the heat from her bones before she returns to the fire, snowflakes begin to drift down from above. There are only a few at first, spinning like tops, but as she watches, they begin to crowd the sky, falling faster and faster. Soon, the dark landscape is all but blotted out in the torrent of snow. Panicked, Lien quickly stumbles back to her tent before the snow obliterates her path and makes walking impossible. Though she is not far from her tent, she recalls vividly when several men were lost in a blizzard the first week on the mountain, found the next morning only a few feet from their dwelling, unable to make their way to safety in the disorienting whiteness.

Bao is standing at the tent flap, pulling on his boots. He looks relieved to see her.

"Li! I was going to come find you," he says. "It's not safe in a storm."

Lien is touched by his concern, but doesn't dare show it.

"I was at the latrine," she says.

"Of course," Bao replies, his mien equally icy.

Without another word, they go to their cots, where Lien lies awake, listening to the breathing of the sleeping men, thinking only of how she is likely to meet her death tomorrow. She whispers many prayers to the ancestors, wondering whether Fa did the same. In the wee hours, she finally finds sleep, but it is a restless sleep and she awakens many times in the night to the frightening feeling of falling from a great height.

The next morning finds Lien dangling over a cliff face in a huge basket of woven reeds. The basket is large enough to hold a man twice Lien's size, but the job is easier if the contents are as light as possible, and the dynamite takes up its share of the container. As she does every time she is lowered over a precipice, Lien eyes the dynamite in the bottom of the basket warily, knowing how volatile it is. Their hands cold, the men lowering her over the cliff with a rope are stopping and starting more than usual, and the jerking movements of the basket remind her of the seasickness on the voyage from Qwangtung to California. She closes her eyes and thinks of warm summer fields full of wildflowers. She thinks of hot, soothing tea and her mother's kind smile. She thinks of Bao's brown hand brushing hers so carelessly. She thinks of anything other than the dizzying height, the bone-numbing cold, the jerking rope, and the unstable explosives.

Finally, the jerking stops. She looks up at the lip of the cliff. A boy appears and gives her a hand signal. She signals back and scoots around in the basket so that she can slowly tip it towards the cliff wall. She braces with her feet and knees until she is perched perilously on the side of the basket. The woven reeds creak and groan beneath her weight.

She grabs the dynamite, heedless of the danger, ignoring the terrifying possibility that the basket might break beneath her. The cliff face is already defiled with the marks of an explosion and Lien shakes her head. Why would they blast the same place over and over again? She wants to cry, thinking of Fa and how her life will be wasted alongside his in this careless manner, but she marshals herself. The Chinese workers are no more valuable to their white masters than hammers or chisels – they are simply tools to do a job, interchangeable and replaceable. This is their fate – this is *her* fate.

Sighing, reluctantly resigned to her doom, she jams several dynamite sticks into the shallow crevasses of the cliff's face. Once they're secure, she lights a match on her teeth, presses the match to the wicks, and drops the match without watching its descent. She takes a deep breath and observes the flames' progress with the skill of experience; this is the part of blasting that requires finesse. Timing is everything.

She silently thanks Fa for his wisdom as the wicks burn faster than usual, spurred by the cold, dry air. She presses her feet flat against the stone and then pushes with all her strength, rolling backwards so the basket tips upright again, hopefully protecting her from the blast.

The hard, frozen stone refuses to give way to the dynamite, and the explosion has only one outlet. Instead of tunneling into the cliff, the blast explodes into the open air, pushing Lien's basket away from the cliff face. Above, the men gripping the rope struggle to maintain a hold on her lifeline, the explosion yanking the rope over the edge of the precipice with such force that they can't hold it for long. They cry out in dismay as the rope is torn from their protesting fingers, the pulley on the edge snapping under the pressure, the basket spinning away from the cliff and falling, taking Lien with it to the ground.

~

Lien dreams of women in bonnets and children in straw hats. She can't see their faces, and their voices are strange and muffled, so that no matter how much she strains to hear their words, the sounds remain elusive. They sit in the dark, clustered around a tiny fire. Around them, the night is an empty, starless void. They are small and vulnerable, and the children are shivering in their cotton clothes, but she can't find any blankets in the dark, and the women don't respond when she tries to tell them the children are cold. The figures and their fire seem to grow smaller and more indistinct. Then they are simply gone and Lien is alone in darkness.

She awakens to warmth and light, but above her is the starless void. She realizes gradually that she is not in her tent, on her cot; she is lying on hard, frozen earth, without a blanket, and her limbs are stiff with the cold. She tries to sit up and screams as pain sears through her head.

One of her legs is immobilized. In the dim firelight, she can see that it has been splinted with slender branches. It aches dully and attempting to move it results in a sharp, grinding pain that takes her breath away. She must have broken it in the fall, she muses, though her thoughts are hard to grasp, slippery as eels.

She wakes again later to more light and warmth, the fire having been fed and burning brightly. A few feet away, on the ground, she sees the shape of another person, lying prone. She slowly sits up, fighting pain in her head as she does, until she can make out some details.

"Fa?" She cries, recognizing the bruised face turned toward the fire. Fa's eyes are closed. Even though she calls his name several times, he does not wake. She fears for a moment that perhaps he's dead, but then sees that his chest is rising and falling with slow, even breaths. His right arm and right leg have both been splinted in the same manner as hers.

With the fire burning so brightly, Lien can at last make out her surroundings. She is ensconced in a cavern with vaulted ceilings so high they are hidden in shadow. She can't determine which way is the entrance; she licks a finger and raises it as high as she can, hoping to feel the chill breeze coming off the mountains, but the air is still.

Terrified and desperate, she tries to crawl around the fire to join Fa, hoping to find comfort beside her teacher. Constant pain sings in her head and every movement of her broken leg is excruciating. She is sobbing in agony by the time she reaches him. She grasps for one of his limp hands; unconsciousness swells up and over her and drags her down into darkness.

Again, Lien dreams, but this time, there is a pale man at her side, ministering to her injuries. He is mumbling in some foreign tongue, so quietly that she can barely make out the sounds. She tries to speak to him, but her words are only gibberish and he ignores her. She tries to make out his features, but they are indistinct; she can't determine the colour of his eyes or the shape of his mouth, no matter how intently she focuses.

When next she wakes, she is still beside Fa, but she is on her back, once again looking up at the ceiling shrouded in darkness. Beside them, the fire burns low and a copper tea kettle nestled in the flames is whistling, the shrill sound echoing in the massive cavern. Baffled, Lien looks about for the invisible caretaker who put the kettle on the fire. The cavern remains empty and mysterious, giving up none of its secrets.

Her head protesting the whistling, Lien crawls to the fire and snatches out the kettle, barely avoiding burning her fingers. A copper cup rests beside the fire ring and she fills it with boiling water from the kettle. The scent of coffee rises up with the steam and Lien grimaces; she despises the American drink. She is desperate enough to drink a few mouthfuls of the bitter brew, however, much as she detests the strong flavour.

Next, she pours coffee for Fa, and awkwardly – ignoring the burning in her head and the cramping in her leg – she raises the cup to his lips. She pours a little into his mouth, and he sputters and spits it out without waking. The second time, she is more successful and he drinks a little, smacking and pursing his lips in displeasure.

Exhausted, Lien drinks a little more coffee and then returns to her prone position beside Fa. Her stomach burbles hungrily and she wonders whether their mysterious benefactor will provide them with food. She feels, at least, less afraid and more hopeful, with warm drink in her belly. She drifts off into a dreamless sleep.

When she wakes again, she is cold. The fire has died down to mere coals, and a fierce breeze has entered the cavern and spoiled their warm hideaway, carrying with it a flurry of snow.

Lien thinks she hears voices and sits up, crying out wordlessly and then shouting, "Here! We're in here!" Her head feels as if it will split in two, so she collapses back to the dirt and remains silent, until the voices are louder and she can be sure she isn't imagining the sound. She calls again. This time, she receives a faint reply.

"Li? Li?"

Is that … Bao?! She sits up again and calls to him, then has to stop because the pain in her head is unbearable. Darkness threatens to take her into unconsciousness again, but she won't let it, not so close to rescue.

Finally, the voices are nearby, and she hears Bao saying, "Li? Li, is that you? You're alive!" He appears beside her, his brown face suffused with joy, his smile wider than she has ever seen it.

"And Fa, too," says another familiar voice: Foreman Storbridge, whose lumbering bulk appears behind Bao, looking down with disapproval at the injured workers. Several other workers, all Chinese, gather around him. They're wearing heavy furs and boots. Some carry lanterns and climbing ropes.

"I'm alive; someone's been taking care of us," Lien tells Bao. Tears stream from her eyes. "They made us a fire and put splints on our broken bones. And there was coffee." She casts about for the copper tea kettle with its matching cup, but both are gone.

Bao's expression is worried as he looks at her broken leg.

"Who did this?" he asks.

"I don't know," Lien says. She starts to shake her head, but has to stop because of the pain.

"I only remember a pale man. I must have been feverish; I don't remember much."

"It's good work," he confesses. "This stranger saved your life." Then he sighs and turns to her with earnestness sparkling in his black eyes. "I have to tell you; we thought you were dead. We came down here to look for a tunnel and collect your bodies."

"But we're not dead!" Lien declares.

"And it's truly a miracle!"

Storbridge says something gruffly to Bao, so low and rapid that Lien doesn't understand with her limited English. Bao replies; Storbridge walks away with a curt nod.

"We're going to set up camp here and explore these caverns," Bao explains. He gets up and goes to check on Fa, who remains unconscious, then returns to Lien. "I wish we knew who was taking care of you."

"I'm sure he'll return. He has to," Lien offers. Her stomach growls and she laughs. "Until then, do you have some food?"

The workers are experienced in setting up camp rapidly. Tents are erected, the fire stoked to a healthy blaze, and tea kettles set to whistling within the hour. Both Lien and Fa are fed, though Fa is still unconscious and is given primarily tea. Lien devours dried fish and fruit from Bao's rations, and gulps down hot tea while it's still boiling.

The Chinese workers sit near their injured brethren and listen to Lien describe the pale man who cared for her wounds. When she describes how she couldn't focus on his face and make out his features, they start murmuring. She hears the whispered word "demon".

"Stop being foolish," Bao chides the men. "We owe a debt of gratitude to this mysterious stranger, not whispered accusations."

"He saved my life!" Lien confirms.

But when the stranger doesn't return that evening, the murmurs grow and Lien catches suspicious glances from the other workers. She asks Bao to sleep beside her that night.

"I don't trust the others," she confesses.

Bao nods.

"They're superstitious because this is all so mysterious. We really weren't expecting to find you alive."

Something about his guilty expression makes Lien ask, "Exactly how long have we been down here?"

Bao swallows.

"Three days. That fall should have killed you, Li."

Lien's stomach churns. She thinks of the stories about demons and ghosts her parents told her as a girl and mutters a quick prayer to the ancestors.

"Can we set up a shrine?" she asks.

"That's a good idea. The others will be comforted by a shrine, as well. We don't have incense, but we can make do." Bao goes to tell the others, and they begin to construct a small, makeshift shrine with the items available in their packs and in the cave. They build it closest to Fa, who clearly needs the most help from the ancestors. Soon, small offerings of dried rations and tea are sitting before a chalk outline of the characters meaning "noble ancestors".

With Bao's help, Lien limps to the shrine, where she says a prayer and lays an offering of dried fish. She doesn't feel different as she returns to her position near the fire, but at least the other workers aren't glaring at her, anymore. She is able to sleep, though her leg throbs after the movement and wakes her many times during the night.

Once, she wakes and swears she sees movement near the shrine. She sits up and squints to see a figure hovering over Fa. She calls out to the figure, and it turns and disappears into the darkness. Beside her, Bao is deep in slumber, undisturbed by the noise, so Lien assumes that she must be dreaming and lies down again.

The second time, she wakes because something is prodding her broken leg and the pain rouses her. She looks down to see a hulking figure crouched by her leg: Storbridge, barely visible in the dying firelight.

"Stop that!" she cries and tries to pull away from him; she gasps with pain when she tries to move the throbbing limb.

Storbridge turns and regards her, eyes narrowed in suspicion. There is something dark and menacing about him. She doesn't like the way he looks at her, rather like a cat observing a bird with a broken wing. Lien reaches for Bao, but finds to her horror that his cot is empty.

"Your friend went to answer nature's call," Storbridge says, and though she doesn't understand all the words, Lien comprehends that Bao has stepped away, leaving her unprotected.

"Leave me alone," she warns him. She's trying to sound intimidating, but instead, she sounds mewling and womanish.

The huge foreman tilts his head and regards her with increased interest.

"There's something not right about you," he says, his voice low, speaking more to himself than to her.

"Go away," Lien says. She looks about for help; the other Chinese workers are safely in their tent, far from the fire, and Fa remains unconscious beside the shrine.

Was that movement she saw in the shadows behind the shrine?

"Help me!" Lien calls out in English. This time, her voice definitely gives her away; she has dropped all pretense and sounds like the woman she is.

Storbridge looms over her, his eyes fixed and unblinking. With shocking alacrity, he reaches down and tears at the blanket covering her. Lien screams as he rips open her tunic to reveal her chest; she tries to cover her small breasts with her arms, but her lie has been undone, the truth of her sex as obvious as her Chinese heritage.

Storbridge guffaws once, but then his shock turns rapidly to disbelief, as he remembers that Lien is a member of his crew, and then rage as he recalls how quickly and skillfully the Chinese workers blast new tunnels and lay new rails, putting his white workmen to shame. And here, all along, there was a woman hiding among them. Maybe there are others; maybe the little yellow men have made a fool of him all along.

Lien screams as the foreman rushes her with a growl. The fire suddenly dies and engulfs the cavern in blackness.

Lien covers her face, expecting to be beset at any moment, but she remains miraculously unmolested. Slowly, she uncovers her eyes and looks about; she can see nothing in the total darkness, but she can hear the sounds of combat: the smack of fists on flesh and the thud of someone heavy hitting the ground, the soft "oof" of someone being punched in the gut.

Then she hears Bao's footsteps, unmistakable to her after their months together and her growing infatuation, and she calls out to him, "Bao! Help me!"

Bao rushes over to her, his hands seeking her in the dark. She reaches for him and they embrace clumsily. When the fire suddenly flares to life again, they both look down to see that her bare breasts remain exposed, pressed against his chest, and she quickly pulls the torn tunic closed over them.

"You're ... you're ... a woman!" Bao stutters, backing away from her.

Lien won't look at him. She clutches the tunic closed.

"I thought you knew. *Xiong* figured it out."

Bao looks down to see the foreman beside him, on the ground, so bruised and battered that his face is barely recognizable. One of his arms hangs limp from the socket, twisted underneath his torso at an unnatural angle.

"What happened?" Bao asks, looking at her accusingly.

"You really think I could do that? To *Xiong*?" she asks.

Bao looks at the man on the ground – who groans softly and gurgles some blood onto the cave floor – and shakes his head.

"I don't know. You're ... you're ...."

"Female, but not a demon – not strong enough to do *that*." Lien gestures to the crumpled body of the Foreman. Tears rise to her eyes as she says, "After all this time together, you really think I'm capable of that?"

Bao starts to say something in retort, but the other workers come rushing out of the tent just then, pulling on their boots, stalling his words. The men rush over to the Foreman, taking in the scene with expressions of shock and horror, and then glance at Lien. The tableau of her sitting helpless on her cot tells them a story. She holds her shirt closed with shaking hands, her face averted in shame.

The men all look to Bao, their eyes seeking. Lien knows that Bao holds her future in his rough brown hands; with a word, he can condemn her or save her. Finally, without looking at her again, he sighs and says, "Help me," and lifts the Foreman's ankles.

"What are you doing?" Lien demands as the workers gather up Storbridge and begin shuffling toward the cave entrance.

"If he lives, you'll never be safe again, Li – if that is your name," Bao says.

When the men return from dumping Storbridge's body in the snow, the others go to their cots in the tent and Bao feeds the fire. He makes sure Fa has slept through the adventure, and then he returns to sit beside Lien, in a meditative pose, saying nothing.

"Lien," she says softly.

He looks at her, his eyes searching her face for the truth.

"My real name is 'Lien'," she repeats. "My parents called me 'Li' and pretended I was a boy, because I was their only child. I left to get away from them, but I don't know how to be a woman, so I stayed Li even when I came over the ocean."

"Did you kill *Xiong*?" Bao asks.

"No."

"Then who did?"

"I don't know," she insists and begins sobbing uncontrollably. Her careful house of lies has been demolished. Without her secrets, she feels exposed and afraid. And now her closest friend, the man she thinks she might love, can't trust her and thinks she committed murder. "He attacked me," she tries to explain.

To her surprise, Bao places a hand on her knee and pats it comfortingly. "I believe you. But if you didn't kill him, who did?"

"He's dead?" she asks.

Bao nods.

"His neck was broken. He died while we carried him outside. Unless you truly are a demon, you don't have the strength to kill a man like that. So, I believe you, because even if you aren't the man you claimed to be, I can't believe that you're a demon."

Lien hugs him in relief, tears flowing even more freely now. "I don't know … what happened … the fire died …," she says, through sobbing hiccoughs.

Bao lets her cling to him. "Did you see what happened?"

She shakes her head against his chest.

"The white men say this place is haunted."

Lien looks up at him.

"They do?"

"A lot of the white men didn't want to come here. About twenty years ago, some settlers moving west were trapped in this valley during the winter. They all died. The survivors … they ate their dead. They're cursed people, now, and Donner Valley is cursed by their memory."

Lien shudders, remembering the women and children huddled around the tiny fire. Were these the victims of the hungry, wives and children devoured by their fathers and husbands?

"How horrible," she whispers, her dreams taking on sudden dark import.

Bao holds her close and strokes her hair.

"But not all ghosts are evil," he says, staring out into the dark of the cavern, unafraid. "Some are just waiting."

~

The sun rises to find the group of Chinese rail workers already on foot, making their way slowly up the ravine to the mountain. The small group of eight men takes turns carrying the two invalids, both of them fortunately small and hardly burdensome. In the evening, they make camp on a rocky promontory, overlooking the valley. One of them, the smallest, who has a broken leg, limps out of the tent at sunset to watch the glorious colours retreating in the sky as night settles over the ravine.

The others now know Lien's secret, but they've sworn to keep it as best they can. She knows it won't remain secret for much longer – if Shen finds out, word will be all over camp faster than a swallow flies. As she watches the sun set, she thinks with dread of returning to the camp and lying about the fate of Storbridge. But what is the truth? What difference does it make whether he fell from a cliff wall or was pummeled to death by ghostly hands?

When darkness slides across the landscape, she retreats to her cot in the tent beside the other men. They sit in awkward silence, unsure how to behave now that her secret has been laid bare. She asks that they leave a lamp lit, even when they sleep; the darkness is unbearable for her now. She swears that she can hear Storbridge's husky breathing, or the soft murmurings of the pale doctor who bandaged her wounds. Even years later, married to Foreman Bao and mother to his children, she will not sleep without a lantern's glow or a stoked fire. She does not want to dream of the faceless, bonneted women and their strange children, or remember the frozen nights spent in that mysterious cavern.

But when the winter nights are bone-numbingly cold, her healed leg aches with remembered pain, and her dreams are dark and haunted.

Sarah Hans is a Buddhist, steampunk, and horror writer. Her work is appearing in several anthologies this year, including *Historical Lovecraft* and *The Crimson Pact: Volume 1*. You can read more of her work, and follow her adventures aboard The Airship Archon, at her website: http://sarahhans.com/

The Forgotten Ones

By Mary Cook

Come and see us now, Mother; this is where we lie
In this dank and distant place with not a glimpse of sky.
Fasten back the turf, Mother, like the man next door
When he dug this grisly grave for when we breathed no more.
He gave us sweets and shiny things – said we mustn't tell.
The doorway to his ghastly house became the mouth of Hell.
This is how we sleep, Mother; neat as in our beds
But now our bones are white and bare, with only skulls for heads.
Don't you feel some shred of guilt, some tiny prick of pain?
The two of us were led away and never seen again.
Look upon us now, Mother; this is where we lie
Since you let our wicked neighbour bring us here to die.

Mary Cook is a UK-based writer and editor whose articles, short stories and poems have appeared in numerous publications, both in print and online. Her main writing interests are humour, horror, and the writing craft. Her collection of humourous horror poetry, *Collywobblers – Perverse Verse for Guys and Ghouls*, is available at Inkspotter Publishing: http://inkspotter.com/bookstore/index.htm.

Nine Nights

By T. S. Bazelli

Marianne opened her mouth, but no breath escaped. Something pressed against her chest, drove out the air so that she could not scream. She fought to raise her sweat-bathed arms, but they rested on the white sheets like lead. If anyone walked by, they would never notice anything was wrong. Marianne fought, voiceless, sucking up the darkness and choking on it like water. Scissors gleamed in the moonlight.

"My Lovely Marianne." A whisper of a voice, vaguely female, amused. *Snip.*

The girl had dark eyes, dark skin, and dark hair, like her own, but the girl was too thin, too hungry, too short. Marianne knew she must still be dreaming. She fought to wake, her eyes blurring over as she sought air and screamed.

It was a hollow, faraway sound, but at once, humid air flooded into her lungs, smelling of citronella, fried fish and decay.

Marianne kicked the blankets and mosquito net away. *It was just a nightmare*, she breathed, slowing her heartbeat. Who would not have nightmares when there was a coffin in the living room?

She did not feel at home in her grandparents' house, in the Philippine heat. She'd grown up in Canada, beneath cool, rainy skies. Even at 14, she was too tall, too pale, too fat, compared to the tiny women in her family. She scratched at her legs, drawing blood, as the itch of a hundred mosquito bites flared up again. Marianne wanted to go home, but she couldn't. It was the dead girl's fault.

Her mouth burned and her head ached. She needed water. She stumbled downstairs in her pajamas, vaguely aware of the sound of a guitar strumming and the smell of cigarettes.

There were still three days until the funeral. Until then, there was always someone awake with the body. There was no avoiding it. Marianne had to walk past the coffin to get to the kitchen. Aunties congregated around empty plates of food, staring at her as she walked past.

Marianne kept her eyes on the table. There were only a few egg rolls, pieces of chicken, rice, bits of glassy noodles stuck to a metal serving dish,

a few bits of roasted pork. In the morning, the containers would be full
again, and more people would come.

Her father looked up from the couch where he sat with her grandfather. They were both dressed head-to-toe in black, despite the tropical heat. It did not seem right. Her father's eyes were red, as if he'd been
crying. She'd never seen him cry. Marianne couldn't cry for the girl in the
glass coffin, whom she knew nothing about. She'd come for the white sand
beaches, palm trees and coconuts, not for this.

One of the older women stopped her as she passed. She had no choice
but to smile, and take the old woman's hand and press it up to her forehead respectfully for a blessing.

"*Kumusta, po,*" Marianne said in Tagalog. Her accent grated on her
ears.

"What is your name?"

"Marianne, *po.*" That was how you addressed your elders, she
remembered.

"So pretty." The old woman patted her cheek. "You look like your
cousin Carmelita."

It came back to the girl in the coffin, as always.

"She was such a smart girl. She wanted to be a doctor, but her parents
couldn't afford to send her. It's so sad ...."

Marianne mumbled an excuse, slipped away, knowing she'd probably
offended the woman. She walked over to the fridge and grabbed a cool
bottle of water.

She stared at the water-stained ceiling as she drank. White paint
flaked away in places. The shadows of moths were silhouetted in the light
fixture. More fluttered about, coming in and out as people walked in and
out of the house. There would be no sleep in the house until the body was
laid to rest.

The family watched over the body in shifts. It was a blur of faces and
smiles. Marianne tried to remember the names and faces of all the relatives she had never met. It seemed her family was related to everyone in
the town.

A lizard skittered across the wall. The movement caught her attention.
She watched it climb over into the next room and she followed.

She shut her eyes as she passed the glass coffin, but she couldn't erase
the memory of the girl's face. The girl wore a borrowed white dress, edged
in lace. In her mind's eye, she saw the girl open her eyes and grin at her.

Marianne felt the edge of the coffin scratch against her bare arm. She gasped and nearly knocked over a candle.

In the coffin, not the dream, Carmelita's eyes were shut, as if she were sleeping. Marianne ran out the door and into the next room.

It was a big house, bigger than any she'd lived in, back in Canada. It was an old colonial-style mansion, left over from Spanish times. The Padilla family had been important people once, but the house had not been maintained. Some of the old stonework was crumbling and blackened with pollution. But Carmelita's family was poorer yet, so her grandparents had offered to let them hold the wake in their house.

In this room, an old piano leaned against the wall, scratched with years of misuse, by cousin upon cousin. The chandelier was dull brass. She tried the light switch, but the bulb burnt out in a blast of light, leaving her in darkness. Despite the humidity, the heat, she shivered, as if a cold breeze filtered past her.

Someone stared at her from across the room. She froze, looking into a face so similar to her own. She could not move. She thought her heart went still.

"What are you doing here in the dark, *anak?*"

The elder lady, the house help, flicked on the light switch. It turned on without a fuss, in an electric hiss. Marianne let out a breath, staring at the mirror. It had just been a reflection.

"Nothing, *po.*"

"Carmelita loved to play the piano. She would sit here for hours. Do you play?"

"No."

"Call me 'Yaya'. Your father used to call me that when he was a boy." She smiled. "Oh, what a terrible boy he was."

Yaya patted her cheek, then frowned, as she put her hand to Marianne's forehead. "You are burning up. Fever. Come, you'd better lie down."

Marianne stared at the mirror, transfixed by the reflection lit by the electric light, and the moon. Her skin seemed too pale, a shade of death. Her hair seemed uneven on one end, as if …

She trembled, as she stumbled back past the body, and collapsed onto the floor.

〜

Marianne rolled out of her bed, wiping the sweat off her neck with cold fingers. Her head still throbbed and she wondered how long she'd been sleeping. As she put her feet onto the wooden floor, a cockroach swept past her toes, into the darkness under the bed. She let out a little shriek, before shaking out her slippers, and sliding her feet in only after inspecting the insides.

There was the sound of chanting, as she walked downstairs, using the worn wooden banister to steady herself. Her legs felt like jelly. Talk picked up louder, as she entered the living room, and people were dispersing, rosaries in hand. The tables were piled up with food again, but there were fewer people and the coffin was missing.

"*Ate*, Marianne?"

A young boy in a baseball cap and a young girl in a floral dress came up to her, hesitant. Marianne searched through her memory to recall names and faces, but she couldn't.

"Yes?" she replied, aware she was dressed in pajamas, while everyone else was in black or white.

"Can you finish the scary story you started to tell us at the *libingan*?" The boy searched for the word in English. "Funeral."

Marianne frowned. "The funeral?"

"Yesterday. I can't sleep until I find out what happened!"

Marianne's mind was blank.

"I'm sorry. I don't feel so well. I need to find my mom and dad." Marianne walked fast, trying to avoid everyone as she wound through the mourners. She heard her parents' voices out in the yard.

Marianne paused at the screen door because her mother was yelling. She could see their silhouettes, against the concrete wall, away from the florescent lights of the house. Her father tossed a cigarette onto the dirt and rubbed it into the ground with his feet. He'd given up smoking years ago.

Her mother stormed towards the house. Her cheeks were red with anger.

"You should have told me," she said, as she flung open the door, and stopped just before crashing into Marianne.

"Oh, Marianne, are you feeling better, dear?" She placed a hand on Marianne's forehead, patted her back, but glanced over her shoulder at her husband's hunched form in the yard. "The fever's gone."

"Mom, how long have I been in bed?"

"You were well enough to go to the funeral. You seemed fine, yesterday."

"We already had the funeral?"

"The medication must have been too strong." Her mother frowned. "You don't remember?"

Marianne shook her head.

"Go back to bed, dear. You look so pale. Get some rest."

"When can we leave, Mom?"

"Not until the nine-day novena for the dead has finished. If you're well enough, after then, we can still go to the beach."

Nine more days of food and family. Her mother walked away.

Marianne felt a chill in her chest, as if she'd been stabbed with an icicle. Her heart stopped beating for a moment and she grasped at the walls to steady herself. She looked around the room, to call for help, to say something, but no one was looking in her direction. As abruptly as the feeling came, she felt fine again.

Marianne walked back to the children.

"What kind of story did I tell you?" she asked, but the children did not seem to hear. They ran past her after a black-winged moth.

Yaya looked straight at her, eyebrows crossed together. She was not a relative but her father's one-time nursemaid. Her brown skin was wrinkled, her hair white. A cockroach ran over Yaya's feet, and the old woman crushed it with the heel of her slipper.

~

The mosquito bites stopped itching. Her head was clear for the first time in days, but outside, the sky was dark and rain drenched the house in sheets. Wind rattled the balcony door and water dripped down into a pool in the middle of the hardwood floor. She paused, trying to listen for people downstairs, but it was quiet. The window shutters slapped shut, leaving her in the dark for a moment.

She panicked, as the dream of nights before came back, but a moment later, the light returned and she let out a breath. Fever and nightmares, nothing more, she tried to remind herself.

She could see the light in the kitchen from the stairwell. She could smell garlic rice and sausages. Breakfast smells. She couldn't remember the last time she'd eaten, but neither did she feel hungry. She made her way down the steps, oddly light. The heat was bearable for the first time. It was all very odd.

She walked into the kitchen, but no one looked up from their meal. Yaya was at the sink, washing out a pan. Marianne realized then that it must be a dream. She saw Carmelita seated at the table, cutting the sausages with a dull knife, spooning rice and some tomatoes into her mouth.

"I can't wait to go home, Mom." The girl at the table smiled.

"I thought you wanted to go to the beach, Marianne."

"But I can't swim," Carmelita replied.

"All those lessons and you've forgotten? You can't just forget …."

"I mean, it's been a while." Carmelita laughed.

Marianne felt her blood freeze over. She walked up to the table and cleared her throat, but no one turned in her direction. She slammed a fist against the table. A glass of water vibrated. Nothing more. Not even a glance from her mother or father.

"Mom, Dad!" Marianne waved her hands in front of their faces.

Her father continued to flip through the channels on the TV from his chair. Yaya dropped the pan in the sink and turned away, apologizing, scrubbing frantically.

"That's not me," Marianne breathed.

"Do we really need to stay for all nine days? It's not like Carmelita was that close. She was just a cousin."

Her father set down the remote, his eyes bloodshot still. "She's still family."

Carmelita frowned, as she shoved more sausage into her mouth. Her mother winced, looked away from her father.

Marianne pushed at the chair, but though she could feel the cold metal beneath her fingers, it did not move. She swung at the pitcher of water on the table, but glass did not shatter.

"Why can't you see me?" she shouted, her eyes filling with tears.

The room began to swarm with cockroaches and moths and lizards. They crept in through the cracks in the windowsills, up through the pipes in the sink, beneath the door to the rear of the house, filling the kitchen.

Her mother screamed and Yaya crushed a few cockroaches with her pan. Her father jumped up onto the couch.

"What's going on?!" They began to huddle together, everyone except Marianne and the girl who wanted to steal her life.

"I think it's the storm. They're just trying to get out of the rain …."

Her mom squealed as she swatted away the insects from her legs.

Carmelita caught Marianne by the wrist. She stared into her eyes. *So, she can see me*, Marianne thought, triumphant for a moment.

"Begone, little ghost." Carmelita said, digging a nail into Marianne's wrist. Marianne shrieked as a drop of her blood dripped onto the tile floor.

The insects rushed away as if it were poison. Carmelita smiled, open-mouthed, and Marianne thought she saw two yellow eyes staring back from inside the girl's mouth.

The world went dark.

~

Marianne tossed the mosquito net aside and ran out of the bedroom. Outside, the moon was shining again. The storm had gone and she did not know how many days had passed. She could hear her parents in the next room and ran to find them. Her father's hands were balled into fists. Her mother's cheeks were red again.

Marianne walked into the room between them. They stepped away from Marianne, so that they were still facing each other, as if to ignore her. She wanted to shout, to get their attention, but she was afraid that Carmelita would hear her. The lights in the room flickered and her parents both looked up for a moment.

"We should leave, Renee. Have you seen how upset Marianne is? This is all too much for her."

"I said no. Carmelita was my daughter, too. I can't abandon her now."

"What difference does it make? You ignored her for 17 years and now she's dead. You never told me. I know you feel guilty, but what about me, Renee? What about Marianne? You never told me you had another daughter. You have no right to make us suffer for what you did."

"It wasn't right." Her father was near tears.

Marianne had never seen her parents cry.

"If I had sponsored her to come to Canada, she could have had better medical treatment. She might never have died. I should have never have left her behind."

Marianne stepped back out the door. She had a sister. She stumbled back against the wall and a lizard ran up it, a black streak. She'd always hated being an only child. She felt numb. Carmelita was her sister.

She hates me, she realized, remembering the look in Carmelita's eyes at the kitchen table. *She wants my life.* Marianne shivered, pressed up against the wall. She sucked in her breath and walked down the steps. They creaked beneath her feet. She saw Yaya look up, rosary in hand. Their eyes met for a moment and she looked away as she walked straight towards the kitchen.

Marianne saw Carmelita seated with the two children, huddled together as if to tell a story.

Marianne ran past. Carmelita could see her, when everyone else could not, but there was someone else who could see her, too. She raced into the kitchen, heart pounding. The crowd parted to let her past, but no one looked at her. It was as if she were invisible. She walked up to Yaya and placed a hand on her shoulder.

The old woman shivered and adjusted her dress. She turned her back to Marianne and walked out of the kitchen to the piano room. Marianne followed.

"Yaya, I don't know if you can hear me, but I know you can see me. Please, help me." Marianne slammed her hands against the piano. The keys rang loud and off tune.

Yaya shut the door.

"I'm not a ghost. Please," Marianne pleaded, but she could not feel the tears sliding down her cheek. "Carmelita's stolen my life. Please help me. What is this? What's happening?"

Yaya crossed herself and kissed the cross on her rosary.

"*Mangkukulam.*" Yaya looked at her in the eye, but did not go any closer.

Marianne searched for the meaning. Witchcraft?

"Come, *anak*, do not let her see you. She will try to leave before the nine days is over. You cannot let her."

She opened the door and light flooded back into the dark piano room. She walked straight through the kitchen, the back door, and out the gate into the streets of the town. There were people out, playing card games under florescent lights.

Marianne caught up to the old woman in the street. Yaya was careful not to touch her. She walked a few feet away and did not look at her. Her slippers clacked against the street.

The moon was bright enough to see by, as they moved away from the main road, towards the church. The face was in shadows, ornate and baroque, blackened windows. Marianne felt as if people were watching her from the shadows, but she could see nothing. They kept going until they reached the concrete wall of the cemetery.

The cemetery was not large, but it was full. There was no green, only concrete. Some graves were marked by slabs on the ground, but others were stacked in layers. In between, several larger mausoleums were scattered around. Old bones flashed white in the moonlight.

Marianne stepped back and away from the wilted flowers and graves, keeping to the middle of the narrow path. They walked towards a concrete mausoleum. The door was made of iron bars and, inside, three concrete graves. Her great-grandparents were buried there, Marianne thought. The third ... she shuddered as Yaya tried the door. It swung open noisily.

A dog growled, appearing behind them. Dark fur, yellow eyes, its shoulders hunched low. Marianne saw other dogs moving between the graves.

Yaya held out a hand, said a word and flicked her fingers. The dogs disappeared with a whimper, melting back into the shadows.

"Help me if you can," Yaya said, as she knelt down slowly in front of the newest grave, her knees clicking with the strain. Marianne pushed against the slab. It opened a fraction.

There were growls from outside. Marianne looked back, hoping the bars would keep the dogs out. She and Yaya kept pushing until the slab was free. Yaya started digging through the coffin. Marianne stared at the girl inside. It was her face that stared back. Carmelita looked as if she were still sleeping. Her body had not yet begun to decay. Her mouth was partly open. Her eyes closed.

Yaya pulled something out from under the pillow beneath the body's head. It was a rag doll made of black cloth, a dark ribbon tied around its waist, holding several clippings of hair close to the doll's body.

Marianne knew whose hair it was.

"How do you ... Who was Carmelita's mother?" Marianne stepped back, seeing, only then, the resemblance between the dead girl and the old woman. Yaya said nothing, as a snake pushed its way out from between the dead girl's lips. Marianne thought she might be sick.

"Close it!" They both shoved at the slab, knocking it back into place, sweating and panting, both. Yaya rubbed at her back, but her other hand still gripped the doll. She walked right out of the mausoleum and Marianne walked after her.

A woman stood there, with long, dark hair, pale skin, almond eyes. Marianne did not recognize her. She scratched at the head of a black dog with long fingernails. Her dress was too large, the flesh on her arms too loose. She looked as if she had been beautiful once. Her eyes were as yellow as the dog's.

"Traitor," she hissed at Yaya. "You always treated the Padilla family better than your own flesh and blood, Mama. Why are you helping that spoiled, fat, coddled child? Her worthless father should never have left Carmelita here. I begged him to take her, but he refused. He gave his new family everything and left us with nothing. Don't you want your granddaughter to have what she should have?"

Clouds hid the moon as the wind began to whip against Marianne's cheeks. The first drop of warm rain hissed down from the sky, hot as blood.

Yaya stepped forwards, blocking Marianne's path. "Not this way. It is not right, you devil girl." Yaya took a small knife out of her pocket.

The madwoman yelled and jumped at her mother, grabbing at the knife. The doll went tumbling. Metal fell onto the ground.

There was a hiss. Cockroaches, lizards and moths began to come out of cracks between the tombstones, pouring over the wall like a dark wave, even as the rain began to drench them.

Marianne ran for the knife, feeling around the slick earth for the blade. It pricked her hand as she grabbed for it through a pile of legs and wings, and biting, scratching mouths.

The two women struggled in front of her, swallowed up by the insect horde.

Marianne plucked the damp doll off the wet dirt and cut the ribbon that bound it around the waist. Dark locks of hair fell into the puddles and Marianne screamed. The insects blotted out the light.

~

Marianne scratched at her leg and blinked awake. The room was full of sunlight. It lit the mosquito net like a cathedral. She jumped out of bed.

She found her parents in the kitchen with her grandparents.

"Where's Yaya?" She asked.

"We haven't seen her, today, Marianne. Why?"

Marianne began to run down the street, past the church, towards the cemetery, remembering the way in the daylight.

Mourners had come to visit, bringing flowers, tidying their loved ones' graves. They looked up at the tall, Canadian-born girl who raced into the cemetery towards the Padilla mausoleum.

She pulled at the door, but it was locked, shut tight with a padlock. She searched through the cemetery and nearly tripped on the body of the old woman, slumped between two concrete graves.

Clutched to Yaya's chest was a black rag doll, a ribbon hanging off of it. A few scattered hairs were caught in the folds of the rags. Marianne tucked the doll in her waistband, beneath the loose top of her shirt.

Her parents found her there, sobbing beside the body. Someone ran to find the doctor and the police, but she knew there was nothing anyone could do.

"I want to go home, Mom, Dad." She cried. "I don't care about the beaches. Can we go home, please? We don't have to stay for all nine days, do we?"

Her father looked pale. "No, let's go home. It's enough."

Back at the house, her sorrow and guilt abated. Marianne re-tied the ribbon around the doll's waist, looped a hair between it, and smiled. All fixed again. She spat a frog out of her mouth and packed it in her suitcase, just in case.

T. S. Bazelli is a writer from Vancouver, Canada. By day, she writes software manuals and by night, she writes speculative fiction.

Vodka Attack!

By Meddy Ligner

Early 1942, Somewhere on the Eastern Front

As he emerged abruptly from the enveloping fog, the building he was searching for finally appeared in front of him. It seemed to be an old factory with grey walls, half-destroyed and turned into a field hospital for the occasion. In the distance, he heard the cannon thunder. The cold and snow froze his bones, as he increased his pace to get away from them.

Once inside, Captain Piotr Simonov received a shock. Before him was a chaos of torn flesh, bloodstained linens, bits of torn skin. Chloroform and the sharp odour of medications mixed with sweat and grime, while moans and atrocious complaints resonated in the immense room. On camp beds, hundreds of eyes, wherein death danced, observed him. Somehow, the visitor slipped past the deformed bodies and finally collared a nurse who was wandering around the vicinity.

– Tell me, Comrade! Where can I find Dr. Yuri Iliev?

– At the end. In the operating theatre.

Simonov headed in the direction indicated and and finally arrived in front of an old office equipped as an operating room. On the heavy metal door hung a red sign, where was written, "Do not enter. Operation in progress." It was necessary that he be patient a little longer before reuniting with his old friend Yuri.

While waiting, the officer leaned against the decrepit wall. There, an unfortunate who was missing one eye handed him a copy of the evening edition of *The Red Star*: the journal of the *frontoviki* – the soldiers on the Front who defended the Motherland against the Fascist hordes.

Simonov accepted the gift and flipped through the pages, smeared with mud and some bloodstains.

As usual, the news was generally good. In the various articles, bad news was everywhere restrained, nay, rejected. Under orders of the genius Comrade Stalin, the glorious Red Army would begin the counteroffensive, which would permit them to continue until Berlin, in order to kick dear Adolph Hitler's ass.

Of course, all this was only propaganda. Aided by experience, Simonov knew how to read between the lines. Even if the situation was no more catastrophic than at the beginning of the hostilities, the war was far from won. Because the Germans were still occupying Soviet soil and committing atrocities there. Simonov recalled a young Muscovite student of the name of "Zoya Kosmodemianskaia". The young partisan had been arrested, tortured and executed in the province of Tambov. Before the Fascists had hanged her in the main square of the village, she cried, "You can never hang all of us! My comrades will avenge me!" The officer remembered a photo of the young woman, of her dead body, half-naked, lying in the snow. This shot had made her an icon of the regime that had received the posthumous medal of Hero of the Soviet Union.

The slamming of the door drew Simonov out of his thoughts. Immediately, he recognized his old friend, Yuri.

– Piotr! What a surprise! What are you doing here? cried the doctor.

– My company has been sent into this sector and I knew that you worked around here. I took advantage of my day off to come see you ... And you? How are you?

– Each day, I must butcher these poor devils, said he, referring to the patients, who were lying on the floor. And as you can see, the conditions are more than precarious. We work without stop, in urgency, with few means. But follow me; we'll go into my office. We'll be more comfortable there.

When they finally arrived in his office, Iliev removed his shirt soiled with blood. Then he washed his hands, sat facing his friend and invited him to do the same.

– Here, at least, one can talk undisturbed.

– You have something to hide?

– Not particularly, but I prefer to keep the commissars of the NKVD[1] at a good distance. Here, one can easily fall afoul of them. Those shits track down any they call "deserters by injury". Once they have a doubt, when they suspect self-injury, they execute the man in question under the pretext that he has betrayed the nation. They are always on our backs,

---

1   The secret police of the USSR, who purged the Soviet Army repeatedly through the 30s and 40s.

digging ... No counting the number that can always swing should they be considered *deviants* ... So, that's the routine! And you? How goes it with you?

– Nothing original. The war.

As the conversation prepared to turn to another subject, the door to the office opened abruptly. A man with Asiatic features entered the place.

– Hello, Ruslan! exclaimed Iliev. Let me introduce to you my old friend, Piotr Alexeievitch Simonov. We were born in the same village. Our families were very close and we went to school, together ... Peter, this is Ruslan Solotin.

– Hello, and welcome to our field hospital, responded the latter. I share the office with Yuri. But I don't want to disturb your reunion. I have two or three things to do and then I'll leave you alone.

– No, of course not, Ruslan! You're not disturbing us. Do what you have to do, no worries! insisted Iliev. Can I get you a little vodka? In the name of friendship!

– You musn't refuse, said Simonov, smiling.

– Ruslan?

– Maybe later, thanks!

And the man went into the back of the room to let them go about their business. Iliev revised the conversation.

– And since the Battle of Moscow, where have you fought?

– I was assigned to a new artillery unit on the central front. We pounded Fritz relentlessly, hoping soon to be sent home. But, as you know, the situation is far from well-regulated. The Fascists are still besieging Leningrad, and it is murmured that they're preparing a vast offensive to the South come spring, and ... and ....

– And what? asked Iliev, who was listening.

– And ... but what is your colleague doing? asked Simonov in a deep voice.

Iliev turned toward his colleague and called:

– Hey, Ruslan, can you explain to my friend what you're in the process of fucking up?

– I'm lighting a variety of candles. And here is a small altar dedicated to our gods, Ruslan explained, showing them the object.

– Though he had received a perfectly good Soviet education, Ruslan continues his shamanistic practices, Iliev explained. Like all Buryats.[2]

– Exactly. Where we live, in far-off Siberia, there is a sort of communion between the spirits of the taiga and men.

– You are a shaman? asked Simonov.

– Yes, for seven generations. For my people, shamans are, at the same time, priest, doctor and mage … We have the power to communication with the spirits and the divinities, to whom we make offerings: food or vodka, for example … This drink is very prized by Those who live Beyond our World ….

Simonov was taken aback by what he had just heard. For him, Siberia represented the hell of the camps.[3] Many people of his acquaintance still languished there. Yet, in this vast country, lived mysterious peoples who fascinated him. He wanted to ask for more details, but suddenly, someone knocked on the door.

– Yes, enter! ordered Iliev.

A tall, strapping man, wheat-blonde, saluted his superior and presented his request without losing a second.

– Comrade, we've made prisoner a German soldier. He is wounded. I just had to hold back my men from killing him. He needs medical attention.

– Very good, Sergeant. Put him in the operating room. I'll arrive at once.

– I didn't know that you helped even the *Fritzes*! laughed Simonov.

– A doctor occupies himself with helping the whole world. And also, contrary to what our superiors would have us believe, they are not all brutes. Here, come with me in lieu of aggravating me … Ruslan, what are you doing?

– I'm coming with you, responded the Siberian.

When the trio approached the prisoner, they immediately noticed that the German was terrified. Iliev leaned over him and observed him with great attention. He decided that the injury had caused significant damage. His verdict was without appeal.

---

2   A semi-nomadic Mongolian group of tribes from southeastern Siberia. They are the largest surviving Siberian ethnic minority. The actor Yul Brynner was Buryat.

3   The Gulag prison system made famous by Alexandr Solzhenitsyn.

– He needs a blood transfusion, without which he'll croak. Piotr, you can jabber in German, no? You can explain the situation to him?

– I can try, Simonov replied nonchalantly.

Simonov had always appreciated the language of Goethe. While he was a student, he had taught at the University of Leningrad. He was then far from imagining under what circumstances it would serve him … At that time, the war seemed so far away.

He approached the wounded man and began to explain to him what it would be necessary to do to save him. With a visage pimply and hairless, the other had the look of a kid having barely left adolescence. In his grey uniform of the Wehrmacht, he gave the impression of being in disguise. He listened attentively to what Simonov told him. As the Soviet officer spoke to him, he lost his composure. In response, he cried, eyes rolling:

– *Nein, nein!*

Simonov tried to calm him, insisting on the gravity of the situation, but nothing helped.

– He categorically refuses any blood transfusion. He doesn't want Slavic blood. He doesn't want the blood of an *untermenschen* – a 'subhuman', as the Nazis designate us. This man has been brainwashed by the propaganda of Goebbels.

– If he doesn't undergo the transfusion, he'll die within two or three hours, said Iliev.

– I've explained all that to him. He doesn't want to hear any of it.

– Ah, well, then, he's dead. We're not going to waste any time on this kind of fool … Leave him.

– Wait! I want to try something, cried Solotin.

– What do you want to do? asked Iliev.

– A sort of experience. Wait for me. I'm going to my office to find something that I need.

With these words, the Buryat left the room like lightning. Iliev and Simonov stayed with the wounded man, who weakened with the passing minutes. His voice became less and less audible and his strength progressively abandoned him. He finally lost consciousness.

– He still lives, but he won't for much longer, Iliev said.

– And your colleague? He wanted to try what, exactly?

– No idea. You know, with that kind of guy, we can expect any … The Buryats don't think like us. They don't have the same cultural references. But wait; here he comes.

In the same fashion that he had gone out, Ruslan burst into the room. In each hand, he carried a bottle of vodka. Around his neck hung an animal-skin bag.

– And what are you going to do with all this alcohol? asked Iliev, who was beginning to worry.

– Don't be uneasy, Yuri. I repeat that this is a simple experiment. In any case, this man is condemned. And anyway, he is a Fascist bastard, no?

– All right. As you wish … Do you have need of us?

– No, but you can stay here if you want. Move away and let me be.

The two witnesses did just that and sat on stools that were situated in the back of the room. From there, intrigued, they observed the merry-go-round of the Siberian: He deposited the first two bottles next to the German then poured a part of their contents into a graduated cylinder connected to operating tubes. He also prepared the vials and the syringes. Iliev understood, then, that his colleague was about to effect a transfusion in defiance of all medical ethics.

– But … you want to inject him with vodka? My word! he exclaimed.

– Yes, but that is not all. Have a little patience.

– I hope you know what you're doing, Comrade ….

The Buryat did not flinch at this warning. He continued his preparations with seriousness and precaution. Iliev and Simonov attended the scene with apprehension, asking themselves what was going on in the head of the Siberian.

The latter took out his little altar, which he placed on the operating table. He added a small ceramic cup, into which he poured a little vodka. He then lit two candles and a stick of incense. With his two hands, he delicately fanned the grey smoke toward his face, which shone with a sort of ancestral bliss.

The Siberian closed his eyes. While grey vapours enveloped his weather-beaten face, he reached into his sack and extracted a small drum with white skin.[4] Without warning, he began to strike it sharply, at regular

---

4   The signature instrument of the Siberian shaman. The NKVD murdered shamans throughout Siberia during the 20s and 30s, taking special care to confiscate and burn their drums.

intervals, launching a strange litany. He chanted prayers that, for Iliev and Simonov, went back to the dawn of time. The words of the shaman were to them incomprehensible, though Simonov thought they were addressed to obscure Siberian divinities. There, in that far country, on the banks of the great Lake Baikal, spirits had certainly begun a great dance. Before this spectacle of another age, the two men were struck dumb, unable to move and interrupt their comrade in his enigmatic ceremony.

When he had finished his recital, Solotin got up and poured the vodka on the floor. On tiptoe, he returned to the wounded man and, suddenly, stuck a needle in his bruised arm. The vodka began to invade the body of the Teuton. Iliev dared not flinch, but he knew that the experiment was going to be cut short, that without a doubt, the German would kick the bucket in a minute or two! His blood would be poisoned by *Product 61*, the name given to the vodka brand by the Soviet soldiers because of the rank it occupied in the list of articles with which they were furnished. A product of the first necessity, which permitted the combatants to withstand the hell of war.

At first, the *Fritz* did not move. Then, after a few minutes, came some slight convulsions and, once the vodka had inundated his entire being, there were violent spasms that shook the unfortunate man. He began to bellow like a madman.

– Quick! Hide yourselves! Solotin cried, rejoining his confused comrades. They hid themselves in the back of the room. Brusquely, the wounded man got up. He staggered as his entire body was dismantled by fits and starts of unspeakable brutality. His head spun without end. Iliev could not believe it. This man should have died several minutes before because of all the vodka in his veins! Instead, against all medical logic, he had succeeded in standing up!

– But, good God, Ruslan! What have you done? shouted Iliev.

The other man remained tight-lipped. Totally caught up in what he was seeing. Iliev and Simonov, quickly understood that they were in the middle of assisting in a metamorphosis.

Indeed, the German had only a distant connection with the human that he had once been. His arms were transformed into powerful legs, ending in sharp claws. His skin cracked into multiple scales of a copper colour, shredding his grey uniform into a thousand tatters. Petrified, Simonov never ceased to cross himself and invoke all the saints of Russia. As for Iliev, he trembled like a leaf, searching desperately for a way to flee that accursed place. Solotin, for his part, did not lose sight of what was happening.

The groans redoubled in intensity, when the mutation neared its end. Finally, it gave birth to an infernal hydra. Part-human, part-dragon.

In seeing this monstrosity, the three men experienced an ambiguous feeling, mixing at once the worst of fears and the most unhealthy of curiosities.

They believed their final hour had arrived when the beast's eyes, yellow and saurian, fell on them. The sight of this filthy being greatly disgusted them, including the thick slime dripping from its reptilian mouth, studded with sharp fangs. The men were medusaed, hypnotised.

In a burst of lucidity, Simonov grabbed his pistol and shot at this *thing* which faced him. At the same moment, two armed soldiers, alerted by the cries of the beast, entered the room. They were instantly roasted by a wave of fire. The beast spat anew and grilled another soldier who had just come in. Others followed, their guns rattling. Then the fire broke out, charring, burning, carbonising everything in its path.

Several bullets pierced the armour of the dragon, whose blood flowed purple on the floor. Entering into a maddened rage, he vomited new flames, deadlier than ever. In one bound, he escaped, breaking the glass of the windows in the room. In an instant, he had vanished in the dark. Outside, they heard gunshots and cries of terror. Then silence fell upon the plain.

– Damnation, what is this circus, Ruslan? bawled Iliev.

– I wanted … Let's just say that I wanted to practice … something that my master-shaman had taught me, explained the Buryat, hanging his head.

– What?! You're mad! My word!

– Of course not. It was the curse of the man-dragon. I took the opportunity to test it … and it worked beyond my expectations ….

– It's not possible, lamented Iliev, raising his eyes to the ceiling. We'll have to find him and eliminate this demonic creature at once! Then I don't know what canard we'll serve the NKVD. If we tell them the truth, it's the firing squad for us! At any rate, they'll never swallow this unlikely story!

– It's going to be easy to find, said Simonov, who was leaning out the window. His wounds left traces of blood in the snow. We mustn't lose one minute!

Indeed, the monster was quickly located. He was hiding near the hospital, in the ruins of an old school. Illiev had commandeered a score of men to lay siege around the lair of the beast. They circled the place carefully with several batteries of machine guns placed at regular intervals. Each waited for the release of the prey, fingers poised nervously on the trigger.

While snow fell in fat flakes, cold tore the flesh of the combatants. And in this atmosphere frozen by ice, everyone could hear the rattle of the creature.

– It's dying, said Simonov.

– Yes, it's suffering like a martyr, added Solotin.

– Oh, you're unfeeling, Ruslan! May I remind you that this thing was human not so long ago! And that, without all your bullshit, we wouldn't be where we are, Iliev snapped.

The Siberian clenched his teeth, but refrained from answering.

– Be on your guards! If this trash raises its nose, shoot it! We're waiting for reinforcements before the attack. Be ready, Iliev ordered all the soldiers.

– When I tell this to my wife, she's going to think I'm nuts! Simonov said with amusement.

– I am truly sorry, Solotin said.

– You got lucky this time, my friend! I just learned tonight that the NKVD guys aren't here. So, we can arrange everything as we like, Iliev reassured him.

The voice of the medical officer was then smothered by a rattling noise coming from behind the line of soldiers. An enormous machine that crushed everything in its path appeared from the shadows.

– The T-34![5] We can say that they haven't slacked off with reinforcements! Iliev cried, delighted.

– With that, we will polish our friend's scales! cheered Simonov.

Solotin, alone, remained silent, as if absorbed in internal, abyssal meditations.

The chariot came and stood with them, the barrel aimed straight at the shadows, where hid the man-dragon. His growls were now interspersed with ferocious outcries.

– Come on! Finish it! Fire! cried Iliev, dropping his arm.

---

5   A Soviet medium tank, the most common design produced during WWII.

And the tank fired at its mark. An explosion took out almost all of the pile of stones left over from the school. In unison, the machine guns began to vomit their deadly poison. The wounded creature could not hide and, with the energy of despair, tried to force a way out of the blockade. His flames carried off some unfortunates, but his body was soon riddled with bullets. Too handicapped to advance, he stopped and continued to defend himself with his hard skin. While his scales were now purple with blood, the beast still gave some blows with his claws until, in a last rattle, he sank into the fresh snow, lifeless. Iliev immediately ordered a ceasefire.

They all approached with extreme caution, before realizing that their adversary was definitively no longer a threat. A circle was being formed around the body when Iliev spoke:

– Comrades, look well, because you will never again see anything like it … Needless to say, what happened this night must remain between us. Anyway, who would believe you? No one! They'd send you directly to the madhouse. In the meantime, I can guarantee you that any tattletale will have to deal with me. Any questions? All right, burn *that*!

Without a word, the troop obeyed and, when all was finished, the men dispersed. On the horizon, bursts of artillery streaked the sky, as if the war wanted to recall their good memory.

With heavy steps, Iliev, Simonov and Solotin reentered the hospital together. Silent, grave, they thought back to those moments they had just lived through. Simonov decided to lighten the mood.

– And what do you say to a little vodka to celebrate? he asked.

The laughter of the three companions went up into the starless night and resonated until dawn.

Meddy Ligner was born in 1974 in Bressuire, a small town in the western part of France. He spent his first 18 years there. He goes back frequently to see his family and to play baseball with the famous Garocheurs. He studied history and afterwards, he taught French abroad in Finland, Russia and China. Since 2003, he has worked as a teacher of history and geography in Poitiers, France, where he lives with his wife, his daughter and his son. His website is: http://meddyligner.blogspot.com

The Ascent

By Berit K. N. Ellingsen

Some say screaming is embarrassing and shameful, but under the right circumstances, or perhaps the wrong circumstances, screaming is actually very liberating. Because there are times and places when you would really like to scream, when you would absolutely love to scream, and feel a great and pressing need to do it, but you can't.

~

One of those places is at the bottom of the swimming pool, when you're lying there behind the wetsuit that's too tight in all the wrong places, and the round, white swimming goggles that make you look perpetually startled. You're trying to relax, trying to stay calm, trying to maintain that delicate balance between the need to breathe and the greed for another breath-hold record. All while your lungs ache for air, your throat swallows for the same, and the muscles in your body, down to tiny little flexors you didn't know you had, burn from lack of oxygen, and the only thing that's silent is your mind. Because this is mind over matter, brain over muscles and you over water. After the initial few minutes of hypoxia, the acute need to breathe vanishes, and you enter a free-floating state where it feels like you can go on forever.

Of course, you can't; it's just a question of how long your body can remain conscious on the small amount of oxygen you brought with you from the surface. In order to stretch the breath-hold time as far as possible without fainting, you have become intimately familiar with the signals from your body that say it's about to black out: the pins and needles starting in your fingers and toes, like cruel little whispers, like the warm sun being momentarily obscured by a cloud. The prickly sensation invades your hands and feet, and slowly creeps up your wrists and ankles. There's a round orb pulsing behind your eyes. For every contraction, the sphere changes colour, from deep electric blue, to warm glowing gold, back to blue, again. It doesn't go away, even when you blink. The edge of your vision is framed by a moving spindly black, like a mass of dark spiders crawling around your eyes, only you can't feel them. As the blue orb pulses slower, the black cloud starts to eat its way towards the middle of your eyes, the spiders multiplying. That's the true signal, the body's black flag of unconditional surrender to oxygen deprivation. You know exactly when to break off, when to push hard away from the blue tiles at the bottom of the pool and stick your head out of the water and breathe.

Sometimes, the surge of air rushing into your suffocating lungs and brain and muscles is so sudden and liberating that you black out, anyway, but then you're caught by friendly hands and the record is still yours.

~

You think the static breath-hold records are a little stupid in themselves, a child's play at the bottom of the pool. But despite that, you are proud of them. How many people can hold their breath for more than eleven minutes?

~

The exercise does have a purpose, though. It's an appetizer for the main course, preparation for the real dives into black water. Those trips are another game, completely. There, you stand on a sled, a slim metal frame with a tank of air connected to two balloons, bright yellow for visibility in low-light conditions, wrapped shut. The sled moves along a thick wire, of the kind that's used in sailing, and plunges into the deep to a predetermined depth. The sled uses its own gravity and your weight to fall into the blue. All you need to do is hang on, equalize the raging pressure in your ears by using a little of your own breath from a plastic bottle tied to your leg, tolerate the increasing cold and darkness, and refrain from screaming. After less than two minutes, the sled reaches the bottom of the line. Then you just need to be lucid enough to pull the strap that opens the tank and the main balloon, wait until the balloon has inflated and hang on hard while the sled rushes you up to the air and the light.

Some people think using a sled is cheating compared with swimming down yourself and then back up again, which requires considerably more energy and strength. But with the sled and a brief decompression at ten meters on the way up, you can go deeper than 200 meters and up again in one breath. For you, the purest challenge is not the swimming or the climbing, but withstanding the depth and the darkness and the lust for oxygen as long as possible. To go as deeply as humanly possible. The fight against the pressure and the water is an addiction to you and your over-developed diving reflex.

～

It's for real, now, a new-record attempt at what is called "No Limits Diving". No limits. The sled takes you down much faster than your body alone can. After just a minute, you're down deeper than most divers go with air on their backs, the sled shrieking along the wire. You start in bright daylight in tropical waters and end up in a temperate dusk, where the water is cold enough to bite your hands and stiffen your cheeks. Together with the weight of the water that bears mercilessly down on you, it's only just tolerable, even for the brief time it lasts. As you plummet down, the deep makes your heart slow and the blood to retreat from your arms and legs. Your organs squeeze up against your spine and your lungs fill with blood plasma to avoid damage.

～

Beyond the whirr of the sled as it falls on the wire, the deep is always quiet. It's so quiet it sometimes feels like the building pressure in your ears is caused by the silence and not just the weight of the water. Riding the sled down is a little like lying at the bottom of the pool, only now you need to clench one hand around a handle, the other around the plastic bottle, and wriggle your lower jaw back and forth so your ears pop to equalize the brutal pressure. The cold makes certain you don't go fully into that silent breath-hold space of the bottom of the pool. You reach the edges of it but not further. That's why you can hold your breath for more than eleven minutes in a warm and brightly lit pool, but only for seven, or so, on the sled. There is also another thing. An ancient instinct refuses to let you close your eyes in the deep. Some divers fear sharks or eels or jellyfish while they're down. But there are scuba divers at the top part of the wire and they look out for dangerous animals. If they see one, the competition is delayed until the animal has passed.

No, your fear is much older and more primitive than that. It's the true fear of the deep. You have dived in many places of the world, from Arctic to tropical waters and everything in between. But everywhere, the deep looks and feels the same. It's devouringly dark, jealously cold and crushingly heavy. It doesn't need to strike or bite or poison you, like other dangerous things do. No, the deep simply uses its own weight to pacify you. It sits on you until you give up and leave, or stop flailing your arms and legs. Fortunately, the deep is mindless and doesn't know you're there. You regard that as a blessing. Still, you always keep a knife in a sheath on your thigh. Other divers laugh at you, ask if you plan to catch some fish while you're down there, and wonder if you're going to bring a harpoon at the same time? You say it's for cutting yourself free if you get tangled in the wire or the balloons, but you know better. It's for the ancient fear of the deep.

∿

The sled and you reach the end of the wire. You're doing fine, not feeling too cold or anoxic. No fainting in sight, the spiders stay away from your eyes, the trip up should be fine. You pull the cord on the tank. Then it is quiet for a few seconds as the air streams into the balloon and the yellow plastic starts to fill up. This is the worst part of the journey. There is nothing to do but take in the view of the hollow gloom around you and the gaping dark below you. On the way down, you fight against the cold current of descent and the increasing pressure. On the way up, you enjoy the view of the flood of bubbles from the balloon and the increasing light as you ascend. Then the depth releases its hold on you, and you are born again into the air and the sun. But that's more than two hundred and ten meters away in the vertical, a long climb with a merciless angle of ninety degrees. You are literally in too deep. If the main and the back-up balloon don't inflate, you haven't got enough air or power in your body to climb back up the pressure well. Then your only hope is the scuba divers watching you further up.

Finally, the balloon plumps up and the sled starts whirring in reverse. You hold on to the thin handles and rise along the wire, relieved to have escaped the deep once again. But this afternoon, against what is possible, against what is natural, the deep senses you, and acts.

∿

Something terribly fast rushes out of the darkness below, blurs past you and curls around the inflated balloon. The current of the sudden motion slams against your body, almost takes you away from the sled. Whatever it is swats the ocean's weight like a fly. You can only imagine the power needed to move at that speed at this depth.

What looks like a giant coil of maroon rope, as thick as your thigh, curls around the yellow plastic. Pale suction cups the size of your fist squeeze out of the red like jellyfish. They look soft and smooth, but you know they hide a circle of knife-like cartilage, nature's own *vagina dentata*. If those bowls kiss you, it's goodbye. Now you want to scream, but you can't. You can only stare in terror as the arm pulls at the balloon and shakes the sled, stopping your ascent to the light. The coils curl sinuously, almost sensuously, around the balloon, increasing their hold on it.

In the horribly slow thinking of the deep, you realize the arm wants to pull the entire sled into the abyss. You pull out your knife and start sawing at the neck of the balloon to release it. All movement is heavy and painful. Your muscles are not built to fight against the deep. Your heart is blasting and your lungs are on fire. You have no air left for the way up, but the only thing you can think about is getting the sled free.

The yellow plastic rips, releasing a torrent of tiny bubbles into the dusky water. The sled tilts back to the wire. You pull the cord for the back-up-balloon. It fills quickly and, with the hold of the tentacle gone, the sled starts screaming up the cord. You hang on and feel the speed take you away; you're on your way up. But then something cold and ancient wraps itself around your leg and takes hold like a giant anaconda. You don't have to look to see what it is. You can feel the suction cups dig through your wetsuit and into your leg. The sled bounces and swings. You hold onto the handles as hard as you can and slowly, slowly bury your knife into the red flesh. You really want to scream, but you can't. The diving reflex is too strong. Your throat and epiglottis have closed shut. All you can see are the black spiders scuttling quickly over your eyes.

～

Some say screaming is embarrassing and shameful, but under the right circumstances, or perhaps the wrong circumstances, screaming is actually liberating. Because there are times and places when you would really like to scream, when you would absolutely love to scream, and feel a great and pressing need to do it, but you can't.

One of those places is in a coma after terror. If you're lucky, you're still breathing on your own, and can gasp and hyperventilate and heave your breast as much as you like, while whatever it is that makes you feel like screaming plays out in your vegetative mind.

If you're unlucky, however, the centres in your brain responsible for breathing have shut down, been shocked into silence. So, while your mind is screaming loudly, the machine that's pushing air into your inert lungs and body, thinks breathing steadily and calmly takes precedence over self-expression, and keeps moving in an entirely too-slow pace. Then you can't scream, however much you want to. You can only stare in horror at whatever is coming at you, stare paralyzed and helpless, and let it happen to you, again and again. But finally, the breathing centers in your brain come back online, you ignore the slow breathing of the machine that's kept you alive for three weeks, cut yourself free from the net of tubes and wires and needles that are tangling you, and scream and scream! And it is very, very liberating.

Berit Ellingsen is a Norwegian literary and speculative fiction author. She is also a science journalist and has a dark past as a game, film and music reviewer. Her fiction has or will appear in various online literary journals and in print anthologies, most recently in *The Subterranean Literary Journal*, *OverClock Zine* and *Zouch Magazine*. Berit admits to pining for the fjords when abroad. Her debut novel, *The Empty City*, is inspired by the philosophy of nonduality.

Nightmare

By Wenona Napolitano

Darkness gripped me like a ferocious lion,
ripping and shredding apart helpless prey.
Reaching out, I begged you to stay.
But you left and my soul started crying.
My fears slowly took me over.
Nightmares set in, taking over sweet dreams.
My heart stops when I wake and drown in screams,
Lonely without a comforting lover.

Once, I drank in the dreams and dreamed the wine
that flowed over satiny cherubs' wings.
I could hear my guardian angels sing.
Sweet voices soared to eternity's time.

Now I can no longer feel my own soul.
I just hear the wind blowing in my mind.
My sweet seraphim are no longer kind.
Angry devils tear me, leaving a hole.

With trembling hands, I drink the poisoned wine
That will forever stop bad dreams in time.

Wenona Napolitano is a freelance writer, poet and the author of *The Everything Green Wedding Book*. Her specialty areas include: natural health, green living, gardening, crafts, and wedding planning. When not writing, Wenona loves to spend time with her family, craft, garden, and go on treasure hunts at local antique stores, flea markets and yard sales. To relax, she loves nothing better than to curl up with a good book. Contact her at: everythinggreenweddings@yahoo.com.

Copyright Acknowledgments

About the Anthologists

Silvia Moreno-Garcia's stories have appeared in publications such as *Fantasy Magazine*, *The Book of Cthulhu*, *Evolve 2* and *Shine: An Anthology of Optimistic Science Fiction*. She co-edited the anthology *Historical Lovecraft* together with Paula R. Stiles. Find her at silviamoreno-garcia.com.

~

Possessing a quixotic fondness for difficult careers, **Paula Stiles** has driven ambulances, taught fish farming for the Peace Corps in West Africa and earned a Scottish PhD in medieval history, studying Templars and non-Christians in Spain. She has also sold fiction to *Strange Horizons*, *Writers of the Future*, *Jim Baen's Universe*, *Shine*, *Futures*, *Black Gate*'s "Warrior Woman" issue, and other markets, as well as a co-written supernatural mystery novel, *Fraterfamilias*. She is Editor in Chief of the Lovecraft/Mythos 'zine *Innsmouth Free Press*. You can find her on Twitter (@thesnowleopard) and Facebook, or at: http://thesnowleopard.net.

Other Innsmouth Titles

HISTORICAL LOVECRAFT

Historical Lovecraft, a unique anthology blending historical fiction with horror, features 26 tales spanning centuries and continents. This eclectic volume takes the readers through places as varied as Laos, Greenland, Peru, and the Congo, and from antiquity until the 20th century, pushing the envelope of Lovecraftian lore. William Meikle's inquisitor tries to unravel the truth during a very hostile questioning. Jesse Bullington narrates the saga of a young Viking woman facing danger and destruction. E. Catherine Tobler stops in Ancient Egypt, where Pharaoh Hatshepsut receives an exquisite and deadly gift. Albert Tucher discovers that the dead do not remain silent in 10th century Rome. These are tales that reimagine history and look into the past through a darker glass. Tales that show evil has many faces and reaches through the centuries. Tales that will chill your heart.

~

FRATERFAMILIAS

French artist Paul Farrell kills four people in Paris and walks into a hail of police fire at JFK Airport. A Russian history professor and shaman with a dark secret steals the body. Police on both sides of the Atlantic are on the case, but they each have secrets of their own. And a powerful enemy watches from the shadows, one who could destroy them all. This is *Fraterfamilias*, an urban fantasy thriller now available in print and as an e-book.

~

Find more information about these titles at InnsmouthFreePress.com